# SCARCROSSED

## CASTLES OF THE EYRIE
## BOOK THREE

### EVIE MARCEAU

# CHAPTER I

**A WEDDING AND A CORONATION . . . witnesses . .
. a lost crown . . . headstones**

Winter weddings were unheard of in the kingdom of the Mirien. It was known as a land of warmth, sunlight, and rich harvests, where tradition dictated that Mir couples held their wedding on one of the long summer days that stretched lazily from sunrise to sunset. The expectations were no different for royalty: Bryn's parents had married on a mid-summer day with blue skies overhead; the previous king and queen had wed on the warmest day of that year, and so on the custom went.

And yet the wedding of Mars Lindane and Illiana Joster broke tradition in three ways: first, it was held in winter, when frost crept over the fallow fields. Second, it was brief at barely half an hour, instead of a multi-day affair. And third, it was private.

No grand crowds, no visiting dignitaries.

Only the couple and a few witnesses.

Bryn huddled in a velvet shawl against the chill trawling through Castle Mir's council room. The gathered wedding party was painfully small: Mars and Illiana; ancient Lord Randall, the castle's chief scholar, to serve as official; Illiana's mother, Mam Nelle, and brother, Christof; and Bryn and Rangar.

"Here. Take my cloak." Seeing Bryn shiver, Rangar slid out of his bearskin cloak and draped it over her shoulders.

Lord Randall used his arthritic fingers to flip to the royal marriage oath passage in an ancient book. "You may face one another," he said to Mars and Illiana.

Illiana clasped Mars's hands, guiding him to face her. The wedding was rushed, and the bride's dress was an old lace gown that a servant had found in storage, yet Illiana beamed with as much joy as if she was draped in gold.

Mars's expression was harder to read, in no small part because of his cloudy, unfocused eyes. The infection that had taken hold of him after his near-death experience had robbed him of his sight, yet he'd quickly learned to adapt. Still, even with his unfocused gaze, his softened jaw and firm posture made it clear he was just as joyful as his bride.

"Mars Lindane of the Mirien, firstborn prince of King Deothaniel and Queen Helena, do you bind yourself with this woman?"

Mars gave a solemn nod. "Forever, I do."

As they stood witness, Rangar slid his arm around Bryn's back, hooking his hand around her hip to draw her close. She hadn't realized until that moment how tense she'd been holding herself. She couldn't help but think about her own doomed wedding to Trei Barendur, Rangar's eldest brother. The tradition was different in the Baersladen. The common folk had shouted a loud three-call chant after every vow that had made her heart rattle.

Here, the few gathered witnesses remained quiet as stone.

"And Illiana Joster of the Mirien, daughter of Nelle Joster, do you bind yourself with this man?"

Illiana's soft gaze fell adoringly on Mars. "Forever, I do."

Rangar's hand tightened on Bryn's waist. He leaned in to whisper in her ear, "You're next, princess." He quietly pressed something into her palm.

Bryn felt a jolt of anticipation as she looked down and saw his engagement ring. It was the second time he'd given it to her. She'd had to throw it back in his face the first time to convince Captain Carr that she cared nothing for Rangar, and ever since then, she'd felt the ring's loss keenly.

She looked down at her palm, hiding her smile, but

before she could close her hand around the ring, Rangar suddenly took it back. Her lips parted, confused.

"Not yet," he whispered hotly in her ear. "I want to put it on your finger myself—and this time I want it to *stay* there." His lips grazed her ear, giving her wicked shivers.

Old Lord Randall cleared his throat, bringing Bryn back to the present. The officiant's shaky fingers flipped to the next page as he pronounced, "The Second Amendment in the Third Law of Succession declares that a member of Mir royalty may marry a commoner so long as they are not the crown heir. Mars Lindane, do you swear by honor and reason that you hold no claim to the Mir throne?"

All eyes—except for Mars's clouded ones—turned to Bryn.

The seemingly insignificant Second Amendment of the Third Law of Succession was the reason for this rushed marriage instead of a proper grand summer ceremony in front of the entire populace. Mars could only marry Illiana if he weren't the crown heir—a title that Bryn currently held. But she needed to surrender that title back to him soon, so that she and Rangar could return to the Baersladen. Every day, King Aleth's health grew poorer. They didn't dare wait until summertime to return, while the kingdom's enemies might see Aleth's condition as a weakness.

"I swear by honor and reason," Mars stated. "I

recognize my sister, Lady Bryn Lindane, as crown heir to the Mirien."

Lord Randall adjusted his spectacles. "Then it is my honor to declare this marriage as valid. Mars Lindane and Illiana Joster, you are now one."

Both of them broke into grins, then Mars pulled Illiana into a kiss. Mam Nelle clapped, and Christof Joster gave a whistle of congratulations. Once the couple finally broke the kiss, Bryn approached them.

"Mars. Illiana. I'm so happy for you." She squeezed her brother's arm. "This is a blessing for the kingdom, and I'm so pleased to see my brother with a smile on his face."

"Thank you, Lady Bryn," Illiana said. "For all you've done."

"Don't think of it," Bryn said, waving away the witch's thanks. "Though we are anxious to return to the Baersladen. If we could handle the remainder of the paperwork . . ."

"Yes. I have it right here, my lady." Lord Randall shuffled through parchments on his wooden stand. He held up one document, squinting at it. "First is the marriage certificate. I'll need two witnesses."

Mars and Illiana signed the certificate, then passed the quill to Rangar, who wrote his name as witness, and to Bryn, who signed hers.

"Excellent," Lord Randall said. "Now that the marriage is formalized, we can begin the transfer of succession. This parchment decrees that Lady Bryn is relinquishing her claim to the Mir throne into the possession of her brother, Prince Mars." He paused, giving Bryn a keen look. "You are certain this is your wish, my lady?"

Once more, all eyes fell on Bryn. She gave a firm nod. "I am."

"I must impress upon you the magnitude of this decision," Lord Randall stated. "It is no small thing for a crown heir to give up a throne. Many people have killed, died, and warred to possess what you now possess. Do you swear by honor and reason that you give this up freely, of your own will, under no duress?"

Bryn squeezed the quill in her hand. She knew many people throughout the kingdom doubted her decision. Mars hadn't proved himself to be an effective leader the first time he'd been on the Mir throne, so was she thrusting her people back under the uncertainty of an unproven ruler?

And yet, as she watched Mars holding Illiana's hand, she knew this was the right choice. Mars wasn't the same headstrong, arrogant prince he'd been in their youth. In fact, he'd *never* been that person. It had been an act to convince their parents that he was on their side. Yes, he had made mistakes trusting Captain Carr, but now he had Illiana. She was a voice of the common folk—not to mention a witch highly skilled in hexmarks—and he finally had put his trust in the right place.

"By my own free will," Bryn said, "I relinquish the crown."

Lord Randall nodded and turned to the velvet

pillow resting on the Little Table that held the golden crown. It had graced Bryn's father's head for as long as she could remember, and seeing it now gave her a small stab of pain.

She missed her parents, despite their sins.

"Sign here," Lord Randall said, indicating the bottom of the parchment.

Bryn squeezed Rangar's hand before she approached the wooden stand. This was an important step in their future but not the only hurdle they faced: Rangar was still technically a fugitive. Until they could clear his name of his brother's murder, he wouldn't be welcomed back into Barendur Hold—except into its dungeon.

While his dark eyes watched, she signed her name to the parchment and set down the quill, stepping back. Lord Randall picked up the crown and placed it on Mars's head, reciting the coronation vows.

At the back of the room, Rangar took Bryn's hand. "You gave up a kingdom," he said quietly.

"I'm gaining a new one," she answered, meeting his gaze. "Once we clear your name."

His attention fell to her lips as though he was debating sweeping her into a kiss right there. She stepped closer to rest her forehead on his broad chest. She briefly let her eyes sink closed.

*No longer a queen. Not duty-bound. Only bound by soul—to him.*

His fingers stroked her long hair. "I don't care if

you're a princess, a queen, or a shepherdess, Bryn Lindane. As long as you're mine."

She tipped her head up and, while the rest of the small gathering watched her brother be crowned King of the Mirien, kissed her prince.

After the marriage and coronation, Bryn took one last walk through Castle Mir. Under Captain Carr's reign, much had changed from the childhood home she remembered, yet each room was still as familiar as the various parts of her own body. She spent time in her old bedroom, where the music boxes and silver hairbrushes were a reminder of the girl she'd once been, then visited her parents' former bedroom. The bed was still shrouded with a black cloth, as was the full-length mirror, out of tradition. They would only be lifted when the new king and queen took residence, and Mars and Illiana wanted to redecorate first.

She shivered, feeling as though her parents' ghosts lingered.

She walked through the cavernous ballroom and down to the kitchen level, where a few cooks gave her smiles, and then through the servants' entrance to the remembrance garden. She wound among the still-blooming rosebushes until she reached the gravestones. She stopped in front of two of the newest markers.

*Deonthanial Lindane, King of the Mirien*
*Helena Lindane, Queen of the Mirien*

Resting a hand on her father's headstone, then her mother's, she whispered a blessing of eternal peace.

"... to the earth we all return," she finished.

The grass rustled behind her. She spun to find Rangar leaning against one of the older headstones. He said thoughtfully, "You've done the Lindane name proud today."

She lifted her skirt to walk through the grass to where he was, then perched on the low headstone next to him. Facing her, he caught her chin between his thumb and first finger.

"I want to take you away from here. From these bad memories. I want to take you the Baersladen and make you my wife."

On impulse, she reached up to touch his scars. "I want that too."

His voice lowered as he moved his lips to brush hers. "I want to take you *here*, as well."

A spark jumped between them. Night was falling, and they were alone, but the remembrance garden was hardly what she'd consider private.

"Not here," she whispered urgently against his lips. "A servant could walk through at any moment."

His lips grew insistent against hers. "I promised you I'd finish what we started in your bedroom. I mean to fulfill that vow."

Already breathless and feeling his same urgency,

Bryn glanced over her shoulder at the weeping evergreens on the far side of the garden. Once, she'd hidden in those boughs to spy on Rangar and Valenden when she thought they'd meant to start a war.

"I know a place," she whispered with a wink and, taking his hand, tugged him away from the headstone and toward the deep, dusky shadows.

# CHAPTER 2

**LOVE IN THE GARDEN . . . a black cat . . . only two
brothers left . . . a golden ring . . . time to go home**

Rangar took her hard and hot beneath the
evergreen boughs.

Running her hands over his broad
shoulders with her head tipped back against the cool
grass, Bryn couldn't believe they were here—together.
For so long, fate had toyed with them: crashing their
lives together with the wolf attack, then hurling them
apart for a decade, only to have them collide again and
be thrust apart once more like two birds floating in a
storm. Her fingers curled into his shirt, determined not
to let him go this time.

Both of their breaths were fast as they coupled in
the shadows, knowing it was risky to do so outside of

the privacy of a bedroom. But Bryn liked having Rangar bed her beneath the bare moonlight with the garden smells around them. Here, she felt connected to the earth. To Rangar. To her own hopes and dreams.

"I thought I loved you when you were a princess," Rangar murmured as he pressed his palm against her hip to adjust the angle, "I had no idea how much I'd want you as a queen."

"Not a queen . . . not yet." Bryn's lips parted as an aching pressure built between her legs. She rocked to meet his final thrusts as he braced his hand in the grass and finished inside her.

Pleasure crested over them before surrendering into a sweet calm, leaving them panting visible breaths into the cool night air. After a moment, Rangar rolled off her and buttoned his pants. Bryn adjusted her skirt and started to button her blouse, but he stopped her hand. Slipping his rough palm against her bare ribs, he ran his hand along her scars.

"You don't mind that the scars leave me imperfect?" she asked.

His hand pressed flat against her ribs. "The scars are my favorite thing about your body. They are a badge of your curiosity. Your strength. Even at a young age, you dared to tread where no one else would."

"Except you," she pointed out softly.

His hand moved up her skin until his thumb grazed the bottom of her breast. "That night, when I saw your lantern at the edge of the forest, something called to me. I knew I had to follow you." He moved his hand to cup her cheek. "Do you believe in fate now?"

He looked more handsome than ever in the blue shadows of the moon. She tenderly ran her thumb along his own scars. "I don't know about fate, but I believe in you, Rangar Barendur."

He claimed her mouth in a softer kiss, but they were interrupted when a door creaked open on the far side of the garden. Going still, they both listened. But it was only a maid letting out a cat, and the door soon shut again.

Bryn sat up, finally closing the buttons on her blouse. She looked at the night sky beyond the evergreen boughs and let out a small sigh.

Rangar plucked stray pieces of grass out of her hair. "Will you miss this place?"

"Parts of it," she admitted.

He matched her gaze up at the stars. "It's the same night sky in the Mirien as in the Baersladen. The moon and stars don't change. We can't take Castle Mir's tapestries with us, but we can take the sky."

She settled against his chest, and he stroked a hand down her arm. Tipping up her chin toward him, she asked, "Is there any more news of your father's condition?"

Pain flashed briefly in his eyes, but then his expression hardened—always a soldier, never wanting to appear vulnerable, even to her. "No more letters have come in the past few days."

She sensed the worry in his voice. For all he acted

like emotions didn't get to him, she knew how much he loved his father and the extent of his concern.

"He might yet recover," she said softly.

His jaw tensed. "My aunt wouldn't have summoned us back if recovery was likely. My father is dying, and it does no good to pretend otherwise. It's going to leave the Baersladen vulnerable. I must track down Broderick and prove he is Trei's murderer before my father passes. Otherwise, the Bear crown will be in uncertain hands."

"We'll find Broderick." She rested her head on his shoulder while watching the black cat slink through the rosebushes, barely more than a shadow. "When your father passes, do you think Valenden will make a play for the crown?"

Rangar gave a harsh snort. "Not Val. He has no ambition for the crown."

"It's hard for me to believe that, when so many others would kill to be king."

"Is it?" He cocked an eyebrow. "You yourself just gave up a crown."

"I have my eyes set on another one."

Rangar combed his tangled hair back off his face as he sat up. He explained, "Val and our mother were very close. They both had an inclination toward excess and dark thoughts, but she was able to overcome her shortcomings. She kept Val on the right path when she was alive, so when she died, he was lost. He told our father he wanted to relinquish his place in the line of succession. Without our mother's guidance, he didn't trust himself to make good decisions. And there's the issue of progeny, too. Val was reckless with his affairs—a disease left him unable to have children. That alone technically invalidates him from being king, though, of course, there would be ways around that if Val so wished."

"What ways?"

"There are many orphans in the Baersladen."

Bryn lifted her eyebrows in surprise. "You mean he'd pass off an orphan child as his own blood? A false heir?"

Rangar chuckled lightly. "Bryn, that kind of thing has been happening throughout every kingdom for years. If not an orphan, then there are other ways for a wife to become pregnant by someone who isn't her husband and pass off the child as his."

"He wouldn't mind another man siring a child on his wife?"

"Val? He'd probably *prefer* it."

Bryn huffed a deep breath. "And yet, despite all that, he's still older than you, which puts him next in line. Even if Val swears now that he doesn't want to be king, we don't know who might try to whisper in his ear, just like what happened with my own brother. Advisors could try to manipulate him. Even turn the two of you against each other."

Rangar seemed unconcerned as he plucked another piece of grass from her hair. "Our father taught us the strength of family. For all the times Val's follies have tested my patience, nothing can break my bond with my brother."

Bryn's own rocky family history made her doubt his words, and yet it was true that the Barendur family had always stood united. Rangar's father and brothers had risked their lives to save her from the siege solely due to the belief that, as Rangar's Saved, she was part of their family. Trei had even sacrificed his own future with Saraj to marry her to keep the kingdoms safe. He had even died for his family.

"I hope you're right," she murmured. "The Baersladen will need its two remaining princes united."

Rangar said evenly, "The Baersladen will need its new queen, too." He reached into his pocket and took out the engagement ring with the maiden rose stamped into the metal band. Taking her hand, he slid the cool circle around her finger. For a moment, they both admired it glinting in the moonlight.

Bryn swallowed a nervous lump in her throat. She toyed with Rangar's ring as she said, "Are you so certain the Baer people will accept a foreign-born princess?"

"They already have." Rangar took her hand to keep her from nervously twisting the ring. "When I saved your life, you became part of my family, and thus part of the Baersladen. My people have the same beliefs I do about the *fralen* bond. In any case, you've already proven yourself to have what it takes to thrive in our lands. A prim Mir princess spending days hiking through mud to find a single lost lamb told them everything they needed to know."

She studied their entwined hands but still bit her lip in doubt. "And you . . . Are *you* ready to be king when your father passes?"

Rangar didn't answer right away. His eyes drifted to the headstones of the fallen Mir royalty from the past centuries. Finally, he said, "I always thought Trei would rule. It never felt possible that anyone but him would sit on our throne. He prepared for it his entire life."

She squeezed his hand. "You prepared for it, too."

He barked a laugh. "In name, perhaps. I was required to learn history and politics just the same as my brothers, but I always thought I would serve my kingdom in a different way. My father intended for me to be captain of the Baer army."

"Captain of an army and king of a kingdom aren't so different."

His dark eyes found hers as he searched her face with a flicker of amusement.

"What?" she asked, suddenly self-conscious, checking her hair for more grass.

He cupped her cheek. "I'm lucky to have you, Bryn. I wanted this for so long. You. A woman to go through life with. Someone to promise me that I won't fail as king, when I doubt myself."

She placed a gentle hand on his chest. "You'll be the greatest king the Baersladen has ever seen, Rangar Barendur."

The black cat wound over to them and purred as it nuzzled its head against Rangar's side. He stroked the cat in amusement. "Baer lore says black cats are a sign of good luck."

She smiled. "Mir tradition claims they're *bad* luck."

"Well, then, I suppose it's a good thing you're about to be a Baer queen, Bryn Lindane." He wrapped a hand around the back of her neck and pulled her close enough for his lips to scorch their way across her jaw and neck, finally settling on her own lips. When he broke the kiss, he kept his hand on her waist. "Are you ready to say goodbye to your home?"

She took one last look at her parents' headstones, then shifted her gaze up to the stars again.

*It's the same night sky in the Mirien and in the Baersladen. The moon and stars don't change.*

"I'm ready," she said.

# CHAPTER 3

**GOODBYES . . . a falcon overhead . . . a warning of wolves . . . no maiden roses . . . honey**

The first time Bryn had left the Mirien, she'd fled with nothing to her name, sharing a horse with Rangar and sleeping in the open. This time, a closed carriage and team of horses waited to transport Bryn, Rangar, Valenden, and Saraj. Bryn wasn't a disgraced princess fleeing a siege anymore, but rather the future queen of the Baersladen. And yet, if she was being honest, she had to admit that she missed those days of riding in Rangar's arms on a single horse.

While Saraj helped the maids load baskets of food for the five-day journey, and Valenden and Rangar checked the horses' harnesses, Bryn prepared to say her goodbyes.

"Bryn," Illiana said, reaching out to squeeze Bryn's hands. "We wish you a safe and swift journey."

Bryn took note of the ornate wedding ring on Illiana's finger. It would be a tumultuous few weeks for them in the Mirien as they tried to win back the trust of their people. It didn't help that the wedding and coronation had been so rushed.

"Yes," Mars said, "Send word as soon as you've arrived safely at Barendur Hold. This time of year, the roads can be treacherous. In winter, bandits are more desperate. The rain and snow can bring flooding, too. We've also received reports of wolves attacking travelers near the Vil-Kevi border."

Rangar, finished with the horses, came over and placed a hand on his sword hilt. "Wolves tend only to attack single travelers on foot, or the weak and elderly."

"Not these wolves, so I hear," Mars cautioned. "Apparently, they brought down an entire team of horses."

"We'll be fine," Bryn assured her brother, folding her hands together as she took one last look at Castle Mir.

Rangar rested a hand on Bryn's back. "The carriage is ready as soon as the last of the luggage is loaded. Valenden will take the first shift driving."

Valenden looked up from where he'd been tightening a bridle and gave a snort. "I volunteered nothing of the sort."

Rangar patted his brother on the shoulder with a wicked grin. "*I* volunteered you."

Saraj finished helping the maids stow the luggage and dusted off her hands. "Good thing we're traveling light, since we only have a team of two horses."

"We can spare another pair," Mars offered. "It will get you to the Baersladen faster."

Rangar shook his head. "We'll manage, and your soldiers will need those horses. You should prepare for trouble among the common folk. Not everyone will agree with your decision to bring magic to the Mirien."

Mars gave a solemn nod. "We'll be prepared."

Valenden still grumbled as he climbed up into the driver's seat. Bryn embraced Illiana one final time, then her brother, while she tilted her head up to whisper in his ear, "I'm with you, Mars. The Mirien and the Baersladen will lead the Eyrie into a new era of peace."

Mars felt for her shoulders and gave her a grateful squeeze.

Rangar held the carriage door open, but Saraj pointed up at a castle parapet where her falcon, Zephyr, perched. "I'll ride up front with Valenden for a while," she said. "Zephyr wouldn't like being cooped up in the carriage. He'd rather fly along with us."

She whistled for Zephyr, who took off in a circle overhead.

Bryn climbed into the back of the carriage with

Rangar and settled in as Valenden drove them out of the castle grounds and through Mir Town. Watching out the window, Bryn tried to gauge the mood of the populace. Some of them had been loyal to Captain Carr and weren't pleased to hear of Prince Mars's miraculous rise from the dead, sudden marriage, and coronation.

She flinched, startled, as Rangar rested a hand on her knee.

"Sorry," she breathed, touching her chest. "I'm jumpy."

"Worried about the journey north?"

She glanced back out the window. "More worried for Mars and Illiana. Half the Mirien is on their side, but the other half isn't."

"Have faith in your brother," Rangar said. "A true leader learns from his mistakes, and I believe Mars has done just that. An untested king is an invitation for weakness."

Bryn sighed. "I'm grateful that we could be here for their wedding, at least."

His mouth hitched. "And now you have your own wedding to plan for."

A flush of nerves rushed through her at the idea. Was she truly, finally, going to marry Rangar? "I was never the type to dream about my wedding day," she confessed. "I assumed I'd be betrothed to some dull old minor lord like Baron Marmose. And that my mother would plan the wedding according to tradition, and I'd hardly be involved except to recite the vows."

"I wish to give you the wedding that you deserve," Rangar said, gently brushing back a loose strand of her hair. But then sadness crept into his eyes. "A second wedding, I should say."

Bryn swallowed a lump. "You're thinking of my wedding to Trei?"

Rangar continued to smooth down her errant curls, his eyes a little distant. "It would be a lie to say I don't wish I could have been your first—and only—husband."

She clutched his hand tightly and looked him straight in the eye. "We'll have a special wedding, Rangar. I'll make sure it's nothing like my first wedding. I don't want those doomed reminders, either. No maiden roses, no honey cakes, no dais in the village square."

He cocked an eyebrow. "No honey cakes?"

A brief grin played at the corners of her mouth. "Very well, the honey cakes can stay. But I'm serious, Rangar. I want something new between you and me. Old traditions are being shattered across the Eyrie; let us be a symbol of change as well. Perhaps we'll marry on a ship at sea. Or in a forested glen. Or at midnight around a bonfire."

A mischievous light crept into his eyes. He gathered her up around the waist and dragged her into his lap, stroking a hand down the side of her face. He purred, "I like hearing you talk about our wedding. I'd like to discuss our wedding *night* even more."

Bryn slid her arms around his neck as she gave him a playful, scolding look. "You've already tarnished me, Rangar Barendur. I'll hardly be a virgin bride."

His fingers squeezed the folds of her dress as his eyes simmered with growing desire. "Do you feel like being tarnished again?"

She threw another glance at the carriage window. They were on the outskirts of Mir Town now, but a few houses and farms still flanked the road.

"We should wait until we're at Barendur Hold," she said.

"It's a journey of five days," Rangar answered in a low rumble. "If you think I'm waiting that long before *tarnishing* you again, you are gravely mistaken. I've waited years to have you perch in my lap and taste your sweet mouth. I plan on having you every night, my queen."

Warmth bloomed in Bryn's cheeks. As she adjusted her position in his lap, she could feel Rangar's growing desire. "It's daytime," she pointed out.

"Every night," he corrected himself steadily. "*And* every day."

He tugged the curtain closed with a swift movement, then crushed his mouth against hers. She drank him in as her body began to crave him in equal measure. Her hands around his neck clung on, unwilling to let go. The carriage bounced, and he gripped her harder around the waist.

"On second thought," he murmured as his lips found the outline of her jaw. "Perhaps waiting until tonight to bury myself inside you will make it all the sweeter. For now, I'll just have a taste."

Bryn moved in for another kiss, but he caught her chin and shook his head. A wicked gleam lit his eyes. "Not that kind of a taste, princess."

She blinked at him, not understanding, until his fingers slowly gathered the hem of her skirt up around her knees. She clamped her hands on her skirt protectively as she squelched a gasp. "Rangar!"

But his hands didn't stop pulling up her skirt until it was up around her thighs. His thumb slipped under the band of one stocking, dragging it down to expose her inner thigh. "You're mine, Bryn. That's my ring on your finger. If I want a taste of you, I'll have it. Anywhere on your body I want."

Her body turned to fire as he kneaded the sensitive skin on her bare thigh. Gasping, she challenged, "You think you can do as you wish because I wear your ring?"

His darkened eyes taunted her as his hand continued to stroke her thigh. "Tell me you don't want this."

She clamped her jaw shut, narrowing her eyes. Want it? Lords and ladies, she was craving it more than anything she'd ever wanted in her life. She was practically panting to have him touch her more. But she wasn't about to give him the satisfaction.

"Right," he barked at her silence. "That's what I

thought. Now sit back on the seat and spread your legs."

Her eyes widened. Her body was already quivering, and with shaky limbs, she slid off his lap and onto the velvet bench seat. Reclining against the backrest, she eased her knees open a few more inches.

"More," Rangar grunted as he wrenched her knees apart. Her thighs tried to clamp together on instinct, but Rangar was already on his knees on the carriage floor. He balled her dress's hem in his fists as he slid the fabric up to her waist.

The carriage jostled, and Bryn squeaked as the motion awakened her already-alert body. She found her gaze pinned on Rangar's hands as he stroked his way up her thighs and pressed his thumb against the buzzing place at her center.

"Saints," she gasped.

"Be quiet," he threatened. "Or Valenden will stop this carriage to see what the commotion is. I'd rather not have my brother see my bride naked *again*, but his interruption won't stop me from taking what I want, whether he watches or not."

Her jaw fell open at his bold threat, but she was buzzing too much to be scandalized for long. Rangar shoved her panties aside and dipped a finger into her cleft. She cried out again.

At his warning look, she clamped a hand over her mouth.

He licked his way from her knee to her upper thigh until he replaced his finger with his tongue. Bryn went breathless as the buzzing feeling intensified. With one hand still clamped over her mouth, she gave soft sighs as Rangar nipped and licked and sucked. Her other hand twisted in his hair, holding on like a stallion's mane.

Rangar devoted his time to getting the taste he was after, but with the rhythmic rocking of the carriage over the bumpy road, it wasn't long before Bryn cried out in a rush of unstoppable pleasure, clamping her thighs tightly against the side of his head.

Rangar wiped his mouth with the back of his hand and looked up at her wolfishly. "That'll be enough to satisfy me until we stop at an inn for the night. I'm going to have you there. *And* the inn after that. *And* the one after that. I'm going to bed you in every village from here to the Baersladen."

She was still heaving for breath when Rangar straightened her clothes and opened the curtain again. Her vision had gone blurry from the things he'd made her feel, and it took her a moment to center her sight on the surroundings.

They were beyond Saint's Forest, on the way to the village of Cinde. She recognized the dairy farm with the long stone fence that, until a few months ago, had been the furthest she'd ever gone from Castle Mir.

Rangar brushed her hair off her shoulder to nuzzle his mouth against her ear. "You have no idea how many nights I lay awake wondering what you'd taste like." His voice went gravelly. "Honey. It's honey."

# CHAPTER 4

**THE CHESTNUT INN . . . dangers further north . . .
sausage soup . . . talk of war . . . wolves**

The road north passed through winter-dead fields where stone cottages' chimneys pumped out steady smoke. By the second day on the road, they'd traveled into the upper boundary of the Mirien kingdom. Famed for its flat ground and silty soil, the land until then had made for easy travel. But now, taking a turn in the driver's seat with Rangar, Bryn spied the foothills ahead that would slow their progress.

"That's the boundary with Vil-Kevi." Rangar pointed to a ridge line in the distance. "We'll be there by this evening."

Bryn drew a wool blanket tightly around her. "Do

you think it's already snowed in the higher mountains?"

"Without a doubt," Rangar said, glancing at her thin dress beneath the blanket. "When we get there, you'll wear my bearskin cloak."

She didn't argue—she'd seen Rangar tromp practically shirtless through the frigid cold and be utterly unbothered. But *she* wasn't yet so hardy. "I'll get used to the cold eventually," she murmured, more to herself than Rangar.

Holding the reins in one hand, he rested the other on her knee reassuringly. "No one expects a princess who spent most of her life in the Mirien's warm climate to have as thick skin as the Baer people. There is no shame in finding the cold difficult."

She gave a shrug, still worried. "The future queen of the Baersladen shouldn't need to huddle by the fire."

His hand squeezed her knee. "I'll keep you warm, my love."

His flirtatious tone made her mood lighten. Watching the road ahead, she shaded her eyes. "Is that an inn?"

Rangar nodded. "It's the last inn before we enter the forest. We'll stop for our midday meal before pressing on toward Vil-Kevi." He knocked twice on the side of the carriage, and after a few seconds, Valenden stuck his head out with a scowl.

"I was napping, you oaf."

"We're arriving at The Chestnut Inn," Rangar informed him.

Valenden squinted ahead to see the inn, then, after a yawn, his face turned serious. "We'll be ready."

When he ducked back inside, Bryn asked, "Why did Val seem worried? Do you anticipate danger? The inns we stopped at yesterday were fine."

Rangar's jaw was set hard as he steered the carriage horses toward the inn. "Those were closer to Mir Town, where it's safer. There are Mir soldiers patrolling in those areas. Out here, we're on our own. As we near the border, there are more travelers from all different towns and kingdoms, and some of them can be desperate."

"Bandits, you mean." She raised her eyebrows as she recalled her days on the road with Valenden. "The last time I ran into bandits wasn't so bad—I was reunited with my sister. I have to admit, it did change my perspective on banditry."

"Not all bandits are secret dukes and duchesses who give their spoils to the poor," Rangar cautioned. "And it isn't only bandits we should fear. When people from different places come together, even the most law-abiding folk can clash."

The inn was a two-story wooden structure that had seen better days, though it was in good repair. One other carriage was parked in front, along with a few horses tied to a hitching post. An old woman drew water from the well at the side of the building.

Rangar pulled up beside the large black carriage

and helped Bryn climb down. "A public carriage," he said, nodding toward the other one. "Transporting travelers to Ardmoor, most likely. Public carriages don't go further into the mountains beyond that."

He unharnessed the horses to let them rest and drink water from the trough at the hitching post while Valenden and Saraj climbed out and stretched. Bryn noted that Valenden's sword was now strapped to his side for the first time since leaving Castle Mir.

"Where's Zephyr?" Bryn asked Saraj, tipping her head upward.

"I crated him for now," she said. "Falcons tend to draw attention."

"So do famous princesses," Valenden muttered, looking Bryn over. "It wouldn't be the worst idea to cover your fair hair until we're in the Baersladen."

Bryn touched the tips of her hair with a frown.

Rangar dropped a heavy hand on his brother's shoulder. "You aren't on the run anymore, Val. There is no need for disguises."

Valenden's face remained grave. "Not everyone is thrilled to have the Lindane family back in power."

"That's their problem, not ours," Rangar said. "Besides, I need to ask around for any clues that could lead us to Broderick, and I *want* him to know it's me pursuing him. I have no wish to hide my identity."

Valenden didn't seem quite so confident, but he strode toward the door regardless. "Well, in any case, I'm starving. And I wouldn't say no to an ale."

Saraj slid her arm between Bryn's and muttered wryly, "Has Val *ever* said no to an ale?"

Inside, there was a young couple with a baby, and two men wearing the green of Vil-Kevi's army, and a few other men alone at tables with ale. All eyes turned to them when they entered. The old woman Bryn had seen at the well came over as she dried her hands on her apron.

"My Lord, what an honor," she said in surprise and deference to Rangar, taking note of his fine clothes, then glanced at Valenden with a little more uncertainty. "My Lords, I mean." When her eyes fell on Bryn, they widened considerably. "Goodness! Lady Bryn! Is it truly you?"

Bryn gave a kind nod. "We're seeking a meal and some rest from our travels."

"Certainly, princess." The woman wiped off a table by the front windows. They took their places, and she brought them mugs of ale and warm sausage soup. Rangar disappeared to the backroom to speak with the innkeeper, doubtlessly asking if anyone with Broderick's description had passed through.

Bryn had finished half her ale when the young mother at the next table cleared her throat. "If I may be so bold, Lady Bryn, is it true about your brother? Prince Mars lives?"

Bryn turned to face the woman with the baby at her breast. "Yes, it is. Hasn't the official messenger already spread the word?"

The woman shook her head. "We've heard only

rumors so far, my lady. We weren't sure what to believe. There's been so much, ah, uncertainty these last few months."

*Uncertainty.* As in her parents swinging from the gallows.

"I assure you," Bryn said gently. "My brother is alive and well and has been crowned king of the Mirien. There will be a formal celebration of his coronation soon at Castle Mir."

One of the solo travelers made a gruff sound in his throat. He was a heavyset, bearded man with a dangerous air to him, and it wasn't lost on Bryn that Rangar chose this moment to return to the table.

"Begging your pardon, my lady," the man said gruffly, "But isn't Prince Mars without sight?"

Bryn straightened her spine. "It's *King* Mars, and yes, my brother's eyes were damaged, though he does not need sight to rule."

"Not with a witch at his side," one of the other men muttered snidely.

Valenden whirled around in his seat, one hand on his sword as he asked sharply, "What was that, good sir?"

The second man, with gray hair threading at his temples and heavy wrinkles on his brow, didn't look cowed by Valenden in the slightest. "They say the new king intends to bring magic to the Mirien. That's why he married a witch."

Bryn felt the energy shift around her. At her side,

Rangar's muscles went rigid. Saraj's eyes scanned the room as though expecting danger at any moment.

Rangar started to speak, but Bryn rested a hand on his arm. She said to the man, "And what of it? Magic would put great power into the hands of the Mir people. We've always prided ourselves on placing logic above superstition. So, is it not logical to use what tools we can to better the kingdom?"

The young mother looked alarmed by the mention of magic, but the older men didn't balk.

The heavyset one said, "Perhaps, my lady, but I've come from Zaradona, and there is much discontent at the idea of permitting the free use of magic. Here in the Mirien, we may be ruled by logic, but the southern kingdoms are ruled by religious tradition. Magic is a sin in Zaradona. In Ruma and Dresel, too."

"I was also taught that magic was a sin," Bryn said steadily. "And I believed it until I saw for myself what a blessing it could be."

Saraj leaned close to Bryn and whispered, "Perhaps we'd best continue our journey now, Bryn."

Bryn shook her head. "I want to know what the common folk think." She faced the two men again and said loudly, "Speak plainly. You won't be punished for any treasonous talk as long as your words are the truth."

The gray-haired man pressed his lips together tightly, but the heavyset one continued, "Your brother has chosen a difficult path, princess. He may drag the Mirien kicking and screaming into accepting magic, but he has no say over the other kingdoms."

"The Baersladen already permits magic," Valenden argued. "As do Vil-Kevi and Vil-Rossengard."

"Zaradona, Ruma, and Dresel will fight him over it," the man countered. "Perhaps also the Wollin."

"So?" Valenden said hotly. "Zaradona and Ruma and Dresel can do what they wish on their own lands."

"Magic is like an infection," the man said gruffly. "Just like all new ideas, it spreads. Borders do not stop it. You think the rulers of Zaradona and Ruma and Dresel will stand by quietly while the new Mir king brings magic right to their doorstep?"

A heaviness sank into the pit of Bryn's stomach, but she refused to be intimidated. "Some new ideas are necessary. They *should* spread."

"Even at the cost of war?" the man challenged, looking boldly into her eyes.

Rangar jumped up, drawing his sword. "You're addressing a princess; may I remind you."

Bryn shook her head quickly. "Rangar, it's all right. I asked him to speak plainly. We cannot fault him for it now."

Saraj stood and slipped the old innkeeper a few coins. She herded Bryn up and out of her seat. "We should get back on the road if we want to make Bergil Town by nightfall."

Back in the carriage, Bryn still felt shaken. It didn't help that the road grew bumpier and rockier as they entered the forested hills. She wanted to talk to Rangar about what the burly man at the inn had said, but he was up front driving the carriage.

"You look troubled," Saraj noted. She had Zephyr out of his crate and perched on her gloved arm, and was feeding him strips of dried venison.

Meanwhile, Valenden had sprawled out on his bearskin cloak on the carriage floor and had managed to fall asleep despite the bumpy movements.

"I can't stop thinking about the prospect of war," Bryn admitted. "When Mars and I discussed bringing magic to the Mirien, we knew it would be met with resistance both within and outside of the Mirien, but that man's warning about the southern kingdoms . . ." she shook her head, troubled. "I worry that our aims might bring more pain than power to the common folk."

Feeding Zephyr another strip of dried meat, Saraj observed, "War has been at the Eyrie's doorstep for a decade now, ever since the sighting of the black fawn. Tensions between the kingdoms were high long before Mars's decision to allow magic. The monarchs of the southern kingdoms rule with absolute power; if that is ever to change, magic is the means."

Bryn gave a nod. "You're right. My greatest fear now is—"

The carriage jolted, immediately followed by the panicked whinny of one of the horses. Bryn grabbed the windowsill to steady herself. Saraj clamped Zephyr's leather hood over his eyes to keep him calm.

On the floor, Valenden stirred groggily amid muttered curses. "What the devil . . ."

A horse whined sharply again. The carriage drew to such a rough halt that Bryn tumbled off her seat and crashed onto Valenden. For a brief moment, they were a tangle of limbs as the carriage rocked back and forth.

"If you want me that badly, princess," Valenden muttered, "You needn't throw yourself on me."

Bryn ignored his comment as she twisted toward Saraj, who was already thrusting open the window to look outside.

"Stay in the carriage!" Rangar called urgently from the driver's seat.

"What's happening?" Saraj called.

Bryn's skin turned clammy with a dark premonition. Her dress suddenly felt too tight, like she couldn't breathe. She pressed a hand over her ribs, struggling for full breaths, feeling the scar lines hidden beneath the fabric.

"Wolves," Rangar said darkly from outside.

# CHAPTER 5

**WOLVES ON THE ROAD . . . clash of swords . . . a lucky knife . . . animals or demons . . . into the night alone**

*W*olves.

Instantly, Bryn was six years old again and lying in the snow at Saint Serrel's shrine, bleeding out as a pack of wolves tore into her flesh. Digging her fingers against the scars along her ribs, she fought her rising panic.

Outside, a wolf howled, and then the carriage jolted again.

Wide-eyed, Bryn met Saraj and Valenden's equally concerned looks before she thrust her head out the window. Twilight was falling, and the thick forest cover overhead made the evening that much darker.

One of the horses was bleeding from its shoulder. Both animals were stamping their hooves, eyes flashing wildly as though they might bolt at any moment.

Something rustled in the brush on the side of the road. Bryn caught a quick glimpse of gray fur. "Rangar?" she called in alarm.

He twisted to look backward at her call. He had his sword in one hand, the reins firmly in the other to keep the horses from bolting. "Bryn, get back inside the carriage! And tell my damned brother to get out here with his sword!"

"Wolves don't attack large groups," she pressed, her voice rising in pitch.

A moment of sympathy softened his face. He, more than anyone, knew what wolves meant to her. For ten years, they'd haunted her nightmares. She feared wolves more than anything else.

"These wolves are different," he said. "Larger. More violent. Now get Valenden out here *now*."

Bryn ducked back in, chest rising and falling quickly. "Val." Her voice was hoarse. "Rangar needs you."

For all his cursing, Valenden couldn't hide the fact that he was actually quite fearless. He didn't hesitate to climb out of the carriage, closing the door behind him to keep the women safe.

A howl sounded from somewhere close by in the woods.

"What's happening out there?" Saraj asked in a rush.

"A wolf attacked one of the horses," Bryn explained. "I don't know if we'll be able to continue. It looked badly wounded."

Saraj's brow furrowed.

Bryn wet her lips and said in a shaky voice, "Mars warned us of reports about wolves attacking travelers —" Before she could finish, growls sounded outside, followed by one of the horses shrieking. The carriage suddenly rocked violently.

They heard a man grunt—either Rangar or Valenden, Bryn couldn't tell—and slash at something with his sword.

Rangar suddenly yelled, *"Behind you!"*

Valenden let out a determined cry as he slammed into something. The carriage rocked violently again. Saraj tightened her jaw and pressed a hand on Zephyr's back to keep him calm. She reached for the door handle.

"What are you doing?" Bryn said breathlessly. "Don't go out there!"

"Zephyr can help fight off the wolves," she insisted.

A minute later, Bryn was left alone in the carriage as more growls sounded outside. She heard Zephyr's shriek, followed by a wolf's pained yip. Rangar and Valenden shouted warnings to one another.

*"Val, another one to your left!"*

*"That's not a wolf, that's a gods damned demon!"*

Their swords clanked as the two men fought off

the wolves. One of the horses let out a scream that sounded all too human.

"Lords and ladies," Bryn muttered under her breath to rile up her courage. "I'm not eight years old anymore. I can help, too."

She unsheathed the small knife she kept strapped to the outside of her boot and opened the carriage door. Before she could even step out, a flash of gray fur bolted past her. Shrieking, she clutched the door jamb with one hand and the knife with the other.

The wolf was *huge*.

For a second, she felt like she was back in the battle of Saint Serrel's shrine, only instead of soldiers against rebels, it was monsters attacking. Several wolves snarled at the head of the road, where Rangar stood between them and the horses. One of the horses was already dead, its carcass weighing down the harness and spooking the other, who was covered in blood but still standing.

Valenden was frantically trying to free the living horse.

Saraj whistled, and Zephyr dove out of the sky. Bryn whirled to find two wolves creeping up on her.

She gasped.

Zephyr suddenly slashed its talons at one's eyes. The other locked its sight onto Bryn and snarled. She had just enough time to raise her knife as it rushed her. Her instincts took over. As the beast lunged for her with lips drawn back and teeth flashing, her hand came down. She slashed the knife against its muzzle.

Its weight crashed into her, knocking her to her feet, but she had enough time to raise her knife again before it doubled back.

It snarled low, preparing to strike again.

*Black eyes*, she thought in a confused rush. *Its eyes are black and weeping black tears.*

But she didn't have much time to wonder what was wrong with the wolf before it pounced. She dug her heels into the ground, ready to fight. When it was close enough, she drove the knife into the side of its neck, though it managed to get its teeth around her arm.

"Bryn!"

Rangar was by her side in an instant, sword raised. He brought the blade down over the wolf's neck. Such a blow would have sliced the head off a regular wolf, but this one seemed like its bones were made of steel. Rangar's sword lodged in the wolf's spine. He wrenched it out with a vicious battle yell and brought it down again.

This time, the wolf stayed down.

*Dead—finally.*

Breathing hard, Bryn looked in a daze at the blood seeping from her arm, then at the dead wolf. She grabbed her knife out of its neck, clutching the hilt tightly in preparation for the next attack.

"Valenden, protect the horse!" Rangar shouted.

"I'm trying, gods be damned!" Valenden answered. With his back turned, he didn't see a wolf stalking out of the woods behind him.

But Bryn did.

She screamed as the wolf threw itself on Valenden in a storm of teeth and claws. Valenden was fast—he gripped the animal by the neck and tried to wrench it off him, but it had gotten its teeth deep in his side. With the wolf blocking access to his sword, Valenden had only his fists as weapons. He slammed a punch into the wolf's head, but the beast only bit him harder.

Rangar was on his feet immediately. He picked up his sword with both hands and, giving another battle cry, leaped on the wolf, using his momentum to slam the blade into its back. The wolf yipped, wounded, and released Valenden. It scrambled back a few steps, blood rushing from the deep cut, but then it turned on Rangar with those strange black eyes.

Saraj gave a sharp whistle. Zephyr circled overhead, ready to dive again. "Bryn, get Val into the carriage!" Saraj said. "I'll cover you!"

While Rangar faced off with the wolf, Bryn skirted around it, breathing hard. Its eyes shifted to her, but Zephyr swooped down with flapping wings to block its vision. Rangar gave another yell as he swung his sword at the wolf, though it moved with incredible speed out of the way.

Valenden collapsed to the ground, clutching his ribs.

"Val!" Bryn sank to her knees beside him. She tugged his arm around her neck. "Stand. Hurry!"

He winced as she helped him to his feet.

"We have to lay you down in the carriage," she ordered.

She helped him crawl into the carriage, where he groaned as he lay flat on his bearskin cloak. She rested a hand on his shin while glancing back at the fight. Rangar raised his sword again. The wounded wolf feigned an attack to the left, but Rangar sensed its deception and swung the sword to the right just as the wolf moved that way instead.

The blade lodged deep into the animal's skull.

The wolf shuddered before falling to the ground, dead. Rangar immediately went to where Valenden had been working to extract the horse from its broken harness. He cut through the tangled strap, freeing the animal.

Eyes rolling in fear, the horse reared up, drawing the attention of the wolf pack. Rangar slapped the horse on its hindquarters, and the panicked animal took off at a gallop down the road. Immediately, the entire wolf pack gave chase, disappearing into the twilight mist.

Bryn exhaled in both relief and exhaustion. She clutched Valenden's leg hard, her attention turning to him as the next most immediate danger.

Rangar was by her side quickly. His eyes scanned her to make sure she was unhurt, his hand going to her tangled hair. "Your arm—"

"I'm fine. It's Valenden who needs attention."

"Damn thing tried to eat me alive!" Valenden wailed.

The tight set of Rangar's shoulders eased. "If he can complain, he's well enough to survive. Saraj?"

The falconer climbed into the carriage to inspect Valenden's wounds. "Let me see the wound, Val. Dammit, stop moving . . ."

While Saraj tended to Valenden's injury, Rangar led Bryn to the carriage's front, where the lantern shone brightly. He pressed a hand to her cheek to guide her to look him in the eye.

"Tell me you're all right."

"I'm all right, Rangar."

He pulled up her bloody sleeve to inspect the bite mark. His face was grim in the twilight shadows. "It's fortunate the beast didn't get its jaws around you— this is only a gash from its incisors. It will heal, though it might . . . scar."

She swallowed, feeling suddenly numb. *A scar is only a scar*, she wanted to reassure him, but couldn't find the words.

Instead, she said in a rasping voice, "The horse?"

Rangar shook his head. "It would have bled to death anyway. The wolves had already fatally wounded it. With luck, it will draw them far off before they bring it down."

She stared at the blood pooling on the road around the other dead horse. "Will the wolves come back?"

"Not likely after we killed two of their pack. Besides, the horse that led them off should feed the lot of them. Wolves only attack when they're hungry."

"Those weren't normal wolves." Bryn couldn't

keep the panic out of her voice. "You saw them, they were enormous! And fast. And their eyes . . ." She pressed her lips together.

Rangar rubbed her shoulders, making soothing sounds like he would calm a spooked horse. "It'll be all right."

"What about the carriage?" she pressed. "We can't go anywhere without horses."

Rangar was silent for a few moments before he said, "I'll have to go seek help."

She gripped his hand with a strength she didn't know she had. "You can't go off on your own! There could be more wolves!"

"We have no choice. I'll start a bonfire here for you and Saraj and Val. Even hungry wolves fear fire. Stay near the fire and they won't dare venture close. You can always lock yourself in the carriage, too."

"It's *you* I'm worried about!"

"I don't fear wolves." He paused, then added, "Not any longer."

Thinking of their shared past pulled Bryn out of her panic. Taking a few deep breaths, she blinked a few times and then said, "I don't want you to go."

"The dangers of the forest are nothing new to me. I'll hike back to Bergil Town and then return with fresh horses before dawn."

She wanted to argue but couldn't think of any alternative solution. Her worries were interrupted when Saraj stuck her head out of the carriage. "I've bandaged Val the best I can manage. He's sleeping now. He dug a bottle of whiskey out of his bag and drained the entire thing."

Rangar and Bryn returned their attention to Valenden, who was now snoring on the bearskin cloak. Saraj had removed his bloody clothes down to his waist and wrapped his wounds in strips torn from one of his shirts.

"How bad is it?" Rangar asked.

"He'll recover as long as it doesn't get infected. We need to make haste back to Barendur Hold so the mages can treat him properly."

Rangar explained his plan to return to Bergil Town, and Saraj agreed it was the best course of action. The three of them dragged fallen logs from the forest to the side of the road, where Rangar used a hex to light a fire. By the time the flames rose, night had fully fallen, and sparks glittered in the darkness.

Sitting on a log between the fire and the carriage, Bryn hugged her blanket tighter around her shoulders as she watched Rangar gather extra weapons and coins to purchase new horses.

Finally, he came to stand in front of her, then dropped into a crouch. In his bearskin cloak with dirt and blood streaking his face, he looked as much a beast as the wolves themselves.

"I'll return before dawn, Bryn."

She stared at their clasped hands, unable to look him in the eyes for fear that she might never see his face again.

"I *will*," he insisted. "I've spent my entire life

wanting you by my side. I made an oath when I saved you—I'm responsible for keeping you safe."

"I made an oath, too," she said quietly. "I'm responsible for your life as well, Rangar. So, you'd better come back to me in one piece, if you have any hope of me believing in fate."

His mouth twitched in a brief smile. "You'll believe, Bryn Lindane."

He sealed the promise with a soft kiss.

As he disappeared into the darkness, Saraj came to sit beside Bryn, wrapping an arm around her back as the fire crackled. Far off in the distance, a lone wolf howled.

# CHAPTER 6

**BONFIRE TALKS . . . berserkir beasts and fairy tales . . . science and magic . . . a welcome sight . . . departure**

"There's something unnatural about those wolves," Bryn said as she and Saraj huddled in front of the bonfire. Out of the corner of her eye, she spied on the cadaver of one of the fallen beasts.

"They're the biggest wolves I've ever seen," Saraj voiced her agreement. "And did you see how their eyes have some black substance in them?"

"I thought they were crying black tears. Have you ever heard of such a thing?"

Saraj shook her head. Her hands knit in her lap as the crackling fire painted an orange glow over her face.

In a low voice, she said, "Do you know the legend of the berserkir beasts?"

The name alone gave Bryn enough of a chill to pull her blanket tighter. "My nan told me a lot of stories growing up, but not that one."

"I'm not surprised," Saraj said. "I imagine the bedtime stories they tell princesses tend to be pretty fables about rabbits and wishing wells. Common folk tell their children darker tales meant to warn them away from dangerous acts, such as wandering too far into the woods on their own."

Bryn glanced at the two dead wolf carcasses. A puddle of blood had spread from their bodies toward the fire. She shivered and moved her foot away from the encroaching puddle. "Go on."

"In the orphanage where I grew up, the older children told the younger ones that berserkir beasts were wild creatures who had been possessed by evil spirits and patrolled the places where two environments meet: forest and field, or sea and village, that kind of place. The evil spirits inhabiting the animals granted them astonishing strength and size. Berserkir bears could easily tear down a redwood tree. Berserkir foxes could slaughter an entire stable of sheep. They had a vicious bloodlust; they rarely even ate their victims. They were only after the violence."

Bryn squeezed her hands together tightly. "You think these are berserkir wolves? They've been taken over by an evil spirit?"

Saraj shook her head. "It's only a made-up story.

There were never any real berserkir beasts. And even from what I know of mages who practice dark magic, I've never heard of possession like that." She took a deep breath as she, too, studied the wolf corpses. "I'll admit, however, that the first thing I thought of when I saw those wolves was the old stories."

"So, if berserkir beasts aren't real, then what are *those*? Could they be sick?"

Bryn stood up and moved apprehensively toward the closest dead wolf. She crouched a safe distance away in case it did have some sort of contagious disease, and used a stick to examine its lifeless body.

Saraj joined her with a lit torch to shine light on the carcass. The two women inspected the dead wolves as best they could from a distance.

"I don't see any rashes or sores," Saraj noted. "And they weren't foaming at the mouth like dogs who have *lyssa*."

Bryn used the stick to push the fur back from the wolf's eyes to get a better look. "That oily substance almost looks like it's coating its entire eye. I'm surprised it could even see."

Saraj nudged the beast's hindquarters with her shoe. "It has muscle on top of muscle. Not at all like regular wolves, who are lean and bony."

Bryn tossed the stick into the forest, wiping her hands on her dress. She'd never wished for warm water and soap more in her life. An owl hooted far off in the woods, and Bryn and Saraj returned to the fire. They shared a humble meal of hardtack and cheese that Saraj supplemented with some late-season dandelion leaves she found on the roadside. As they sat in silence, Bryn's mind filled with worries about the wolves and Rangar being out there on his own.

She glanced back toward the carriage as a new fear entered her head. "Val was badly bitten; if the wolves *are* sick, he could be infected."

Her own arm had been injured, but the wolf hadn't sunk in its teeth as it had with Valenden, and from what she knew of diseases from animals, a solid bite was usually required.

"He hasn't shown any sign of illness yet," Saraj pointed out.

"Still, we should take the wolf carcasses with us to Barendur Hold so the healers can examine them in case he does sicken."

"That's a good idea, but the healers in the Baersladen aren't like the ones in the Mirien," Saraj said. "Your people rely on science; we look primarily to magic. Our healers can bandage scrapes and make fortifying teas, but most of our people go to mages for any grave health concerns."

As part of her education, Bryn had been taught the fundamentals of biology and the human body. It surprised her to think the Baer people might not have such basic knowledge, and she wondered if perhaps the Baersladen could gain as much from studying science as the Mirien could from embracing magic.

"There is a place for both science and magic," Bryn said. "Our healers are skilled, though I envy the fact that Mage Marna could mend a broken bone with just a few words."

Saraj added another log to the fire, standing back as smoke billowed upward. "You're right that both take skill and years of practice to master. I'm sure if I saw a Mir healer sewing a cut closed with thread, it would look like magic to me."

Bryn peeked at the bandaged wound on her own arm as she wondered what it would be like to have the ability to heal herself. "I hope for the chance to learn more magic when we're back in the Baersladen. I have only three hexmarks—four if you count the translation one, but that one draws off Mage Marna's magic, not mine."

"Three hexmarks are three more than any other Mir citizen I know of," Saraj said kindly.

Bryn tipped her chin questioningly at Saraj. "How many do you have?"

"Twenty-two."

Bryn gaped, impressed. "What do they all *do*?"

Saraj smiled as her hand drifted to her shoulder to feel the raised scars beneath her clothes. "Everyone receives the same hexmarks at the beginning. The finding spell, the spark spell, the sleep spell—that one helps yourself fall asleep, not put others to sleep, which is much more advanced. Those three don't require much skill beyond being able to speak the words and learn the hand gestures."

Bryn snorted. "They weren't that simple for me. It

took me days to get the finding spell to work. It kept leading me to Rangar instead of the lost lamb."

Saraj laughed softly. "Well, you didn't grow up surrounded by magic. Baer children pick up the ways of hexmarks from a young age."

"And your other marks?"

"Many are to help me hunt with Zephyr. Superior eyesight, the ability to move quietly through the woods." She dropped her voice. "Did you know there are some to enhance pleasure . . . with a man?"

Bryn raised her eyebrows.

Saraj winked. "I'm sure you'll want to get those hexmarks once you and Rangar are wed."

Before Bryn could reply, a weak voice called from the nearby carriage, "As though Bryn and Rangar haven't already ravished each other. In fact, I know for certain that they have."

"Val!" Bryn jumped up, running to the carriage where he lay on blankets on the carriage floor. "You're awake. How are you feeling?"

"Like I was attacked by wolves." He sat up, wincing, and gingerly touched the blood-soaked bandage around his side. "And then drank an entire bottle of ale."

"That last part is your own fault," Saraj chided. "Bryn, help me change this bandage. There are water jugs in the trunk at the carriage's rear."

Bryn fetched a water jug, and together the women cleaned the dried blood off Valenden's torso and eased a fresh bandage around him. Saraj looked worried as she tied off the bandage. "The wound is deeper than I originally thought. There's no way to clean it out fully."

Wincing, Valenden eased himself back down to the blanket. "My aunt can burn out any infection with a spell once we get to Barendur Hold."

"It isn't infection I worry about," Saraj muttered, glancing at Bryn. "At least not *just* infection. These aren't normal wolves. Bryn and I examined one of the dead ones—we think they may be sick."

"Sick? What kind of illness gives a creature strength and speed like that? Those were the healthiest damn wolves I've ever seen."

Bryn patted his bare shoulder. "I'm sure you will be fine, but you should save your strength. Try not to move more than you need to." She frowned at Saraj. "He's shivering. Should we move him closer to the fire?"

Saraj considered this, then said, "It's too much of a risk. If the wolf pack returns, you and I can likely make it to the carriage in time, but he wouldn't be able to. I think it's best he stays here. We'll load him up with blankets."

They unpacked every wool blanket they'd brought, and buried Valenden under it. After it was done, Bryn yawned, rubbing her eyes.

"You should sleep, too, Bryn," Saraj said. "I'll keep watch by the fire, and we can trade places in the morning."

Bryn was too exhausted to argue. The carriage

floor was just wide enough that she could lay down next to Valenden, curling under his blankets. She wrapped an arm carefully around his unhurt shoulder to keep him warm.

"Good night, princess," he muttered, already half-asleep again.

"Good night, Val." After a few minutes, she whispered, "I fear for Rangar alone in the woods."

But Valenden started snoring, and Bryn sighed and closed her eyes.

"By the gods, I left you alone with her for *one night*, Val."

Bryn's eyes shot open at the familiar voice. Early morning sunlight streamed through the carriage windows. Rangar stood beside the open door, scowling down at Bryn and Valenden entwined together under the blankets.

"Rangar!" She shoved to her knees and crawled over to throw her arms around him. "Are you well? What happened?"

He pressed a kiss to her forehead. "No more wolf sightings, though I did hear them howling to the east. I was able to buy two new horses in Bergil Town. We can continue the journey." He touched Valenden's boot beneath the blanket. "How is he?"

Still snoring, Valenden didn't stir.

"He's well, considering," Bryn said.

Rangar grunted. "If he's so well, explain to me why you felt the need to sleep at his side all night?"

She leveled an impatient look at him. "Tame your jealousy, Rangar. We have greater concerns." She climbed out of the carriage, away from Valenden's hearing if he should wake. Saraj was heating water over the fire for tea. She whispered to Rangar, "We think the wolves might be sick. Valenden could be infected."

Rangar's face turned serious. Bryn pointed out the wolf carcass, and Rangar knelt to inspect it. In a grave voice, he said, "We'll wrap the bodies in blankets and stow them in the luggage rack. Mage Marna can examine them."

Bryn, Saraj, and Rangar wrestled the giant wolf bodies into blankets, then stacked them on top of their wooden trunk. The two horses Rangar had brought back from Bergil Town hung back skittishly on their lead ropes, as though they smelled the lingering scent of wolves.

"We should go," Rangar said, looking up at the sun. "It's still several days' voyage to Barendur Hold, and the sooner we get Val to my aunt, the better."

He hitched the horses to the carriage and put out their campfire. Bryn climbed in the driver's seat with Rangar, while Saraj took a turn in the back.

The horses took them deeper into Disworth Forest.

# CHAPTER 7

**ACROSS THE BORDER . . . Lady Enis returns . . . growing discontent . . . wolf carcasses . . . happy to be home**

Rangar drove the horses as swiftly as possible over the uneven forest road. They entered the kingdom of Vil-Kevi around midday. The trees were larger here and seemed to make clicking sounds, almost like they were communicating with each other. Bryn had briefly visited Vil-Kevi once before when the Barendur family had brought her on an ill-fated attempt to rendezvous with Mars, and she'd been both disturbed and enchanted by the strange forest kingdom.

That night, they slept in a small inn that was barely more than the back room of a farmhouse, and the following day continued deeper into the forest, where the mountains began to make the road more difficult to traverse. Valenden stirred in and out of consciousness, demanding they stop for more ale from the few inns they passed. There was no obvious sign of infection in his wound, but Bryn didn't like how pale he was growing day after day.

When they stopped at an inn that night, she asked Rangar, "How much further until we reach the Baersladen border?"

"Tomorrow if the weather holds, then another day and a half to Barendur Hold."

Bryn looked apprehensively at the twilight sky. It had been snowing light flurries on and off all day. The higher mountain elevations visible from the road were blanketed with thicker snow.

The inn was larger and livelier than any they'd come across thus far in Vil-Kevi. With stone walls and a tiled roof, it was the grandest building in the small hamlet of farmhouses that surrounded it. Several horses were tied to the hitching post out front.

"Gods, I'm starving," Saraj said as she climbed out of the carriage. She sniffed the air. "Beef stew?"

Valenden, moving gingerly, painstakingly climbed out. "*You're* starving? I'm practically dying here, Saraj. I need sustenance."

Rangar helped Valenden hobble to the inn. Bryn walked ahead and held the door open for them. Warm firelight and the rich smell of savory dishes floated out, bolstering her spirits. A fiddler played a rousing tune by the inn's fireplace. There were a few women and even children dining around the wooden tables, and more people than the few tethered horses outside suggested, which meant the inn must also serve as a public house for the small village.

Rangar spotted a pair of men in traditional Baer logging garb. "I'm going to ask about Broderick, and then I'll see about us getting rooms for the night."

While he went to speak to the Baer men, the rest of their traveling party took their seats. A sweet girl who couldn't have been older than twelve served them stew, which was even more delicious than it had smelled.

"I see you've returned to Vil-Kevi, princess," a female voice said from behind Bryn. "It must have charmed you on your first visit."

On alert, Bryn turned to find a middle-aged woman with long blond hair and angular features dressed in a forest-green gown, with slits on the side to allow her to move freely in the breeches beneath.

"Lady Enis!" Bryn said, pleasantly surprised. "How fortunate to see you again. Saraj, Lady Enis is a countess in Vil-Kevi. She helped us the previous time we were in this forest."

Lady Enis looked dubiously at Valenden's bandages beneath his partially unbuttoned shirt. "Prince Valenden, you're looking significantly worse than the last time we met."

Valenden threw back the rest of his ale and

explained, "We met with some trouble on the road a few days ago."

Lady Enis's thin eyebrows rose. "What kind of trouble?"

Bryn cleared her throat and said in a quiet voice so as not to upset the nearby diners, "We were attacked by unusually large wolves a few miles before reaching the Vil-Kevi border."

Lady Enis's mouth pursed knowingly.

"This isn't the first you're hearing of such an attack," Saraj guessed.

"No, unfortunately, it isn't. We've had reports from several villages and farmsteads of these large wolves you speak of. My cousin, Prince Anter, sent out hunters who have yet to find anything."

Bryn leaned in over the flickering candle. "We killed two of the beasts. We have their bodies in the carriage."

"Do you truly? Prince Anter would be exceedingly interested to examine them."

"Feel free to take one," Valenden muttered. "Personally, I think it's macabre to ride around with dead monsters wrapped in blankets." He doubled over, coughing.

Bryn frowned. "Val, you should rest." She spotted Rangar speaking to the innkeeper behind the bar. A few keys traded hands. Bryn waved Rangar over.

"Lady Enis," Rangar said, acknowledging the countess with a nod. "It's a pleasure to see you again."

"Rangar, you'd better get Val up to a room," Bryn suggested.

Valenden didn't argue as Rangar helped him to his feet, though he did swipe a bottle of mead off the bar on their way to the stairs.

Once they were gone, Bryn turned back to Lady Enis. "What does Prince Anter think of the attacks?"

She answered measuredly, "He doesn't believe it's a coincidence that strange creatures appear at the same time as so much turmoil in the Eyrie."

"You're speaking of Mars's coronation?" Bryn asked.

Lady Enis gave a small nod. "Among other things, including King Aleth's poor health in the Baersladen and what that will mean for its future. But yes, the Mirien is the most powerful kingdom in the Eyrie; everyone is waiting to see how its people will fare under Mars's rule. The rumors that Mars intends to allow magic have been met with mixed opinions even here in Vil-Kevi, where we've practiced magic for generations."

"Why would the forest folk oppose magic?" Saraj asked.

"Because of the wolf attacks. Some say they are caused by dark magic meant to weaken the Outlands. Perhaps even from Mirien."

"Mars would never do such a thing!" Bryn argued. "He knows nothing of magic himself; it will be years before he and his advisors even settle on the right path forward to introduce magic to the common folk."

Lady Enis folded her hands. "You don't have to convince me, Lady Bryn. The royal forest families of Vil-Kevi and Vil-Rossengard will support King Mars. We wish to squelch these superstitious rumors as much as you do."

Bryn was relieved to hear they would have the support of the forest kingdoms. The Eyrie was rapidly becoming divided on the subject of magic, and they needed all the allies they could get. "We'll give you one of the wolf carcasses for Prince Anter," Bryn assured her. "And share any insights we might glean from our own investigations."

Rangar soon rejoined them, and they spent the remainder of the evening discussing the political changes with Lady Enis before retiring to their rooms. Bryn tossed and turned all night until Rangar folded her into his arms, where she at last surrendered to sleep. But her dreams were of wolves and a wind so fierce it kept them from returning to the Baersladen.

The following day, the road led them high into the mountains. They crossed the Baersladen border as a heavy snow began to fall. Bryn joined Saraj and Valenden in the carriage while Rangar hunched under his bearskin cloak to drive the horses. As they crested the pass, Bryn tried to spot the ocean in the distance, but the snow was falling so hard she could barely see ten feet ahead.

There were no inns in the remote mountains, so they had to spend the night in the carriage, huddled around a fire Rangar had started in a silver tin, eating the last of the food Saraj packed. When Bryn woke in the morning, squeezed onto a carriage bench with Rangar, she was relieved to see the storm had calmed. A blue sky now stretched over the snow-blanketed mountains, giving way to the shimmering ocean in the distance. When she squinted, she could see the squat tower of Barendur Hold far down along the coast.

"We're almost home," she breathed as a rush of joy overcame her.

But Rangar's mood was darker as he peered down at the castle. "If my father is as ill as we've been told, that means my aunt will be in charge. I don't know how she'll respond to my return. There might be some people at the Hold that still believe I committed Trei's murder."

"Your aunt won't put you back in chains, surely," Bryn insisted, though worry crept into her voice. Mage Marna was a fair woman but exceedingly tough; she wouldn't take sympathy on Rangar only because he was her nephew. "Valenden sent the letter explaining Broderick's guilt."

"But without evidence, it's only our word."

"No one can find Broderick to *get* evidence," Bryn argued.

"Not yet," Rangar said darkly.

The horses had a hard time descending the mountain pass in the icy snow, but they eventually pulled the carriage into the valley. Bryn's heart soared as she began to recognize the villages along the road. And yet when they stopped at the small hamlet of Mahoven to fix a loose wheel, and common folk gathered around to see what the commotion was, doubt crept in.

Did *they* believe Rangar was Trei's murderer? Would they welcome him as their new crown heir, or call for him to be thrown in the dungeon again? And would they still embrace her, given all the turmoil with the Mirien?

A handful of children ran out of a farmhouse, running up to Bryn. "Lady Bryn!" the children called excitedly. "You're back!"

She smiled and squeezed their offered hands. "I've missed my home here. I'm so happy to have returned."

Now that the children had made the first interaction, a pair of middle-aged women shyly approached her. "We've been worried for you, my lady."

"I'm quite well," Bryn assured them, glancing back at Rangar and Saraj fixing the wheel with some of the local farmers who had volunteered to help. "Is there any further news of King Aleth's health? We came as soon as we heard."

One of the women shook her head sadly. "They say he is bedridden and unlikely to recover."

The other women added in a hushed voice, "There is much speculation about who his successor will be: Prince Rangar or Prince Valenden. Personally, I never once believed Prince Rangar capable of what they accused him of. He'll make a fine king, and you, my lady, will be the queen we've always wanted."

After the worrying news they'd received on the road about the wolf attacks and the discontent growing in the villages over the use of magic, Bryn was exceedingly relieved to hear such welcoming words.

"Are there marriage plans in the works?" the first woman whispered, glancing at Rangar.

Bryn's cheeks reddened as she took off her glove to show them the engagement ring with the maiden rose petal imprint. "That is something I hope to work on once we're back in the Hold, depending on King Aleth's health, of course."

"Oh, it'll be good for the kingdom to have a joyous royal wedding!" the second woman said before slyly raising an eyebrow. "And perhaps young heirs not long after that?"

Bryn's eyes widened at the suggestion of children, but then she smiled and gave a small shrug, though her heart started pounding.

*Did* they want children?

Rangar finished with the wheel and thanked the gathered villagers. Most of them shook his hand enthusiastically, but there were some who hung back with suspicion on their faces.

*Rangar is going to have an uphill battle winning over all his future subjects*, she thought. He desperately needed to clear his name—it was the only way he'd ever be accepted as Aleth's successor.

"Ready, my love?" he asked while holding open the carriage door.

"I'll ride up front," she said. "I want to see Barendur Hold as we approach."

Pride shone in his eyes, though as he looked her up

and down, it transformed to one of flickering desire. As he settled next to her in the driver's seat, he rested a hand on her knee.

"We'll be home soon," he said. "This time, I'm bringing you back as my fiancé. No one is going to come between us again—and I'll be calling you my wife before you can imagine."

# CHAPTER 8

**RETURN TO BARENDUR HOLD . . . a fair punishment . . . "get your hands off her" . . . a deathbed . . . grief and lust**

One of the Mahoven villagers must have ridden ahead to alert Barendur Hold of their impending arrival, because as soon as Rangar pulled the carriage into the village square outside of the castle, they were met by a dozen soldiers.

On alert, Bryn's body instantly went rigid.

Rangar rested a calming hand on her knee. "Let me handle this. These soldiers know me—we trained together. They will not act rashly."

"This isn't exactly the warm homecoming I had hoped for," Bryn muttered.

He squeezed her knee. "All will be well. Do not lose hope."

As they descended the carriage, Mage Marna strode across the drawbridge in her white and gray robes. Her white hair was pulled back in a simple braid. Deep lines etched her face. "Nephew," she said with a nod, coming to stand before the line of soldiers. "Lady Bryn."

Rangar returned her nod. "Aunt. We received your letter about Father's health and came at once. Valenden was wounded on the journey and needs your attention. Furthermore, I would like to see my father immediately."

Mage Marna signaled to two of the soldiers, who went to the carriage to help Valenden. He was groggy and weak, and they ended up fashioning a stretcher out of a blanket and two poles.

Mage Marna did a quick inspection of Valenden, frowning at his wounds. "Take him to Ren in the mage quarters. Tell Ren to prepare a draught of yarrowberry juice. I'll be up shortly."

As they carted Valenden off, Mage Marna turned back to Rangar with a deep line carved between her brows.

"Aunt, if I may—" he started.

She cut him off. "We've decided to put you under house arrest, Rangar."

"*We*?" he said tensely. "Did my father also agree to this?"

"*I* decided it," she corrected herself. "Aleth has

been unconscious for the last two days. Trei's murder case has yet to be solved. We received the information about Broderick but have been unable to locate him. It provides enough doubt to keep you out of the dungeon, but for the time being, I cannot allow you to move freely about Barendur Hold. You'll be restricted to the third-floor suite."

Rangar's jaw clenched but he didn't argue. All in all, Bryn didn't think the mage's decision was unreasonable. Though it wasn't absolving Rangar, nor was it locking him back in the dungeon.

"I need to see my father," he insisted. "He isn't on the third floor."

Mage Marna's stern expression eased. "Yes, you may see him first. Guards, let Prince Rangar through to see the king, then lock him in the suite."

Rangar took Bryn's hand and started to move toward the draw bridge, but Mage Marna held out a hand. "Wait. You go on, Rangar. Let me speak with Bryn alone."

Rangar hesitated, but Bryn squeezed his hand. "It's fine. Go see your father. I'll be right behind you." Two guards followed Rangar as he disappeared into the great hall.

Alone on the drawbridge, Mage Marna gave Bryn a searching look. "You must not interfere with our way of justice," she warned. "We will free Rangar only when there is clear evidence of his innocence. You may visit him in his arrest and stay with him in the third-floor chamber, if you wish."

"I understand. I promise to abide by your decision." She rubbed the bandage on her arm. "There's something more you should know."

Bryn informed Mage Marna about the wolf attack and showed her the remaining carcass. Mage Marna ordered it taken to the mage quarters so she could study it, while also watching Valenden carefully for any sign of sickness.

"There's more," Bryn informed her. "On the road, we heard stirrings that villagers are blaming a dark mage for the wolf attacks. They believe nefarious magic has created some kind of monsters."

"Berserkir wolves," Mage Marna muttered. "Like the old fable." Bryn nodded. Mage Marna looked deeply troubled by this, but she was distracted by Bryn's bandage. In a more gentle tone, she said, "Shall I heal that for you?"

She reached for Bryn's hand, but Bryn held it back. Mage Marna looked confused until Bryn said, "Thank you, but to be honest, I'd rather heal it myself."

Understanding crossed the mage's face. She nodded, approving of Bryn's interest. "So, you still want to apprentice under me?"

"I do."

"We will discuss this more at length, you and me. With Aleth's health in jeopardy, my attention must be on him for the time being." She gave Bryn another approving look. "But I shall keep your interest in mind."

She stepped aside to allow Bryn to cross the drawbridge. As Bryn swept into the great hall, memories rushed back to her. Straw covered the floor as usual, and a few lambs were still curled by the hearth, not yet chased out to pasture by the shepherdess. She recognized her wayward troublemaker lamb among the flock and fought the urge to squeeze him up in a hug—she had more pressing matters.

As she climbed the stairs, she mulled the fact that this wasn't the triumphant return she'd imagined. Rangar was under house arrest, King Aleth was at death's door, Valenden was wounded, and there was the mystery of the berserkir wolves, too . . .

She made her way to the mage chambers, where they had sequestered King Aleth in the largest bedroom. She paused at the door, overwhelmed by the shadow of death that clung to the walls. The king lay in a wooden bed raised off the ground, buried in blankets that clung to his much-diminished shape.

Rangar sat at his father's side, holding his pale hand.

Bryn stepped into the room cautiously. Her lips parted in shock. "Is he . . ."

"He's asleep." Rangar's voice was gruff. "Ren says he hasn't woken in days."

Bryn sank next to Rangar on the bed. "What ails him?"

"The wasting disease," Rangar said quietly.

"Rangar. I'm so sorry. I . . . I didn't think his ailment was this severe."

"Nor did I," Rangar said.

They sat in fraught silence as King Aleth wheezed in his sleep. Despite Mage Marna's urgings that they return immediately, Bryn had still anticipated that they would have months to prepare for King Aleth's possible passing. But seeing the king with her own eyes, she worried they may only have a matter of weeks. Or even less.

They sat with King Aleth for some time before Mage Marna appeared in the doorway. "So you see," she said softly, "why it was imperative that you and Val not spend the winter in the Mirien."

Rangar stood, his expression grave. "There is no chance of recovery, is there?"

Mage Marna shook her head sadly. "The wasting disease exceeds my healing ability. We brought in mages from the forest kingdoms; they were also unable to help him other than to ensure he isn't in pain."

Bryn's heart faltered. King Aleth, gruff as he was, had become like a father to her in the few months that she'd known him. He had opened his home to her and even risked his life to save her.

"How long does he have?" Rangar asked.

"A few weeks, at most."

Rangar filled his lungs, letting the breath out slowly. Bryn rested a gentle hand on his arm. The air felt thick with what everyone wasn't saying: at King Aleth's death, a successor would need to take the throne. Valenden had surrendered his place in line, so Rangar was the natural choice. But was Rangar ready to be king? Would the common folk accept him as their leader if he wasn't able to clear his name first?

"Rest," Mage Marna urged them. "I'll have a meal brought up to your suite."

Before heading to the third floor, they checked on Valenden in his room down the hall, though he was asleep. Ren had replaced the makeshift bandages with clean ones and washed the remaining blood off Valenden's chest.

When they finally reached the door to the third-floor suite, two soldiers stopped them.

"Lord Rangar," the first one said. "I'll need your sword."

Rangar bristled but didn't argue as he unstrapped his sword and handed it to the soldier.

"And any other weapons you have on you. You, too, Lady Bryn."

Rangar produced a number of daggers from hidden places along his body, surprising even Bryn. The soldiers patted him down and nodded for him to enter. "If you'll pardon me, Lady Bryn." The soldier moved to search Bryn for weapons, but Rangar growled low.

"Touch her, Oliver, and I won't need a knife to end you. My fists can do the job."

The soldier, who by his unfazed look was a friend of Rangar's and used to Rangar's temper, said evenly, "You know the rules."

"It's fine, Rangar," Bryn said, holding out her arms.

Rangar narrowed his eyes as the soldier, Oliver,

slid his hands along her curves and then stepped back with his hands raised and a hint of teasing in his eyes. "Done. Was that really so hard, Rangar?"

Rangar scowled at the soldier, grabbed Bryn into the room, then shut the door. Bryn hadn't had many opportunities to visit these chambers before; they were reserved for traveling dignitaries who would expect more comfort than sleeping on a pallet on the great hall's floor. The furniture was heavy oak but simply adorned, with a single wool woven tapestry on the wall.

Bryn placed her hands on the sides of Rangar's face. "Look at me, Rangar." His jaw was so tense she felt the muscles popping beneath her palms. "Your father loves you. He knows on some level that you're back."

Rangar twisted his head to hide the pain that crossed his face. Bryn shook him slightly to force him to look at her again.

"I know what it's like to lose one's father. You were there for me when mine passed. Let me be here for you now."

"He isn't gone," Rangar muttered. "Not yet."

But pain broke across his features, and he folded himself into Bryn, burying his face against her hair. His hands gripped her waist so hard someone would have to pry them apart. She slid her hands over his shoulders.

"He knows you had nothing to do with Trei's death," Bryn reassured him, gently stroking the back of his head. "He always trusted and believed in you. I knew it after spending just a few days with your family. He built a strong Barendur legacy, and you will continue that."

Rangar pulled back, his eyes wet. "They won't accept me as king as long as I'm under arrest in my own home. Nor should they."

Bryn clenched his shirtsleeves in her fists, shaking him out of his brooding nature. "Then *make* them accept you."

"How, without proof?"

"Get proof. You told me you were going to hunt down Broderick. So do it. Drag him back here and make him confess."

Rangar's eyes wavered as his hands tightened around her waist. "And leave you here alone? And my father on his deathbed? And Val?"

"I'll care for your family," she assured him.

Tension was coursing through him. Rangar's eyes were damp, but he didn't cry—*Rangar Barendur never cries.* His muscles were tensing and untensing erratically. Breathing hard, he pressed his forehead against hers.

"I'm no murderer, Bryn."

"I know that, Rangar."

His lips were close enough to hers to brush them when he spoke. A spark shot between them. There was such tension throughout Barendur Hold that it felt as though a storm had settled within the walls. Bryn expected thunder and lightning to crash around them at any moment.

Rangar's hand fell lower on her hip. He palmed her dress's fabric like he wanted to tear it off. "Tell me again that you love me."

"I love you."

"Tell me you belong to me."

"I do—and you belong to me."

He captured her lips in a fiery kiss. There was lust behind it—there was always lust in Rangar's kisses—but Bryn would have been a fool not to have also picked up on the pain there. There was grief and fear and doubt all tied up in his embrace, lending it an almost violent urgency. His teeth grazed her bottom lip hard.

Before she knew it, he picked her up around the waist as though she was a log for the fire and tossed her onto the bed. She fell on the mattress with a squeak.

"Rangar—"

"No. Enough talk." He stalked toward her like a cursed beast himself, his damp eyes hardened now. He prowled his way on top of her, caging her head with his arms, and looked down at her on the bed like he wanted to devour her to quench his own grief. "I've had enough talk for a lifetime. Now, I want you to moan for me."

# CHAPTER 9

**MERCILESS . . . house arrest . . . three gifts . . . brave Calista . . . a brother who doesn't want the throne**

Rangar's lovemaking was merciless. Bryn knew that his reputation as a savage was unwarranted—mostly—but he seemed determined to prove her wrong as he ripped at her clothes, letting his hands and mouth claim every piece of her.

She tossed her head back and gave in to the rush of desire that threatened to consume them both. It was clear that Rangar needed this. He was so filled to the brim with pain that he was practically trembling. If he'd had his sword, he likely would have gone out and fought some pine trees to work out his grief that way, but this way also had its benefits.

*I need it, too.*

Bryn had been so focused on how Rangar felt about his homecoming that she hadn't realized that she'd neglected her own emotional peaks. She, too, had much to grieve and even more to fear. She clung to Rangar around his neck, fingers twisting in his shirt.

"Take this off," she ordered breathlessly, pulling urgently at the fabric.

Rangar tore his lips off her neck long enough to drag his shirt over his head and toss it aside. Then he fell on her again with a visceral need. His knee thrust between her legs, parting them. Her skirt was a tangle around her lower half, and he wrestled it up around her waist.

"I'd sooner you never wear clothes again," he said in a growling voice.

"What kind of queen would that make me?" she teased.

"The perfect kind."

He burned his lips over her skin. She squeezed his shoulders so hard it must have been painful, but he only seemed to crave more. He kissed the hexmark on her ear, then the one on her left shoulder, then the one the side of her wrist.

"I want to take you from behind," he panted as he dropped her wrist. "Turn around."

Her eyes widened as she did as he ordered. She'd heard about people coupling in this way, like animals

—she hadn't known it was *true*. He thrust her skirt around her waist so her ass was bare except for her chemise. He soon shoved aside that silk garment, too. His fingers gripped the sides of her hips hard. Then he leaned forward, his weight pressing her down against the bed, and hissed in her ear.

"I've been gentle with you thus far, Bryn Lindane. Do you want me to be merciless?"

Her breath rushed in. Her pulse thundered in her ears. Her whole body felt on fire with Rangar's weight on top of her, poised to enter her.

She whispered, "Yes."

"What was that?"

"*Yes.*"

He freed his cock from his pants and ran the tip along her cleft. She felt a sudden rush of pleasure, but it came paired with an excruciating need. She pushed her hips back in an attempt to feel more of him, but he held off, torturing her.

One hand stroked and teased between her legs while the other seized her breast. "As you wish."

He thrust into her from behind. Her whole body quivered as she let out a cry. His weight pushed her face against the pillow, and she muffled her moans in the soft fabric. He wrapped his hands around her hipbones to hold her steady as he rode her. Bryn's hands fisted in the sheets, twisting them into knots.

What was he doing to her? Was he trying to break her?

"Rangar," she panted as his thrusts made her ache with desire.

His need was great, and his thrusts were unforgiving; but Bryn held on, shivering from the pleasure that radiated up from the base of her belly. It was no surprise making love to Rangar held a lot in common with two soldiers going at each other with swords.

When he finally finished, Bryn's legs were quivering. An eruption of tingles had spread throughout her whole body until her vision had practically blurred. They panted together until Rangar finally sat up and dragged her into his lap. His hands captured the sides of her face.

"Bryn Lindane." His breath staggered between words. "You're going to be the death of me."

She gently bit her lip, bruised from his kisses. "I saved your life. Took your soul from Death's grasp. *I* say when you die, Rangar Barendur. And it won't be for a long, long time."

He kissed her deeply until their pulses returned to a steady beat. Then he dragged her beside him, and exhaustion finally overtook them both.

When Bryn woke, dusk was falling outside. She was alone in bed. She sat up, confused. Didn't Rangar understand what 'house arrest' meant? But then she heard a splash of water from the adjacent dressing room, and in another minute, he came in with a freshly washed face.

He sat on the edge of the bed, stroking her arm. "You slept a long time."

"Didn't you? You needed it."

"I woke early. I had plans to make."

She sat up, instantly on alert. "What plans? What can you do while locked in these chambers?"

"I sent a message to my aunt through the guards. Oliver is an old friend. I'm going to ask her permission to leave Barendur Hold with a small group of soldiers to find Broderick. You were right. The Baersladen is going to need a king soon, and I can't serve my people while locked away."

She took his hand. It was frightening to think about being apart from him again, especially knowing he'd be pursuing a dangerous spy and murderer. But she had learned that if they were to be genuine leaders for their people, they'd have to both be brave.

He brushed his thumb over her cheek and said softly, "I spoke with Oliver, too, about other plans."

She shook her head, not understanding. "What other plans?"

He lifted an eyebrow. "We're engaged. I owe you three wedding gifts."

She scoffed lightly. "That's a Mir tradition, not a Baer one."

"And you're a Mir bride. You were cheated out of three proper gifts when you were engaged to Captain

Carr, since you had to use them to keep me alive. Now, I want you to have everything a princess could desire."

"Gifts? Rangar, I really don't need—"

He silenced her with a kiss, then whispered, "You'll get your first gift tomorrow."

She felt a prickle of curiosity as she smoothed the wrinkles out of her dress and rebraided her hair. "I should check on Val. It doesn't feel fair that I can leave this chamber and you can't."

"As long as you come back," he said, pressing his lips to her knuckles. He held on briefly when she started to pull her hand away. "Wait. You, too, have a duty, Bryn. My father won't live long. We should hold our wedding as soon as possible. I'd like for him to be there to give his blessing, of course . . ." His face darkened. "But it's not only that. If I'm to be king, it behooves us for you, as my wife, to be crowned queen at the same coronation. There will be less debate over our marriage's legitimacy if we marry before assuming the throne."

"Under what grounds would anyone object to my coronation as queen?"

"The same grounds my family forbade me from marrying you before—two siblings cannot rule competing kingdoms."

"That was an entirely different situation," she said, blinking furiously. "That was under the assumption that Trei would rule the Baersladen, and you would be king of the Mirien. Mars is now king. He's my brother, yes, but not yours. A brother-in-law doesn't fall under the same rules, surely."

"I agree, but there are some who may not."

She rested her hands on her hips. "That's ridiculous."

"I think you underestimate the lengths our enemies will go to sew discord among our kingdoms. Already, foreign rulers will be whispering that Valenden has a greater claim to the throne than me. Never mind that Val doesn't want it." He smoothed back an errant curl on her forehead that had come loose from the braid. "Mars and Illiana were smart to wed before their coronation; we should follow their lead."

She twisted his ring on her finger, nodding. "I'll plan the wedding. It won't be the first—" She was about to say that it wouldn't be her first time planning a Baer wedding but stopped herself. Neither of them needed to be reminded of the heartache of her first wedding.

"I'll handle it," she said softer.

As she went to check on Valenden, it felt strange to have free rein of the castle while Rangar was restricted behind guards. Bryn had forgotten the smell of Barendur Hold: It was like a winter feast on a snowy night, all savory meats from the kitchen and woodsmoke and the earthy smell of livestock. The castle had nothing of Castle Mir's architectural grandeur, but she liked its simple construction. There were no secret passages here or hidden stairs for servants to use; Barendur Hold felt honest in a way her home never had.

When she entered the mage quarters, Ren looked up from a book. He cleared his throat. "Prince Valenden woke not long ago, if that is why you've come."

She picked up a mortar and pestle to occupy her hands while she said, "It is, but I also wanted to talk to you." She took a deep breath, unsure how to broach a subject that had been weighing on her. "At the battle of Saint Serrel, Calista . . ." Her words trailed off. Calista and Ren had been the only two mage apprentices at Barendur Hold, friends as well as fellow pupils. She swallowed down a lump before continuing. "I'm sure you heard the details of what happened, but I wanted you to hear it from me directly because I was there and saw everything with my own eyes. Calista kept an entire legion of rebels and Baer fighters protected. She fought bravely and with deft hexwork. Her death . . ." Bryn's voice broke. "We are all worse off for having lost her."

She set back down the mortar and pestle quickly, smoothing her hands on her dress.

Ren nodded slowly. "You speak the truth there, Lady Bryn."

When she made her way back to Valenden's room, she was pleased to find him sitting up, though he was scowling. "What's wrong with you?" she asked.

Val groaned. "My aunt says I'm to stay away from

the bottle until I heal. That ale will only tax my body further."

"She's absolutely right."

He rolled his eyes. "I should have known you'd be in league with her." Then he narrowed his eyes as he studied her dress. "And what have *you* been doing, princess?"

Her hand flew to her collar, where she realized she'd done up her buttons wrong. Blushing, she quickly put them right again. Valenden cackled, though it turned into a terrible cough. Once he had downed some tea for his throat, he said, "Eager to give my brother an heir, eh? We haven't even been home for a few hours."

"Val, stop. How are you, really?"

His expression grew serious. He took another long sip of tea, then grimaced like he wanted something much stronger. "Ren used a hex to rid my wound of infection, but the bite marks are deep. He suspects the wolves' saliva had a substance in it that keeps the wounds from being healed by any of our usual hexes. I'm going to end up with scars just like you and Rangar." He smirked. "Do you like that, princess? I know you're partial to scars."

"You're already covered in scars, Val. Everyone in the Baersladen is."

He snorted. "Fair point."

Bryn glanced down the hall toward King Aleth's room. The door was closed. "And . . . your father?"

Valenden didn't meet her eyes. "No better, no worse."

She sighed. "Let me ask you something, Val. Be honest with me for once, since I don't have a hexmark to tell me if you're lying." She dropped her voice. "Do you truly not want the throne? As the eldest living prince, it could be yours by right."

Valenden took his time finishing his tea, then eased himself further into his sitting position. The lantern on his bedside table cast half his face in orange, half in darkness. "I don't want the throne," he said, studying the shadows. "I relinquished my claim long ago, and I don't anticipate anything changing that. If you fear some stone chair will drive Rangar and me apart, you can calm your fears."

She relaxed, but the truth was, no one knew the future. As much as both Rangar and Valenden reassured her that no questions of succession would ever come between them, she had seen families torn apart before over much less.

She went to fetch supper from the kitchen to take back to Rangar—who was a prisoner once more.

# CHAPTER 10

**RANGAR'S FIRST GIFT . . . a naughty lamb . . . goodbyes . . . Fable and Legend . . . a snowy ride**

The following day, heavy snow fell at Barendur Hold. Bryn wanted to spend the morning snuggling with Rangar under their reindeer pelt blankets, but with him under house arrest, it was up to her to tend to Valenden and spend time in the village to get a sense of the common folk's sentiments.

As soon as she set foot in the sheep barn, animals and farm girls alike flocked to her.

"Lady Bryn!" The head shepherdess, a woman a few years older than Bryn with a sleeping baby swaddled in a sling around her chest, gave a wide smile. "What good tidings to have you back! We feared you would never return from the Mirien. Look at your troublemaker little lamb—he's all grown up now, eh?"

Bryn knelt in the straw as the lamb, now almost a full-grown sheep, gave her shoulder a gentle head butt. She grinned and scratched his head. "And this little one made her arrival!" Bryn stood and dusted off her hands before patting the sleeping baby. "A healthy delivery?"

"It was." The shepherdess beamed. "You've my gratitude for managing my flock while I was on bed rest. I didn't think a princess would be tromping up to the high pasture every day with them!"

Bryn waved away the concern. "I enjoyed it. Besides, the Baer princes are always pitching in with the farm work."

"Oh, they're used to it," the woman scoffed. "They're lords in name, yes, but you're a real *lady*."

Bryn picked some sheep hair off her skirt and asked hesitantly, "What are people saying about our return?"

The shepherdess's face slowly grew serious. The other farm girls suddenly found their chores of pressing concern. "Well," the woman said, patting her baby gently, "There's the ugly business of Prince Trei's murder going unsolved. Few believe Prince Rangar had anything to do with it, but there's still a murderer somewhere out there on the loose. People have been nervous. And King Aleth's failing health has everyone on edge. No one knows what will happen with the succession." She fished an errant piece of straw out of

Bryn's hair tenderly. "But everyone is happy for you and Prince Rangar, my lady. About the engagement. Will we be seeing a wreath of maiden roses in the village square soon?"

Bryn's mind flashed back to her doomed wedding with Trei, which was announced by hanging a wreath of maiden roses in the public square.

*That's in the past*, she assured herself.

She cajoled herself to give the shepherdess a smile. "Perhaps you will."

The farm girls, who had clearly been eavesdropping, giggled excitedly to think about a royal wedding.

When Bryn returned to Barendur Hold, she felt in better spirits to know that public sentiment supported her and Rangar. In their chambers, she found Rangar with Oliver going over a map stretched out on the dining table.

" . . . and we'll save the north for last. It's unlikely he'd head that way," Rangar finished.

Oliver nodded, glanced at Bryn, and rolled up the map. "Yes, my lord."

He strode out of the room, and Bryn turned to Rangar. "What was that about?"

Rangar prowled around the room as he gathered a rucksack and began filling it with *statua* pipe tobacco and extra wool undergarments. "My aunt has given me leave to hunt down Broderick. I'll depart this evening with a team of soldiers."

"We only just returned yesterday!"

He paused in packing his bag, then resumed.

"You've seen my father's state. Time is not on our side."

Bryn refolded the wool clothes he'd carelessly thrown in his pack and tucked them in more orderly. "Are the soldiers coming along to help you find Broderick, or to keep you a prisoner?"

"A bit of both, I think."

She rubbed her face, trying to process everything. "Well at least I discovered that most of the townspeople don't think you killed Trei."

"Oh, good," Rangar muttered darkly. "People I've grown up with, known my whole life, broken bread with and starved with at times, too—I'm glad they don't think I'm a murderer."

Bryn quietly gathered a blanket and tucked that into his bag, too, knowing he never bothered to take care of himself against the cold.

At her silence, he sighed and pinched his nose. "I'm sorry, Bryn. My mind is elsewhere. If I can just find Broderick . . ."

"I know." She placed a soothing hand on his chest.

His tight muscles eased. He tucked a strand of her hair behind her ear. "You'll be all right here alone?"

"I'm not alone. I have your family. And a royal wedding to plan, and your fool of a brother to nurse back to heath, and berserkir wolves to investigate, and . . ."

At her abrupt pause, he raised a questioning eyebrow. "And?"

She dropped her voice. "And your aunt said she'd

take me on as an apprentice. I know you once opposed the idea. I wonder if you still do."

He smoothed his hands over the curls at the sides of her face. "I told you that your soul is mine, but your life is your own. I tried to stop you from learning magic before because I feared my aunt was pushing you toward dangerous, untested hexes . . . but now I realize that magic is a tool, just like a sword or a bow. Such tools are more dangerous in unskilled hands than skilled ones. If you study hexes, you'll be stronger. And that is never something I'd stand in the way of."

She pushed to her toes to kiss him. His hand cradled her jaw, holding her steady as he deepened the kiss. When they parted, he said in a rumbling voice, "I have something for you before I leave."

"Oh?"

"I promised you a first engagement gift."

A flutter of curiosity stirred to life in her chest. A smile crossed his face, and she felt a matching one stretch across her own.

"Come," he said. He pulled her to the window, which overlooked the village square on the far side of the drawbridge. "There's frustratingly little I can do while locked in these rooms, but Oliver has been my hands for me. Look."

Standing in the snow, Rangar's horse, Legend, was tied to the hitching post in the center of the village square.

She looked at Rangar questioningly. "I don't understand—oh!"

Oliver came out of the barn leading a beautiful dapple gray mare, which he tethered next to Legend. A wreath of dried wheat berries circled its neck.

Bryn clapped a hand over her mouth as she whirled on Rangar. "Wait, you mean . . . ?"

"Her name is Fable," he said. "She belonged to a farmer in the valley, but his daughter married and left, so he no longer needed her. The mare has a pleasing temperament. She's fast, but she listens. A good horse for a beginner."

"You're gifting me a *horse*?" Bryn's voice rose in excitement.

He dragged his thumb over her cheek. "I'd get you anything you desired, princess."

She threw her arms around him. Their lips met again, and Bryn wanted nothing more than to stay here and kiss him senselessly . . . except perhaps to go meet Fable.

Rangar chuckled as Bryn threw impatient looks out the window. "Go on. Meet her. Oliver will show you where she'll live in the barn. I need to finish packing, anyway."

Bryn plied him with one more kiss before running down the castle stairs and out into the snow, barely remembering at the last minute to grab one of the cloaks hanging in the foyer. She stopped a few feet away from Fable, taking in the beautiful animal with reverence.

Oliver held out a carrot. "She's partial to these."

Bryn swallowed, suddenly nervous. What if Fable

didn't like her? Horses liked and disliked people, just as humans did. But as she took the carrot and held it out in her palm, she was relieved when Fable blinked her soft brown eyes and gently took it from her. Bryn touched the mare's neck, running her hand over her soft hair. Her mane was a pale gray the color of snow clouds.

"She's a good horse," Oliver assured her. "Doesn't buck and rear like this one." He motioned to Legend, who was eyeing Oliver's pocket for any more carrots.

"Oh, don't worry, I like you, too." Oliver patted Legend's forehead.

Bryn felt like she'd stepped into a dream as she ran her hands over Fable's sturdy back and powerful legs. It was humbling to be in the presence of such a large animal. Her heart squeezed with the sincere hope they'd become a trusting team.

Fable nuzzled her shoulder, and Bryn smiled and scratched her neck.

"Do you want to ride her?" Oliver asked.

Bryn's jaw slackened. "What, here? Now?"

"That's right." Fable had no saddle and no bridle other than the simple rope halter that was traditional in Baer horsemanship. On the road with Valenden, Bryn had practiced riding with stirrups and saddle, but she supposed if she was to make the Baersladen her home, she needed to learn to ride like a Baer.

She looked up at Barendur Hold, where Rangar watched down from the third-floor window. She pressed a kiss to her fingers and held it up to him.

He returned the gesture.

"Well," Bryn said with nervous excitement, "I guess this is as good a time as any."

Oliver made a stirrup with his hands, and Bryn clambered up onto the horse. Fable stood patiently as Bryn wiggled her way inexpertly into a straddle and gripped the rope bridle.

Oliver mounted Legend, giving the stallion a calming pat.

Bryn glanced again up at the castle. "I thought Rangar was very particular about who rides Legend."

"Oh, he is," Oliver grinned wickedly over at Bryn. "No one is allowed to ride Legend but Rangar. But Rangar can't do much while he's locked up, can he? Besides, these two need to get used to one another."

Bryn shook her head at Oliver's daringness, though she supposed it was good for Rangar to have a friend who was just as much a troublemaker as he was.

"Ready, princess?" Oliver asked.

She took a deep breath. "Let's go."

She nudged Fable with her heels to follow behind Legend as Oliver led them through the village toward the coast. She kept her elbows at an angle and close to her body as Valenden had taught her. Fable was much larger than the horses she'd ridden before, but the mare had such a smooth gait and confident step that it wasn't long before Bryn settled back, getting the feel of her.

As soon as they passed the docks, Oliver glanced over his shoulder. "Ready?"

"For what?"

His response was to kick Legend into a trot. Bryn shrieked as Fable started trotting behind him. She made a fist with one hand in Fable's mane while holding the reins with the other. Her thighs clamped tightly to keep her balance. A few snowflakes swirled around them as Oliver led the way onto the snow-covered beach.

Bryn was just starting to feel confident when Oliver nudged Legend into a full gallop.

"Wait!" Bryn called, but Fable took off after Legend without her prompting. Suddenly the wind was swooshing by her face. Sand and snow flew at her from where Legend kicked it up ahead. Panic made her grip Fable's mane even harder. She'd only ever ridden this fast on horseback with Rangar's arm around her and his command of the horse. It had been terrifying enough then, but now she was the only one in control.

*Don't fall off, for the love of the saints. Don't fall off!*

The two horses charged down the beach, kicking up sand. They veered into the frigid surf up to the tops of their hooves, then back onto the flat expanse of sand. The ocean stretched far to the left, the rocky hills of the Baersladen to the right. Bryn was overcome with thrill as much as terror.

Fable was *hers*.

Oliver finally slowed once they reached a rocky

outcropping that blocked the sandy beach. He eased Legend to a stop, then patted his neck.

Bryn's chest heaved in and out with ragged breaths. Once she caught her breath, she yelled, "I didn't say I was ready for a *gallop*!"

"Gallop?" Mischief glinted in Oliver's eye. "That wasn't a gallop, Lady Bryn. That was a nice, gentle canter."

She balked at the idea that they hadn't even been going at top speed. She patted Fable, then grinned and looked up at Oliver. "I'm very relieved I didn't fall off."

"You liked it, didn't you?"

She grinned wider. "Yes."

They rode the horses at a walk on a trail through the forest to return to Barendur Hold. Bryn's legs were aching, but she marveled at seeing the woods from horseback. The height gave her a new perspective on everything, and she felt great power working as a team with Fable.

By the time they returned and housed the horses in the stable, Bryn's head was buzzing as badly as her thighs were aching. She made her way dreamily back to their chambers, where she threw her arms around Rangar.

She kissed him square on the lips. "Thank you."

"Better than your previous first gift?"

"Seeing you in chains? Well, that wasn't *entirely* unwelcome."

He smacked a hand on her ass, then captured her lips in another kiss. Bryn felt the magic of the winter horseback ride with Fable sing through her body, melding with her love for Rangar and his wild homeland.

He trailed his lips down her jawline while he muttered, "As much as I want to bed you once more before leaving, I have a feeling your thighs are already exhausted enough and couldn't take much more *riding*."

She slapped him playfully, but then tipped his face up to meet hers. "I wish you didn't have to go."

He grew serious as he smoothed a hand down the side of her face. "I'll return to you a free man with my name cleared."

"*That* is the best gift you could give me."

They kissed once more in the candlelight as the snow swirled outside before Bryn had to say goodbye to Rangar and watch as he and his soldiers rode off into the darkness.

# CHAPTER 11

**BOOKS WITH NO ANSWERS . . . a healed troublemaker . . . the dead wolf . . . talk of enemies . . . brandy and dresses**

Heavy snow followed for a week after Rangar's departure, and Bryn began to feel like a prisoner, too. She'd been warned about how bleak Baer winters could be, but it was a different thing to experience it for herself. She began to call it a *Bear* winter in her head and think of the season as a blustering old bear that settled in somewhere at the first chill and refused to leave again until spring.

How could Rangar track anyone in this weather, let alone a spy? Bryn could barely make it to the village square without losing both her boots in the snow. She tried to ride Fable a few times, but Oliver had left with Rangar, and she'd barely made it past the docks on her own.

"Ah. My nurse. And what a lovely nurse you make." Valenden sat up in bed when Bryn entered his sick room, already licking his lips at the sight of the soup bowl in her hand.

She thrust the bowl at him and sat on the foot of the bed as he started shoveling venison stew in his mouth. "I hate to break it to you, Val, but I think you're healed. You're going to have to get up and start fetching your own supper."

"Shh!" He glared at her over the bowl. "Don't say such awful things."

"Let me see your bandages."

He begrudgingly finished his stew and then tossed aside the covers to swing his legs out of bed. A bandage hugged his torso over a poultice of *witrath* moss. Bryn rolled back the bandage and peeked under the poultice. The wolf's bite marks were still red, but the wounds had mostly closed with no sign of infection.

"Ren wrapped this poultice?" she asked. "He's very skilled. I haven't seen a wound heal this fast, even under the care of the Mirien's best healer."

"Ren is a marvel at healing hexes and potions," Valenden said as he smoothed down the bandage. "That was always his focus; Calista handled weather and communications."

Bryn again felt a stab of regret to think of the

apprentice they'd lost at the Battle of Saint Serrel. She wished she could have gotten to know Calista better. "Well," she said, "I'm impressed with his work. And you're sure you don't feel . . . odd?"

"Odd how? Odd like I might grow fangs and an insatiable bloodlust at the next full moon?"

Bryn wrinkled her nose. "Well, yes."

"I think if the berserkir wolves had any illness, I escaped it. I feel depressingly just like myself."

Bryn paced the length of his room, toying with the chain around her neck that held his and Trei's rings. "Where did Mage Marna put the wolf carcass?"

"In the dungeon," Valenden answered. "It's cold enough down there to freeze the body to preserve it."

"Are you strong enough to show me?"

He grumbled but got out of bed and into some clothes and, after she'd grabbed some supplies from the mage stores, they made their way to Barendur Hold's dungeon. The last time Bryn had been here, Valenden had snuck her down to say a final goodbye to Rangar before they fled from would-be assassins. The memory haunted her as they splashed through frigid puddles in the dank tunnels. She felt sorry for any poor souls that were incarcerated down here during the thick of winter. It was cold enough to see her breath clouding in the air.

After speaking with the dungeon guard, Valenden led her to a vacant cell where the wolf's body was wrapped in canvas. Bryn crouched before it cautiously. She pulled on gloves and peeled back the canvas.

Fortunately, the cold kept the wolf's body from smelling, though it was stiff enough to be nearly a block of ice. Cuts had been made in the wolf's side and at the top of its skull.

Bryn used a knife blade to poke at the cuts. "Mage Marna's work, I assume? Did she discover anything?"

"She found no signs of *lyssa* or any other illness. She noted the wolf's abnormal size but said there was no obvious cause. She brought in a huntsman from Clarentry who's killed over a hundred wolves; he said it's no subspecies he's ever come across."

Bryn used a pair of clamps to pull back the skin Mage Marna had cut open and peered at the wolf's flesh inside. There didn't seem to be anything off with the beast's organs except for their size. "Dark magic?" she asked Valenden in a low voice.

He shifted from one foot to the other. "I don't see what else it could be, though it's no spell I've ever heard of."

Bryn packed away her tools while staring at the wolf. "Maybe the question isn't how someone created these wolves, but why? Who would want vicious wolves attacking villages?"

Valenden leaned against the cell's bars. "The villages were in the Mirien and Vil-Kevi. So it must be one of their enemies, not ours."

Bryn wished more than ever that she had a better understanding of politics. With King Aleth unconscious, they couldn't exactly discuss the realm's enemies with him. Still, she shook her head. "It happened in the borderlands near where the Mirien, Vil-Kevi, and the Baersladen converge. It's all the same forest. Wolves can't tell where one kingdom starts and ends."

"You don't think it was targeted, then?"

She pressed her lips together. "If it was, then it was targeted against the entire Outlands region, not any one kingdom."

They rewrapped the wolf cadaver and returned to the warmth of the mage quarters. While Valenden went to visit his unconscious father, Bryn explored the castle's library, looking for any texts that might have an explanation for how dark magic could have created the berserkir beasts.

After perusing a few books, she groaned in frustration.

"Everything all right?" Ren stuck his mop of dark curls through the library door.

She closed a thick book with a sigh. "My translation hexmark lets me speak Baer but not read it, so many of these are illegible to me."

Ren glanced at the book's title. "Ah. Well, that's a book on digestive health in elderly women." She slumped further in her seat. He offered, "What are you looking for?"

She told him about the berserkir wolf attacks, and together they spent the afternoon pouring through the reference materials. They continued the search the following day, but after browsing every title in the mage library, they had to admit defeat.

"There's nothing about dark spells to make animals attack," Ren said as he shelved the last book, but then paused. "We can't be the only ones who are reminded of the berserkir legend. It's almost as though someone took inspiration from those old stories."

"What do you mean?" Bryn asked.

"Perhaps instead of researching spells, you should look into the origin of the legend."

Ren's suggestion occupied Bryn's mind for the next few days. Every time she sat down with the castle's head staff to discuss wedding planning, she thought of wolves, and every time she asked around the village about the berserkir legend, she thought about the wedding.

"I assure you, my lady, it'll be the grandest feast Barendur Hold has seen in years," Roxin said while wiping down the kitchen's butcher-block table. "All you need to decide upon is the menu, and we kitchen maids will handle everything."

Bryn swirled her finger in a spot of flour dotting the table. "I suppose my one request would be, well, to make it as different as possible from my previous wedding."

Roxin met Bryn's eyes, and the cook nodded with understanding. "Sad business, that. We all feel Prince Trei's loss keenly. Hasn't been the same without him."

Bryn sighed, twirling Trei's ring on her necklace. "For that feast, you did such an incredible job of weaving Mir ingredients into traditional Baer dishes. I think for my wedding feast with Rangar, we should do only Baer foods. A celebration of these lands. My new home."

Roxin nodded as she stroked her chin. "Yes, I can work with that . . . venison from the forest, salmon from the water, pheasant from the sky. An ode to all the Baer's environments."

Bryn smiled genuinely. "That sounds perfect."

A sly look entered Roxin's eye. "I'll be needing to know a date."

Bryn stilled her hand on the necklace. "We don't have a date yet. We want to hold it as soon as possible, given King Aleth's health, but until Rangar . . ." She trailed off. Silence was better than having to say that her fiancé still hadn't been cleared of murder.

Roxin poured more flour on the table and started rolling out dough. "Not to worry, my lady. This time of year, our cold larders are pure ice. I'll start putting away the wedding feast ingredients, and they'll be ready when you are." She wiggled her eyebrows. "How about we serve more of that fig brandy, eh? I can have the kitchen girls make another batch."

Bryn recalled how all the kitchen girls had joined hands and come together to amplify Roxin's fermentation hex to make the brandy—and how deliciously warm it had left her belly.

"Sure," Bryn smiled.

With the menu set, she still needed to meet with the seamstress about a dress. Helna had sewn her the most beautiful traditional Baer gown of dark grey velvet and obsidian gems for her wedding with Trei—

a dress that had ended up with his blood staining the cuffs. She found herself putting off any chance to visit Helna, afraid she'd be faced with that dress again and have to relive Trei's death.

"Oh, Trei," she whispered as she gazed out her window at the falling snow. "This place isn't complete without you. Maybe it should have been me . . ."

"Bryn?"

She turned sharply at Mage Marna's voice in her doorway. The mage's face glowed in the light from a candle she held. The lines on her face were deeply etched. She clutched a mysterious package under one arm. Bryn was overtaken with a premonition the mage bore news of more death . . .

"Oh no," Bryn gasped. "Is it . . . King Aleth?"

Mage Marna's face relaxed. "The king still lives."

Bryn pressed a relieved hand to her chest. She couldn't imagine the grief Rangar would endure if he was absent when his father passed.

Quietly, the mage handed Bryn the package. "It's time, Bryn."

Confused, Bryn unfolded a bundle, which turned out to be linen mage robes much like the ones she'd worn before, though these had a red thread sewn into the collar and sleeves: the mark of an apprentice.

Bryn had seen these exact robes before. They were Calista's.

She sucked in a breath.

*Mage Marna bears the reminder of someone's death after all . . .*

Though Bryn mourned Calista, the gravity of what she was holding wasn't lost on her. Thrill mixed with her feelings of melancholy and uncertainty. Before she could ask Mage Marna for clarification, the mage said curtly, "The forest. Ten minutes. The hollow oak stump."

The mage turned sharply, taking the candlelight with her, leaving Bryn with a dead woman's clothes—and a chance for magic.

# CHAPTER 12

**A COLD INITIATION . . . a hollowed-up stump . . .
flame too small . . . keep yourself alive . . . word
from Rangar**

Bryn knew the hollowed-out oak stump Mage Marna spoke of: it was a quarter-mile inland, near the path to the high pastures. When she'd worked as a shepherdess, she'd let the lambs stop there to drink from its collected rainwater. She'd always wondered at the small charms nailed into the old stump: wooden stick figures, bits of yarn, buttons. The place had always whispered of magic.

Mage Marna was waiting for her when she arrived, breathless after having jogged through the snow to get there in time. In contrast, the mage wasn't out of breath at all, even at her advanced age.

"Take that cloak off," were the stern words Bryn was greeted with. "And your boots."

Bryn hesitated. Calista's robes were made of thin linen, so she'd grabbed a cloak on her way out of the castle. She wanted to point out that Mage Marna herself wore a heavy cloak against the cold, but held her tongue.

*This is a test. Training has already begun.*

She toed off her boots and hung her cloak on a nearby branch. Shivering, she returned to the stump. The hollowed basin was crusted with ice. Bryn curled her toes in the snow, trying not to squeal from the cold. How long could she go before getting frostbite?

"As apprentice, you will address me as 'lady mage.' I'll warn you that this is a significant commitment. You'll reach the point of exhaustion physically, mentally, and spiritually. It will take time away from your relationship with Rangar. Did he grant you permission to apprentice?"

"He supports my endeavors," Bryn said evenly. "But I don't need his permission. My life is my own."

"Good."

An owl hooted somewhere overhead. With faint moonlight filtering through the trees along with the snow, the forest took on a strange feel, almost as though they'd stepped out of time. Shivering, Bryn clutched her arms tighter.

Mage Marna laid a hand on the edge of the giant stump. "Break the ice."

"Yes, lady mage."

Bryn's bare feet crunched through the snow as she made her way to the edge of the stump. She looked around for a branch, but Mage Marna clarified, "With your bare hands."

Bryn silenced an objection. Was that even possible? She pounded her fist against the thick ice. It took three times and a bruised hand before the ice finally cracked, and frigid, dark water soaked her robe's sleeves. Her feet were losing feeling—she couldn't last much longer standing barefoot in the snow without getting permanent damage.

"Now, climb into the water," Mage Marna commanded.

Bryn gaped at her openly. Soaking in freezing water would result in almost instant hypothermia. Was this another test, this one meant to show how far Bryn would blindly follow Mage Marna's commands? Or to see if she had enough sense to defend herself against what could only be considered a death order?

Mage Marna watched expressionless, and Bryn took a deep breath.

*Trust in magic.*

Wincing, she climbed into the stump before she lost her nerve. The ice water pool was about the size of a small bathtub, deep enough to submerge her entire body. Her skin screamed at the shock of cold. Her eyes shot open as a cry rose to her lips, but she swallowed it down. Clenching her jaw, she focused on her breathing.

*Breathe.*

*Breathe.*

"Good," Mage Marna said curtly. "Now get out and warm yourself before you die."

Bryn needed no further encouragement. She scrambled out of the stump with limbs that screamed in pain. Her extremities were already dangerously numb. Soaking wet, she fell on hands and knees in the snow. Her heart pounded so erratically she was afraid it might give out.

"I must . . . get back . . . to the Hold," she stuttered.

"It's too far. You'll freeze before then. You have to warm yourself here. *Now.*"

Bryn tossed her head up in incredulity, but the mage was serious. She suddenly understood the nature of this test. It wasn't to see how much Bryn was willing to suffer . . . it was to judge the extent of Bryn's current abilities.

"The spark spell," Bryn gasped out between shivers. She held up her cupped palm. Her hand was snow-white and turning blue at the nail beds.

"*Kora yoquin,*" she whispered in a trembling voice. Nothing happened. She tried to steady her shivering hand as best she could and focus on her pronunciation, as Valenden had taught her on their long days on the road.

"*Kora yoquin!*"

A small flame sprung to life in her palm. It died in the blink of an eye—but it had been there.

"See?" Bryn looked up desperately at the mage. "I did it. Please, I have to go back now—"

"I already told you there isn't time. That one flame won't warm your whole body. You'll have to find dry firewood."

"The forest is covered in wet snow!"

Mage Marna kept her lips pressed tightly together. Bryn let out a frustrated cry. She couldn't feel anything below her ankles. The chill had settled so deep into her bones that she felt them clacking together in her ribcage.

"Do you *want* me to die?" she yelled.

"You won't have ideal conditions when you need to cast most spells. You must be able to cast when you're hurt, distracted, sick. Now go on. *Save yourself.*"

Bryn's mind was numb with the cold, but she circled frantically through all of her options.

*The finding spell?*

She closed her eyes and focused all her attention on sensing the location of dry wood. She ignored her shivers and clattering teeth. She pretended her robes were dry instead of freezing into ice.

"*Jin jan en veera,*" she whispered.

A tug pulled her attention to the left. Eyes snapping open, she crawled on hands and knees through the snow, not trusting her legs to hold her upright, to a fallen log on the far side of the stump. It had collapsed over a small, rocky outcropping that made a sort of rooftop ledge. Feeling beneath it, she discovered winter-dead moss and some dry twigs sheltered from the snow.

Her heart squeezed briefly with hope.

Scrambling back to the stump, she quickly arranged a fire with the moss and twigs, though her shaking hands made it take twice the amount of time it should have. Tears sprung up at her eyes, though she didn't dare spare a moment to wipe them away. Her body thrummed with urgency: she had to get warm *now*.

Would Mage Marna stand there and watch her die? Would the mage save her life at the last moment? Bryn didn't want to find out.

"*Kora yoquin*," she whispered with enough control that a flame sprung up on the dry moss and caught. Bryn blew on the flame until it spread to the twigs. Soon, a small fire roared on the dry wood.

Bryn sagged with relief as she held her frozen fingers over the flame, but they were too numb to even feel the warmth. Desperate, she started untying the sash around her waist to shed the wet clothes, but her hands were shaking too badly.

"I . . . can't," she breathed. "The fire . . . It's not enough."

"No," Mage Marna agreed. "A small fire like that can't warm your body before hypothermia sets in."

"But then . . . *why*?" Bryn's mind was numb. Her vision darkened around the edges. Her heart had stopped thumping hard in her chest . . . she could barely feel her own pulse.

"Think," Mage Marna said sharply. "You have other hexes."

*The fire*, Bryn realized. Maybe the point of the fire wasn't to warm her. *It was to make ash.*

As she felt her whole body going numb, she put all her remaining energy into dipping her fingers into the hot coals. If her fingers got burned, she didn't know—she'd long ago lost her sense of feeling in them. But they came away with fresh ashes, and she shakily touched her own face.

Her eyes met Mage Marna's before she whispered, "*Ana somna mortinya.*"

She didn't see the mage's reaction.

After that, she didn't see anything at all.

Bryn dreamed she was following Rangar through a snowy forest.

He rode Legend, and she was atop Fable. He clutched the knife that had killed Trei as he silently pursued a dark shadow moving through the trees ahead. Bryn tried to call out to him, but he couldn't hear her. Suddenly, the shadowy figure stopped. Was it Broderick? But as soon as it seemed to be the shape of a man, it shifted into something more animal-like.

*A berserkir wolf.*

Bryn tried to call out to warn Rangar, but the shadow changed again. It spread like dark smoke in a circle around Rangar and Legend, and before Bryn could spur Fable to reach him, it had swallowed him whole.

She woke with a gasp, sweat running down her temples. It took her a moment to place where she was. Thick steam filled the air just like the smoke from her dream. However, it came out of a simple small copper boiler filled with scented water. She was in her chamber in the mage quarters, dressed in clean, warm apprentice robes.

Throwing off the blanket, she hurried to examine her fingers and toes to see if she'd lost any to frostbite. To her relief, they were all intact.

"Healed by magic," a voice said. Ren was bent over the boiler, stirring the bubbling concoction within. "Frostbite can be cured with a maple sap salve and warming hex," he continued, wafting the steam toward her bed. He nodded at her torso. "That, however, has to heal on its own."

Her eyes widened to find a bandage around her ribs. Worried, she felt along her skin.

"It's on your back," Ren explained. "The amplifier hex. Mage Marna carved it on you in your sleep."

Bryn continued to feel along her back until she noted the raised bumps of a scar beneath the bandage. "Mage Marna brought me back here?"

Ren nodded. "Every apprentice undergoes a test of their initial abilities at the commencement of training. They need to be pushed to the limit to see what they're capable of."

"*You* once froze in that stump, too?"

Ren gave her a puzzled look. "Stump? *I* nearly drowned in a fishing net. I was twelve and had to use the finding spell to locate a sharp shell to cut my way out."

Bryn hugged her arms across her chest, still shivering despite the steam pumping into the room from the boilers. "Does the test always have to be so violent?"

"Magic isn't a game."

She took a deep breath, testing her lungs, and then felt again at her back. "And the amplifier hex?"

"Every Baer citizen gets it at eighteen as a rite of passage. A symbol that they're an adult member of a community. We rely on one another. It's one of a handful of basic hexes everyone receives."

"So, the finding spell, the spark spell, and the amplifier spell," Bryn said. "Those are the basic hexes. I guess now I'm caught up to most of your children," she groaned.

Ren took out a hunk of cheese and strip of dried venison wrapped in wax paper from his pocket and handed it to her with a wry smile. "You passed the initiation, and you aren't even Baer. You grew up without magic. I'd say that's something."

She gave him a grateful smile.

He said, "Mage Marna asked me to teach you the amplifier spell wording. We can get started whenever you're ready, but first, I thought you'd want to know that word has come from Rangar."

Bryn scrambled out of bed so fast that her whole body ached, reminding her that she'd very nearly died.

"What does he say?" she asked breathlessly. "Is he all right?"

Ren pulled a folded scroll from his robes and extended it to her. "This was delivered this morning, sealed, with instructions to give it only to you."

Bryn snatched the letter and ripped open the seal, anxious for Rangar's news.

# CHAPTER 13

**AN UNKNOWN RIDER . . . Rangar's letter . . . Broderick's fate . . . rushed wedding plans . . . a snowy reunion**

Bryn devoured Rangar's letter with her eyes, anxious for any scraps of news.

*My love,*
*I know your heart must be filled with fear to receive this letter, but I have good tidings to report. My men and I located Broderick south of Disworth Forest, where he was hiding out among a small logging operation. The unfortunate news is that he is dead. He died of cholera mere days before we arrived, and thus, we are left with no means to force a confession from him. Regardless, I have*

*managed to obtain strong evidence of his guilt. I'm bringing it home to let my father judge its merits.*
*Rangar*

Bryn reread the letters several times to make certain she wasn't imagining his words.

*Rangar is coming home. He's safe.*

Her breath came fast with relief, and yet the shadow of Broderick's death darkened her hope. The only way to completely exonerate Rangar was for Broderick to confess. What other "evidence" could Rangar have found?

She cleared her throat, aware that Ren was still standing in the doorway. "Rangar is returning."

Ren nodded solemnly. He wasn't the sort of boy to show his emotions plainly, but Bryn got the sense this was very welcome news. "Shall we practice the amplifier spell?"

"Soon," Bryn said, swallowing down the last of the cheese as she shuffled into her house shoes. "I must tell the Barendur family this news."

She hurried through the castle looking for Valenden, pausing every so often to catch her breath and remind herself she needed to take it easy until she was fully healed. Since receiving word that Rangar was coming home, everything about the castle seemed brighter. The hearth fires burned brighter, the workers' smiles seemed especially kind. She plowed through the kitchen on her search and was about to head back up to the yew courtyard when Roxin popped out of the pantry.

"Oh! Lady Bryn. I wanted to ask you about desserts for the wedding feast . . ."

"Yes, yes, later today," Bryn said breathlessly.

She eventually found Valenden with Mage Marna in the council chambers. The two of them sat alone at the far end of the table, whispering among themselves. When Bryn stopped short in the doorway with Rangar's letter clutched in hand, they silenced.

What had they been whispering about so solemnly?

"What is it, Bryn?" Valenden prompted.

She thrust out the letter, eager to share the news. "Rangar is returning. Broderick is dead, but Rangar believes he has proof of his guilt."

Both Valenden and Mage Marna took their time reading the letter. Bryn frowned as she studied their expressions; they didn't seem nearly as cheered by this good news as she expected.

"Is something wrong?" she asked hesitantly.

Valenden and his aunt exchanged a long, cryptic look. Then Valenden sighed. "It's good news about Rangar. Very good news. Depending on whatever proof he has, of course."

Bryn toyed nervously with her necklace. "So why doesn't this feel like a joyous occasion?"

Mage Marna placed her hands on the table and said quietly, "King Aleth has taken a turn for the worse."

Bryn pressed her hand to her mouth. Her first thought was of Rangar. What if he didn't make it home in time before the king's passing? It would kill him not to see his father one final time.

*Besides, the king needs to exonerate him!*

A heavy silence fell over the council chambers. Bryn sank into a wooden chair, resting her clasped hands on the table. "How much time does he have?"

"A matter of days," Mage Marna said quietly. "He won't last the week."

Bryn touched a shaky hand to her forehead, trying to make sense of it.

Mage Marna slid Rangar's letter back across the table to Bryn. "Let us pray that Rangar returns swiftly. If the wedding doesn't happen before Aleth's passing, it will have to wait until after the grieving period. We hold no celebrations in the month following a king's death: no weddings, no birth celebrations, no holidays. The only exception, of course, being the coronation of the next king."

Valenden added, "That means that Rangar will be named king, but you cannot formally become queen until after the grieving period, when you're married."

Bryn felt her shoulders raise in a shrug. "So be it, then. I am in no rush to be queen."

"Yes," Valenden clarified, "but that gives more opportunities for our enemies to try to invalidate your engagement on the grounds that siblings would rule two kingdoms."

"Siblings-in-law," Bryn emphasized. "It's completely different."

Valenden and Mage Marna's stony looks said that while they agreed with her, others might not.

Bryn leaned forward and rubbed her tired eyes. "What can I do to help?"

"Be as ready as you can to marry Rangar the moment he returns," Mage Marna informed her.

For the next two days, Bryn threw herself into wedding planning. She finalized the menu with Roxin, ordered a wreath of maiden roses to be woven and ready to hang in the town square, and sat down to write a letter to Mars.

*Dear brother,*
*It is an uncertain time in the Baersladen. King Aleth may pass any day. It is my hope to be able to marry Rangar before his coronation, but much may yet stand in our way. I would love to have you and Illiana attend the wedding, but I fear there is not time for you to make the journey. Please know you will be here in spirit.*
*Mouse*

Finally, she couldn't put off getting fitted for a wedding gown any longer. She met with Helna in the seamstress's sewing room, pausing at the door as she recalled the last time she'd been here, when Trei was being measured for his wedding suit, standing half-naked with his hexmark scars on full display.

Now, her former wedding dress hung on a dress-maker's form, its beautiful obsidian gems glittering in the lantern light. Someone had cleaned Trei's blood-stains from the cuffs.

"Lady Bryn?" Helna prompted. "Are you well? You look pale."

As though waking from a dream, Bryn blinked. "Y . . . yes. Sorry."

Helna motioned to the dark gray wedding gown. "I've been informed time is of the essence. The quickest option would be to modify your former gown. I can alter the neckline, add a train . . ."

"No," Bryn whispered, unable to tear her eyes off the doomed gown. "Please. I—I can't wear that again."

Helna pressed her lips together in concern. "The fabric I ordered for a new gown comes from Zaradona. I thought I'd have more time. It will be weeks before it arrives . . ."

Bryn tore her gaze away from the gown, shaking her head. "I was wearing that dress when I found Trei's body. And Rangar will loathe the idea of marrying me in the same dress I wore to bind myself to his brother. Can't we alter a different gown? There must be some way."

"I suppose I could dye a wool dress a darker shade . . . It might not be as elegant as this one . . ."

"No, that's perfect," Bryn said in a rush.

Helna gave her a sympathetic smile. "I'm sure Rangar would think you the most beautiful bride in the Eyrie even if you were wrapped in a sheet. Now, let me take your measurements."

Bryn couldn't stop imagining Trei's ghost in the sewing room as the seamstress stretched her measuring string across Bryn's chest. That day, Bryn and Trei had come to an agreement to remain friends and not to try to force love. They'd both admitted their hearts belonged to other people.

*I miss you, Trei.* And now, the kingdom was about to lose another Barendur.

That night, after sitting with the ailing, unconscious king for some time, Bryn's mind was tied in such knots that she was desperate for a distraction. She couldn't stop glancing out the window at the road every five minutes, looking for Rangar atop Legend.

She plunged into the mage library, going back through the books written in Mir to see if she and Ren had overlooked anything about spells to create beasts out of animals. She read about the history of magic in the Mirien before it was banished two hundred years ago. Back then, magic was practiced throughout each of the Eyrie kingdoms. Hexes governed the weather and farming, health and prosperity, and even solved disputes to keep the peace. There was an account of a blight on a winter gourd crop that would have resulted in famine throughout the Mirien's western villages if not for a group of mages who came together to amplify a spell to cure the blight.

As she read, Bryn got madder and madder. Magic had the potential for so much good. It should never have been taken out of the common folk's hands. Of course, it hadn't happened all at once. No ancient king had suddenly declared it illegal to practice. Rather, with the rise of science and academics, magic was derided as backward until practicing it became shunned.

*But magic is just as useful as science,* Bryn thought. *There is a place for both. They're different sides to the same coin.*

She read until the candle burned down and, yawning, rested her head on a pillow of books. She had just started dreaming of wolves again when she was shaken awake.

Ren's eyes glittered in the dying candle's light. "Bryn, wake up. Rangar has returned."

Bryn barely knew the time of night as she barreled down the stairs to the great hall. It must have been well past midnight, with most of the common folk asleep on the floor with the slumbering livestock. She picked her way excitedly among the sleeping bodies to the entrance, where Valenden already waited.

Breathless, she started to dash out into the snow,

but Valenden snagged her arm. "Not so fast, princess. He isn't here yet." Valenden pointed to the roof. "The scouts spotted a rider approaching on the southern road."

"It's Rangar? They're sure?" she gasped.

Valenden nodded. "He lit two lanterns when he passed Thetly Village—that's the signal."

Bryn clasped her hands as she paced in the foyer, watching the town square for any sign of him. How long did it take to ride from Thetly Village to the Hold? After a painstaking few minutes, she finally spotted two lights shining through the snowfall.

Shrieking, she darted toward the drawbridge, but once more, Valenden stopped her.

"Wait!" Valenden sighed and kicked off his boots. "Here. Put these on. Those house shoes won't hold up for five minutes in the snow. And take a cloak!"

Bryn snatched a cloak off a hook and tossed it over her shoulders as she hurtled into the snow. The few lanterns in the village square cast orbs of light on the snowflakes swirling overhead. Valenden's too-big boots threatened to trip her as she ran toward the approaching riders.

With all the riders cloaked against the snow, it was Legend she recognized first. But as soon as Rangar spotted her running toward him, he slid off the horse and closed the distance between them in a few strides.

"Rangar!" she cried.

He swept her into his arms with enough force that she twirled in a circle, Valenden's boots nearly falling off her feet. He set her back down and captured her face between his gloved hands, holding her steady for a kiss.

"Bryn." His breath steamed in the cold air. With chapped lips, he pressed more kisses on her cheeks. "Gods, it feels good to hold you."

She clutched his shoulders as she peered up at him with questions in her eyes. "You really found proof of Broderick's guilt?"

Rangar peered over his shoulder at the other riders, who were dismounting in the village square. Oliver was among them, as well as a few other soldiers Bryn recognized, but there was a new horse and rider, too.

"Let's get inside." Rangar squinted up at the snow. "Before you freeze."

She let out a gruff laugh, thinking of the mage apprentice initiation. A few minutes in the cold with boots and a cloak was nothing compared to what she'd endured.

When Rangar gave her a questioning look, she shook her head. "I'll tell you later. Come."

One of the soldiers led Legend to the barn, and Bryn and Rangar moved into the foyer where Valenden waited. Rangar greeted his brother, who delivered the troubling news of King Aleth's health.

But Bryn's attention turned away from their conversation as the extra rider stepped into the foyer, dusted snow off his cloak, and pushed the hood back.

"Alain?" she said in surprise.

It was Broderick's father, the Mir refugee who had doubted her at first but later pledged his support when she'd agreed to marry Trei for the good of their kingdoms.

Broderick might be dead—but it seemed his father knew his secrets.

# CHAPTER 14

**NO GREATER PAIN . . . fathers and sons . . . a turn for the worse . . . a pivotal lie . . . long live the king**

"Alain," Bryn repeated, moving closer to the old farrier. "I thought you'd returned to the Mirien with the other refugees."

The elderly man placed a stern look on Rangar—it seemed clear he wished to be anywhere but there. Then again, he wasn't in chains, so he must have come of his free accord.

"My lady," Alain said gruffly. "The Saints demand justice, so here I am, though it is not my wish."

She stared at him in bald shock. Was he really going to denounce his own son as a murderer? From what little that she'd known of Alain, he'd been utterly dedicated to the Mirien's wellbeing, but it was hard to believe any father would place duty to kingdom over duty to his son's reputation.

Rangar acknowledged Alain's sacrifice with a nod. "Rest, Alain. Fill your belly. At first light, we'll convene and present what you have to say."

A sharp voice came out of the foyer's shadows. "I'm afraid it cannot wait until first light." Mage Marna stepped forward, her face pinched. A terrible weight sank in Bryn's stomach like a rock in the sea. "Aleth won't last the night," the mage reported. It was one of the first times Bryn had ever heard the woman's voice tremble.

Alarm flashed in Rangar's eyes. Valenden let slip a curse. Bryn moved close enough to Rangar to slip her hand into his and give it a squeeze.

After his shock faded, Rangar took a deep breath and asked, "Where is he?"

"We moved him to the bathhouse," Mage Marna answered. "Not even Ren's magic could summon enough steam to keep him warm in the mage chambers. I've given him a draught of dryad's clover to pull him out of his stupor, but it won't last long."

"Take me," Rangar said.

Along with Alain, they wound through the Hold's dark lower tunnels. All the while, Bryn felt like she was moving in someone else's body. Everything was happening too fast for her to process.

*The king will die this night . . .*

*Rangar will be made heir as long as Alain clears his name . . .*

*If Valenden doesn't make a last-minute play for the throne . . .*

*And what about our wedding?*

Finally, they reached the steam-filled hallway outside the bathhouse. Two guards moved aside as they approached. Initially, the bathhouse was so full of steam that Bryn could barely see a few feet in front of her. It was seldom occupied this time of night, and she felt certain Mage Marna had ordered it vacant for the king's arrival.

Once she got used to the steam, she saw the king laid out on one of the marble tables used for scrubbing and massage—which was also used for preparing the deceased for burial. At first, she feared they were too late, and the king was dead.

But then Aleth let out a wracking cough. Valenden and Rangar, as though a spell had broken, rushed to either side of their father.

"Father," Rangar said, tugging off his glove to feel his father's forehead. "I've returned. I'm here."

"R—Rangar . . ." Aleth muttered, disoriented.

"I'm here, as well," Valenden said, his voice nearly breaking.

"Valenden," the king whispered. He hacked a few more times and then murmured, "Trei? Where is Trei?"

The room fell silent as everyone exchanged looks over the king's head. At last, Rangar said evenly, "Trei is always with us, Father. You have all your sons here."

King Aleth moaned in pain, and Bryn turned to

Mage Marna with a grimace. She whispered, "Can't you do something for him?"

"My hexes to get rid of his pain also make him unconscious; I had to clear them in order to bring him back to consciousness with the draught."

Bryn's heart hurt to hear the king in pain, though she knew he didn't have long to suffer.

"Father," Rangar said, shaking the king back to cognizance. "I've brought Alain, the leader of the Mir refugees. We found him in Ardwallow, a logging town. He'd gone to locate his son, Broderick, just as we had. The son is dead, but Alain has crucial information."

At Rangar's beckon, Alain stepped forward, wringing his hands. He cleared his throat. "Your highness, your family took us in as refugees. Gave us food, a place to sleep, a role in this community. Though I would do anything to protect my children, my son is dead, and my words can no longer hurt him. They can, however, save your own son."

Bryn wasn't certain if King Aleth could process Alain's words in his semi-delirium. His lips moved wordlessly like he was muttering strange hexes.

Alain, uncertain, crossed himself before continuing. "Though I do not wish to make this confession, the Saints require honesty. It is my great shame as a father to confess that my son took Prince Trei's life. I swear to you that I did not know it at the time. I was aware that Broderick distrusted Lady Bryn, as we all did—if you'll pardon us, my lady—but I firmly believed in her once I got to know her. It seems Broderick didn't share my change of heart. He went that night to kill her and assassinated Prince Trei instead. Afterward, he fled to Ardwallow, which was when I suspected the truth. I knew for certain it was my son when the murder weapon was revealed—I saw that knife in Broderick's possession days before the murder."

Alain heaved a deep sigh as though unburdening his secret had lifted a weight, and yet sadness hung in the air.

*They wanted to kill me*, Bryn thought. *It's true. I was the target.*

Valenden rested a comforting hand on the old man's shoulder, leading him away to speak with him out in the hall.

Mage Marna stepped up to the table. "Did you hear that, Aleth?"

The king muttered groggily, "Trei . . . my son. Where is he?"

Mage Marna met Rangar's gaze. Bryn felt a ripple of fear. King Aleth was the only one who could absolve Rangar and had just heard proof of his innocence, and yet he still seemed to believe in his delirium that Trei wasn't even dead.

"Aleth." Mage Marna rested a hand on the king's chest. "Alain of the Mirien has cleared Rangar's name. Rangar had nothing to do with Trei's death. It was a Mir spy by the name of Broderick, whose life fate has now taken in turn. Rangar is innocent. Do you agree?"

King Aleth turned to cough again. His eyes were

bloodshot, and his lips were white. Bryn felt as though she could see the life fading out of him before her own eyes, disappearing into the steam.

"He's so cold," Rangar muttered, smoothing a hand over his father's brow.

Mage Marna's jaw slackened. Her eyes darted as she murmured, "His aura is changing. It's . . . fading."

"Val!" Rangar barked, and his brother immediately returned to the table.

"Aleth," Mage Marna tried one more time. "Declare that Rangar is innocent! You must speak it!"

The king mumbled a few unintelligible words before breaking into coughs again. Bryn clutched her hands around her necklace, praying to the saints and gods alike to give him a moment of clarity with which to spare Rangar.

His coughs slackened into a moan, which transformed into a hiss, which then became silence. Bryn stared, jaw parted.

*He's dead.*

For a moment, no one spoke. Steam continued to rise in loud bursts from the boilers. The room felt shrouded by it, like they had all escaped into the secrecy of a storm cloud.

Mage Marna tossed a quick look toward the bathhouse's curtain door to ensure the soldiers and Alain were outside. Then she extended a long look between Rangar, Valenden, and Bryn.

She raised her voice loud enough so that the soldiers outside would hear. "Yes, my king. Understood, my king. Rangar Barendur is absolved of all accusations."

A current of danger crackled in the air.

*She lied for Rangar's sake.*

Bryn could hardly fault Mage Marna—in fact, she was grateful for the deceit—but it was a chief sin, even treasonous, to make false claims for a king. Mage Marna could be hung for it. Yet it was only the four of them in the room—Bryn, Rangar, Valenden, and Mage Marna. They exchanged silent looks for a few breaths until Valenden gave the first nod.

Then, Bryn nodded.

Then, Mage Marna.

Finally, Rangar dipped his head.

Mage Marna took a few deep breaths, then let out a low wail. "He's gone . . . Aleth is gone!"

The soldiers rushed into the room to see for themselves. They immediately removed their helmets, bowing their heads.

"May his spirit be guided," one said.

"May his spirit be guided," the other echoed.

Mage Marna took a moment of grief and then cleared her throat. "Fetch Ren and the Deathkeepers to perform the rites on the body. Send word to the royal messenger to relay the announcement that the previous king has passed and that—" Her eyes snapped to Rangar, "—Prince Rangar shall be crowned as his successor on the morrow, after which the month of grieving shall commence."

Dimly, Bryn registered that they'd missed their

opportunity to get married. Her hurry had been in vain. Now they would have to wait an entire month to wed, opening them up to possible accusations of illegitimacy.

*If we could have wed today*, she thought, *nothing further could stand in our way.*

But as grave as those concerns were, she set them aside and focused on the tragedy in front of her. King Aleth had been like a father to her. She felt his loss keenly, and she knew Rangar's heart must be breaking. She crossed to him, folding herself into his arms, and held him fiercely.

He pressed a trembling kiss to the top of her head. "May his spirit be guided," Rangar whispered.

She closed her eyes. *It's okay*, she told herself. *Rangar is back. He's safe. He's cleared of the charges . . . granted, because of a lie.*

"Valenden," Rangar said quietly. "I will ask you one final time, brother. As elder son, do you wish to challenge my place as successor?"

Bryn couldn't meet Valenden's eyes for fear of what she might find there. In this last moment, would he suddenly gain kingly aspirations? The silence stretched until Valenden bowed his head and said, "I swear loyalty to you, Rangar Barendur, King of the Baersladen."

He knelt before Rangar and his father's dead body. On cue, the two soldiers knelt and bowed their head, and Mage Marna followed suit.

"My king," the each repeated.

Bryn started to kneel, but Rangar clasped her arm and shook his head. "Not you, Bryn. You never need kneel to me."

"You're the king," she whispered, glancing at the others. She knew enough about tradition throughout the kingdoms to know *all* subjects were required to kneel.

He shook his head again. "You're my Saved, and I am yours. We are forever bound. Soon, I'll call you wife and queen, and we will rule together, neither bowing to the other."

Such a breach of tradition made her nervous, though she was touched by the sentiment. His hand still on her forearm, Rangar pulled her close. He lifted her hand to kiss the engagement ring on her finger. Her lips parted slightly as the magnitude of what had happened settled over her.

Rangar was king.

A king was kissing her . . . a king she was going to wed.

She began to tremble from the idea of it, as well as sheer exhaustion. Rangar frowned and braced an arm around her.

"Lady Bryn needs rest," he said. "Aunt, brother, I will take her to our bedroom and then meet you in the council chambers to discuss tomorrow's coronation."

"Rangar, no," Bryn objected. "It's the middle of the night. You need rest, too. You've been on the road for days."

"She's right," Mage Marna agreed. "Tomorrow will

be a pivotal day. You must project strength and good health, Rangar, so your people feel confident in you. Sleep. Eat. Bathe the dirt from your travels off you. Valenden and I will make arrangements for the funeral and coronation."

Rangar started to object, but Bryn shushed him sharply. She pressed a hand to his sweat-bathed face. His scars were slick against her palm. "Rest, my love." She brushed her thumb over the scars. "My *king*."

# CHAPTER 15

**TRUE ROMANCE . . . this and this and this . . . funeral sashes . . . smells of the forest . . . a mage queen**

Bryn tumbled into a troubled sleep as soon as her head touched the pillow. It didn't help that, given the lateness and Rangar's unexpected arrival, they'd returned to the third-floor chambers despite Rangar no longer being under house arrest. The room felt cursed, and dark premonitions worked their way into Bryn's dreams. Growls haunted the hallways. Yellow animal eyes glowed in the shadows. She was back in the dungeon, where the frozen wolf carcass suddenly lifted its head, snarling with undead rancor.

Breathing hard, she snapped awake. Sunlight

filtered through the window. Rangar was by her side, still wearing his riding gear except for the boots, his face twisted in his sleep as though he was having his own nightmares.

For a moment, Bryn took this opportunity to study him. It was rare to see him vulnerable like this. His hair was filthy, his shirt caked in sweat. His lips were chapped from being out in the cold for so long. As she gently brushed the hair away from his scars, she wondered what he'd endured while on the hunt for Broderick. He looked as though he hadn't slept a single night or stopped for a single meal.

He stirred awake at her touch, capturing her hand with a warrior's swiftness to place a kiss against her palm.

"My love," he said quietly.

"Today, you become king," she said softly.

"And bury my father," he muttered, rolling over onto his back.

She smoothed the sheets off him and started unbuttoning his dirty shirt. His hexmark scars flashed on his bare skin, and her stomach tightened. She had the urge to trace them, to get to know him through his scars—the intentional ones as much as the accidental ones—but stayed her hand.

"You need a bath," she stated firmly.

"Do I smell that bad?"

"I don't mind the smells of the forest—but yes."

He snorted and leaned up to capture her lips in a kiss. It stretched for some time as Bryn's heart began to dance. She'd feared so much for him, but now they were here together. Grief might hang over them, but they were free.

Rangar pushed up to a seated position and slid the rest of the way out of his shirt, never breaking the kiss. His lips were urgent, as though *she* were the only meal he'd craved on the journey.

"Rangar," she said, breaking the kiss. "Really. You need a bath, and proper clothes. I'll call for a maid—"

"Don't you dare leave this bed," he threatened.

He trailed his lips down her jawline and onto her neck. It felt wrong to do this under the shadow of King Aleth's death, and yet Bryn recalled how much their coupling after learning of Aleth's illness had eased Rangar's tension when they'd first returned to Barendur Hold.

She hesitated.

*She* had needed the release then, too, just as she needed it now. Faced with so much uncertainty, what she craved more than anything was to feel one with him. It would be a month before they were bound together in matrimony, and after so much separation, she hungered for that connection *now*.

He brushed her hair off her shoulder and kissed up to her chemise strap. He slid the strap down and replaced it with his lips as his other hand cupped her breast through the fabric.

She sucked in a breath, then let it out slowly. It felt impossibly good to melt into his strong hands. He smelled like wood smoke and horses and pine trees, and she closed her eyes and imagined they were in the forest.

"Lay back," he ordered.

She let herself collapse against the soft blankets. He climbed on top of her, bracing himself with his hands on either side of her head as he kissed her again. Her hands massaged his tense shoulders, gliding over his many hexmarks until she reached his belt. She slipped a finger under it to touch warm skin.

He groaned and pulled back to let his gaze worship her.

"I thought about nothing but you," he whispered. "I wanted to find that bastard Broderick just so I could return here as fast as I could and do *this*." He dipped his head to capture her nipple beneath her chemise in his lips. "And this." His hand hardened over her other breast. "And this."

His knee pushed between her legs, teasing the sensitive area that was already growing wet. Bryn slid her other strap down, freeing her breasts. With his mouth, Rangar sampled her nipples until she felt breathless. She wove a hand in his tousled hair, holding his head steady.

Suddenly, he straightened and dragged Bryn closer a few inches until her hips were flush with his. He started undoing his belt. Her breath came fast as she watched him remove the remainder of his clothes. He was beautiful, her prince—no, her king. She'd so rarely had a chance to admire his naked body in a season of heavy wool clothes and bearskin cloaks.

He pulled her chemise all the way over her hips and treated himself to a long caress over her curves.

"My queen," he breathed.

"Not yet." Her voice was barely a whisper, given how hard her heart was pounding.

He dismissed her words with a grunt. "You've always been a queen. You could be a peasant, and you'd still be a queen."

He straddled her widest part as his lips possessed hers, unrelenting. Tingles of pleasure flooded her body as she felt his cock nudging against her entrance. She angled her hips to allow him to slip inside her, urging him to take her.

*A funeral . . .*

*A coronation . . .*

*Stop it*, she commanded herself. All she wanted to think about was Rangar. For years, he'd believed that her soul belonged to him after he'd saved her life. The *fralen* bond. She had thought it frightening and backward at the time, and there was still something so boldly possessive about it . . . and yet now that she had also saved *his* life, she couldn't deny that their souls felt intertwined in a way that could never be separated.

Her nerves burned as she wiggled her hips, begging him to fill her. He was only too happy to oblige. He spread her knees as his cock pierced her swollen heat. She shuddered with pleasure as he pulled out and drove into her again.

He wove a hand in her hair to hold her steady as he

continued his thrusts. Her whole body was growing feverish. Her breath came faster than she could count. She curled her legs around his hips, urging him to go even deeper still.

He pushed into her one more time, and a wave of tingling crested over her. As she let out a gasp, feeling her pleasure peak, he emptied himself inside her, dripping sweat onto her face.

She sighed deeply, her body going limp. Both breathing hard, they weren't prepared for the knock at the door.

Bryn sat up sharply.

"My lord? My lady?" It was Lada, one of the maids who'd been helping Bryn with wedding planning. Another timid knock came at the door. "I have your grieving garments here . . ."

"Not now!" Rangar growled.

Bryn shot him a look and called out kindlier, "Just a moment, Lada." She reached for the robe at the foot of the bed, but Rangar held her hips firmly against his.

"I'm not done with you," he said in a dark growl. "What if I want you again?"

She rested a firm hand on his scarred chest and shimmied off the bed, sliding into the robe. She tossed him another robe. "I'm serious about that bath. You can have me again when you're presentable."

Though he grumbled, he donned the robe, and Bryn let in Lada. The girl's eyes instantly went to the rumpled sheets, but she said nothing. She laid two folded bundles of clothes on the table. "Helna sent these. There are also sashes to wear while grieving—I don't know if your traditions are the same in the Mirien, my lady."

Bryn nodded. "They are."

Lada patted the other sets of clothes. "And these are garments for the coronation. Your gown from the Harvest Gathering, my lady, and for King Rangar . . ." She hesitated. "Well, all we have on short notice are the garments Helna had prepared for Trei." She rushed to add, "He never wore them, though. Before he could, he—"

*He died.*

Bryn quickly spared the girl her flustered nerves. "Thank you, Lada. King Rangar will be down for his bath shortly."

Lada nodded curtly. "I'll let the attendants know."

Bryn closed the door to find Rangar's gaze fixed low on her hips, and she wagged a finger at him. "To the bathhouse with you. I'll . . ." she swallowed. "I'll see you at the funeral."

His mood grew sullen at the mention of the bathhouse. Though Bryn was certain the Deathkeepers would have already relocated King Aleth's body, she hated that he was going to have to return to the site of such fresh pain.

She sniffed her own armpits. "Hmm, I suppose I need my own bath—"

She shrieked as Rangar captured her around the waist, pulling her back to the bed. With him sitting and her standing, his head was at the level of her chest, though his gaze was pinned to her face.

Reaching a hand to smooth over her cheek, he said, "First, tell me what happened here while I was away."

"Wedding planning, mostly. Mage Marna had hoped we could wed before your father passed to avoid waiting for the grieving period."

His eyes dropped to her curves. "I had hoped for that, too. You have no idea how much I'd prefer to see you dressed today in a wedding gown instead of a funeral sash." His hands squeezed her waist where the sash would later hang. "And Fable? Did you ride her?"

Bryn smiled. "Some, yes. She's a dream horse, Rangar. I trust her footing completely." The smile faded as she hesitantly admitted, "Though I didn't ride her as much as I'd have liked. I was busy with the wedding planning, and Ren and I spent time researching spells that could have created the berserkir wolves, and I . . . " At her pause, he raised an eyebrow for her to continue. "I underwent the mage apprentice initiation."

His hands tightened protectively around her waist. His eyes scoured her body as though searching for any wounds he might not have seen while making love to her. "You did? When?"

She told him about the hollowed-out tree stump and the death slumber hex. It was impossible to keep the excitement from her voice as she recounted the thrilling events, and when she finished, she was surprised to see an amused smile on his face.

"You're *pleased* that I almost died?" she challenged.

"Of course not," he said, the smile stretching wider. "I'm pleased you *lived*. You know, Mage Marna isn't training you because you have an interest in magic. She's doing it because she's getting older, and with Calista gone, the kingdom will need a head mage after her death."

Bryn was taken aback. It hadn't occurred to her that Mage Marna might intend for *Bryn* to take her place one day. "But Ren is far ahead of me in his studies."

"Ren is on a path to replace the healer," Rangar explained. "His studies are focused on that aspect. A head mage must be well versed in *all* aspects of hexes and even experiment to forge new ones. Calista was in line to take my aunt's place."

Bryn was almost at a loss for words. "There must be so many people more gifted at hexes than me."

"That is true," Rangar conceded. "But none who will be queen. A Mage Queen? It hasn't been seen in a hundred years. My aunt wants to leave the kingdom in the hands of someone with as much political power as magical power."

Bryn sank onto Rangar's knee, her head spinning with the prospect of one day being not only the kingdom's queen but head mage as well.

*A Mage Queen.*

If anyone could bring together science and magic, it would be someone in that position.

Another timid knock came at the door.

Lada was back, looking sheepish. "My lord? My lady? The baths are ready and, begging your pardon, a crowd is already gathering in the village square." She cleared her throat. "For you."

Bryn's arm tightened around Rangar's neck.

She allowed herself to revel in this one brief moment—the two of them, not yet king and queen, just a boy and girl mad with love for each other.

Then, they stood and prepared themselves for a funeral and a coronation.

# CHAPTER 16

**A FUNERAL AND A CORONATION . . . the Baer princess . . . crown of gems and claws . . . a flaming arrow . . . a king**

To hold a funeral and a coronation on the same day would be too much for most people, but the common folk of the Baersladen were made of tougher stock—and Bryn was now one of them. The weather had cleared by midmorning with only hazy clouds over pale blue winter skies. Fresh snow covered the town's rooftops, though the village square had been cleared, salted, and dusted with sand.

Since they hadn't anticipated King Aleth's death happening as soon as it had, Bryn was foisted into the ceremony with little preparation. Lada squeezed and cinched her into her old Harvest Gathering dress and attacked her hair with intricate Baer-style braids that circled her scalp like honeybuns. They fastened mother-of-pearl pendants on her ears and draped strings of pearls around her neck. Even with the extra attention to her presentation, however, the style was still spartan compared to the Mirien's extravagant styling. There was no rust dusted on her cheeks and arms, black kohl lining her eyelashes, or shimmering silk threads woven painstakingly into her hair. When she looked in the mirror, a Baer maiden—with blond hair, granted—looked boldly back at her.

She didn't see Rangar, busy with his own ministrations, until right before the funeral. Her heart raced with nerves as Lada led her through the great hall, which was being hastily decorated for the coronation feast, into the foyer. At the same time Bryn arrived, Oliver was urging Rangar to hurry from the other end as he went over some last-minute details on a scroll with his advisors.

Rangar stopped in his tracks when he saw Bryn. His eyes unabashedly raked down her body from the crown of her hair to the toes of her slippers, drinking in every detail of her appearance. She felt suddenly like she was back in the woods, facing some hulking wolf that wanted to devour her.

*Only I wouldn't mind a bite from this particular wolf.*

Not only was he devastatingly handsome, but she'd never seen him looking so regal. As a prince, his clothes had always been presentable but never what she'd call refined. Rangar's normal linen and fur clothing couldn't be a starker contrast to her brother Mars and his fastidiously elegant suits. Rangar was always half-hidden beneath a bearskin cloak, with his mess of dark hair pulled down to hide his scars.

But today, the castle maids had wrangled him into winter-gray trousers with a crisp white shirt and a dark blue velvet cloak that flattered his complexion. A mantel of northern gemstones and bear claws graced his shoulders. For perhaps the first time in his life, someone had convinced him to brush his hair back off his face. The scars were clearly visible, yes, but so were his handsome features.

*A king's features*, Bryn thought. *A king's eyes, a king's lips . . .*

Lips that had just been all over her. She blushed, and that seemed to draw in Rangar for the attack. He stalked toward her until he could take her hand, pressing a kiss to her knuckles.

"My queen," he said in a rumbling low voice that made her toes curl.

"You look very dashing, my king," she answered breathlessly. Rangar's spirit was too wild to allow him to ever look like the elegant princes from her childhood storybooks, but in his fine clothes, she couldn't tear her eyes away from him.

He grunted as he tugged on his velvet cloak. "I can't wait to take the damn thing off."

She fought the urge to roll her eyes. *Always a savage.*

"My lord," Oliver said. "They're ready for you and Lady Bryn in the square."

Rangar held Bryn's hands in his. "Ready?" he said low enough so only she could hear.

"Ready," she whispered back.

He didn't tear his gaze off her. "I want you by my side in all things, Bryn. Today and forever. In this world and the next."

She dipped her head in a nod, not breaking their gaze. "In this world and the next. You, always."

Her heart shot to her throat as Rangar led her out into the square before the gathered crowd. Soldiers had brought Legend and Fable from the stables, their manes braided and their bodies painted with hexmark symbols. Oliver helped Bryn mount Fable.

A team of soldiers emerged from the castle's cellar with a wooden casket decorated with sea stones and maiden roses. Bryn felt her breath catch. She closed her eyes briefly and silently prayed to the saints for King Aleth's soul.

The soldiers carried Aleth's casket toward the ocean while drummers pounded a steady, slow rhythm on a mournful drum. Bryn and Rangar rode behind the casket onto the beach, with Valenden and Mage Marna following on foot, and the common folk rounding up the end in a long procession.

The funeral march proceeded down the length of the beach until they reached a rocky outcropping, where a straw-lined raft floated in the surf. The drummers pounded a new rhythm while soldiers splashed into the surf to mount the casket on the raft. Once it was secure, they awaited the signal from the drummers, then pushed it out to the open sea.

Oliver approached Rangar on Legend to offer a longbow and arrow. Rangar accepted it with a nod. Turning briefly to Bryn on Fable, he explained, "It is tradition for the new king to fire the funeral arrow."

She watched in a mix of fascination and sorrow as Rangar whispered the spark spell to ignite the oil-soaked end of the arrow. A flame leaped to life. He raised the arrow toward the heavens, then released it. It sailed toward the distant horizon in a graceful arc that landed in the center of the raft. The straw immediately caught fire.

A wooden flute played a mournful funeral dirge as the crowd watched the raft burn. In the Mirien, people buried their bodies in the ground, so this custom seemed strange to Bryn until she realized the ground was too frozen most of the year in the Baersladen to dig a grave. She let the flute music call to her heart until the raft finally sank beneath the distant waves.

She glanced at Rangar from the corner of her eye, wondering what was going through his mind. When she'd first crossed paths with him at the Low Sun Gathering half a year ago, she'd thought him so brave as to be foolhardy. But now she knew a tender heart was hidden behind his outward courage. He felt the same fear, doubt, and grief as anyone, even if his stony face rarely showed it. She wanted nothing more than to lead Fable closer to him and squeeze his hand—but this was his custom, not hers, and she needed to follow his lead.

The procession slowly returned along the beach back to Barendur Hold. A dais had been hastily erected during the funeral, and the crowd now gathered closely while Oliver took Fable's lead and helped Bryn dismount.

"Rangar is fortunate to have you," Oliver whispered. "He'll need you now more than ever."

Bryn felt a little dizzy as she climbed the dais behind Rangar and Mage Marna. The throne from the great hall sat in the center of the dais, flanked by benches on either side. Valenden was already on the stage along with Ren, the captain of the army, and Saraj. It gave Bryn courage to see her friends close by, especially when Saraj gave her a reassuring smile.

"This is a sad day for the Baersladen," Mage Marna announced, her strong voice ringing like a winter echo. "King Aleth Barendur's legacy is one of greatness and fortitude. Under his forty-two-year reign, the Baersladen saw unparalleled prosperity. His negotiations with the southern kingdoms kept us fed. His allyship with the forest kingdoms kept us protected. The Baersladen army defeated the Zaradona coup thirty-five years ago, and defended the realm from Mir incursions and banditry. His line is proudly carried on by his two surviving sons, Prince Rangar and Prince Valenden, while he joins his late wife, Anathalda, and his son, Prince Trei, in the gods' realm. His soul now belongs to Death."

The crowd responded with applause for the former king's successes. The sincerity on their faces touched Bryn. More than one elderly face in the crowd had tears streaming down it. These people had deeply loved and respected their king.

Would they love Rangar the same? Would they love *her*?

Mage Marna motioned to Ren. "Apprentice Ren Kotkel will lead us in a funeral hymn."

Ren took a deep breath before closing his eyes and clasping his hands. A silence fell over the crowd as he sang the first few notes of a beautiful but strange melody.

*"We lift our horns and sing,*
*To the gods on high above,*
*We ask that they embrace our king,*
*With their boundless love.*

*Onward to the afterlife,*
*Where the gods and heroes wait,*
*We send Aleth with honor,*
*To the great hall's golden gates."*

Many in the crowd sang along, but others cried too hard to find the words.

Silence followed the dirge. Bryn could hear the ocean in the distance. Its waves had always been a steadying presence for her. Now, she had a feeling that whenever she heard them, she would think of Aleth Barendur.

Mage Marna let the silence linger before announcing sharply, "We bid farewell to the old king but welcome the new. Valenden Barendur, the eldest living son of Aleth Barendur, has surrendered his claim to the throne in favor of his brother, Rangar Barendur. King Aleth supported this amendment to the line of succession. Shortly before his death, he absolved Rangar of any previous charges. We are grateful to know the name of Trei Barendur's slayer, and that the blackguard shall be punished by Death's hand in the afterlife."

The crowd voiced their support, but Bryn still felt nervous. King Aleth had said nothing of the sort—he'd been too delirious to say much of anything. The lie weighed on her. She glanced at Valenden, curious and worried. As much as he claimed he didn't want the throne, he had all the ammunition he needed to declare Rangar ineligible if he ever changed his mind.

*Val wouldn't do that*, she reassured herself. *Just because my own family was duplicitous doesn't mean that everyone's is.*

"Saraj Swiftly, Lead Falconer of the Baer Army, will present the crown."

Clutching a velvet-wrapped bundle, Saraj stood from the bench. She unwrapped the fabric to reveal King Aleth's crown, which had been polished, shined, and now glittered beneath the winter sun. It was cast in heavy bronze, made to look like a ring of bear claws.

"This crown was forged three hundred years ago," Mage Marna pronounced, "Under old King Vestal's rule, after the great war of the Northern Eyrie . . ."

Bryn's attention faded as she spotted a familiar face in the crowd. It was a tall man with long auburn hair and the forest-green cloak of Vil-Kevi's army, though his epaulets and fine boots indicated he was no mere soldier. Though she was certain she'd seen his face before, it took her a few minutes to place him.

*Prince Anter Jarkkinen*, she recalled.

He was one of the younger sons of King Otto Jarkkinen of Vil-Kevi, cousin to Lady Enis. He had attended her family's High and Low Sun Gatherings with his family on more than one occasion.

Her stomach churned with unanswered questions. What was a forest prince doing here, among the commoners?

She was so distracted by Prince Anter's presence that she didn't realize Rangar had approached the throne. As far as thrones, this one was simple, in keeping with Baer style, made of heavy oak with a bear carved into the backrest.

Mage Marna announced, "Rangar Barendur of the Baersladen, third son to the late King Aleth and late Queen Anathalda, I invoke the gods to bless you with wisdom and strength as we crown you the King of the Baersladen, High Captain of the Baer Army, and Protector of the Northernmost Realm of the Eyrie."

Rangar looked every bit the king as he bowed his head so Mage Marna could set the glistening bronze crown atop his backswept curls. Bryn's heart thumped with pride as she clasped her hands together.

*I should be with him*, she thought with a stab of sorrow. If he had only returned a day sooner, she would be at his side, wearing the late queen Anathalda's matching crown instead of seated at the far end of the dais as, what, the royal harlot?

"My people," Rangar called in a booming voice that echoed his father's gruff tone. "This oath I swear to you: Our lands shall be under no kingdom's rule but our own. Our forest shall be full of deer, our seas plentiful of fish, our fields rich with grain. Each village, farm, and house within the Baer border shall be protected by the full power of the Baer army. Should any of these things not come to pass, I will fight without rest until they are so."

The crowd cheered with such vigor that Bryn's heart jumped in her chest.

"I ask you now to swear your own oath to me," Rangar bellowed. "As you once swore it to my father."

Almost as one, the crowd kneeled on the sand sprinkled throughout the village square. Bryn felt a swell of awe to see people who truly believed in their ruler, not out of fear but of trust.

*Rangar has helped these people his entire life*, Bryn

thought. He'd chopped wood with them during long winters. He'd herded sheep during the sheering season. He'd fought at the borders to defend them. *He has earned their trust not with a crown but with the strength of his two hands.*

"We declare our allegiance to you and your reign," cried the people.

Amid her pride in seeing the crowd bowing to their new king, one figure caught her eye. Prince Anter Jarkkinen stood at the edge of the crowd, unkneeling. It was no surprise—a royal did not need to swear an oath to another royal of a different kingdom. But he stuck out enough among the lowered crowd that Mage Marna and Valenden and even Rangar himself seemed to finally take notice of his presence.

A flutter of nerves pattered in Bryn's chest. Why had Prince Anter come unannounced—and why was he armed so heavily?

# CHAPTER 17

**THE FOREST PRINCE . . . deer hearts and dances . . . a visitor with a request . . . a journey into the woods**

I t was done.

Aleth Barendur's body had been given to the sea, and Rangar Barendur sworn in as the next king of the Baersladen.

Bryn couldn't take her eyes off Rangar throughout the duration of the coronation feast. In his glittering bear claw crown atop his swept-back curls, he didn't look like the brooding boy hiding his scars who'd approached her at the Low Sun Gathering. He looked every bit like a king. Her heart felt torn; she loved both versions of him equally, though something simply felt right about seeing him raising his glass to the kingdom's prosperity and being answered by vociferous bellows.

Everything about the feast was unrefined, wild, earthy—just like the Baersladen itself. It was why she had fallen in love with these untamed lands, and with Rangar himself as an embodiment of them. Roxin had prepared the food she'd stored for their wedding feast into a coronation banquet full of roasted meats, hearty winter stews, plentiful ale, and even raw deer hearts. Though he maintained his composure as king, Rangar drank heartily with his fellow soldiers and citizens, and it wasn't long before his gruff voice rose in song and jest with everyone else.

Bryn took a sip of fig brandy that had been intended for her wedding. She ran her fingers over the white grieving sash around her waist that she'd wear for the next month, according to Baer tradition.

"Won't you try the deer heart, darling?" Rangar sank into his throne at the dining table and leaned over to kiss her cheek messily.

She wrinkled her nose. "I'm not queen yet. I don't have to partake in *every* Baer tradition."

He laughed huskily as he smoothed a hand over her intricate braids. "Soon, you will wear my mother's crown. The people already accept you as their queen. As my wife."

With a devilish look in his eye, he pulled her out of her chair as musicians started a *velta*. She joined him in a dance with other couples, smiling to see him so engaged with his people. His hands tightened on her waist as he spun her in circles. His palms moved scandalously low on her backside, but no one seemed to mind their king pawing at his fiancée. She rested her head on his shoulder as they swayed, closing her eyes briefly.

There were dangers still, but did she ever think she'd be this happy?

It came time to trade partners, and Bryn was reluctant to surrender him to Aya and dance with Oliver instead, though he was a skilled dancer. She moved on to one of the blacksmiths next, then a fisherman, and then two twin brothers from a farm outside the village. She was quite exhausted when she finally broke away to search for some water.

As soon as she'd located a chalice and drank, Valenden appeared at her side. "Bryn. A moment?"

She wiped her mouth. She was still out of breath from the dancing. "Give me a rest, Val, then I'll dance with you."

Valenden was in a rarely serious mood, though. "I'm not talking about a dance." He nodded toward the yew courtyard, where Prince Anter of Vil-Kevi stood waiting.

Bryn's good mood faltered. She set down the chalice and swallowed. "Right."

Valenden placed a guiding hand on her back as he ushered her toward the forest prince. "Prince Anter has news I think we need to listen carefully to."

As they stepped outside the great hall's warmth, Bryn wrapped her arms around her chest. Though a roof covered the courtyard's passages, the sides facing the yew were left to the open air, and it was a cold night.

"Prince Anter," Bryn said with a nod. "I noted your presence at the coronation. I haven't seen you since the Low Sun Gathering in the Mirien. Much has changed since then throughout all corners of the Eyrie."

The forest prince's green eyes shifted to Rangar among the crowd back in the great hall. "Very true, Lady Bryn."

She fought the urge to shiver in the cold. "How did you receive word of the coronation? Messengers couldn't possibly have reached you in Vil-Kevi in time."

His eyebrows lifted as he folded his hands, and Bryn saw an echo of his cousin, Lady Enis, in his features. "In fact, I didn't know about the coronation. I came to ask King Aleth for help, unaware of his illness. Vicious wolf attacks have hounded villages across Vil-Kevi. It's growing direr by the day. These aren't normal wolves. My cousin, Lady Enis, brought me a carcass you killed, and she reported on your own attack."

That explained how well-armed he was, Bryn realized. He wasn't stocked with swords, a longbow, and knives for fear of any human attacker—it was to protect himself in his travels from the wolves.

"Berserkir wolves," she said.

"Pardon?"

"That's what we've started calling them, after the old story."

He nodded, aware of the tales. "Yes, these berserkir wolves, as you call them, have slaughtered over two dozen of our forest folk. We've examined the victims' bodies and found that the wolves did not appear to attack them out of hunger. Our warriors managed to capture one berserkir wolf alive. I came to ask if one of your mages would travel to Higharbor Keep in Vil-Kevi to inspect it. Our own mages are at a loss."

Suddenly, the cold air didn't seem so harsh compared to Prince Anter's chilling words.

Bryn glanced over her shoulder back at the party. "Let us meet tomorrow with Mage Marna and others who have been helping us investigate the berserkir wolves. I'll have the maids prepare a room for you to stay the night."

Prince Anter shook his head. "I cannot stay, I'm afraid. My people are dying. I must return tonight."

"Won't you at least eat something before you go?"

"I would appreciate a small package of food to take with me on my return trip."

She sent for Lada, who prepared provisions for Prince Anter. He stowed them in his satchel and then fastened his cloak around his neck.

"I'll speak with Rangar," Bryn promised him. "We'll come to Higharbor Keep as soon as we can."

Prince Anter bid his farewell to her and Valenden. Bryn rejoined the festivities, but a shadow darkened her mood as she worried about the berserkir wolves.

She didn't yet mention Prince Anter's visit to Rangar, wanting him to enjoy his well-earned celebration for one night. Still, the mystery of the wolves wouldn't let her mind go. Even later that night, when Rangar was making love to her, she thought of wolves—and touched the scars across her ribs.

"We must go to Vil-Kevi," Bryn pronounced. "They need our aid."

She sat around the council table with Saraj, Ren, and the Barendur family, anxious after explaining Prince Anter's urgent news.

"If the berserkir wolf attacks are that bad," Saraj said, "Shouldn't you stay here, Rangar? Defend your own people?"

"The wolf attacks haven't yet spread into the Baersladen," Rangar said, looking exceptionally kingly, his tight fist resting on the table. Bryn still wasn't used to how much the bronze crown suited him. "And if we do not wish them to spread here, we must come to the aid of our neighboring kingdom. Helping Vil-Kevi helps the Baersladen, too."

"I won't argue with that," Saraj said. "But you were *just* crowned king. The grieving period for Aleth has only begun. Is it the time for you to leave? Send Val and me instead. Mage Marna, your wisdom would also be of great use."

"I cannot leave during the grieving period," Mage

Marna lamented. "I must lead the community in daily prayer for Aleth's soul."

"I will go," Rangar announced firmly, leaving no further room for debate. "I have faced these berserkir wolves myself. I understand what they are like, and I want to study this live one Prince Anter has caught. Saraj, you will remain here to ensure the realm's safety, along with the captain of the army."

"You should take a mage," Saraj insisted.

"Ren is the Baersladen's best healer," Rangar said. "If these wolves do attack closer to Barendur Hold, he must be here to heal our people."

"Then take Bryn," Mage Marna said evenly.

Bryn's hand went automatically to the hex scarring her ear. "I wish to go, but I'm only at the start of my apprenticeship."

"All the more reason to go," Mage Marna said. "A mage needs experience outside of her studies."

Rangar squeezed Bryn's hand, giving her a measured look, then nodded decisively. "You, Val, and I will go. We all have experience with the beasts. And I want you close to me—especially if there's danger."

"When do we leave?" she asked.

They decided to depart after the following day's prayer for Aleth's soul. Mage Marna pried Bryn away from Rangar to ply her with books and scrolls for her to take on the journey to study and to share with Vil-Kevi's mages.

"Remember," Mage Marna advised, "how you

survived the initiation. You may not have many hexes, but you can use the ones you do have wisely."

Bryn nodded solemnly. Her heart was racing when they saddled their horses and departed Barendur Hold. The fastest path to Higharbor Keep was over Barkksin Pass, which was too steep for a carriage. But it was a journey of only one day, and despite the danger, Bryn looked forward to the ride on Fable.

"I've never been to Higharbor Keep," Bryn said once they'd traversed a few miles on the road. "My parents thought it too unrefined for my siblings and me to visit."

"It's a beautiful castle," Valenden told her. "From the inside, at least."

"What do you mean?" Bryn asked.

"Oh, perhaps it's also beautiful from the outside, but it's hard to tell. It's shrouded by towering evergreens that keep its exterior largely hidden even in the winter. A defensive measure."

"The Jarkkinen family and the Barendurs have always been allies," Rangar explained. "As well as the Viklund family of Vil-Rossengard. For centuries, the three northern kingdoms of the Eyrie were isolated before better roads were built. We had to rely on one another. If one of us needs help, the others answer."

The path soon took them up into the mountains, where the snowfall was deeper, but Fable was sure-footed. Rangar watched her riding with a curious grin.

"What?" she asked. "Remember, I'm new to riding. Don't criticize me too harshly."

"My love, I would never. On the contrary, I was admiring your form. You'll be an excellent rider soon." He leaned in closer. "As excellent as when I ride you in the bedroom."

Valenden, overhearing, groaned.

Bryn gave Rangar a scolding look as she nudged Fable ahead on the narrow path, but she only teased. Her mother would have condemned her for making love with a man who wasn't yet her husband, and it was just another reason Bryn was glad to call the Baersladen her home now. Married or not, coupling with Rangar couldn't possibly be a sin—it was heaven to have his hands on her body, feel their two bodies join.

Her cheeks started to warm as she remembered the last time he'd pleasured her. Maybe "heaven" was the wrong word. There was nothing saintly about what they'd done . . .

"I hope you're prepared to be parents," Valenden pointed out wryly. "With as often as you two have been going at it."

Bryn paused to wonder about the risk of getting pregnant. They had only started to consummate their love, and she knew it could take months for a woman to fall pregnant, yet she'd also been warned it could happen as soon as the first time. She gently touched her belly. While it wouldn't be the worst thing to fall pregnant with Rangar's child, she still had so much she wanted to learn before becoming a mother: how to ride, how to cast magic, how to speak Baer without the translation hex's aid.

"Val has a point, Rangar," she said. "Perhaps I'll speak to Ren when we return to Barendur Hold about teas that could . . . prevent such things until we're ready."

Rangar scowled. "Ready? I was ready to put a baby in you the first time I bedded you."

Her cheeks warmed. "We aren't married yet."

He dismissed that concern with a head shake. "We will be before any child would be born."

"Rangar, be reasonable. There is no harm in waiting a few months, maybe years, to try . . ."

He stopped Legend short and turned around to face Bryn. "You don't want to bear my child?"

Valenden groaned. "Here we go . . ." he muttered, settling back on his horse to watch the two bicker like it was a spectator sport.

# CHAPTER 18

**A BREAK IN THE JOURNEY . . . crossing the border . . . magic and a nap . . . on her knees**

"**O**f course I want to bear your child!" Bryn exclaimed. "Just not yet. I'm still young."

"Many in the Eyrie bear children younger than you."

She squeezed her fist in Fable's mane. "That doesn't make it right. Besides, I can't study to be a mage apprentice with a baby on my hip." Rangar's eyes narrowed as he couldn't argue against this point. She emphasized, "If you want a Mage Queen, you'll have to wait to sire a child on me."

Rangar's eyes dropped to her belly. "And if you're already with child? Val is right. We haven't been taking precautions."

Her cheeks warmed again. "I'm not. A woman . . . can tell these things."

At least, she didn't think she was. She didn't *feel* pregnant, but her mother had hardly given her much information regarding such things. Sex and pregnancy were taboo subjects in the Mirien, for all the kingdom purported to support science.

*It supports science when it comes to men*, she thought bitterly. When she was queen, she would ensure every girl and woman understood the process clearly, as well as every one of their husbands to support them.

But the truth was, her monthly courses weren't due for a few more days, so until her bleeding came, she supposed there was a chance she might already be carrying Rangar's baby after all . . .

She spurred Fable on, holding her head high. "I'll be a mother to your children one day, Rangar Barendur, but not yet."

Rangar brooded at this, and Valenden delighted in his brother's sour mood as they rode on.

The mountain pass between the Baersladen and Vil-Kevi was higher than Bryn had ever been. She marveled at the rocky peaks that seemed to stretch endlessly. They were fortunate to have a clear day, for she wouldn't have wanted to make the journey during rain or snow. They spotted snow-white rabbits munching bark that were so unused to people they didn't even scamper away. Unfortunately, that meant one of them ended up on the end of Rangar's arrow and roasted over a campfire for lunch.

They crossed the Vil-Kevi border, marked with a pile of stones, and descended into the forest valley in the afternoon. When they'd come to the forest kingdoms before for the rendezvous with Mars, Bryn had been frightened by the towering trees that seemed strangely aware. Now, she marveled at them as wonders of nature. Some were so big around at their base that she doubted five men could hold hands around them. They creaked and clicked as the riders passed.

"Magic is strong in the forest kingdoms," Valenden said as Bryn looked around at the clicking sounds. "The forest folk are even more tied to nature than we are. They worship the trees and believe their magic flows from them."

"I might believe it, too, if I lived here," she murmured, gazing up at the towering trunks.

The path eventually flattened as they wound through the forest and came upon a cluster of houses that made a small village. They dismounted to let the horses forage and drink water. One of the forest folk emerged from the closest house, lowering her head out of respect when she saw their fine clothes and Rangar's crown.

"My lords. My lady," she greeted them. "Prince Anter informed us that you might be soon passing this way. We've prepared nourishment for you."

"That's very kind of you," Bryn said as the woman returned from her home with a basket of fresh acorn flour cakes and apples. After they visited momentarily,

Bryn asked tactfully, "These wolf attacks we've been hearing about—have there been any here?"

The woman's face paled. She pressed a hand to her chest. "Not here, thank the gods. But about an hour's ride south in the Sagshaw Valley, yes. The beasts attacked a trapper's home in the middle of the night, killed the poor man's wife, and maimed his children before he could kill it."

Bryn silenced a gasp. "How awful."

"Yes, my lady."

"What are the forest folk saying about the beasts?" Valenden asked.

"We're no strangers to wolves in this forest," the woman informed them. "They're predictable creatures. They stay out of our way other than sometimes stealing rabbits we've snared in our traps. Before now, I'd be hard-pressed to recall a time when a wolf attacked a person. These beasts are different." She hesitated, her eyes going somewhere distant in thought, before saying, "They're more like dogs."

"Dogs?" Valenden asked in surprise.

"Not lap dogs," the woman clarified. "But hunting dogs. My husband has trained dozens of hunting dogs. How these wolves stalk their prey and work together feels . . . organized somehow, as though someone trained them to do it."

With a shudder, Bryn recalled the berserkir wolf attack on the road to Barendur Hold. "We thought they might be mindless beasts, perhaps overtaken by a disease."

The woman raised her shoulders. "Could be, my lady. They are certainly vicious. I'm only giving you my opinion."

As they continued on their journey, Bryn couldn't stop worrying about this alarming new idea that the wolves *weren't* crazed monsters driven by bloodlust but rather in complete control of their actions. She practiced her hexmarks to clear her mind, sparking fire in her palm as they rode.

"You're getting good at that one," Rangar observed.

"I need more experience with the amplifier hex."

He gazed ahead where a small meadow beside a stream made for a good place for them to stop to water the horses. "Val and I can help you with that."

While they let the horses drink from the stream, they sat on cloaks over the snowy meadow and joined hands as Ren had taught Bryn.

"Which spell do you want to amplify?" Valenden asked. "And if you say the purge one, forget it."

"The finding spell," she answered, pitching her gaze up at the trees. "To find a, let's say, warbler."

The three of them closed their eyes as Bryn had seen the kitchen maids do while concocting the fermenting hex. Bryn whispered under her breath, "*jin jan en veera.*"

When she'd used the finding spell previously, she'd had to focus all her energy on perceiving the slight tug which told her the vague direction to look in. She was prepared to feel the tug now, but it wasn't gentle this time. It felt like an invisible hand grabbed her jaw and wrenched her head toward a tall hemlock.

Her eyes snapped open. It took her only a few seconds before she spotted a warbler on one of the branches.

"There it is!"

Her jaw softened in awe, but she immediately felt exhausted.

Valenden yawned as he let go of her hands and wiped his palm down his face. He, too, suddenly looked tired. "Congratulations, princess. Now, I'm going to close my eyes for five minutes. Wake me when it's time to get back on the road."

Bryn turned to Rangar as she hummed with excitement. "That was incredible. I truly felt it—" She, too, stifled a yawn.

"That's the price of the amplifier spell," he explained, lightly pinching her chin to indicate her yawn. "No magic comes without cost. Most require skill and study, and of course, scarification. But pooling our efforts to serve the amplifier spell leaves its casters depleted."

"*You* don't seem tired."

He snorted. "When you've been a soldier going on five nights of no sleep and daily combat, finding a bird isn't too depleting." He took her hand, glancing at the napping Valenden. "Walk with me."

As they strolled along the icy stream bank, he told her more about how spells that required more than one caster worked and what toll they demanded in return. They discussed Bryn's apprentice training and how she might balance it against the realm's needs for her as the future queen. They passed a thicket of reddish-brown ferns that Bryn recognized from one of the books in the mage library.

"Oh, water sprite ferns!" She fell to her knees and brushed snow off the ferns. She turned one over to reveal dark red spores. "Ren told me about these."

She broke off a few ferns, wrapped them in a handkerchief, and then tucked them into her blouse. She was thrilled over identifying the fern, but when Rangar helped her back to her feet, the frown on his face made her smile fade. "What is it? What's wrong?"

He lowered his voice. "Do you truly not wish to fall pregnant?"

"Oh, Rangar." She pinched the bridge of her nose as she groaned. "I told you. I do wish to carry your child, only when the time is right . . ."

"That's not what I mean," he said, smoothing a gentle hand down her curls. "If you feel that way, we should take more care with how we pleasure one another. I wouldn't have filled you with my seed if I knew that wasn't what you wanted."

"*Rangar.*" She hissed for him to be silent as she glanced back toward the meadow where Valenden napped, embarrassed by his straightforward talk. Her cheeks burned brightly. She whispered, "I told you I'll speak to Ren about the tea to prevent pregnancy."

"We won't always be at Barendur Hold." His

fingers curled at the base of her neck as a fire sprang into his eyes. "With Ren and his tea."

Her heartbeat sped as she recognized that lusty look in his eyes. Giving him a stern look, she said, "What, you plan to bed me at Higharbor Keep?"

"No," he purred. "I plan to bed you right here."

Her jaw parted, and she couldn't quite find the words to speak. She sputtered, "We're in the middle of a journey. Prince Anter awaits us, and there are still hours to ride . . ."

"And Val is taking a nap."

She heaved a sigh to express how impossible he was.

His hand slid around the back of her neck until he could curl her in closer. His other one traced over her curves until he had a handful of her thigh. He settled his mouth near her ear and said in a dangerously low voice, "All this talk of putting a baby in you has left me unable to think about anything else."

She felt a ripple of desire pass through her as his breath grazed her ear. Her thigh tingled all around his touch. What was wrong with her for even considering this? They had a mission to accomplish. And Valenden was asleep just steps away!

"The whole point of our talk was that it *isn't* time for a baby . . ."

"I know. That's *my* point. That there are other ways to please one another. Now, kneel in the grass. Here, on my cloak." His voice was husky, impatient.

Her eyebrows snaked up at the bold command.

"I'm not so innocent that I don't know what women do on their knees, Rangar."

"Good. So do it."

Aghast, she was about to tell him to drop to his own knees, but the look on his face made her reconsider. Rangar looked like he very well might take her up on it and put his tongue in places that would make her forget why they were even in the middle of a forest, and have her moaning loud enough to wake Valenden, and the warbler, and every animal in the forest while she was at it—including any wolves.

Narrowing her eyes, she sank onto her knees on the cloak. "So now that you're my king, I can't refuse you? Is that what this is about?"

"No, my love, it's about sticking my cock between your pretty lips."

Her breath rushed out at his boldness, but she had to admit it stirred something within her. Well, she was already a harlot who'd made love before marriage—what difference did it make if she was on her knees now?

Besides, a wicked part of her wondered if she'd like it.

He undid his trousers and freed his already stiff cock. Bryn's eyes widened—it was one thing to have his manly part beneath the sheets, quite another to have it directly in her face. And yet, as he wrapped one of his hands around his cock and tipped up her chin with the other, her curiosity got the best of her.

"I've never done this before," she admitted.

"Good. I'd be tempted to kill the man who had your lips around him first. Don't use your teeth. Take as much as you can."

She took a deep breath before placing a tentative kiss on the tip of Rangar's cock. A groan slipped from his mouth, and his hand around her chin tightened. He moved it to the back of her head, fisting her hair to keep her head steady.

"That's it, my love. Just like that."

Bryn let herself test and toy and lick, gaining boldness as Rangar's reaction made it clear he enjoyed everything she was doing. He tasted salty like the ocean, not altogether an unpleasant thing. Her efforts grew bolder as she took more of him into her mouth. His hand on the back of her head guided her in a rhythm until he groaned and pulled out, turning away to spill his seed into the snow.

Breathless, Bryn sank back onto the cloak. She delicately touched her lips, shocked by what she'd just done—and how much she'd enjoyed it.

Rangar cleaned himself up, then dragged her to her feet, claiming those lips that had just been on his most intimate part.

"If I fail at being king," he moaned into her mouth, "It's because I'll be too busy ravishing you every chance I get, instead of tending to my kingdom."

# CHAPTER 19

**HIGHARBOR KEEP . . . a hidden castle . . . a waterfall . . . Val and his wine . . . tunnels to the wolf**

As they approached Higharbor Keep, more homes and farmsteads cropped up in the forest. With little farmland, the forest folk took advantage of every meadow and sunlit clearing in the forest to grow their meager winter greens and vegetable crops. A few scrawny goats munched on forest brush. According to Valenden and Rangar, most of the forest folk filled their bellies from hunting, fishing, and gathering wild edibles from the forest.

Bryn kept glancing over her shoulder at Valenden on his horse, wondering if he'd truly been napping or had overheard Rangar and her by the stream. She finally comforted herself with the knowledge that he doubtlessly would have teased them about it mercilessly if he had.

"There. Ahead. This is the town of Woodmark." Rangar pointed toward a small town hugging the edge of the forest. There was a small square and what looked like several taverns and an inn, and all the small shops and businesses one would expect from a kingdom's main commerce center, though this was smaller even than Barendur Village.

"But where is the castle? Where's Higharbor Keep?" Bryn asked.

She'd been warned that the structure was nearly invisible behind the trees, but this was ridiculous—no sign of any castle existed.

"This way." With a cryptic smile, Rangar led Legend into the small town, passing a few vendors and children chasing after a stray chicken. He then led them up a path behind the town into the towering trees. A rushing sound like water came from somewhere ahead. He looked over his shoulder. "Do you see it now?"

Bryn drew in an awe-filled breath. Amid pines that stretched higher than she'd ever seen trees grow, she could make out glimpses of an enormous stone-and-wood structure. Unlike Barendur Hold, which was squat like a bear, Higharbor Keep was made to mimic the trees. It was narrow and tall, with turrets that rose amid the tree canopy. A mountain waterfall spilled down a cliff on one side of the castle.

"No one said anything about a waterfall!" she exclaimed.

Valenden and Rangar grinned at her wonder. They spurred their horses over the rocky paths toward the castle and across the wooden bridge that spanned the waterfall's rushing creek. The pine boughs opened on either side of a heavy oak door. The guards stationed at the door must have gotten word of their arrival because attendants were already waiting to take the horses.

After the day-long ride, Bryn dismounted Fable with shaky legs and stroked her horse. "Thank you, sweet girl. Now go eat hay."

The attendants led the horses across another bridge and into a cave that seemed to serve as Higharbor's stable.

"King Rangar," one of the forest guards said, bowing his head. "We're honored by your visit. Prince Anter is expecting you. If you follow me, I shall take you to him."

Bryn's sense of wonder increased as the guard ushered them through the heavy door. Inside, the castle's windows were plentiful and delicate, made out of bits of colored glass so that the entryway sparkled with soft blues and greens. The distant rushing of the waterfall could be heard from every room they entered. The furniture was simple but delicate, unlike Barendur Hold's heavy oak. The kingdom's woodworkers were unrivaled when it came to carving beautiful relief work into the wooden walls.

They climbed one of the circular towers into a windowless room lit by dozens of lanterns, where Prince Anter conferred with advisors over a table laden with books. It was colder in this room than in the rest of the castle, and as Bryn hugged her arms, she looked at the roughly hewn stone walls and realized the space had been carved *into* the mountain.

"King Rangar. Prince Valenden. Princess Bryn." Prince Anter quickly came to greet them. "Welcome to Higharbor Keep." His eyes snagged on their white mourning sashes. "I'm sorry again for your father's passing."

"Thank you. I've seen nothing like this place," Bryn confessed. "This room . . ."

Anter nodded. "Higharbor Keep was constructed overtop of caves in the cliffside. Half the castle is made up of these interior cave portions."

"Amazing."

Her compliment brought a smile to his face, but it soon fell again. "I'm sorry your first visit is for such grave concerns, Lady Bryn. I trust you met with no attacks on the road?"

"We were safe," Rangar assured him. "Though some of the forest folk reported attacks nearby."

Anter nodded, his long auburn hair sleek and smooth. "Yes, and in fact, a messenger arrived not long before you bearing more reports of wolf attacks. The berserkir wolves, as you call them." He took a deep breath. "But you have traveled far. It is nearing suppertime. I'll have someone take you to your rooms to rest, and then we can speak more over a meal."

Rangar dipped his chin.

A young lad in green wool showed Valenden to his room, a chamber built over a cave so close to the waterfall that drips splashed the room's single window, and then took Rangar and Bryn to a tower bedroom whose circular windows looked out among the treetops. More servants silently brought in basins of warm water, towels, and a pitcher of wine before leaving them to rest.

Bryn sank onto the bed, easing off her mud-caked boots. She sighed as she let herself flop backward. "My thighs are killing me."

Rangar went over to the table to pour them mugs of wine. "Don't talk like that, my love, or you'll tempt me to be late to supper."

"Lords and ladies, Rangar. You're insatiable!"

He handed her the wine glass with a smirk. "It's good that you understand the man you're about to marry."

He pinned her to the bed for a long kiss and seemed tempted to make good on his threat to be late for supper, but then groaned reluctantly and stood. "We shouldn't keep our host waiting—though by the gods, it's hard to step away from you."

They bathed quickly and freshened their travel clothes, then were escorted to a private dining area on a balcony overlooking the waterfall. Anter, Valenden, and Lady Enis sat around a roast wild boar.

"King Rangar. Princess Bryn." Lady Enis greeted them warmly and motioned to chairs. "Your brother has already sampled much of Vil-Kevi's cuisine . . . and wine."

Valenden raised his wine glass. From his unfocused eyes, it was clear he'd already downed at least a full bottle. Bryn rolled her eyes.

Prince Anter cut to the chase as soon as they'd been served. "Winter is hard enough in these lands; my people cannot also be fighting off berserkir wolves."

Bryn rested her hands on either side of her plate. "Valenden and I examined a wolf carcass and found no evidence of *lyssa*. Our mages do not believe the wolves are infected. It isn't a sickness we're dealing with, but dark magic."

Anter shared a long look with his cousin. "The same possibility crossed our minds, though our mages cannot identify any known hex capable of such a thing."

"Nor ours," Bryn confessed. She took a slow sip of wine while gazing at the falling waters. "Our head mage sent some of our primary texts to share with your magic casters, though I have examined the books myself and found nothing. Still, yours might discover something we overlooked."

"We'll be grateful to review them," Lady Enis said.

Rangar wiped his mouth and said, "You say you have one of the wolves captured? A live one?"

"Yes," Anter confirmed. "In a pit in a lower portion

of the cave. Our mages cast a hex to put it to sleep after it attempted to bash its head in against the stone walls when we captured it."

"I'd like to inspect it this evening," Rangar said.

They continued to debate what might be causing the berserkir wolves to act so violently and then turned to how to protect the population until a solution could be found. Rangar offered to house any forest folk living near the border in one of the Baersladen's mostly empty fortresses and vowed to send extra arrows to their archers' stores.

"The thing I keep returning to," Bryn said, "Is who has the motivation to cast a spell on the wolves? If it isn't a natural process, as we all seem to believe, then what enemies does Vil-Kevi have?"

Anter leaned back in his chair as he considered this. "Our last war was fifty years ago against the ice folk incursion that came from across the Eyrie's upper sea. We keep to ourselves here with our sister kingdom, Vil-Rossengard. My grandfather had to be dragged into signing the Treaty of Windvalley in the first place. He would have preferred us to remain our own sovereign land."

"Yet you sided against the Mirien when my brother first rose to power," Bryn said.

"In name, yes," Prince Anter conceded. "We were all aware of your late parents' tyranny, and it seemed your brother was posed to follow in their footsteps. It was a tense time. My father swore to fight the Mirien if needed—but war never came, fortunately."

"Yet," Valenden said darkly before downing more wine.

"And now, as I understand it, your brother intends to rule more equitably," Anter said.

"That is true. My brother is not an enemy of your people, nor would he have reason to harm the forest folk."

Not all the kingdoms are pleased with Bryn's brother's decision to allow magic in the Mirien," Rangar said gruffly. "As the largest kingdom, the Mirien sets the tone for all the others moving forward."

"Ruma and Zaradona, you mean," Prince Anter said.

Rangar nodded. "And Dresel. Their spiritual beliefs are staunchly against magic. They're dogmatic about it. If I had to guess, I'd say they were furious about King Mars's decision."

"Furious enough to create berserkir wolves?" Bryn asked.

The table remained silent.

She drew in an unsteady breath. "If that were so, why target the attack on the northern kingdoms instead of the Mirien, their primary enemy?"

"The Mirien is too powerful. Better to attack it from its borders than its capital."

They continued to mull over the possibilities, and then after supper, Anter handed them torches and led them through a deep system of tunnels until they reached the pit where the berserkir wolf was being kept. He sent for their head mage, and while they waited, Bryn peeked into the pit. Her torch's light cast a glow over dark gray fur that rose and fell into unnaturally deep slumber. She moved forward more to see the beast's face, but her foot slipped on the slick rock.

Rangar caught her around the waist a second before she slipped. Gasping, she scrambled back. "Careful," he breathed against her ear.

Footsteps sounded in the tunnel, and a tall woman appeared in flowing robes. She had neither hair, nor eyebrows, and the torchlight glistened on her bald head.

"This is our head caster, Mage Albia," Anter said. "She is the one who put the beast to sleep."

Bryn nodded, feeling the familiar tingle to her skin whenever strong magic was present. The mage signaled to two guards at the edge of the pit.

"Hoist the creature up," Mage Albia commanded. "And chain it there to the wall."

The two men climbed into the pit, wrapped a cloth under the enormous animal's body, and climbed back up. It took their strength, Valenden's and Anter's, to raise the beast and drag it to the edge of the cave, where a guard fastened a chain around its neck.

Bryn couldn't tear her eyes off the creature. This one looked even larger than the ones that had attacked them. Black tears stained the fur around its eyes. Its lips twitched in its sleep over giant incisors.

"*Spectra ka daram*," Mage Albia said, tracing a

hexmark shape in the air. For a moment, nothing happened. Then, the wolf's eye snapped open.

# CHAPTER 20

**BERSERKIR LEGENDS . . . the wolf in the pit . . . memory of orange biscuits . . . old suitors . . . a motive**

Bryn gasped and scrambled back into Rangar's protective arms. "It's okay," she breathed. "The wolf just startled me."

The wolf attempted to push to its feet, but it seemed sluggish from the aftereffects of the sleeping spell. Thick drool rolled from its black tongue.

"Take caution," Prince Anter advised. "We've woken it before. It's a grumpy devil once the spell fully wears off."

Though the beast was chained, Rangar moved to stand in front of Bryn as a precaution. Valenden drew his sword for good measure. The wolf's lips curled back as it let out a low, rumbling growl. Its all-black eyes made it hard to gauge where the wolf was looking —or where it might lunge.

Suddenly, it lurched toward Rangar and Bryn, snapping its jaws. Bryn's body went instantly on defense, ready to run or fight. But the chain tightened, holding it several feet from where they stood. Its snarls echoed throughout the cave as it relentlessly tried to attack.

"Those eyes," Bryn muttered, clutching her dress's neckline. "What would cause such a thing?"

"The tongue is black as well," Lady Enis said. "There are wild animals with naturally black tongues, but I've never seen a wolf with one."

The berserkir wolf's vicious growls battered Bryn's ears. The poor creature strained so hard against the chain that she feared it would suffocate itself. There was something truly unnatural about its bloodlust . . .

*But what if it isn't bloodlust?* Bryn thought. The forest villager had suggested that the wolves' attack on the nearby trapper's family had seemed calculated, like trained hunting dogs.

"Enough," Anter said sharply after watching the creature strain against the chain for a few minutes. "Mage Albia, if you will."

"*Spectra ka hypony,*" the mage whispered, tracing a different hexmark in the air.

The wolf's efforts grew strained until it slumped to the cave floor and eventually closed its eyes. Once it remained still, the two guards approached it to remove the chain and lower it back into the pit.

"Wait," Bryn said, frowning down at the unconscious beast. "Let me inspect it first. The carcass we examined was badly wounded—I'd like to see a living one up close."

"Absolutely not," Rangar snarled.

Mage Albia glared at him as though he had insulted her magical ability. "My hex is effective, I assure you. The wolf will not wake."

Rangar looked ready to throw Bryn over his shoulder and cart her out of there, but she rested a firm hand on his chest. "I'll be careful."

His nostrils flared. "If you think that I—"

"Come with me, then," Bryn said. "And keep your sword drawn if it makes you feel better."

Rangar clearly didn't like the idea but was smart enough to know Bryn wouldn't back down. He muttered a curse under his breath, drew his sword, and aimed it over the sleeping wolf's head as she bent to inspect the animal.

She stretched out a hesitant hand to touch its fur. It was softer than she'd expected, though caked in dirt. She could feel its chest rising and falling. Taking its head in her hands, she gently examined the oily black substance oozing from its eyes. Though the wolf was enormous, it felt vulnerable and delicate in its sleep, and her heart went out to it.

*Someone made it into this monster.*

She carefully pried open its jaw and looked closely

at the oversized teeth that crowded its mouth around the strange black tongue. Finally, she stepped back and wiped her hands on her dress. She took a deep breath. "What will you do with this wolf?"

"Kill it once we have finished studying it," Prince Anter said. "It cannot be allowed to return to the forest."

Of course, he was right, but it pained Bryn to think of the wolf being slaughtered.

That night, she lay in bed listening to the distant sounds of the waterfall. The bedroom's windows showed the treetops swaying in the wind, making her feel strangely out of sorts. Rangar had kissed her senselessly and now slumbered by her side, but the whole time she hadn't gotten her mind off the berserkir wolf.

Letting out a long exhale, she finally admitted to herself that sleep wouldn't come. She got out of bed and lit a candle with the spark spell, then opened one of the books Mage Marna had sent. This was one written in an old common tongue that Bryn knew a little of. It told the history of the berserkir beast legend.

*In the old time, there was a legend of the berserkir beasts - a pack of vicious, rabid animals that roamed the dark forests, hunting for prey with a bloodthirst that knew no bounds.*

*According to the legend, these creatures were once ordinary animals - wolves, bears, and other fierce predators that roamed the wilderness. However, a dark curse befell them, causing them to become twisted and mutated, driven mad with an insatiable hunger for blood.*

*The berserkir beasts were said to be almost unstoppable, tearing through anything that crossed their path with ferocious speed. They were feared by all who lived in the kingdom, and many a brave warrior fell victim to their relentless attacks.*

*Despite their fearsome reputation, there were some who claimed to have encountered the berserkir beasts and lived to tell the tale. These brave souls spoke of the beasts' unending rage and savagery.*

*As time passed, the legend of the berserkir beasts spread throughout the kingdoms, becoming a cautionary tale told to children to keep them safe in the wilderness.*

She closed the book as her mind ran back through the old story. In the Mirien, they told a version of this tale where, instead of animals, a dark sorceress with a vendetta turned soldiers into vicious, bloodthirsty warriors. Bryn tried to piece together all the clues they'd uncovered, yet the puzzle refused to come together in her mind.

She reached for a midnight snack from a tray one of the servants had left. Her hand fell on a biscuit, and she grimaced as soon as she took a bite.

*Orange biscuits.*

It wasn't the flavor that was off-putting, but the memories it invoked. Months ago, Captain Carr proposed marriage with orange biscuits and stuck his disgusting tongue down her throat. Before that, orange biscuits called to mind Baron Marmose's equally off-putting courtship when he'd served her the biscuits and bored her to tears with tales of his yapping little lap dogs . . .

Her breath caught in her throat.

*His dogs.*

Baron Marmose was well known for his hobby of breeding and training dogs. Most of his pets were tiny, fluffy things she might have mistaken for dust mops, but one thing he'd said on that long-ago carriage ride now stuck in her head.

*"One must maintain meticulous breeding ledgers, princess, or undesirable traits may pop up in the offspring. I once bred a whole litter of black-tongued miniature sheepdogs . . . "*

A strange feeling began to curdle in her stomach. Baron Marmose was exceedingly skilled in dog training, and while most of his animals were lapdogs, he was also known for training highly prized hunting dogs used in the Ruma army.

*"The way these wolves stalk their prey and work together feels . . . organized somehow, as though someone trained them to do it,"* the old woman at the inn had said.

*And now the black tongues,* Bryn thought.

She shoved up from the table, breathing hard, staring down at the plate of orange biscuits. Then she rushed to the bed, shaking Rangar awake.

"It's Baron Marmose," she gasped. "The kingdom of Ruma is behind the wolves."

Though the hour was late, it didn't take long to reconvene everyone in Higharbor Keep's council room deep in the caves.

"I'm sorry to rouse you from sleep," Bryn started, clutching her necklace. "But it's important."

"Who said anything about sleep?" Valenden murmured with a hint of a smirk. "I, for one, was becoming acquainted with a lovely Kevi maid . . ."

Bryn didn't even bother to roll her eyes as she set Mage Marna's book on the council table. "We've all noted the similarities between the wolves attacking villages and the berserkir beasts from the old legends. This book contains different versions of that old tale. Each kingdom has a slightly different take on it. In the Mirien, for example, it's berserkir warriors, not animals."

Prince Anter drummed his fingers on the table. "Yes, here, it is creatures that only lust for violence under a full moon."

"Right," Bryn said. "Well, after some more research tonight, I found Ruma's version of the legend. It tells of a cruel coven of witches commanded by the God of Hell to sow evil in our world. They do so by summoning monsters called *berserkins*."

She opened the book to the page and slid it over to

Prince Anter. "I say all this to show that Ruma is well aware of the berserkir legend and its various iterations. They know that real-life berserkir creatures would stir rumors of evil and witches in all the kingdoms that practice magic."

Prince Anter sat straighter, frowning down at the book. "You think Ruma's leadership created the beasts to dissuade the use of magic?"

Bryn explained, "The timing is uncanny. The first berserkir wolves appeared just weeks after Mars announced that he would permit magic in the Mirien. It was just enough time for them to create the wolves."

"And how exactly do you propose they created them?" Anter asked.

Bryn sat down, suddenly feeling her confidence waver. "Well, I haven't figured that out yet, exactly. Ruma claims not to practice magic, but we all know it happens secretly in every kingdom. Still, I have evidence that Baron Marmose is involved. He's famed for training dogs, including hunting dogs. He once confessed to me how his breeding experiments resulted in animals with black tongues."

The table was rendered silent at this. Valenden stroked his chin, then let his hand fall and muttered a curse about Baron Marmose. Anter folded his hands as he gave it deep consideration. Rangar met Bryn's gaze and gave a nod of encouragement.

"This is most interesting," Prince Anter said at last. "If it is true, it explains motive and means, though we may not yet know precisely how it was accomplished.

And yet the question remains—what can we do about it? If true, this situation is far more grave than simply dealing with vicious wild animals."

"I'll write a letter to my brother," Bryn offered. "Ruma is their neighboring kingdom to the south, and they maintain good relations, at least on the surface. It will be easier for Mars to send spies than for us. The Rumese officials would suspect any northern folk asking questions."

"That's wise," Rangar said. "Though it will take weeks for spies to gather the information we need to prove a plot and, of course, Ruma will deny it. What do we do until then?"

"We keep our people safe the best we are able." Anter turned to Bryn. "Your insight is valuable, princess. I'm grateful for the bond between the Baersladen and the forest kingdoms—and that you are now one of us."

"Soon," she said, running her finger over her engagement ring. Then her eyes fell to her white sash.

"Yes, what of the wedding?" Prince Anter said.

Rangar rested his hand over Bryn's. "It will happen as soon as the grieving period for my father is over at the month's end. We would be honored to have your presence, and Lady Enis's."

Anter responded, "I, too, would be honored to attend, though we shall have to see the state of the realm then. If we cannot get these berserkir attacks under control . . ."

Rangar nodded. "We will send the supplies we discussed. Arrows and poison to bait the wolves."

"Again, you have my gratitude."

The group retired once more for the night after Bryn, Rangar, and Valenden made plans to return to the Baersladen the following day. But still, sleep didn't come for Bryn. The distant rush of the waterfall sounded like wolf growls, and the smell of orange biscuits haunted her dreams.

# CHAPTER 21

**DANGERS OF MAGIC . . . spooked livestock . . . suspicious villagers . . . wolves at the gates**

Bryn's heart felt heavy on the journey home to the Baersladen. Though Fable's footing was solid, Bryn's mind spun in dizzying circles. She grew increasingly certain that her former suitor, Baron Marmose, was behind the berserkir wolves' creation. She recalled holding the sleeping wolf's head in her hands, feeling its steady breath. It was a crime to twist an innocent creature into a monster.

They crossed the border back into the Baersladen mid-day but didn't stop to rest along the rocky mountain inclines until they were well into the Baer valley. Bryn's stomach was rumbling when they finally spotted a small village ahead.

"This is Elderwall," Rangar said. "The dairy farmer here is a retired soldier who served with my father. They'll shelter us while we rest the horses."

Bryn felt comforted by the prospect of friendly faces, yet she got a strange premonition as they approached. The village was a small cluster of houses and shops, with the dairy barn as the largest structure, yet everything was completely silent.

Valenden peered up at the sun. "It's mid-afternoon. Where is everyone?"

Bryn's uneasiness grew as they came to the first house, where a wooden sign had hastily been erected. Rangar and Valenden stopped their horses, looking grimly at the sign.

"What does it say?" Bryn asked of the Baer words.

"It reads, 'No Magic.'" Rangar's voice rumbled with displeasure.

"No Magic?" Bryn's face twisted into a frown. "But we're in the Baersladen. We're far from any kingdoms that outlaw magic."

Rangar made a low sound in his throat. "I know. Wait here."

He swung down from Legend and approached the house attached to the dairy barn. For a long while, no one answered his knock. But then the door opened a crack. Rangar exchanged words with whoever was inside, then sauntered back to Bryn and Valenden.

"My father's old compatriot is away, but his son is here. He says we may come in to rest." Rangar's tone was troubled, however.

Bryn dismounted, and they made their way through the strangely quiet village. She spotted wooden signs on several shops and houses with the same Baer words: *No Magic.*

The dairy farmer's grown son nervously waited for them at the door. "King Rangar, Prince Valenden, Princess Bryn. This is such an honor. My name is Jonnah. My father will be deeply sorry to have missed you, but we'd like to offer you all the comforts we can." He whistled to two small twin girls peeking down from a loft. "Suri, Agna, fetch fresh water from the well." He turned back to the travelers. "Please, sit."

As they took their places, Bryn still felt a strange tension despite the farmer's kind words of welcome. The two girls soon scampered back with water to clean their hands and faces, and a pitcher of milk and plate of scones. After thanking their host and making light conversation about the dairy herd, Rangar broached the subject.

"What is going on in the village, Jonnah?"

Jonnah looked tempted to profess confusion at what Rangar referred to, but then he glanced toward the door and sighed. "You're referring to the signs."

Rangar nodded.

Jonnah dragged a hand through his hair. "Two days ago, the cows stopped producing milk. That sometimes happens when they're spooked, such as if a predator gets into the fence and attacks."

Bryn's spine went rigid. "You mean . . . one of the wolves attacked the cows?"

"No, and that's the troubling thing," Jonnah said. "All the cows are accounted for and unharmed, yet we found tracks much larger than ordinary wolves' in the pasture. The wolves *were* there, but they left the cows untouched." He paused. "Several of the village boys reported being chased by a vicious beast into a tree, however."

"The berserkirs are here," Bryn breathed, throwing a worried look at Rangar. It was the first report they'd heard of the berserkir wolves attacking a Baer village.

"And the villagers?" Rangar asked. "They are all unharmed?"

"Yes, no one was attacked. The boys' fathers were able to chase off the wolf with arrows. But they got a good look at the wolf, which frightened them. They said it was no ordinary wolf, but a demon. There was a Ruma priest through here a few years ago who tried to preach that magic was sinful. He was mocked out of town at the time, but since the monstrous wolf's appearance, some in the village have started to believe he was right. That the wolves are demons caused by magic."

"That's ludicrous," Valenden snapped. "Even if they were made by magic, magic itself is not evil *or* good. It's merely a force, like the weather. It's the caster who may be good or evil."

Jonnah nodded. "It isn't me you need to convince, Prince Valenden. We in this house have long valued magic—it's kept us fed on many a long winter when the cows needed more warmth than our wood stores could provide. But people are scared. And when they get scared, they can be easily fooled into believing anything."

After finishing the refreshments, they gave Jonnah some gold coins before continuing on the road. Bryn was more anxious than ever to return to Barendur Hold, where she could write a letter to Mars. But Rangar was correct in that it would take weeks to prove any Ruma plot—and in those weeks, the realm's sentiment toward magic could shift rapidly.

They rode as fast as the horses could manage, stopping only briefly to let the horses drink at streams. Though most of the other small villages they passed seemed untroubled, a few others had the same "No Magic" signs posted. Rangar and Valenden appeared just as concerned as Bryn; their brows held the same deep wrinkles, marking them as brothers.

*This will be Rangar's first test as king*, Bryn thought, though she did not doubt his ability to defend the kingdom. He was new to ruling, yes, but not to managing the Baersladen. He had been at his father's side for all his twenty-two years, helping his people through famine, skirmishes, banditry, and blizzards. If anyone could solve this puzzle, it was the two of them together.

*Rangar knows his people, and I know mine—and Baron Marmose.*

As they crested the last hill before reaching the valley road to Barendur Hold, Bryn released an audible breath of relief. Soon, they'd be home and able to solve this crisis from the safety of stone walls—

She screamed as a gray blur hurled out of the nearby trees with a snarl.

Everything happened so quickly that she barely had time to process it. All she saw were monstrous teeth and black eyes.

*A wolf!*

The berserkir wolf hurtled itself against Fable with enough force to knock the horse to the ground. A searing pain ripped across Bryn's thigh as she crashed onto a sharp rock with the horse's weight on top of her.

She cried out as Fable kicked and thrashed in an attempt to return to her feet, while the berserkir wolf snapped its powerful jaw on the horse's shoulder. Though Fable formed a barrier between Bryn and the wolf, the horse's weight threatened to crush her right leg.

Yells and the slice of steel told her that Rangar and Valenden had swiftly dismounted. She saw a flash as Rangar brought down his sword upon the wolf's back. The creature snarled and turned on Rangar, but Rangar and Valenden positioned themselves to funnel it away from Bryn and the horse. It tried to double back, but Valenden was there in a flash, blocking its path with his sword.

Fable finally rose, freeing Bryn from where she'd been pinned. Wincing from pain, Bryn crawled into the grass on the side of the road, clutching her leg.

Blood streamed down Fable's neck, but the horse seemed okay for the most part.

"Back!" Valenden cried, trying to cut off the wolf's retreat into the forest. He lunged at the wolf, who dodged his blow—but landed right in the path of Rangar's sword.

The blade sliced cleanly through the wolf's neck. Its severed head fell to the side of the road, and a split second later, its body followed.

Bryn's own body was so full of adrenaline that it refused to acknowledge that the danger was over. She was shaking hard and unable to stop. Her throat made little noises she didn't even recognize.

Rangar was by her side in an instant, brushing her tangled hair back off her face. "Shh, my love. It's dead. You're safe."

She threw him a wild-eyed look. "And Fable?"

Valenden had gone to soothe her mare, whispering reassurances to the horse as he stroked around the wolf bite on its neck. "She'll recover," Valenden assured her. "A brave mare—she didn't bolt."

Finally, Bryn started to shift out of the sheer panic that had overtaken her. Pressing a hand to her chest to center her breathing, she gasped, "It came out of nowhere."

"Let me see your leg."

Rangar jerked her skirt up around her thigh. She was too shaken to be embarrassed by Valenden seeing her half-naked as Rangar pressed against her flesh. "The bone isn't broken, but you'll be badly bruised, and you need to take it easy on that knee for a few days."

"I'm fine," she said between heaving breaths.

"You aren't fine. Nothing about this is fine," Rangar growled. Before she knew it, he had scooped her up, tossed her on top of Legend, and swung up behind her. He swept an arm around her waist, holding her flush against him so possessively that the breath nearly rushed out of her.

"Val, take Fable back to the Hold. The stable master will stitch her wound. I must get Bryn back swiftly."

Valenden nodded and began to halter Fable to his own steed. Rangar kicked Legend into a gallop. Bryn felt a rush of terror as the stallion's hooves pounded over the snow-marked road. The frigid wind chapped her face. But Rangar's body was warm, and his arm held her as steady as steel.

With Legend's speed, they glimpsed Barendur Hold on the horizon within minutes. Rangar thundered past the roadside villages, his attention fixed on getting Bryn to safety. She could feel his heart thumping fast but steadily in his chest. A bruised leg was hardly an emergency, but she knew better than to argue with him.

This wasn't just about her leg. It was about the wolves. The animosity toward magic. The pressures of being king.

The village square was still swathed in white banners to signify the grieving period for King Aleth.

They fluttered in the blustering wind coming off the sea as Rangar drew Legend to a halt and slid off. With his hands around her waist, he helped her down but didn't release her once her feet were on the ground. His fingers dug into the skin around her ribs.

"Bryn," he said lowly. "Believe in me. I'll solve this."

She brushed the pads of her fingers over his scars. "*We'll* solve it, Rangar. You aren't alone."

He kissed her almost ferally, as though the adrenaline from the wolf fight was still coursing through him. She was breathless by the time he released her. He scooped her up into his arms and carried her toward the castle.

Oliver came striding out in his military armor to meet them. "My king. My lady . . . "

"Mount Legend," Rangar ordered. "Exercise him. He needs to cool down after our ride."

"Yes, my king."

And then they were swallowed back within the belly of Barendur Hold. The familiar smells of straw and woodsmoke and roasting meats enveloped Bryn, and she pressed her face into Rangar's chest and shuddered with relief to be home.

# CHAPTER 22

**A NEED FOR SPIES . . . stuck in bed . . . a girl and a horse . . . six kinds of pies**

The next few days were ones of tension and turmoil in Barendur Hold. A winter storm moved in, cutting off access to the more remote villages, so Bryn and Rangar were left without any means of receiving reports of more possible berserkir wolf attacks.

Rangar forbade Bryn from leaving bed until her leg healed, and personally brought her stew and ale, and added more wood to their room's fireplace when it grew low. Ren was kind enough to sit with her for long training sessions on the usage of new hexes. But even practicing magic grew tiresome. After long days sequestered, she finally threw off the covers while Rangar was out and tested her leg.

The skin was still tender where she'd been pinned between Fable and the rock, and her knee was painfully sore, but she found she was perfectly capable of walking with only a slight limp.

Of course, Rangar chose that very moment to check on her.

"What are you doing?" he roared. "You're supposed to be in bed!"

"You're a king," she lobbed at him. "You have more important things to do than play nursemaid to me."

He stalked toward her, but she had long ago learned not to bow to his growling temper. She rested her hands on her hips. "I want to check on Fable."

"Fable is fine." He grabbed her around the waist and set her back on the bed. "*You* are not."

"I am," she insisted. "You just want to keep me locked up because you're afraid something worse may happen to me."

"And what's wrong with that?" he said between a clenched jaw.

She shoved his hand away. "A lot, frankly."

His jaw tightened into an even sharper edge, but he stepped back and folded his arms. "I only want to keep you safe, Bryn. It's my—"

"Duty," she said with more sympathy. "The *fralen* bond. I know, I know. Believe me, Rangar, I know how seriously you take it." She crossed to him by the window and gently touched his scarred cheek. "Trust that I know what's best for me. I've been working with Ren on mastering new hexes. One to unlock doors, one to heal minor scrapes, one to thicken my skin against a blade."

His shoulders slowly lowered as he let himself relax into her palm. "You make me proud, Mage Queen."

She pushed to tiptoes to kiss him but then frowned when she broke away. "Who knows if I'll even be allowed to be a Mage Queen by the time I finish my apprenticeship and we marry. The way the tide is turning against magic, it'll be banned throughout the Eyrie before then."

"You shall be a Mage Queen," he vowed, brushing his rough thumb over her lips. "And magic *will* be a tool for the people."

He claimed her lips again, and then as he went to meet with Saraj and the captain of the army to discuss further protective measures for the outer villages, she went to visit Fable in the stables. Taking care with her bruised leg, she limped through the stalls until she found the white mare.

"Sweet, brave girl," Bryn whispered, holding out a crab apple she'd brought from the kitchen. "Not even wolves can bring you down."

Fable munched the apple and then nuzzled Bryn for more. Bryn smiled and stroked the horse's neck around the stitches the stable master had performed on her wound. Bryn had spoken with Ren about the hexes for bonding with horses, and he'd given her a spell to memorize but told her that most of the magic between a rider and horse came not from spells but from trust built over the years.

"I trust you," Bryn whispered, pressing her forehead to the horse's forelock. "And I'll give you every reason to trust me."

That afternoon, they received word that the main road might soon be passable by messengers, so she limped to the library and sat down to write the letter to Mars.

*Dear brother,*

*I have worrisome news from the forest kingdoms. Villages along the Baer and Kevi borders have sustained further berserkir wolf attacks. We were even personally attacked within a mile of Barendur Hold, though we are all well. I examined both dead and live wolf specimens and discovered they possess black tongues. The only other time I've heard such a thing was from Baron Marmose when he described training his hunting dogs. Prince Anter Jakkinen, Rangar, and I believe these berserkir wolf attacks originate from dark magic within Ruma at the baron's hand, with the goal of sewing fear of your plan to permit the free use of magic.*

*I write to request you send some men into Ruma to investigate these claims and discover how the baron might have created such creatures and what we can do to stop them . . . and reassure the populace magic is not to blame.*

*PS, Despite these dark times, Rangar and I plan to wed at dusk on the day of the new moon. Your and Illiana's presence would deeply touch my heart.*
*Yours,*
*Mouse*

She sealed the letter and entrusted it with the Baersladen's swiftest messenger, reminding him that if it fell into the wrong hands, such a bold accusation as the letter claimed could be grounds for war among the Eyrie.

As Rangar continued to be occupied by his mission to strengthen security among the villages—employing every huntsman in the kingdom to scour the forests for berserkir wolves—Bryn dedicated herself to her apprenticeship. Her diligent study with Ren paid off when she proved to Mage Marna that she'd mastered the wording for the minor healing spell and another one to prevent eavesdropping, and was rewarded with two fresh hexmark scars carved into her back.

"An apprenticeship can take years, even a decade," Mage Marna reminded her. "It is not a race to collect hexmarks like badges of merit. There is more to magic than what the skin shows."

"I know," Bryn confessed, running her fingers along the various herb and potion jars in the mage storerooms. "But I'm anxious for it. It's like a hunger. The more sentiment spreads *against* magic, the more I want to master it."

Mage Marna touched her cheek, a rare affectionate

gesture for the stern older woman. "Do not be so anxious to turn your back on your own ways, Bryn, in your desire to assimilate into ours. You were raised with science. That is the sister study to magic."

"I didn't think science was highly valued in the northern realms."

"Perhaps," Mage Marna admitted. "But I've spent many years in many different kingdoms, even ones outside of the Eyrie. There is no one answer to any problem. No single right way."

Bryn nodded as she considered this. Then she asked, "I understand magic isn't to be rushed, but there is one more hexmark I hope to acquire before the wedding."

"And what is that?"

She paused. "To make weeds flourish."

Mage Marna looked at her askance. "Weeds?"

"Is there such a hex?"

"There are many hexes to help plants grow, though none specifically for weeds." She cocked her head. "Still, I might be able to modify one for you. Consider it my wedding present to you and Rangar. Return to me in a few days."

As the days passed, marked each morning by the prayer for King Aleth's soul, the white mourning banners grew gray with sleet, dust, and salt air. Bryn dutifully tied her grieving sash daily and said her own personal prayers for King Aleth, but she also looked anxiously toward the end of the grieving period.

Roxin replenished the castle's stores of ingredients

for the wedding. Invitations went out to royals from other kingdoms as well as villages throughout the Eyrie, though with the caveat that people should only travel if they felt safe to do so. The village children were sent to gather maiden roses to hang in the square, though this time of year, the few remaining flowers were small and withered and had to be woven in with wheatberries to fill out the wreath.

Bryn watched from the drawbridge as the eldest child of the group climbed a ladder to hang the wreath in the village square. Excitement fluttered in her chest. It was only a matter of days until she'd finally be wed to Rangar, and the wreath proved it.

"My lady," a gentle voice said behind her. "If you have a moment?"

Helna stood behind her with a bundle wrapped in rough wool. Bryn's heart began to pound harder. There could be only one reason Helna would speak with her this soon before the wedding. "Of course," Bryn said.

Helna unfolded the bundle to reveal her wedding gown. Bryn gasped at the sight of it. Enough time had passed to allow the new fabric to arrive from Zaradona, and it was a beautiful sea-gray silk with pearl buttons and intricate embroidery in the shape of ocean waves.

"Oh, Helna," Bryn said as she touched the dress reverently. "It's beautiful."

The old seamstress beamed. "You'll be quite the bride in it, my lady. I tried to make it as different as I could from your wedding gown to Prince Trei. This one is lighter but still in keeping with traditional colors . . ."

"It's perfect." Bryn squeezed the woman's hand. "Truly."

That evening, Bryn and Rangar dined in their chambers, and she could hardly contain her excitement about the wedding gown.

"Show me," Rangar grunted, his eyes trailing down her décolleté. "I want to see you in it. And then, I want to see you out of it."

"You can't see a bride in her dress before the wedding," she admonished.

"That's a Mir custom, not a Baer one." He downed his ale and wiped his mouth with the back of his hand. "To us, it's just a dress."

"Well, forget such thoughts. You aren't going to see it a moment before I'm standing in it across from you, with the vicar between us. Besides, I can tell at least one Mir custom has grown on you."

He raised an eyebrow. "Oh? And which one would that be?"

She motioned to the chambers they had settled into as their primary suite. "Having a private bedroom. Not sleeping in the great hall with goats and a hundred villagers."

A playful snort came from his nose. "You liked the goats."

"And you," she challenged equally playfully, "like having a locking door and a bed where you can make love to me whenever you like, without having to abscond to some shadowy corner and hope no one passes by."

He conceded this with a nod as he finished chewing his turkey leg. "I do like that. As a matter of fact, I like that quite a bit." He cleaned his hands on his napkin while he took his time drinking in the sight of her like she was part of the meal. "In fact—"

But a knock at the door interrupted whatever scandalous words were on the tip of his tongue. It was Roxin and two other kitchen maids carrying pies in each of their hands.

Bryn stepped back from the door to allow them entrance. Pleasantly surprised, she said, "What's this?"

"Mince pie, apple pie, fig pie, pear tart, walnut pie, and oyster pie." Roxin counted off the six pies as the maids crowded them on the room's dining table and started taking away their empty dinner plates.

"Goodness, we can't eat all this!" Bryn exclaimed.

"They're to sample," Roxin said proudly. "For you to pick which confection you want with the wedding banquet. Walnut pie is traditional, but I took to heart what you said, my lady, about celebrating the Baersladen's natural environments. I thought you might want something a little different. We'll leave you to it. Tell me tomorrow which one you prefer."

After thanking them and closing the door behind them, Bryn sat back down at the table and twirled her fork over the pies with a smile curling her lips.

"It's been a long time since I've indulged like this," she said to Rangar. "I almost feel like I'm back in Castle Mir, where they brought out pies after every meal." She frowned, though, as her fork glided over the last pie. "I think I'll skip the oyster one, though."

Rangar stabbed his fork into it, taking a hearty bite. "Delicious."

She made a face, then dipped her fork into the pear tart and popped the bite into her mouth. Sighing with ecstasy, she slumped back in her chair. "That is divine. Roxin *must* have used magic."

"Try the apple one." Rangar scooped a bite of the sweet fruit pie and held it out for her across the table. Bryn ate the bite off his fork, licking her lips to capture the delicious crumbly crust. "Heaven," she murmured. "I'll never be able to choose between them."

"Roxin wants to please you," Rangar said as he took a bite of the walnut pie. "Everyone in the castle wants to please you, our beautiful foreign-born princess." He swallowed the bite and met her eyes. "*I* want to please you."

"You do," she said softly, resting her hand over his.

He kissed her knuckles, then briefly left the table and dug through the wooden dresser drawers, returning with a satin satchel. He set it on the table next to the pies.

"Your second wedding gift, my love."

# CHAPTER 23

**RANGAR'S SECOND SURPRISE . . . the castle vaults
. . . morning of the wedding . . . honeybuns**

Bryn hesitated before opening the satin satchel, savoring this magical moment with Rangar. Her curiosity prickled and teased her. His first wedding gift had been Fable, who was rapidly becoming one of Bryn's favorite living creatures in the entire world.

A secretive smile touched Rangar's lips now, as though he knew this second gift would please her even more.

Drawing a breath, she tugged the satin cord open and slid the contents out into her palm. Glittering jewels winked in the room's candlelight. Blue sapphires as large as an almond, set in gleaming gold. Her lips parted, but no sound came out. She stared at the necklace, unable to believe what she saw.

"Rangar," she whispered. "This—this belonged to my mother."

Bryn hadn't seen the necklace in ten years. It had been a gift from a foreign dignitary eager to secure trade deals with her parents. She'd once overheard Elysander whispering to some young noblewomen that their father was furious over the gift. The foreign dignitary had been a handsome man and spent a bit too much time with Queen Helena, even visiting her in private in her bedroom. When the scandal was discovered, their father banished the dignitary and locked the necklace in Castle Mir's vault.

"I know," Rangar replied.

"How could you possibly have gotten this?" Confusion shone in her eyes as she searched his face. "No one gets into the castle vault. It requires multiple keys held by multiple advisors."

"You underestimate my craftiness."

"You *stole* it?" she said incredulously.

He grinned wickedly. "Saraj had a nasty habit of thievery before she was made head falconer. She taught me some tricks in our younger days. Just before Mars's coronation ceremony, I helped myself to the vault. I remember your mother wearing this necklace on the First Night of the Low Sun Gathering. I'd never seen anything so delicate in my life . . . until I saw you. I knew you deserved to have it."

With a shaking finger, Bryn touched one of the glittering sapphires in her palm. "We have to tell Mars. If he discovers it's missing . . ."

"What does your brother care for a necklace? There were countless others in the vault. Besides, you have as much right to it as he does." When she remained speechless, he grunted. "Don't you like it?"

Her attention shot to him in surprise. "What? Are you mad? Rangar, I *adore* it!"

She, too, recalled her mother wearing the necklace at the Low Sun Gathering. At the time, she wondered if she'd ever be as beautiful and refined as her mother. The necklace's value was staggering, but it wasn't what moved Bryn—it was having this small piece of her mother back.

She stood so abruptly that her chair tumbled backward. She clutched the necklace in her fist and threw her arms around Rangar's neck.

"I love it. I love *you*."

His hands slid down her back. "Good," he purred in her ear. "Now, I want to see you wear it."

She turned around and lifted her hair so he could fasten the links around her neck. Turning back around to face him, she brushed her fingers over the jewels, relishing their cool touch against her warm skin.

"Beautiful," Rangar whispered, his gaze fastened to the necklace. "But you misunderstood, my love. I want to see you wearing *only* the necklace."

Her lips parted. Her hand dragged along the necklace's smooth surface slowly, tantalizingly. "Then you'd better make it so."

He needed no more permission. He tugged artlessly at her dress's ribbons until he could pull the neckline down over her shoulders. His lips immediately found the hollow at the base of her neck, just above the curve of sapphires.

She tipped her head back as he nipped at her skin like he'd wanted a taste ever since the pie. One of Bryn's hands went to the necklace as her eyes sank closed. The other tangled in his hair as he continued to dot fiery kisses along her décolleté.

"You're right about the private room," he said between caresses. "The Mir tradition. I can light enough candles here to see every inch of your pretty flesh. I never want to hide in the shadows again, bedding you in the dark."

As though to prove his point, he yanked her dress down over her hips until it pooled at her ankles, leaving her only in her chemise and the necklace.

"This scrap has to go, too." He slid the chemise's straps over her shoulders and pushed it down to join the dress.

Naked, Bryn initially tried to cover herself with her hands, but Rangar grabbed her wrists and held them to her sides.

"None of that," he ordered. "I want a good look at what's mine."

She flushed as his gaze examined and worshipped

and caressed her naked curves. The sapphires were heavy around her neck, her only adornment. He touched his fingers to the jewels.

"They're nothing compared to your beauty," he whispered. "And as for the third and final wedding gift, you'll receive that after the ceremony."

He captured her lips in another kiss while freeing her hair from its braid. His fingers roughly combed through her curls until they were loose around her shoulders. He wrapped the length of her hair around his fist until he'd gathered it like a rope.

His other hand grabbed her ass. "Wrap your legs around me," he ordered.

He lifted her with one hand while she slid her legs around his hips. He carried her to the bed, but instead of lowering her onto it, he sat on the foot of the bed with her in his lap.

One hand went to unbutton his trousers.

"Tomorrow, we'll be wed." His breath was husky. "You've no idea how often I've imagined this day. Calling you, my wife. I've wanted it since I was nineteen and saw you dancing in that field before the bonfire."

"I wish you'd approached me," she panted as his fingers coiled tighter in her hair.

"Gods, I nearly did. Your father would have killed me, but it might have been worth it." He adjusted her on his lap so that she was straddling him. His erection was rock hard between her legs, teasing her bare skin.

"Now," he ordered in the same sharp voice he used when commanding the military, "Sink onto me."

There was something undeniably ardent about being fully naked while Rangar was fully clothed. Though unsure exactly what to do, she lifted her hips and wiggled until his cock pressed against her slick center.

He groaned as she wiggled. His hand tightened in her hair, and the other latched onto her hip to guide her down his length.

"That's it." Holding her by the hip and hair, he guided her to rise and fall as they made love. "By the gods, Bryn. I could do this forever and still not have enough."

His hips thrust up to meet her as she sank down. Her bare skin was extra sensitive as it slid against the rough-spun fabric of his shirt and trousers. The sapphires clattered gently like soft bells as she moved.

He cupped one of her breasts, then lowered his lips to taste her nipple. His cock impaled her in a way that was both rough and not rough enough, and she started moving faster on instinct. He groaned again as he took her mouth in a kiss. His lips held a trace of apple pie: cinnamon and warm buttery crust. Breathless, she moved faster, feeling a delicious need cresting in her.

As her body tremored with pleasure, he suddenly released her coil of hair so he could grab both her hips. Her hair fanned out around them as a moan rose in his throat.

"Gods . . . Bryn . . ."

His body tightened as his hands dug into her flesh. His breath heaved as he pushed into her one more time. A line of sweat dripped from his brow.

Both of them spent, he gripped her jaw, holding her face to look at him.

"*That* is my dessert of choice," he rasped, brushing his thumb against her bottom lip like he was already ready for another bite.

When she woke in the morning, Rangar was gone.

She stared at the ceiling, one hand lightly trailing against the sapphire necklace as she thought, *Today I marry Rangar Barendur.*

Baer tradition, as she knew all too well from her marriage to Trei, required a royal wedding to be held at sunset beneath the open sky. Her previous wedding day had been miserable when a rainstorm had left her and Trei drenched. Of course, that had only portended the tragic events that followed.

*Today will be different*, she thought fiercely. *Today, Rangar and I take our fates into our own hands.*

Before going downstairs for breakfast, however, she took the time to unstring Trei's ring from her chain necklace and press it between her palms. Kneeling before the hearth, she whispered a prayer to her Saints and Trei's gods to watch over his soul.

"Oh, wise Saints of the South, oh mighty gods of

the North, I ask that you guard Trei Barendur's soul across the life bridge to his rightful place among the honored dead." Then, because she wasn't sure exactly what she believed happened to a soul, she whispered to Trei's spirit itself, "You're missed, Trei. You're loved. You aren't forgotten."

She was relieved to see sunlight pouring through the window. *No rainstorms today.* Fresh snow had fallen overnight, blanketing the castle grounds and village square in pristine white. The snow replaced the white sashes and banners of King Aleth's grieving period. Gone were all emblems of mourning. It felt like a good omen. A fresh start.

For the first time in a month, she didn't wear her white sash.

In the great hall, she snagged honeybuns and milk from the kitchen girls passing around breakfast baskets, then spotted Valenden and Oliver eating by the northern hearth. She made her way over, though slowly, having to stop five times to greet well-wishers for her big day. The mood was noticeably lighter throughout the breakfast crowd now that the mourning period was over.

"And what a joyful way to move on from our mourning," one elderly weaver said, clutching Bryn's hand. "With a royal wedding!"

Bryn beamed sincerely. It felt marvelous not to have to pretend anymore. She'd pretended to be interested when Baron Marmose courted her. She'd acted the part of a happy bride with Trei, though her heart had been breaking. She'd even forced herself to smile sweetly at the villainous Captain Carr's proposal.

But now, her smiles could finally be genuine.

*I'm marrying my soulmate.*

She caught Valenden's eye over the weaver's enthusiastic nodding head and begged her leave. She sank onto the bench next to Valenden, taking a bite of her honeybun at last. She groaned with delight.

"If it isn't the most favored girl in the Baersladen," Valenden teased. "Gracing us with her presence."

She rolled her eyes. "Everyone's so kind, but I might have to hide out all morning in my room, or I'll never accomplish anything except talk to well-wishers. Have you seen Rangar this morning?"

"You mean he didn't wake you up with a cock pressing into your back?" Valenden asked.

Oliver snorted so hard that milk frothed at the corners of his mouth.

Bryn flicked a crumb toward him. "Really, Val, you're going to have to tame that tongue of yours if *you* ever hope to one day marry."

"Bah. My tongue has no interest in being tamed." He laughed in his usual cavalier way, but Bryn caught him glance across the great hall toward Winter, the girl who ran the village tavern. Bryn wasn't a fool—she'd often wondered if the reason Valenden frequented The Whale Tavern didn't have less to do with ale and more to do with the girl serving it.

Bryn cleared her throat. "Oliver, have the scouts said anything about carriages on the road?"

Oliver finished chewing his breakfast and wiped his mouth. Speaking gently so as not to disappoint her, he said, "I'm sorry, my lady. They haven't."

Bryn's good mood faltered. She had hoped Mars and Illiana would be able to attend the wedding by some miracle, though she'd known how unlikely it was. Her letter had probably only arrived to Mars a few days before. The king and queen of the Mirien wouldn't be able to drop everything and travel to the Outlands on short notice. Besides, Mars and Illiana had their own issues to occupy them.

*War.*

*Wolves.*

*A rising tide against magic.*

Bryn smiled, refusing to let anything dampen her spirits. Pushing to her feet, she said, "Right. Well, though I'm sure Rangar can simply stride up to our wedding ten minutes before, women don't have that luxury. I have a full day of bathing and preparations before the ceremony."

"Wait, Bryn." The smirk fell off Valenden's face. He stood, pulling her to the side of the hearth where they had more privacy. Dropping his voice, he said, "I know today is a joyous day, but I thought you should know there was a wolf attack in Freville last night."

Her eyes flashed. "Freville? That's a Mir village."

"I know."

"I didn't think the wolves had moved south . . ."

Valenden held out his hands as though to suggest reality was reality regardless of what she thought.

"You can imagine the anti-magic sentiment there. Freville was already staunchly against its use."

"What does this mean?" she said urgently.

"It means," he said, "that you should get married, get drunk, and fuck your husband tonight. Because tomorrow, we'll have fresh concerns to deal with."

# CHAPTER 24

**WEDDING PART ONE . . . toasts with friends . . . sunset on snow . . . a surprise arrival . . . now and forever**

The rest of the morning and into the afternoon, servants bathed, scrubbed, plucked, and scoured Bryn until she felt like a roasting chicken ready for the spit. She was trussed up in Helna's beautiful wedding gown, and Lada wove her hair into braids that hugged her scalp in the shape of maiden rose petals to match the imprint on her engagement ring.

"King Rangar is going to think he has died and gone to the great afterlife when he sees you," Lada giggled.

"And where is Rangar?" Bryn asked.

"Oh, you won't see him until the wedding," Lada answered. "His brother took him to The Whale Tavern."

"*What?*" Great. All she needed was Valenden getting Rangar drunk before the ceremony—but Rangar was smarter than that. He might let Valenden drag him to The Whale Tavern, but he wouldn't get too deep into his cups.

Her attendants chattered in excitement as they preened her, and as bolstered as Bryn was by their enthusiasm, her mind kept turning back to the wolves.

*A wolf attack in the Mirien will be taken very seriously.* She could only imagine the chaos Mars and Illiana must be dealing with as their people questioned the attack. The Mir people would want assurances. They would want answers.

Had Mars gotten her letter? Had he sent a spy into Ruma? How long before they got a report?

A knock came at the door shortly after the attendants had finally taken their leave and given Bryn a moment of peace. Distracted, Bryn glanced at the window and realized it was already late afternoon.

*Sunset will be here soon!*

Roxin and Saraj opened the door, grinning. "Bryn, you look like a vision!" Saraj exclaimed. "That dress is utter perfection."

Roxin uncorked a bottle of fig brandy, whose sweet smell permeated the room. She waved it tantalizingly. "We came to toast the bride."

Bryn rested her hands on her hips in mock seriousness. "Is there some Baer tradition I don't know about to get a couple completely inebriated before the most important ceremony of their lives? Lada told me Valenden took Rangar to the tavern."

Roxin perched on the foot of the bed. "If it's not already a tradition, it should be."

Saraj dragged over a chair and accepted the glass of brandy Roxin poured for her. Roxin handed Bryn a glass, too, and raised a toast. "To our fair queen, may the gods smile upon you!"

"Here, here," Saraj said, drumming her knuckles on the table.

They downed their drinks, and Roxin immediately refilled the glasses. Bryn's throat burned from the brandy but not in an unpleasant way. With a small smile, she laughed, "I don't altogether mind this new tradition, you know. Roxin, the brandy is divine. We should have done this at my first wedding."

The smile on Saraj's face slipped for a moment. She peered down into her glass. "That was a different time. It didn't feel quite so . . . celebratory. Behind the scenes, at least."

Bryn's heart went out to Saraj. Months had passed since Trei's death, but broken hearts could take a lifetime to mend.

"That was a difficult day," Bryn admitted somberly. "For many of us."

Silence filled the room until Roxin belched. "Ah! Pardon me, ladies. Here, one more drink, and then it's off to the village square with you, pretty bride."

Bryn accepted another pour of brandy, though she was wary. Her head was already starting to spin. She took a polite sip and looked out the window. The first tinges of pink hugged the horizon.

"I guess this is it," she said, clutching her chain necklace on habit.

Saraj stood up and rested her hands on Bryn's shoulders. Looking her squarely in the eye, she said, "Today will be a happy day for you, Bryn. Fate brought you and Rangar together all those years ago. It was meant to be."

"Thank you, Saraj." Bryn wanted to tell the falconer how much her friendship had meant to her over the many months of knowing her. The Baersladen was her home now, but it was a harsh land, and if she hadn't had a kind soul to help her ease into life here, she might never have fallen in love with the land and people as she had.

"Would you help me with one last thing?" Bryn asked.

"Of course."

Bryn took out the sapphire necklace from its box on her desk. "Help me put this on?"

When she was ready, the guards escorted her into the village square just as bright pinks and oranges erupted on the horizon, reflecting off the beautiful snowbanks. A crowd was already gathered, and as soon as Bryn stepped across the drawbridge, her breath caught.

Each person in the crowd held a dried wheat berry

stalk. The effect was a sea of golden rays like a fresh dawn. The dais was decorated with more wheat berry stalks and the few remaining maiden roses of the season, all wrapped up in golden ribbons to symbolize Bryn's homeland.

But what stopped Bryn in her tracks was Rangar.

He stood between Mage Marna and Valenden, dressed in his coronation suit with his hair smoothed back and the bear claw crown glittering on his head. He'd never looked more handsome, not even at his coronation. Then, he'd been mired in grief over his father's death and the gravity of accepting responsibility for an entire kingdom. But today, a rare lightness graced his features. As long as she'd known him, Rangar had been all growls and snarls and brooding looks in the shadows. He stood at his full height for once, rivaling even Valenden's stature. His scars only made him all the more beautiful, Bryn thought, because no one else in the world had them.

She briefly touched her own scars outside of her gown.

"My lady?" one of the guards prompted.

She cleared her throat, returning to the present, and picked up her hem over the snow. "Right."

They escorted her to the dais stairs, where Valenden extended his hand to help her. The same old vicar who had married her and Trei clutched the Tome of the Divine, the sacred Baer text, looking even more ancient and tottering this time around, but she just smiled to herself. Something was endearing about the old vicar.

Mage Marna bowed her head. "Lady Bryn. Congratulations."

Bryn couldn't hide her wide grin. Mage Marna had terrified her the first time they'd met. With her white hair and perpetual frowns, she'd struck young Bryn as a cruel enchantress. But Bryn had come to see deep wisdom and good in Mage Marna. Buried under her cold exterior was a woman who cared intensely about her kingdom.

When Bryn faced Rangar and slowly lifted her gaze to meet his, wonder washed over her that they were finally at the altar despite all the obstacles that had stood in their way.

Rangar's lips parted as his head tipped down to fully view her in the gown. Love shone in his eyes, rivaling the gleaming lights of the setting sun. "My bride," he whispered low enough for only her to hear. "I've waited so long for this moment. In my heart, I knew it would always come. I never doubted."

And it was true. Ever since he had approached her at the Low Sun Gathering, Rangar had been unwavering in his belief that they belonged together. Even when she'd wed his brother, he'd insisted fate would find a way for them to be united.

"My wild prince," she replied. "The best thing I ever did was trust you enough to run away with you."

Though the vicar had not yet instructed them to clasp hands, Rangar reached for hers. Yet as soon as his thumb brushed her palm, a commotion in the crowd sent a shockwave through Bryn's heart. Her head spun toward the village square, where at the far end, a sudden bustle had drawn everyone's attention. She stood on tiptoes to try to see what was happening.

"A carriage arrives," Rangar said darkly.

Her teeth clenched together. *No! She and Rangar had withstood so much that she wouldn't let anything stop this wedding now . . .*

Rangar signaled to Oliver at the front of the crowd. "Gather the soldiers—"

Valenden rested his hand on Rangar's arm. "Wait. Look."

As the carriage made its way through the parting crowd, gleaming gold banners on its sides caught the setting sun.

Bryn gasped, recognizing the Mir emblem. "It's Mars! Mars and Illiana have come!" Anger and fear vanished from her heart, overtaken by excitement. She squeezed Rangar's hand tightly. "We must greet them!"

He held her back gently. "They've come from the Mirien for you, my love. Hold your place here, where you belong. Today, let the world come to you instead."

She sank back into his arm as the carriage stopped at the edge of the square. Her heart thumped in antici-pation as the driver climbed down. A team of Mir soldiers on horseback formed a protective circle around the carriage.

The driver announced, "Their royal highnesses, King Mars and Queen Illiana of the Mirien!"

Illiana emerged first, then helped Mars down. Though their travel clothes were rumpled, they both beamed with good health and happiness. Golden crowns rested on their heads, and a black eye mask embroidered with golden threads circled Mars's eyes.

The Mir soldiers moved their horses to form an aisle through the parted crowd to the dais. Hand-in-hand, Mars and Illiana made their way over the packed snow. The crowd's excited murmurs reflected the buzzing in Bryn's heart. She could hardly stop herself from running to the end of the dais and gripping her brother's hands as he climbed the stairs with Illiana's guidance.

"Brother. You got my letter," she breathed. "You came."

"Of course, Mouse. The letter was apprehended, but we got it back in time to read the contents. You were at my wedding, and I'd move mountains to be at yours."

Bryn squeezed Illiana's hands. "I can't imagine how fast you must have traveled—"

Valenden cleared his throat, interrupting her. "I know this is a happy reunion, princess, but let us not forget we're in the middle of *your own wedding*."

Red rose to Bryn's cheeks. Illiana giggled and said, "May we join you on the dais?"

"Of course." Bryn motioned to the place next to

Valenden. "We would be honored to have the king and queen of the Mirien with us as guests of honor."

Once everyone had resumed their places, and the crowd settled down from the excitement, the old vicar lifted his book. "The gods have gathered us here today to bind not only a man and a woman, but a king and his chosen bride. Among our most sacred traditions is the *fralen* bond. When King Rangar Barendur and Lady Bryn Lindane were brought into this world, their souls were separated from the Great Ones and placed in human bodies for an unknown amount of years before they would ultimately return to the Great Ones in death. And while on earth, both of these two faced the God of Death, yet their souls were saved by the other. A life saved is a soul owned, and two lives saved by two souls is the ultimate binding of fates."

The crowd murmured at this, and Bryn caught the words "fate" and "meant to be" muttered frequently. She squeezed her hands together, feeling as though it was impossible to deny what Rangar had always attested: they were fated soulmates.

The vicar flipped a page in his book and turned to Bryn. "Bryn Lindane of the Mirien, do you bind yourself with this man?"

She clenched her hands harder. Months ago, she'd stood on this stage across from Trei, confronted with the same question. Her heart had begged her to say no because her heart belonged to another.

Now, she could finally say exactly what she felt. "I do. Now and forever."

# CHAPTER 25

**WEDDING PART TWO . . . a kiss as husband and wife . . . Bryn's gift to Rangar . . . dancing . . . Saraj's future**

The vicar bowed his head toward Rangar. "And do you, Rangar Barendur, King of the Baersladen, bind yourself to this woman?"

A hush fell over the crowd, or maybe it was only in Bryn's imagination. She felt as though time stood still, and it was just her and Rangar in the whole world. Maybe the gods really had chosen them to be together, she thought, because everything about this moment felt right.

A ray of golden sunset light broke through the distant clouds to illuminate Rangar's face. He murmured, "I do. Now and forever."

Bryn's heart leaped in her chest. A bubble of emotion fought its way up until she felt tears in her eyes.

"You may begin the marriage with a kiss—"

Rangar interrupted the vicar by pulling Bryn into his arms and kissing her with every ounce of his soul. The moment their lips touched, Bryn felt a spark as the dying sunlight sank below the horizon. The spark grew into a flame, which swelled into an inferno. Rangar leaned her backward to deepen the kiss as though hundreds of villagers and soldiers weren't watching.

They were both breathless when they finally broke apart. Rangar pressed his forehead against hers as he whispered, "You are mine. I am yours. I pledge that I shall honor and love you for all your days and into the afterlife."

She gripped his shoulder. "I love you."

The cheering crowd threatened to drown out the vicar's words as he spoke the final portion of the ceremony that officially declared Bryn to be queen of the Baersladen. A rare, wide smile cropped up on Rangar's face and didn't seem inclined to go away anytime soon. With their arms around each other's backs, they waved to their people.

Mage Marna approached Bryn with Queen Anathalda's bronze crown atop a velvet pillow. It was shaped like twigs like Rangar's, yet finer, with only a single bear claw in the front.

"Lady Bryn," Mage Marna said. "It is my honor to name you as our queen."

As her heart thundered, Bryn knelt to receive the crown. Once, she had been the successor to the greatest throne of the Eyrie. The heavy, jewel-encrusted crown atop Mars's head would have been hers. And yet this humble bronze crown on a simple wooden dais in a small village square was exactly where she belonged.

"This is my new homeland," she said to Rangar and Mage Marna. "I shall honor it as queen."

Saraj jumped up and down in the front row, cheering loudly with tears in her eyes. Bryn recognized Helna, Roxin, and even Mam Delice, who had decided to remain in the Baersladen instead of returning to the Mirien. Even Aya, Rangar's former lover for a time, was clapping with sincere enthusiasm.

Guards threw open the doors to the great hall, where the sound of musicians playing a lively tune poured out along with the smell of Roxin's delicious feast. Rangar started to guide Bryn toward the stairs, but she dug in her heels.

"Wait." She pressed her hand against his chest. "You gave me two wedding gifts. My horse and my mother's necklace. I have nothing so fine as jewels to give you, but I want to show a token of my love. I know you plan to give me a third wedding gift . . . but it would be my honor to give you one instead."

Rangar's brow furrowed with a touch of curiosity.

Bryn glanced over her shoulder at Valenden, who

nodded. He signaled to Oliver in the front row, who went to the tall posts where King Aleth's mourning banners had hung. He tugged on a cord. A lattice of fishing nets rolled down the post. He did the same with the three other posts.

Rangar's lips parted in curiosity. "What is . . ."

"Wait," she admonished before turning to face the village square. Taking a deep breath, she raised her hands in the air. "*Vaxa terra friasa,*" she said under her breath while tracing the shape of a hex Mage Marna had given her on her back where her hair had hidden it.

People in the crowd looked around expectantly, wondering what spell their new queen was performing. Surely some recognized the hex shape, but those that did must have been equally stumped, as it wasn't a spell normally associated with gifts or marriage.

"Weeds?" Rangar said uncertainly as he recognized the spell. "Ah, darling, did you mean to . . ."

But his words faded as vines began to burst from the hard ground and snake up the fishing nets. Green leaves unfurled as the vines climbed and climbed, filling out the netting until it looked like spring-green banners had been hung. Once the vines reached the top of the posts, they burst into hundreds of blooms.

The villagers gasped in delight.

"Maiden roses," Bryn whispered, turning to Rangar. "They're technically a weed, but the first thing you taught me when we came here was that weeds have beauty, too. You told me I could flourish and adapt just like them. And I have."

He cupped her cheek, shaking his head softly. "My rose. My beloved. My life."

He kissed her again, softer this time, as the smell of maiden roses wafted into the dusky air.

The crowd made their way into the great hall, freshly plucked maiden roses woven into their hair and buttonholes. Guards escorted Bryn and Rangar, along with Mars and Illiana, to the head table. Bryn took in the great hall decorations in wonder—maids must have decorated it during the ceremony because it now burst with winter greenery and clusters of red berries and even an ice sculpture of a crown.

She caught sight of Roxin and threw her arms around her. "It's all so beautiful, Roxin!"

Roxin wiggled her eyebrows. "Wait until you try the food."

The tables were already filled with villagers digging into the salmon and pheasant and venison. The quartet of musicians was at the far end of the hall from the royal banquet table, but their music was so rousing that it filled the entire room.

Rangar pulled out a chair for Bryn. "My queen."

She couldn't help but smile. "I guess I don't have to scold you anymore for inaccuracy. Now I truly *am* your queen."

He pressed a kiss to her cheek. "You always were." His voice was low, and the smile was gone from his face, replaced by a fire in his eyes. A spark shot through Bryn, sending her heart pounding all over again.

*The wedding night is still ahead of us*, she thought with a thrill. A time just for her and Rangar to celebrate. But as eager as she was to make love to Rangar now that he was her husband, she wanted to thoroughly enjoy the party first. She tore into some butter biscuits dripping with melted cheese and downed a glass of fig brandy.

Illiana, across the table, raised her glass. "A toast to the new King and Queen of the Baersladen. The most star-crossed couple in the Eyrie. Fate smiles on you this day."

Bryn downed more brandy, grinning. "This is a more pleasant feast than my first wedding, it's true." She nudged Rangar in the side. "*Someone* interrupted it and ruined everything."

He licked a trace of brandy off his own lips. "You'd just married my brother. I had to take fate into my own hands, darling."

She nudged him again playfully.

Memories of Trei were heavy in her heart, and as she looked over the happy feast, she wished the past had turned out differently. As glad as she was to be with Rangar, it came at a heavy cost. She would have given anything for Trei to be here now with Saraj at his side. But she'd learned to accept the past—she would always remember Trei, as would everyone in the Baersladen who had loved him.

"Oh, the villagers are starting to dance!" Illiana exclaimed. "Mars, won't you dance with me?"

"You'll have to lead, my love."

Mir guards stood at attention as their monarchs swayed among the Baer villagers. Bryn laughed as she watched, thinking how their parents could never imagine a world where kings danced next to shepherds.

Oliver approached the head table, and Bryn expected him to address Rangar or Valenden, but to her surprise, he nodded to Saraj instead. "Saraj Swiftjoy, might I have a dance?"

No one looked more surprised than Saraj herself. Hardly anything flummoxed the falconer, but Oliver's request had her speechless. Her cheeks turned pink. "Oh . . . ah, yes. Of course."

She looked nervous as he led her to the dancing area, but after a few exchanged words, she smiled.

Bryn leaned close to Rangar. "I haven't heard Saraj speak a word of interest about any man since Trei's death."

He rested his arm on her chair back as he confided, "Oliver was Trei's closest friend. He, Trei, and Saraj spent many nights together at the tavern or training Zephyr. Perhaps Oliver had feelings for her that he could never pursue until now."

It warmed Bryn's heart to think of the possibility of Saraj eventually finding love again after losing Trei. Rangar brushed the hair off Bryn's neck and kissed the exposed skin. His hand moved down her dress to the place on her back where the weed growth hexmark lay.

"You've been keeping secrets from me."

She raised an eyebrow. "Only good secrets. Did you like your gift?"

"It was the most enchanting thing I've ever seen in my life," he murmured, still stroking her back. "But I still owe you your third present."

"Give it to me tonight," she said. With a wink "Now, dance with me."

Before he could object, she pulled him out of his chair and tugged him toward the other dancing couples. Everyone's eyes were on them as she wrapped her hands around his shoulders. They stepped to the melody, a *celestin* dance led by a fiddle.

"This is only the second time you've danced with me," she said, gazing up at him. "The first time, I was terrified of you."

"I wasn't *that* bad of a dancer."

She slapped his shoulder playfully. "I thought you had come to murder my family. And yet when we danced, something happened. I can't quite put a name to it. All I knew was that my heart trusted you even if my head didn't."

He guided her in a slow circle to music. "I'm glad you listened to your heart."

"Me, too."

She rested her head on his broad shoulder. He really was a passable dancer, a fact which still surprised her. When they'd first met, he had been so stiff that she'd been shocked he hadn't stepped all over her toes. Since then, their bodies had come to know one another intimately. From the early days riding on Legend with him to their lovemaking that ignited passions she didn't know were possible.

They danced late into the evening, pausing to switch partners so she could dance with fishermen and farmers, too, then dug into Roxin's delicious apple pie, and then Rangar swiped a bottle of wine and clutched Bryn around the waist.

"Enough of this," he said lowly into her ear. "Everyone else has had their time with their new queen. Now, I want my wife all to myself."

She uttered a small cry as he suddenly threw her over his shoulder, carting her toward the stairs. Whistles and bawdy calls of encouragement echoed behind them as he took her to bed.

# CHAPTER 26

**THE NEW MONARCHS OF THE NORTH . . .
wedding night . . . a gift from a missed mother . . .
two letters**

On their wedding night, Bryn and Rangar's lovemaking was tender and slow. For so long, their desire had been quenched with quick rendezvous behind a barn or a curtain, lustful kisses and tussles they'd engaged in like soldiers on the attack. But tonight, they took their time easing one another out of their clothes, sipping brandy in front of the fire while she perched naked in his lap, and then making love all through the night.

In the morning, Bryn woke lazily, stretching beneath the soft sheets. Her body smelled like woodsmoke and wine and roses, and she knew her hair must look like a wild tangle, but she rolled over and buried Rangar in a kiss.

He stirred awake readily, hands clasping her bare waist. "Mmm," he purred, blinking his eyes open. "You taste like apple pie."

She smiled languidly. "It's hard to believe I'm waking up to my husband in bed with me."

"That reminds me," he said, fingers gliding under the sheets to cup her ass, "I have one more wedding gift for you."

While he went to the dresser, she sat up, holding the sheet around her body. He'd given her jewels and a horse; what else could he possibly have?

He sank back onto the edge of the bed and handed her a wooden box inlaid with mother of pearl. "This isn't a gift from me, actually. It's from my mother."

Bryn's eyebrows rose. Queen Anathalda had died when Rangar was very young, and he rarely talked about her, but Bryn knew that he'd loved his mother fiercely and that she'd adored her sons in return.

A question was posed on her lips. "How—how is that possible?"

"Open it," he said simply. A strange look graced his face.

Bryn lifted the lid to find a small white gown embroidered with a sweet image of a goose. It was just the size for a baby. Eyes widening, she sucked in a breath. "Rangar, we—"

"I know," he said in a calm voice. "We agreed it isn't time for children until you are ready. I'll honor that promise to you. But my mother stitched this while she was on her sickbed. She made one for each of her sons' firstborn children, the grandchildren she knew she'd never see. She wanted us to give it to our wives on our wedding night as a blessing for a large, fruitful family."

Bryn examined the sweet gown. She could only imagine the love and sorrow Queen Anathalda had poured into each stitch.

"It's beautiful," she said sincerely, closing the box. "I'm honored by your mother's thoughtfulness. I'm sorry neither of your parents was here to see you wed."

"They are watching from the afterlife," he said.

She touched his scars gently. "We will have many babies one day, Rangar Barendur."

His mouth hitched in a wicked smile. "I shall enjoy putting them in you, my queen."

As much as Bryn wished for a lazy, careless day together, she wasn't surprised when a knock soon came at the door.

*We're king and queen now*, she thought with a sigh. *There are no lazy days for us.*

It was a messenger summoning them to meet with Mars and Illiana in the council chambers. Bryn assumed they were eager to return to Castle Mir and wished to say goodbye, but when they entered the chambers, a heavy silence portended different news.

"Has something happened?" Bryn asked in alarm.

Valenden, Mage Marna, Mars, and Illiana sat around the table, along with the Baersladen's captain of the army, Ulfmund. Valenden waved a hand toward the captain. "Ulfmund got word late last night of more wolf attacks. Some in the Baersladen. One in Kaldbad." He paused. "Ten people are dead."

Bryn gaped. "Kaldbad? That's no tiny farmstead or village. That's a large town."

"The berserkir wolves are getting bolder," Valenden said darkly. "And multiplying in numbers. The town of Kaldbad is already calling for a ban on magic within its borders."

Illiana looked troubled as she drummed her fingernails on the table. "On our ride here, our guards asked at every village about the berserkir wolves. People are terrified. We often heard that a dark mage is to blame, and only a ban on magic will end the attacks."

"Forbidding magic wouldn't stop a dark mage," Bryn argued. "Someone this evil doesn't care about the law."

"When people are scared," Illiana said, "They grasp at whatever solutions they can. It isn't just about these wolves and the person behind them—it's about growing fear over what magic can do in general in the wrong hands."

Bryn turned to Mars, exasperated. "Were you able to send a spy to Ruma?"

He nodded, stroking his chin. "We sent three, but it has only been a few days; too soon to hear back. I have hopes that by the time we return to Castle Mir, we will have word from them."

"I'll send Zephyr with you," Saraj offered. "He can

fly back here with a message within half a day. It'll be the fastest way to get word to us."

Mars nodded. "Good. Though we haven't heard back directly from our spies, there *has* been word out of Ruma. King Cedric of Ruma has called for a grand parlay between all the royal families of the Eyrie to discuss these wolf attacks and this 'sin of magic' as he calls it."

"That's it!" Bryn exclaimed. "That's practically evidence that the Ruma royal family is behind the wolf attacks and conspired with Baron Marmose to make it happen! This was their plan all along."

Rangar added, "We haven't received word of this grand parlay."

"You will be soon," Mars said. "As will Vil-Kevi and Vil-Rossengard. It takes longer to deliver messages to the Outlands, especially in winter. King Cedric called for the parlay to meet in the Wollin. Queen Amelia Hytooth of the Wollin is too elderly to travel, so we must all travel to her."

Valenden folded his arms tightly. "It isn't an accident that the Wollin is one of the few neutral kingdoms whose vote could throw the results to either decision."

Rangar and Mars both nodded their agreement.

Finally, Rangar paced to the window and announced, "You should return with haste to Castle Mir, King Mars. Send us word as soon as you hear from your spies. I need to look after the safety of my people here in the Baersladen before I can think of leaving. I will work with Saraj and my army captain to reinforce village fortifications and set traps for the wolves while we wait to hear plans for the grand parlay. Though, I must admit, our supplies of poison and traps are running low. If only we had more hunters."

Bryn sat straight as an idea came to her. "What if I could get you more skilled hunters with knowledge of the forest?"

"I'd say do it," Rangar answered. "But who?"

"My sister. Elysander's troupe of bandits live in the woods. They know how to hunt, and during the winter, they have nothing else to do. They could be the exact reinforcements we need."

Valenden grinned. "Brilliant! They know how to have a good time, too—I always love some scandalous nights with bandits. Will you write a letter to your sister?"

She shook her head. "I don't trust letters not to be intercepted, and we're already using Zephyr to carry a message. I think this is one message that must be delivered in person by a trusted individual. Someone who knows them. Who's, say, spent some scandalous nights with them."

As all eyes fell on Valenden, he groaned, "At least you trust me."

"Do you really think Elysander will help?" Mars asked. "As you described in your meeting with her, she was not inclined to get involved in politics. And Dresel's royal family is against the use of magic."

"The royal family might be, but Elysander still

loves the Mir people, and now the Dresel people as well. They're all under threat. You'll just have to be very persuasive, Val."

He stroked his chin, considering. "Shame she's married . . ."

Bryn groaned and rolled her eyes.

"Very good." Mars stood and smoothed a hand over his embroidered blindfold. "We shall await more news, and if the grand parlay is agreed to, we shall see you in the Wollin in a matter of weeks." He turned in Bryn's direction. "I'm sorry such concerns dampen your wedding bliss, my sister."

"Life is full of good and bad," Bryn said. "I'll take what comes." She squeezed his hands again. "I'm so glad you came, brother. I pray that in the Wollin, all three of us Lindane siblings shall be together again."

"If the Saints will it," he said with a nod.

For days after Mars and Illiana's departure, Bryn threw herself into studying more hexes that might help them solve the mystery of the berserkir wolf attacks. Working with Mage Marna and Ren, she earned a hex for silencing a person's tongue and another one for dulling a person's memory. When Ren told her a rumor that Trei had borrowed books that they'd never found, she used the finding spell to locate them in an old chest that had been moved to a storeroom after Trei's death, and pored through them. She read about the history of the Eyrie kingdoms, about the customs of each land, the natural resources of forest and desert and ocean, trying to find any mention of hex spells.

She was helping Rangar and a farming family reinforce their sheep corral against possible berserkir wolf attacks when a shadow passed in the falling snow overhead, followed by a familiar caw.

"That's Zephyr," Rangar said, tipping his head up and squinting into the stinging snow. "Mars must have sent him back with a message. You go—I'll catch up to you when I finish here."

Bryn mounted Fable and rode swiftly back to Barendur Hold, where Saraj was already waiting for her on the rooftop sentry post where the falcon had landed. The post offered meager cover from the snow, but it was enough shelter that Bryn lowered her cloak's hood.

"He bears a message?"

Saraj nodded, stroking the bird as he rested on a perch after his long flight. She removed a small piece of rolled parchment from a wooden tube fastened to his leg and handed it to Bryn.

Footsteps sounded on the roof, and Rangar soon joined them, pushing back his hood and shaking out his hair. "The message?" he said, breathless from his ride back to the castle. "Read it."

Bryn unrolled it with fingers numb from the cold.

"It's from Mars," she confirmed, then read aloud, "*One of my spies was slain by a Ruma guard after inquiring about the wolf attacks in what I suspect was an attempt to keep him from discovering the truth. But one of the other two successfully infiltrated Baron Marmose's manor house. He reports that as many as a dozen of the baron's dog trainers suddenly fell ill and passed away. They say it was rancid poultry, a terrible accident."*

Bryn looked up from the letter. "An accident?"

"More like they were all poisoned," Saraj muttered darkly, "to keep them from talking. But talking about what, exactly, is the question."

Rangar drew a deep breath. "About their role in developing a hex to create the berserkir wolves, I'd wager. So it can never be traced back to Baron Marmose or the Rumese royal family."

Bryn folded the letter and tucked it into her dress. She shivered from the wind. She'd underestimated Baron Marmose's ambitions if he would go so far as to kill twelve of his own loyal workers.

"There's something else," Rangar said. "As I rode into the stables, a messenger awaited me with this." He took an envelope from his cloak with the silver wax seal of Ruma. He read the letter swiftly and summarized, "It's the invitation to the grand parlay. They set out their reasons as Mars said—the berserkir wolf attacks spurred by the 'sin of magic' throughout the Eyrie. Apparently, the Hytooths have agreed to host the gathering at Hytooth Palace in the Wollin on the next new moon."

Bryn quickly calculated the timing as she hunched in her cloak against the blowing snow. "That's in seven days."

Rangar crumpled the invitation in his fist. "According to the messenger, the other royal families have all agreed to attend."

"Even the Viklund family from Vil-Rossengard?" Bryn said. The Viklunds were notoriously independent, usually communicating only with their sister kingdom of Vil-Kevi.

Rangar nodded. "I told the messenger that we would be in attendance as well. We have no choice. We must advocate for the use of magic. If it is outlawed throughout the Eyrie, the Baer people will not be able to sustain themselves through our harsh winters."

Bryn looked out at the swirling snow. "It frightens me, Rangar. The Eyrie has been on the verge of war for months, and now, with tensions this high, every royal family will be together under one roof?"

Rangar drew her close, pressing a kiss to her forehead. His lips warmed her numb skin. "You are always safe with me, my queen. No one would dare raise a hand in violence while I am around—or they'd risk having it cut off."

# CHAPTER 27

**THE SOUTHERN ROAD . . . Zandir the dark mage . . . proof of guilt . . . two riders alone . . . warm in the cold**

As the time neared to set out for the ride to the Wollin, Bryn doubled down on her studies. In one of Trei's old books, she found a passage on the Rumese tradition of holding annual hunts with trained hunting dogs. Thinking of what Mars's spy discovered about the baron's dog trainers dying suddenly, she focused on those pages.

*In the kingdom of Ruma, there was once a dark mage by the name of Zandir who was known for his experimentation with magic. It was said that he had a fascination with hunting dogs and was always seeking ways to improve their speed and strength.*

*Zandir began working with a group of skilled dog trainers, using his dark magic to imbue the animals with otherworldly powers. He called this spell "cannin ka ulrick," which roughly translated to "the speed of dogs."*

*The spell's results were astounding, as the hunting dogs became faster and stronger than any others in the kingdom. They were able to run for longer periods of time without tiring and could take down larger prey with ease, though the spell left the dogs with black tongues.*

*However, Zandir's actions did not go unnoticed, and many feared the consequences of such powerful animals being unleashed upon the land. Some even whispered that the mage sought to use the dogs for nefarious purposes.*

Bryn closed the book and hugged it to her chest. This was it; she felt certain. In league with the Rumese royal family, Baron Marmose had ordered his dog trainers to use the "speed of dogs" hex on a pair of wolves to turn them into berserkirs like in the legend. The berserkir wolf pair must have reproduced, and they'd released the wolves somewhere near the Vil-Kevi border, so far from Ruma as to cast off any suspicion—and to ensure the berserkir attacks were far from their own people.

"Rangar," she breathed when she finally found him conferring with Oliver and the captain of the army in the portico surrounding the yew tree. Rangar dismissed the others with a nod, and Bryn rushed up with the book. "Look at this."

She showed him the passage and gave him time to read it, then pointed out, "The black tongues. The superior speed. The fact that the berserkir wolves don't act with frenzied bloodlust but rather as though they were trained to attack. This essentially proves that Ruma is behind the berserkir wolves."

He closed the book, his face stony as he considered this. "It's astounding, Bryn. You figured out what no mages or spies could. We will take this information with us to the grand parlay."

"No," she insisted. "The Hytooth family is neutral when it comes to magic. And Queen Amelia is rumored to be so elderly that her senses are dulled. She might easily be swayed by the royal families of Ruma and Zaradona and Dresel, especially if they suggest the Woll people are in danger."

"So, what do you suggest?"

"That we leave now. Early. We arrive at Hytooth Palace before any of the other royal families and have a private audience with Queen Amelia. We get her on our side before the others have a chance to influence her."

Rangar dragged his nails through his hair. "Hytooth Palace is normally five days by carriage, but if this snow continues, that could add days to the journey. Even if we left today, a small delay might get us there at the same time as the others."

"So, then we won't take a carriage. We can ride faster on Legend and Fable."

He cocked his head. "Just the two of us?"

"Valenden can rule in our absence."

"Dear gods," Rangar muttered huskily but then drew in a long breath. "Your plan might be our best option. It would be a long, hard ride, though. Are you prepared for that?"

"I can manage. I've been riding Fable every chance I get. Oliver has been a good instructor."

"Not too good, I hope," Rangar said, eyes flashing.

"Oh, don't get jealous. Besides, you know Oliver has his sights set on Saraj."

Rangar handed her back the book. "Safeguard this. I'll speak to Val and tell the stable to ready the horses for a long voyage. We'll leave tonight and hope to miss the worst of the storm. If the weather improves, we could be in the Wollin as soon as the day after tomorrow."

She started to rush to their room to pack, but he captured her arm. "Wait, Bryn." He snagged her gaze and held it. "I promised I'd keep you safe. I mean it."

She touched his scars, letting her fingers trail down their length. "I believe you, Rangar Barendur. And for what it's worth, I don't intend to let anything happen to you, either."

They parted to each complete their tasks. As Bryn stuffed clothes and blankets into rucksacks for them, her mind went to the Wollin. She'd never been to Hytooth Palace, but she had once traveled to the south of the Wollin with her family. She recalled the smell of the orange groves and the gently lapping waves on the sandy beach. She'd never imagined any place could be as serene, yet she feared that serenity would be in short supply on this visit.

Once their clothes were packed, she left the rucksacks in their chambers so as not to invite questions, and went to the kitchen. She'd hoped to sneak into the pantry unobserved, but someone cleared their voice behind her as soon as she was bent over, digging through potatoes.

"Can I help you, Queen Bryn?"

"Roxin!" Bryn straightened, pressing a hand to her chest as she struggled to explain the potato in her hand. "Ah . . . I wanted to surprise the king with a romantic . . . picnic. I was just borrowing some food."

Roxin folded her arms pointedly. "A picnic, eh? During a snowstorm? With a potato?"

Bryn scrunched up her face. "An . . . indoor picnic."

"That's called a *meal*."

Bryn sighed. "Look, as queen, can't I just command you to help me and not ask questions?"

A smile broke across Roxin's face. "As queen? No. As a friend? Yes, I'll help. Now put down that potato."

Bryn described what she and Rangar would need for the trek, and Roxin packed a small bundle with dried venison and cheese and fruit. Bryn dressed in her warmest clothes and carried the rucksacks down to the stable, where Oliver had already prepared Legend and Fable with saddle pads that could double as extra blankets.

She stroked Fable's face. "We have to go out in the snow, but I promise we'll be all right."

Rangar soon joined her in his bearskin cloak, and brought Valenden and Saraj with him. Saraj gave Bryn a sturdy hug. "Please take care. Don't trust any other royal families for a moment, other than your brother."

Bryn returned the embrace, then glanced between Oliver and Saraj, who were standing exceptionally close. "Thank you for helping to keep watch while we're away, Saraj. If you need anything, I'm sure Oliver can help."

Oliver grinned a little sheepishly as he nodded.

Valenden rested one hand on Rangar's shoulder. "Watch your back, brother."

"And you, Val. Don't fuck up the kingdom."

"Well. No promises."

They drummed their fists on each other's chest, and then it was time for Bryn and Rangar to leave. The sun had sunk an hour before, and snow clouds blanketed the darkening sky. Rangar made a stirrup with his hands to help her mount Fable and then swung himself up on Legend. "Let's go."

With a nod to the others, they took off at a trot. Snow stung Bryn's face as she rode behind Rangar. With the heaviest clouds far out at sea, it looked as though they would outrun the worst of the storm. She focused on her form atop Fable, ensuring she was steady and not holding her muscles so tensely that she'd be sore the following day. Fable had a gentle gait even at a fast pace, and seemed to know where it was safe to tread despite the darkness.

They rode on the valley road for several hours, and

then Rangar branched off toward the high southern mountains. The horses climbed a rocky path until they reached a hunting shelter with walls on three sides and a sloping wooden roof.

"We'll stop here for the night," Rangar called back to her through the wind.

They dismounted, tethered the horses so they could forage for grass, and then dragged their possessions into the shelter. While Bryn shed her wet, frigid outer clothes, Rangar gathered dry wood that had been stacked in the rear of the shelter and lit a fire with the spark spell.

Shivering, Bryn tugged off her boots. "It wasn't so bad when we were riding," she said. "But now that we've stopped, I feel as though I'm going to freeze."

"It's always warmer when you're moving and when you have a horse's heat between your legs." Crouching under the low ceiling, he knelt beside her and rubbed her arms. "You'll warm up soon with the fire and some food in you. *I'd* oblige to put some heat between your legs, too."

Despite the fact that she was still shivering, she gave him a slow smile. "We'll see about that if I don't turn to ice."

Once they were in warm clothes with their riding garments hanging near the fire to dry, Rangar portioned off bread and venison for them, and Bryn was finally able to relax into the thick blanket around her.

Rangar gathered her in his arms, blanket at all, and

moved her into his lap. "My strong Baer woman. You don't let snow and wind stop you."

"I thought you preferred delicate women."

"Delicate. Hardy. I'll take you however you are, Bryn Barendur."

It felt strange and wonderful to have his surname following hers. The Lindane family name was cursed, and she felt as though she'd shed some ratty old winter coat by taking his instead.

Snug in the blanket, she shifted in his lap until she could lay her head against his chest. "I can hear your heart beating," she whispered as he pressed a kiss to the top of her head. "Aren't you going to ravish me here, in this place we have all to ourselves?"

He looked down at her in amusement. "Do you wish me to, my insatiable little love?"

She snuggled even closer against him. A part of her felt invigorated by the storm blustering outside and the small haven of their hunting shelter. She imagined Rangar stripping naked and joining her under the blanket, their bodies moving together until they moaned into the wind. But another part of her was content just being in his arms.

"Newlyweds supposedly can't keep their hands off one another," she said.

He chuckled low in his chest. "Darling, it doesn't matter what newlyweds should or shouldn't do. We rode hard today. It's cold. If you want me to simply hold you, I'll hold you."

She realized then that was exactly what she

wanted. There would be other nights of wild passion, but here in the safety of the mountain shelter, she only wanted to close her eyes and fall asleep in Rangar's arms.

# CHAPTER 28

**THE ROAD TO WOLLIN . . . mountain crossing . . . love magic, fear magic . . . a near tragedy . . . hayloft**

Rangar roused Bryn before dawn, and they mounted Legend and Fable to head higher into the mountains as first light broke. The mountain range separating the Baersladen from the Wollin was high but compact as opposed to the mountains that led to Vil-Kevi, which seemed to stretch endlessly. By mid-morning, they had crested a pass and begun to descend into a river valley that would take them to the Wollin's border.

"You spent time in the Wollin as a boy, didn't you?" Bryn called up to Rangar on the trail ahead.

"One summer," Rangar answered back. "My brothers and I were wards of the Hytooths for a few months. They treated us well, given that every other royal family in the Eyrie considered us savages."

"What are Queen Amelia and King Marthin Hytooth like?"

"Haven't you met them?"

"Only briefly at my family's gatherings. The Hytooths attended, but I was the wayward third child, which made me utterly irrelevant."

"King Marthin is a fool," Rangar said thoughtfully. "I do not say that to be unkind. He is a gentle man but no cleverer than a child. It was rumored he was kicked in the head by a horse in his teenage years, but by then, he and Amelia were already betrothed. He could have been a drooling invalid, and they'd still have had to wed."

"Amelia is Woll born?"

"Yes, she comes from the Wollin. She was the daughter of a minor lord with just enough noble blood to count as a royal. I'm told she was quite beautiful in her youth."

"And now?"

"She must be almost ninety years old, but she still has a grace about her. Ever since she married King Marthin, she ruled in her husband's name, and everyone knew it. He might have made proclamations before a crowd, but she decided the Wollin's course of action beforehand. When I was their ward, her mind was not as sharp as I imagine it once was. She was forgetful, would repeat herself often. I cannot imagine it has improved since then."

In her readings, Bryn had come across the progeny charts for each of the royal families of the Eyrie. Queen Amelia and King Marthin had born no children, though there were ample cousins and nieces and nephews potentially in line for the crown.

Once they descended the mountains, the horses could move faster on the valley road. Bryn and Rangar galloped for some miles, hoping to make up time. For Bryn, racing over long stretches of land was both frightening and exhilarating. Her heart rose to her throat with every hoof fall, her torso pitching forward into the wind. Prayers not to fall off spilled from her lips.

They stopped at a farm to water the horses, and the farmer and his wife came out to greet them. Rangar and Bryn had stowed their bronze crowns in their rucksacks so that they might have been any wealthy couple, not royalty.

After trading the farmer some coins for grain for the horses, Rangar asked, "You've heard of the wolf attacks in the north, I assume?"

The farmer and his wife grew serious. "Awful news. I've also heard terrible things from Vil-Kevi and the northern Mirien."

"But nothing around these parts, south of the mountains?" Bryn asked.

The farmer pressed his lips together in a somber frown. "We hear howling at night. It sounds unlike any wolf I've heard. But King Rangar's army came last week and laid traps all through the mountainside, and we've been safe since then, thank the gods."

Bryn fought the urge to extend a knowing look to Rangar. "Thank the gods," she repeated softly, then added more hesitantly, "If you have protection hexes, I advise you to use them."

Silence hung in the air. Bryn had asked the question as a test.

The farmer remained silent, and Bryn was afraid she'd hear the same anti-magic rhetoric as before, but the farmer's wife blurted out, "I agree." The woman rolled up her sleeve to show off several hexes on her forearm. "We've cast every last spell we know that might keep us and our livestock safe."

Bryn's shoulders eased. "So, you don't believe magic is to blame for the wolves?"

"Bah," the farmer's wife said. "Magic is like water —too much or too little can do harm, but if you take care to tame its flow, it is life-giving. All this chatter about the danger of magic . . . pish. Around these parts, we've practiced magic for generations. Stopping magic would be like taking away our breath."

"King Rangar would never outlaw magic," the farmer intimated. "He's wiser than those zealots in the southern kingdoms."

This time, Bryn couldn't help but glance back to gauge Rangar's reaction. He remained stoic as he nodded. "I agree with your thoughts about magic," he said. "Let us hope more people begin to see the same logic."

As they rode through the southern Baer villages, Bryn was heartened by the strong protections against berserkir wolves and the lack of "No Magic" signs. They once came across a handful of anti-magic signs at a settlement that bore the look of Zaradona immigrants, but almost all other homes and farms seemed to continue using magic as they always had.

"See?" Bryn said encouragingly to Rangar. "Reason still prevails. We have many allies yet among our people."

They crossed the border into the Wollin, and the terrain continued to flatten. The Wollin was a long, narrow kingdom that hugged the western Eyrie coast. Woll village houses were made less of stone and timber and more of thatched roofs and clay brick siding.

When the sun began to sink on the horizon, Rangar kept an eye out for places they might pass the night. They entered a village with a tavern, and he dismounted and went inside while Bryn waited with the horses.

"There is no inn for miles," he reported when he emerged. "But they serve meals here and can put us up for the night in the hayloft."

"A hayloft for a king?" she said wryly.

His eyes danced with amusement. "As long as I'm not wearing my crown, I'm just a traveler with coins in his pocket."

Bryn was in no position to complain. She'd spent enough nights sleeping on hard soil that hay sounded positively divine. They went inside, where a woman with the Wollin's famed red hair brought them pints of ale and plates of roasted duck as she juggled a toddler on her hip.

"What a sweet child," Bryn said, smiling at the little girl.

"This is my Mara," the tavern keeper said, beaming as she bounced the girl on her hip. "Already riding her big sister's pony."

The woman disappeared back into the kitchen, leaving Bryn and Rangar to their meal. The duck was tough, but Bryn was grateful for anything besides dried venison strips. On the other hand, the ale had a lovely salty touch that Rangar explained was from filtering the brew with oyster shells from the nearby coast.

A crash came from the kitchen, followed by the tavern keeper's wail, loud enough to wake the dead. *"Mara! My Mara!"*

Bryn and Rangar were both on their feet in an instant. The rest of the tavern was empty, and they'd seen no sign of the tavern keeper's husband or other children, so they rushed into the kitchen to see what had happened.

The tavern keeper's face was pale as snow, her eyes wide. An overturned pot of boiling water rested on the floor. The toddler girl was lying on the ground, unmoving. Red splotches marked the child's bare face and arms.

"The pot . . ." the tavern keeper gasped. "It slipped. The hot water scalded her. She isn't breathing!"

Rangar dropped to a knee by the girl and felt her breath against the back of his hand. He looked up at Bryn with a pained expression. "Her body is in shock from the burns."

Bryn fell to her knees, too, hovering her hands over the toddler. The girl's skin blistered badly as puss bubbled up. "Is there a healer in this town?" Bryn asked.

"No," the mother gasped. "Sara has a few hexes, but mostly for gardening . . . She's visiting her family in Vinmur now anyway . . ."

Bryn clasped Rangar's hand and said firmly, "I need you to amplify a hex for me."

He didn't question her; he only bobbed his head in a nod. Bryn wet her lips. She'd obtained the healing hex with the idea that a queen should have the skill to mend her people's minor scrapes and bruises, but she never imagined she'd be faced with a little girl's *life*— especially not so soon after beginning her apprenticeship. The healing hex on its own wasn't strong enough to reverse the girl's burns, but if she used Rangar's amplifier spell, there was a chance it could save the child.

Clasping Rangar's hand, Bryn traced the minor healing hex shape over the girl's body. She said carefully, "*Cura na agus.*"

A tingle of magic gathered from Rangar's body and

poured into her own. She closed her eyes, centering her intention on the girl.

"My sweet Mara . . ." the tavern keeper wailed in the background.

Bryn pushed all else out of her mind except the girl and the spell. She hung onto the incantation's words in her mind, repeating them silently again and again. Rangar's hand tightened in hers supportively.

Suddenly, the girl moaned.

The mother gasped, and Bryn finally opened her eyes. The little girl blinked awake. Her arms were still splotched with red, but the worst of the blisters had reversed themselves. The deepest burns were now nothing more than a sunburn.

The little girl's bottom lip trembled, and in the next breath, she let out an ear-piercing wail. Her mother rushed in and scooped her up, crying tears of relief. "That's it, my love! You cry. You cry as loud as you need to."

Once Bryn had seen the girl safely in her mother's arms, all her energy slackened. She slumped to the floor, barely catching herself.

Rangar gripped her shoulders hard, holding her up. "Bryn?"

"I'm fine." But her voice was weak.

A handful of villagers who had heard the girl's wails rushed in through the kitchen's back door. They stopped, relieved, to see the mother's calm face despite the girl's crying.

"May the gods bless you," the mother choked out to Bryn.

Still feeling depleted, Bryn nodded. Rangar helped her to her feet, one hand going to her wrist to feel her pulse.

"What happened, Alyse?" an elderly woman asked in concern.

"The boiling water spilled on Mara. Oh, it would have been awful if these two hadn't come with a hex to heal her right up!"

Though most of the villagers murmured comforting words, the elderly woman frowned sharply. "A hex, you say, Alyse?"

A few distrusting eyes shifted to Rangar and Bryn.

"Oh, stop with that, Ester!" the tavern keeper snapped. "Mara might have died if they hadn't used magic!"

"You don't know that," the elderly woman said firmly, tightening her shawl. "We don't know what the gods intend. Magic should be left to them, not to we earthly beings."

"Well, if the gods intended Mara to suffer terrible burns, then damn the gods, and I'll keep my hexes!"

The villagers began to argue over the use of magic, and Rangar pressed his hand to Bryn's back as he whispered, "I think we should go. Now."

# CHAPTER 29

**HYTOOTH PALACE . . . the vast sea . . . a strange greeting . . . red-headed cousins . . . not the first to arrive**

As weak as Bryn was, she was in no position to argue with Rangar. He had to practically carry her out of the tavern and across the farmyard while the villagers continued to argue in the distance. A ladder led up to the barn's hayloft; Rangar took one look at it, then threw Bryn over his shoulder so he could climb with both hands. When they reached the top, he dropped her on a blanket the tavern keeper had laid out over the straw for them.

"Oof!" she said as a cloud of straw floated up around her. "Rangar, I could have managed the ladder on my own."

He crouched in front of her to recheck her pulse. "You should rest. The amplifier spell is a drain."

"On you, too."

"Not as much as on you. You were the caster."

"Well, I'm fine."

It was chilly in the barn despite the blanket and insulation provided by the hay. With her body depleted of its reserves, she couldn't help but shiver. "You heard what those villagers said about magic. Even to save a little girl's life, they distrust it."

"Not all of them."

"Yes, but enough to be a problem."

Rangar eased himself onto the blanket beside her and took out a brandy flask. Passing it to her, he said, "We'll be at Hytooth Palace tomorrow, well before the other royal families arrive. We'll talk to Queen Amelia and get ahead of this anti-magic sentiment. I promise you; we can turn the tide."

The brandy burned down Bryn's throat, but at least it warmed her belly.

They spent the night huddled beneath Rangar's bearskin cloak, listening to the snores of the livestock in the barn below. Bryn's dreams were tainted by images of witches burned by boiling water. In the morning, Rangar left a stack of coins at the tavern's back door, and they departed without alerting anyone, afraid their presence would only further stir the village's disagreement over magic.

Legend and Fable were well rested, and with the flat terrain of the Wollin, Bryn and Rangar made good time. A cool breeze rolled in off the ocean as the road led them toward the coast. They crested a small hill, and the sea view rolled out beyond.

Bryn stopped Fable, gazing at the ocean as a sentiment of awe settled over her. Having lived most of her life far inland, she would never grow tired of seeing the vast expanse of water. Here, the ground sloped gently into a flat, sandy beach, which in turn opened to glistening turquoise waves, dotted here and there by sleepy fishing vessels.

"This coast is so different from the Baersladen's," she observed, listening to seagulls squawking in the distance.

"There is a benefit to a wide-open beach," Rangar agreed. "Much easier to see enemy ships approaching. And fishing is as simple as wading in and casting a net. Still, I would not trade our rocky coastline for anything. These waves are too quiet."

The gentle shush-shush of the distant waves was a far cry from the crashing tides outside of Baersladen Hold, it was true, but Bryn found them soothing.

"There." Rangar pointed to a collection of towers rising over the terra cotta rooftops of a nearby town. "That is Hytooth Palace."

They spurred on the horses as they raced toward the town. The palace was a beautiful, sprawling sandstone structure with a large, domed tower painted yellow, and another portion painted a dusky red, so that the place had a relaxing yet whimsical spirit, almost like a fairy tale come to life. It sat on a seawall above the lapping waves.

The road took them into the sprawling town of Serra, the capital of the Wollin, a bustling coastal port full of fish markets and salt traders. Tall palm trees swayed overhead, providing shade to the streets below. Rangar shed his bearskin cloak, tying it in a roll across Legend's back. There was a slight chill in the air, but it was far warmer here than the frigid Baersladen this time of the year.

When they approached the walled gate to Hytooth Palace, Rangar dismounted to speak to the guards. "I am King Rangar Barendur of the Baersladen, and this is my wife, Queen Bryn Barendur. We've come for the grand parlay."

The guards bowed deeply, though they glanced between one another as though uncertain. An uneasy premonition stirred in Bryn's stomach. Did the guards doubt them? Or was there something else going on?

"Show them our emblem as proof," she said, then faced the guards herself. "We wished to remain undisturbed during our travels, so we came in plain clothes without a carriage."

Rangar removed a chain around his neck to show them the bronze emblem of a bear—the sigil of the Barendur royal family. The guards nodded, apparently accepting their claim but still seemed uneasy.

"King Rangar," the first one said deferentially. "We are honored by your presence but did not expect you nor Queen Bryn so soon. The grand parlay does not start for two more days."

"We feared the wolf attacks might slow our journey," Rangar explained. "And I wished for some extra time to visit with Declan and Phillipa Hytooth—I have not seen them since I stayed here as a ward many years ago."

"Of course." The first guard whispered something to a younger soldier, who hurried into the castle. He then signaled for the door to be raised. "Welcome to Hytooth Palace, your Majesties."

As Rangar helped Bryn down from Fable, and they surrendered the horses to stableboys, Bryn muttered quietly, "They seem nervous, don't they?"

Rangar nodded, having sensed it, too. "A grand parlay does not often occur. They'll be responsible for the safety of every royal family member in the Eyrie—many of whom despise one another. I suppose I cannot blame them for some nerves."

The gate led them into a breezy courtyard dotted with palm trees. The sandstone-colored turrets rose high above into the pale blue sky. Bryn touched the small knife sheathed at her waist as a reassurance.

"King Rangar! Queen Bryn!" A man and woman in beautiful pale blue clothes strode into the courtyard to greet them. Bryn placed them as siblings or cousins by their unruly red curls and matching ruddy cheeks. They looked too similar to be husband and wife.

The man strode up and gripped Rangar's arm in a firm welcome. "How good to see you again, Rangar. And now a king!"

Rangar slapped the man's shoulder fondly. "Declan." He nodded to the woman. "Phillipa. You've both grown a foot since I last saw you."

"And you've gained a wife," the man said, grinning charmingly at Bryn.

Rangar didn't seem to like the man's affable smile aimed at Bryn, so he slid a possessive hand around Bryn's back. "Yes, my wife, Queen Bryn. Bryn, this is Declan and Phillipa Hytooth, niece and nephew of Queen Amelia and King Marthin. When I spent a summer here, they were our partners in crime."

"Guilty," Declan said with a laugh, taking Bryn's hand and delicately kissing it. "Congratulations on your nuptials."

"Yes, congratulations," Phillipa said, "though we were deeply sorry to hear of your brother and father's passing, Rangar."

Rangar bowed his head briefly. "May their souls be guarded."

The two Hytooths bowed their head. "May their souls be guarded."

After the moment of solemnity, Declan slapped Rangar on the shoulder again, his smile reappearing. "Come. We weren't expecting you so soon, but we'll show you to your room. I told the palace staff to reserve the tower bedroom for my brooding old friend —it has the best view over the ocean. We're going to house those miserable Greys from Dresel in a window-less first-story room."

Rangar and Declan fell into conversation about their journey while Phillipa hung back, slipping her arm between Bryn's.

"I've been anxious to meet you, Queen Bryn," Phillipa confessed. "My mother never let me attend your family's gatherings at Castle Mir when I was a girl—they only sent my brothers. But we're heard incredible tales of your adventures these last few months, and I'm dying to know what is true and what is gossip." She dropped her voice as she tipped her chin toward Rangar. "Did he *really* steal you away, only for you to fall in love with him? And was he *actually* accused of poor Trei's murder? Surely no one believed him capable of such a thing. Oh! And you must tell me about the Battle of Saint Serrel's Shrine and that miserable Captain Carr . . ."

Overwhelmed, Bryn pressed a hand to her fore-head. "Yes, of course. Um, perhaps after we rest."

Phillipa squeezed her arm. "Oh, silly me! You must be exhausted from the journey. How curious you came on horses instead of a royal carriage . . . There I go again, rooting out gossip. Don't mind me."

Given the mild climate, Hytooth Palace was largely open-air, letting in the breeze and the sound of the shushing tide. Their guest bedroom was in an upper portion of the yellow-painted tower, which afforded a breathtaking ocean view. When Bryn stood at the door, the wide windows showed sea and sky as far as she could see.

"We'll have your rucksacks brought up," Phillipa said. "Though you packed so lightly, you must be in need of extra clothing and other accouterments. I'll have some things sent up for you."

"We'd be grateful," Bryn said. "Thank you."

"And you must join Declan and me for tea," Phillipa continued. "Traveling always leaves me starving, and it will be so good to grow acquainted . . ."

"Actually," Rangar cut in. "We were hoping to speak to your aunt, the queen."

Both Declan and Phillipa fell into an awkward, uncharacteristic silence. While Phillipa busied herself with a loose string on her gown, Declan cleared his throat. "Queen Amelia is ailing, as I'm sure you are aware. The healers have advised her to focus exclusively on rest before the grand parlay."

"Understandable," Rangar said. "But between us, we did not arrive two days early because we feared wolf attacks on the road. We have reason to believe other royal families are plotting to bring strife to the Eyrie. Queen Amelia must know what evidence we have before the others arrive and can influence her."

Declan and Phillipa exchanged a cryptic, uncomfortable look. Sensing their hesitation, Bryn cleared her throat.

"With all due respect," Bryn added, "We would never want to tax your aunt, but the future of the Eyrie is at stake."

Finally, Declan rested a heavy hand on Rangar's shoulder. "It isn't just my aunt's health, my old friend. The truth is, I'm afraid you aren't the only one with that plan."

Alarm tiptoed up Bryn's spine. "What do you mean?"

Sighing, Declan rubbed the bridge of his nose. "Ruma's delegation arrived yesterday, *also* wishing to speak with my aunt in advance of the grand parlay."

Bryn held in a gasp. "King Cedric and Queen Yves are already here?"

Now she understood the palace guards' strange behavior when they arrived. It had to appear unusual for *two* delegations to arrive early and unannounced, if not outright suspicious.

"Not exactly," Declan said slowly. "The Cheron royal family is scheduled to arrive in two days, with everyone else. However, they sent an emissary ahead of them."

An icy fist formed in Bryn's stomach. She dreaded the name they might say. "Who?"

Phillipa clasped her hands, biting her lip. "Baron Marmose."

# CHAPTER 30

**A TROUBLED QUEEN . . . the snake and his dogs . . . beaten to the chase . . . a confused king . . . Bryn's new idea**

"Baron Marmose?" Rangar roared. "Where is he?"

Declan held out a calming hand against Rangar's flare of temper. "Now, Rangar, we all know you act rashly when you're angry. The baron is in the library . . ." Declan swallowed hard. "With my aunt."

"He's speaking with the *queen*?" Rangar roared louder.

Phillipa flinched. "We tried to tell him the same thing we told you, that our aunt needed rest before the grand parlay, but just like you, he insisted he'd come with urgent business that required her attention."

Bryn's legs, aching from days on Fable, threatened to give out. She sank onto a wooden chair.

*Baron Marmose is already here? He beat us?*

Her hands curled into fists on the armrests, outraged that such a snake had outwitted them.

"In that case, I must speak with Queen Amelia immediately," Rangar snapped, heading for the door.

Declan blocked the doorway, holding out his hands. "Rangar, by the Saints! You're a king now, not some headstrong, backwater prince! Get control of yourself. You think my aunt will be responsive if you storm in making demands?"

Rangar stopped, though his chest still rose and fell heavily.

Phillipa added, "You know how much our aunt values decorum. She was fond of you and your brothers as boys but always thought you were too wild. You must show her you've grown into an honorable man."

"My honor has never been in question," Rangar snapped.

Declan rolled his eyes. "Perhaps not your honor, but your manners. Even *I* would question those. Look at you, my friend. You look like a woodsman who hasn't seen soap in weeks."

Bryn pushed herself to her feet and went to stand with Rangar. "They're right," she said in an exhausted voice. "You don't come from a kingdom that cares about manners, but I do. The Mirien and the Wollin are very traditional in our values. We must present ourselves graciously if we want to influence Queen Amelia."

Rangar's face betrayed his severe displeasure at the idea of manners.

Phillipa scoffed wryly, "There's the Barendur temper. No wonder they call you savages. Listen to your wife, Rangar. Now, come on, Declan. Let's leave them to get cleaned."

"We'll send up fresh clothes," Declan said. "And for the Saints' sake, comb your hair, Rangar."

Once the Hytooth cousins had left, Rangar stalked to the window. He muttered to Bryn, "It's ridiculous. Ceremony and tradition when the kingdoms are in danger."

Bryn touched a hand to Rangar's cheek. "Declan and Phillipa are only trying to help."

"They're trying to help *themselves*," Rangar growled. "While you and Phillipa were talking, I asked Declan about Queen Amelia's succession plans. He confided that she has not designated an heir. Declan, Phillipa, and about ten other cousins are all vying for the crown, and they want to use the grand parlay as an excuse to pressure her into naming her successor."

Bryn's eyebrows rose. "So, they think if they help us, we'll help them?"

Rangar nodded.

Bryn considered this as she gazed at the ocean, toying with the rings on her necklace. "An alliance isn't necessarily a bad thing. You trust Declan and Phillipa, don't you?"

"More than the other Hytooth cousins. Declan and Phillipa have an agreement between themselves. She supports his efforts to be named heir, and when he is the king of the Wollin, he will give her Ambrose Castle in the south."

Bryn squeezed Rangar's arm. "Then, if you believe Declan would make a good ruler, there is no reason not to support them and have their assistance in return. We can use all the help we can get if Baron Marmose is already here and speaking with Queen Amelia."

Servants soon arrived with their belongings, as well as water and soap to bathe themselves, and food and wine. Though Rangar was anxious to meet with Amelia, Bryn urged him to take his time. She stripped him of his dusty travel clothes and scrubbed his scarred body, then commanded him to eat and drink while she bathed herself.

He tore into a small loaf of herbed bread, watching her change into one of the dresses Phillipa had sent up.

"Lords and ladies, all these laces," Bryn muttered as she fumbled with strings. "How do Woll women function trussed up like cooked hens?"

Rangar took a swig of wine, his eyes on Bryn's bare décolleté as she fought the complicated dress. "You know, this *is* improving my mood, after all."

At his husky tone, she gave him an unamused look. "It's hardly the time for flirtation."

"You were the one who said we should rest. That I

should calm my temper." He leaned back in the chair, letting his gaze drip down her body. "You *know* how best to ease my tension."

She managed to tie the final lace and judged her success in the mirror, adjusting the intricate gown over her breasts. Once she was satisfied that she looked presentable, she came over and sat in Rangar's lap. Wrapping her arms around his back, she said teasingly, "I hardly think the queen will think us well-mannered if we arrive smelling of a recent rut."

Rangar adjusted his hips beneath her. "Then you need to stop talking about rutting, my sweet."

She plucked a date from the food tray and stuffed it into his mouth. "There. Let that satisfy your sweet tooth until after we've spoken to the queen."

He frowned as she climbed off his lap and pulled him to his feet. She brushed out his clothes—a crisp white shirt and dark blue trousers—and then unwrapped their crowns from their velvet coverings. She went to the mirror to place hers on top of her curls.

"There." She placed his crown atop his head next. "*Now* King Rangar of the Baersladen is ready to address another monarch."

At the direction of servants, they made their way through the spacious hallways of Hytooth Palace until they reached the library doors, propped open with small dolphin statues. Before they could enter, a tiny dog shot out into the hall, snarling at them.

Bryn sucked in a breath. "It's one of his," Bryn whispered to Rangar.

Rangar growled back at the dog.

More yapping came from inside the library, followed by a man's voice. "Daffodil, come back here!" The tiny dog yapping at Bryn's heels did a roundabout and charged back into the library.

Bryn steeled herself before entering. *That was Baron Marmose's voice—I'd recognize it anywhere.*

She felt Rangar tense beside her and rested a calming hand on his arm. "Remember," she whispered, "Decorum above all else."

His jaw tensed as they entered.

Hytooth Palace's library was a beautiful, airy space with a high ceiling and tall glass windows to protect the books from the ocean breeze. Thousands of tomes lined the walls, with worktables by the windows and a sitting area near an unlit fireplace.

Queen Amelia sat in a high-backed chair near the fireplace with a cup of tea. Her gray hair was piled in curls on top of her head in an attempt to hide its thinning volume. Her skin was as wrinkled as silk left too long in a trunk, and so thin that blue veins were visible in her hands.

Baron Marmose sat across from her, petting one of his lap dogs. He looked unchanged from when Bryn had last seen him many months ago, when he'd come to the Low Sun Gathering with the intention of proposing marriage. His dark skin and hair were in sharp contrast to his elegant white clothes with the thick cuffs typical of Rumese wealth. She had once considered him a handsome enough man, though he was ten years her senior with the start of graying hair, but now she only felt repulsion.

The queen and the baron looked up at the sound of their footsteps. Queen Amelia's eyes were cloudy and distant from age, but Marmose's sharp gaze skewered Rangar and Bryn.

What was the emotion that crossed his face? Surprise? Rage? Perhaps even the thrill of a challenge?

Queen Amelia raised her warbling voice as she squinted across the library. "Phillipa? Is that you?"

Snapping to her senses, Bryn straightened her spine. "Queen Amelia." She gave an exaggeratedly deep bow to ensure the old woman's eyesight would take in the movement. "I am Queen Bryn Barendur of the Baersladen, formerly Lady Bryn Lindane of the Mirien. We've had the pleasure of meeting before at my family's gatherings, though briefly. I'm with my husband, King Rangar Barendur of the Baersladen."

Queen Amelia perked up at Rangar's name. She set down her teacup with an unsteady hand and pushed slowly to her feet. She held out her hand. Bryn and Rangar hurried to her side so that Rangar could take her bony hand in his strong one. "Rangar Barendur? The brooding little boy who sulked around my palace that one summer in need of a hair comb?"

Bryn couldn't stop her laughter at the accuracy of that description, despite the presence of Marmose.

*Maybe the old queen's mind isn't as dull as everyone says.*

Rangar said in a rare warm tone, "The same, my queen. I remember that summer fondly. It is a pleasure to return and visit with you again."

A chill crept over Bryn's skin, coming from the direction of Baron Marmose. Breathing out a long exhale, she turned to face him.

He gave a flat, cruel smile. "Lady Bryn."

"*Queen* Bryn Barendur of the Baersladen," she corrected, then couldn't help but add smugly, "*Esquire* Marmose, is it?"

He gave a mirthless laugh at her dig. "Baron, actually. Not that I would expect you to remember. You've had so *many* fiancés in such a short amount of time. It must be hard for you to keep track."

Rangar, overhearing, rolled his shoulders back, but Bryn quickly rested a hand on his bicep to say she could handle the baron.

"Now, I'm afraid *you* are mistaken, baron." Bryn turned to Queen Amelia and raised her voice, though keeping her tone light. "The baron and I were never formally engaged, your highness, though I heard the strangest rumors that he claimed otherwise when I was the crown heir of the Miren." She feigned confusion. "I can't imagine where such awful rumors began. Someone must not like you, baron, to have accused you of such bald-faced ambition for the Mir crown."

Queen Amelia's brows furrowed, though Bryn couldn't tell if the woman had understood her veiled accusation or not. The queen patted Rangar's hand like he was still a boy instead of a towering warrior in a crown.

"And how was your journey, my dears? Where were you again, Declan?"

Bryn's hopes sank. The elderly queen *was* confused—she thought Rangar was her nephew, and the two looked nothing alike.

After a moment of hesitation, Rangar said, "It was a swift journey, my queen, though we were disheartened to hear of the growing berserkir wolf attacks."

The queen still looked distant and confused, and Baron Marmose took the opportunity to cut in. "Yes, as a matter of fact, Queen Amelia and I were just speaking of the monstrous wolf problem. You aren't the first people I've heard compare them to the berserkir beasts from the old legend."

"Yes," Bryn said tightly. "It's uncanny, almost as though someone planned it."

The baron cocked his head, his smug smile vanishing. He quickly recomposed himself and said, "In any case, Queen Amelia and I agree that dark magic is behind the attacks—and it must be stopped by any means necessary." He gave an exaggerated sigh. "I suspect there will soon be significant changes throughout the Eyrie. I hope you are happy with your hexmarks because, after the grand parlay, I doubt you'll be allowed to get any more."

Bryn narrowed her eyes as her heart pounded. That snake had gotten to the queen and already influenced her! Or at least, he seemed to think he'd won Amelia over to his side . . .

Queen Amelia suddenly tightened her grip on Rangar's arm as though she was faint. A servant standing at attention disappeared to fetch help, and in another moment, King Marthin arrived. He was a gray-haired, sallow-faced man with the habit of leaving his mouth hanging open.

"Amelia," he said in concern, then looked at Bryn. Rangar, and Baron Marmose as though he had no idea who these guests in his palace were. "Come, my wife; you must rest."

Servants moved to escort the queen out of the library, but as she shuffled away with her husband, Bryn felt a moment of panic.

"My queen!" she said, "If we could meet tomorrow, you and I . . . One queen to another . . ."

"I'm afraid she needs her rest before the grand parlay," King Marthin insisted. "But you are welcome to explore the palace. Oh! You must go into Senna and try the roasted octopus from the fish market—such delicate flavor and such a whimsical shape!"

Bryn's hopes sank for the second time in an hour. King Marthin seemed to possess every bit of the child-like mind she had been warned about.

*The queen better name a successor soon*, Bryn thought, *because Amelia and Marthin are already unsuited to rule.*

Baron Marmose stood, setting his lap dog on the rug, where it sniffed around while yapping with his other two dogs. He smiled smugly as he started out of the library.

"You know, I think I will try that octopus," he said languidly to Bryn and Rangar. "I have the time, you see. My work here is *already done*. I'll see you two at the grand parlay day after tomorrow, if our paths do not cross before."

Squeezing her hands into fists, Bryn had a hard time managing her temper as the baron strode out with his gaggle of dogs.

Rangar rested a hand on her shoulder. "We arrived too late," he whispered darkly.

"No," Bryn said through a clenched jaw. "I have an idea."

# CHAPTER 31

**BACON AND FIST FIGHTS . . . eavesdropping . . . Petal, Daffodil, Rosebud . . . wind hex . . . the hypocrite**

For the remainder of the day, Bryn and Rangar toured the palace and the seaside town of Senna with Declan and Phillipa while discussing strategy for the upcoming parlay. Since Baron Marmose had already seemed to draw Queen Amelia to his side, the fate of magic in the Eyrie was in dire jeopardy.

In the morning, Bryn went down to breakfast determined to speak with the queen, though King Marthin informed them that Amelia was spending the day alone in the library to rest.

"Yes, of course, she must save her energy," Bryn

said sympathetically. "Tomorrow, when the other royal families arrive, there will be much talk and excitement. It could easily drain her."

Next to her, Rangar was silent as he tore into his eggs and toast, but across the table, Baron Marmose *tsk*ed and said with a sarcastic edge, "How good of you to think of her health, Queen Bryn."

A dog, curled in his lap, tried to swipe a bite of sausage from the baron's plate. "Petal, no!" Marmose scolded as he set the dog on the floor with the others, muttering, "They're elite animals. I only feed them ground venison or turkey. It keeps their coats shiny and their spirits robust."

The little dogs yapped and begged for table scraps, but the baron shushed them.

Bryn eyed the dogs sniffing each other's backsides and hardly thought "elite" was the right word, whether they were purebloods or not. Quietly, she slipped a piece of her bacon into the napkin in her lap.

"And what will you two do today?" Baron Marmose asked Bryn and Rangar with a barbed tone. "Stroll the beaches again? An odd choice of pastimes when wolves are slaughtering your people. I myself plan to stay here at the palace, close to Queen Amelia, should she need anything."

The threat was clear—he didn't intend to give them a chance to speak to the queen alone.

Bryn clenched her jaw against the anger that rose in her throat. She nudged Rangar under the table when he looked ready to rip the baron's head off.

Forcing a smile, she said, "How good of you, baron. I thought I'd rest as well, as a matter of fact. The journey was tiring, and I, too, want to be prepared for the grand parlay. As you said yourself, people are dying. We owe the parlay our full attention." She slipped her napkin into the folds of her skirt. "If you'll excuse me, King Marthin?"

The king, whose attention was fixed on an ant crawling over the strawberries, barely glanced up. "Yes, yes, Queen Bryn."

Bryn stood and bent down to place a kiss on Rangar's cheek. She whispered, "Give me ten minutes. Then go."

He gave a slight nod.

She made a show of strolling in the tower's direction but then, once out of sight, doubled back to the grassy courtyard where the baron had been letting his lapdogs run freely. A fountain stocked with giant golden fish babbled beneath the palm trees. A small side door for servants' use led back to the breakfast room.

She pushed the door open a sliver and peeked inside to spy on what was happening. The door was tucked away behind a hanging tapestry that obscured the breakfast table, though she was able to overhear Rangar asking King Marthin about succession plans.

"Oh, Amelia won't speak of it," Marthin said. "She thinks the subject morbid."

Rangar pressed, "And yet chaos will reign if no successor is named. Nearly a dozen nieces and nephews have a possible claim to the Woll throne. If you do not want your family torn apart, you must make the decision soon. Declan is—"

She let Rangar's words fade away as she unwrapped the stolen bacon, then stooped to hands and knees. Marmose's lap dogs immediately took note of the smell and padded over to her, out of sight behind the tapestry.

"That's it," she whispered, waving the bacon in the air. "Just a little further, you rascals."

She lured the three dogs into the courtyard, shut the door, and parceled out the bacon. The greedy dogs scarfed it down, then happily scampered around the courtyard, swatting at the fish in the fountain.

Hands twisting anxiously, she paced beneath a palm tree, glancing through the breakfast room window every few minutes. It wasn't long before Rangar excused himself. Baron Marmose stood as well, clearly intending to ensure Rangar did not attempt to enter the library. But then he frowned and called to his dogs. When none of them answered, he rushed out of the room.

Rangar was able to slip quietly in the library's direction.

It wasn't long before Marmose strode into the courtyard. "Ah! Petal. Daffodil. Rosebud. How the devil did you—" When he saw Bryn, his face went rigid. "Oh. I see. I thought you were *resting*, my lady."

"I find a stroll very restorative. Apparently, so do your dogs."

"I'm sure you have no idea who let them out of the breakfast room."

She shrugged.

He sneered and started back inside, but she quickly called out, "I know about the speed-of-dogs hex."

He froze. He didn't move a single muscle for a second but then slowly pivoted around with pursed lips. His eyes searched hers as though judging how much she knew. In a flat tone, he said, "I've never heard of that."

She folded her arms, stalking toward him. "Oh no? That's strange, because I found a reference to a Rumese mage who learned how to enchant dogs to attack. The hex left them with black tongues. And the berserkir wolves we found? They also had black tongues. Quite the coincidence, don't you think?"

The baron's hands tightened to fists at his side. He sneered, "That isn't proof of anything. Look at my dogs. Sweet, harmless little things. They—and I— have nothing to do with vicious animal attacks."

"You also train the Cheron family's hunting dogs. *They* do hunt, and kill, and bite."

Marmose went quiet as he looked her over. They were alone in the courtyard, and the privacy must have emboldened him to step closer and say, "Is this why you arrived early? To tell Amelia about my supposed sins? To get her on your side?"

"Yes," Bryn said bluntly. "And you came early to do the same."

His smile turned uglier in triumph. "Perhaps, and

if that is the case, then I won. You were a day too late. Mark my words; the Wollin queen will side with Ruma during the grand parlay. Magic will be banned throughout the Eyrie. You and your husband's scheming is for naught."

Though her temper flared, she forced herself to remain calm. She knew confronting Marmose with her evidence was the only way to distract him long enough to keep him in the courtyard. So, she needed to provoke him more.

"We have the Baersladen, the Mirien, Vil-Kevi, and Vil-Rossengard on the side of magic," she challenged.

He scoffed. "And we have Ruma, Zaradona, Dresel, and now the Wollin on the side of reason. The two forest kingdoms are insignificant—as sister kingdoms, their votes only count as half."

She pretended to let out an audible curse. "Damn—I'd forgotten about that."

He smiled cruelly at her small show of vulnerability. Stalking toward her, he took his time looking her over like she was another one of his prize-winning dogs. "You made a mistake in marrying that wild prince. You should have married me."

She didn't have to pretend to be disgusted. "You? You wanted my sister, not me! I read your note to our mother on the night of the Low Sun Gathering!"

"Ah, so you feel slighted because Princess Elysander caught my eye. You can hardly blame me—she was the picture of refinement and elegance, and you were like a skittish colt that just wanted to skip around the pasture. But you've always been beautiful. I would have happily taken you as my wife, even if it meant training you to behave."

She let out an incredulous exhale at his audacity. "How *generous* of you. And I'm sure the fact that I became crown heir to the richest kingdom in the Eyrie played no part in your renewed insistence at an engagement?"

Holding out his hands, he said, "Every man wants to be king of a land like the Mirien. Especially a baron who has little chance of rising in station in his own kingdom. And you were a fool not to accept my offer."

"Well, as you said, I must be a fool, but at least I'm not fool enough to fall for *you*."

Angry now, the baron seized her arm. She tried to pull away, but he held her with a powerful grip. In a dangerously low voice, he said, "You cost me a throne, girl. Do not think that will go unpunished. Your parents intended for you to belong to me." Scouring his hot gaze down her body, he growled, "One way or another, I'll make sure that bargain is fulfilled."

She narrowed her eyes. As much as she wanted to knee him between his legs, she'd learned something from her interactions with men like him and like Captain Carr, who thought they could take anything they wanted.

Those kinds of men always had secrets.

She grabbed his shirt collar with her free hand and tugged hard as though trying to pull out of his grasp. He sneered and captured her around the waist, pinning her to his side. But she managed to rip off his top button, pulling the shirt partially over his shoulder.

She hissed in a breath when she saw the hexmarks there—just as she'd suspected.

"You rambunctious whore," the baron said, oblivious to her true aims, capturing her wrists in his hands. The skirmish seemed to stoke his passions. "So eager to get me unclothed, is that it?"

Seething, she spit on his cheek. "Let me go! I'm a queen!"

"Queen, whore, I don't care. You're still that same silly girl who didn't even know what was happening in her own kingdom—"

Fast steps sounded behind them, and then a wall of wind slammed into Marmose with enough strength to send him staggering backward. Bryn was able to stumble away as Rangar attacked again with another blast of the wind hex, one hand tracing the symbol in the air as his lips murmured the incantation.

"By the Saints, Rangar!" The baron shouted indignantly. "You dare use magic? Here, where it is banned? And against me, a staunch critic of its use?"

"You don't like magic?" Rangar said evenly, striding forward. "Fine. I don't need magic."

His fist slammed into Marmose's cheek. A garbled cry slipped out of the baron's lips. Rangar pulled his arm back for another swing, but Marmose scrambled a few steps away, holding out his hands. "You brute! You're as savage as they say!"

Rangar jabbed his finger like a dagger. "Touch my wife again, and I'll break off each of your fingers and feed them to your dogs, you deceitful fraud."

Rangar had at least seventy-five pounds of muscle on the baron. And though the baron was arrogant, he was also smart enough to realize that, too.

Clutching his bruised jaw, he narrowed his eyes. Turning to Bryn, he spat sharply, "Stay away from my dogs, *girl*." And he strode off as though he could pretend that the fight had merely been about bacon.

Rangar immediately pulled Bryn into his arms, touching her cheeks delicately in case she was hurt. "He had his hands on you."

"He didn't hurt me."

"I will kill him. I swear, I will."

"Shh." She kneaded her hands over his tight shoulders. "I provoked him intentionally. You know that was the plan."

Rangar briefly closed his eyes as he pressed his nose against her hair, breathing in her scent. "I don't care. I go mad when I see another man touching you."

"He's nothing."

"He almost married you!"

She cupped her hands on Rangar's cheeks, guiding him to look at her. "But he didn't. I married you, Rangar Barendur. You are my Savior, and I am yours. I have no such bond with any other man in the world, and I never will. Don't let your temper guide you. We always knew Marmose was a bastard. He's only proven it."

Rangar took a deep, shuddering breath as he tried to tame his rage.

Bryn stroked his scars gently, lowering her voice even further. "He's proven something else, too."

Rangar tilted his head. "What's that?"

"For all his talk against magic, he has hexmarks. A hypocrite just like Captain Carr was." She raised her eyebrows meaningfully. "But most importantly, he has an *influence* hex."

# CHAPTER 32

**EIGHT ROYAL FAMILIES . . . a mage to battle a mage . . . tense meetings . . . High Priest Red . . . a young queen**

Back in the privacy of their bedroom in Hytooth Palace's tower, Rangar reported what he'd discovered while Bryn was distracting Baron Marmose.

"I found Queen Amelia in the library," he informed her. "She was just as disoriented as before. When I spent the summer here as a boy, her mind was already dulling, but this felt different. Less like a slipping mind and more like an *influenced* one. She recalled everything about me with uncanny detail but refused to speak of the present situation in the Eyrie. When I pressed her about supporting a free magic society, she repeated the same phrase: *Magic is killing our people.*"

Bryn's lips pressed together grimly. "Marmose must have cast an influence spell over her. That's why she's siding with him so staunchly. And why the baron seemed so confident."

Rangar nodded.

Bryn muttered a curse as she paced the length of the bedroom. "Do you know how to break an influence spell?"

He shook his head regretfully.

"Are there mages in Hytooth Palace with whom we could consult?"

"As far as I know, there aren't any official mages in all of the Wollin. Magic is technically forbidden here, though the Hytooths do not prosecute anyone found using it."

Bryn groaned as she leaned against the windowsill. Outside, a cool breeze rolled off the ocean. She hugged her arms and said worriedly, "Then we'll have to wait for Illiana to arrive. If any magic caster knows how to break such a spell, it will be her."

Hytooth Palace crackled with tension the rest of the day and into the morning, though King Marthin and Queen Amelia appeared too distracted to notice it. Baron Marmose kept his dogs locked in his room and scowled at Bryn and Rangar every chance he got, who in turn, kept their distance and made sure to keep knives on their bodies.

More Hytooth cousins arrived early in the morning, making Declan and Phillipa nervous. Though everyone was outwardly cordial, it was clear the cousins were ready to fight tooth and nail amongst themselves to determine who would succeed Queen Amelia.

In the late afternoon, a servant came to Bryn and Rangar's room. "Begging your pardon, my king and queen, but Declan asked me to inform you that the other royal families have begun to arrive."

Bryn exchanged a knowing look with Rangar. They had already dressed in elegant finery for the occasion, including donning their crowns to make a powerful first impression.

Rangar peered out the window at the courtyard below. "It's the Greys, judging by their carriage colors."

Bryn joined him and watched as wizened old King Angus Grey of Dresel climbed out of his carriage with significant effort, followed by his scandalously young wife, Queen Hanna Grey, who couldn't be more than sixteen years old. Their clothes were rich white fabrics draped around them like robes, in keeping with the arid style of the southern portion of their kingdom.

"Do you know them?" Rangar asked.

"Only by reputation," Bryn answered. "They never came to the Mirien, but they sent Duke Dryden to court Elysander as a means of allying our two kingdoms. According to the duke, the Greys do not share our sentiments about a free magic society."

"So, we cannot rely on them," Rangar said regretfully. "I had hoped Duke Dryden had perhaps influenced them to our cause."

"There's a reason the duke turned to banditry to help the Dresel common folk. Dresel's own monarchs won't lift a finger to help them."

As the Greys entered the palace, greeted by Phillipa, a sentry blew a trumpet to announce the arrival of another royal carriage. Bryn and Rangar waited until a crimson-painted carriage with iron bars on its windows pulled up.

"King Salvator Surin of Zaradona," Rangar said distastefully. "He's even more dogmatic in his hatred of magic than the Greys. He's a widower, never remarried."

A tall, thin man with dark hair, despite his advanced age, climbed gracefully out of the carriage and made the sign of prayer against his chest. Behind him, another man emerged. Dressed in a red robe, the second man wasn't much older than Rangar, but he had a graveness that instantly set Bryn's nerves on edge.

"Who is that?" she asked.

"High Priest Felisian Red. King Salvator travels everywhere with him. He insists he needs the priest's heavenly blessings five times a day, but it's no coincidence Felisian Red is a skilled warrior as well as a priest."

Bryn raised her eyebrows. "A bodyguard, you mean." She took a deep breath before grumbling, "I suppose we should greet the new arrivals."

The Hytooths had arranged for all the royal delegations to meet in the library after settling in, and while the Greys took the time to bathe and change, King Salvator and High Priest Red did not change out of their dusty, rumpled travel clothes. Bryn was surprised to find them already in the library, standing stiffly by the fireplace with Baron Marmose.

They'd been whispering among one another but stopped when she and Rangar entered.

Sensing the tension, Declan immediately jumped up. "Ah, King Rangar and Queen Bryn. It's my honor to introduce you to King Salvator Surin of Zaradona and—"

"Yes, we're acquainted," Rangar cut him off. "High Priest Red. We trained together as boys for a time in Vil-Kevi."

The priest gave a slow nod, though a sour look crossed his face. "Ah, yes, I'd almost forgotten. My soldiering days are so far behind me."

"Yes, I was surprised to hear you were now a devotee of the Saints. Back then, you certainly didn't say no to wine and women—"

"Queen Bryn." King Salvator interrupted Rangar and whatever incriminating information he was about to reveal. "What a pleasure to meet you. I knew your parents well. Devout servants of the Saints. May the Saints keep their souls."

Bryn bristled. Only a fellow zealot would dare to compliment her despotic parents' former reign. "May the Saints keep their souls," she repeated tightly.

Tensions hung in the air until the doors swung open, and the Greys entered. Old King Angus leaned on his young wife's arm, his eyes as cloudy with cataracts as Queen Amelia's. Queen Hanna helped her elderly husband down to the sofa, then beamed in relief to see Bryn.

"Queen Bryn!" she said, rushing over to clasp Bryn's hand. "I've been so looking forward to meeting you." She glanced among the older men and said more quietly, "Another young woman is a welcome sight."

Bryn's heart went out to the young queen. Bryn had escaped the fate of marrying a much older man, but Hanna hadn't been as fortunate. She warmly squeezed the girl's hands while she wondered if they could use Queen Hanna's naiveté to their advantage. If Hanna held sway over her husband, perhaps she could whisper in his ear about magic . . .

"Indeed," Bryn said with sincere kindness. "I hope the two of us have a chance to get well acquainted while here. I want to know all about Dresel. You know, my sister now lives there, married to Duke Dryden."

"Yes, of course! Elysander and Duke Dryden rarely come to court, but it's always such a pleasure when they do. And I'm dying to hear about your adventures! It's been the talk of high society ever since the siege on Castle Mir!"

Bryn chatted more with Hanna while quietly

trying to feel out the girl's personal sentiments regarding magic, while Rangar and Declan went to the whiskey cart and started pouring themselves drams. The delegation from Zaradona remained by the fireplace, looking stiff and uncomfortable.

"Announcing King Mars and Queen Illiana of the Mirien!" a servant announced from the library doorway.

Bryn practically squeaked as she pivoted to find her brother and Illiana stepping into the library, looking dazzling in a golden suit and gown, with their glistening jeweled crowns freshly polished. They, too, had clearly wanted to make a powerful first impression.

"Mars!" Bryn threw her arms around her brother, who grinned beneath his golden blindfold and hugged her close.

"Mouse." He pressed a kiss to the top of her head.

Bryn greeted Illiana next while Rangar came over to speak to Mars. Out of the corner of her eye, Bryn noticed the cold looks King Salvator and High Priest Red exchanged with Baron Marmose.

Under the scrutiny of so many eyes, Bryn could hardly speak openly with Mars and Illiana about Marmose's influence hexmark that she'd discovered. Limiting her conversation to the weather and bland exclamations of distress over the berserkir wolf attacks was painful.

Later that afternoon, the two forest kingdom delegations arrived in unison. King Hans Viklund and

Queen Karin Viklund from Vil-Rossengard entered in forest green wool clothing with their long dark hair in matching braids, and just behind them, Prince Anter Jarkkinen with his father, King Otto.

Bryn was relieved to have their allies finally present. Prince Anter caught her eye and strode over, giving her a deep bow. "Queen Bryn. It does one good after a long journey to be in the company of friends."

"I feel the same, Prince Anter." Her gaze shifted briefly to Baron Marmose and the delegates from Dresel and Zaradona. Lowering her voice, she said, "Tonight, after the welcome banquet, meet us on the beach, just south of the palace wall."

"The beach?"

"Easier to ensure we aren't being overheard in a wide-open space."

The delegates engaged in polite yet tense chatter as the sun began to drop, when their hosts finally joined them. Queen Amelia and King Marthin, arm in arm, entered the library.

"Friends from across the Eyrie," Marthin announced. "We are honored by your presence. We've received word that the final delegation from Ruma has been delayed. They will join us tomorrow morning just before the grand parlay begins. In the meantime, our chefs have prepared a welcome feast to showcase the Wollin's oceanic bounty. Please, join us in the banquet hall."

The formal speech seemed to have strained King Marthin's diplomatic abilities because a servant had to come and lead him off toward the banquet. Bryn kept her attention on Queen Amelia, however. The elderly woman had a dazed, distant look, and when Prince Anter approached her to thank her for housing them, she seemed not to know who he was.

The banquet was just as strained as the conversations in the library had been. While servants brought them course after course of grilled fish, fresh oysters, and seafood stew—with ample wine between each course—everyone seemed reluctant to speak, saving their words for the grand parlay the following day.

As soon as the final course was set out, Queen Amelia started mumbling something under her breath. Bryn, seated three chairs away, leaned in. She thought she'd heard the word "hex."

"What was that, my queen?" she asked.

Baron Marmose, at the far end of the table, snapped sharply, "Queen Amelia looks taxed. We've worn her out with our arrivals."

King Marthin, who'd been entirely focused on his stew for the last half hour, blinked in surprise. "Oh, yes. You there, the butler. Help her."

Two staff hurried over to help the queen to her feet.

"Wait," Bryn started, but Rangar rested a hand over hers. He silently shook his head. She closed her mouth and threw a scowl in Baron Marmose's direction.

"If you'll excuse us," King Marthin said, dabbing his mouth. "We wish to be rested before the grand parlay tomorrow. It will begin at noon in the library. No blades, no weapons. The same rules as any parlay."

King Salvator of Zaradona cleared his throat. "And *no magic*, I believe the rules stipulate, isn't that so, King Marthin?"

"Ah, yes, of course. That as well."

Once their hosts had departed, the delegations took their leave one at a time, all claiming the same desire to rest after the long journeys, though Bryn knew that the night would be filled with long, secretive meetings, scheming sessions, and perhaps even the threat of violence.

She and Rangar also claimed they were retiring early, though once they were in their room, Rangar shed his formal clothes and dressed in simple breeches and a tunic top. He strapped a short sword to his side.

Bryn went to the window, looking out at the last rays of the sinking sun over the horizon. "Were you able to speak privately to Mars and Illiana?"

"Yes, they're meeting us on the beach at first star's appearance. Prince Anter?"

Bryn nodded. "He'll be there, too."

"Good. He speaks for both Vil-Kevi and Vil-Rossengard."

Bryn changed into a less formal gown; her movements distracted. "And if we're overseen conspiring out in the open?"

Rangar gave a dismissive shrug as he laced his boots. "It isn't a conspiracy if it's in the open, is it?

You're merely meeting with your beloved brother and his wife. And Anter is an old friend."

"No one would ever believe that."

"It doesn't matter. As long as we aren't overheard, no one will be able to prove a conspiracy. Besides, don't you think the families of Zaradona, Dresel, and Ruma are also meeting tonight in secret?"

They waited until the servants lowered the lanterns throughout the palace, then pretended they were going for a romantic walk along the secluded section of beach reserved only for palace officials. The first star appeared overhead as they reached the southern wall that divided the palace beach from Serra's beach, open to common folk and fishermen.

The ruins of an old sandstone chapel marked the palace's end. Bryn settled on a broken pillar, hugging her arms against the cool breeze. The tide was coming in, lapping at her shoes. She kicked them off and let her toes dangle in the water.

"This feels nice. The Baer Sea is always too cold for wading," she observed.

"For a Mir princess, perhaps," Rangar teased lightly, a rare break in the evening's tense mood. "Not for a Baer queen. You still have some toughening up to do."

Bryn made a face at the idea of wading in frigid water.

A lantern appeared at the far end of the beach, and Bryn went silent. She'd been expecting Mars, Illiana, and Anter, but only one solo person walked toward them, a shadow in the moonlight.

"Who is that?" Bryn asked. "It's a woman in a dress, but she's too tall to be Illiana."

Rangar rested a hand on his sword. "Take care," he warned. "I feared one of our enemies might take this chance to try to move against us before the grand parlay."

But as the woman approached, her features began to take shape in the light of her lantern. Bryn's eyes went wide. She shoved up from the broken pillar, feet splashing in the surf.

Crying out in joy, she ran forward toward the stranger with Rangar calling after her.

# CHAPTER 33

**THE BEACH AT NIGHT . . . a secret rendezvous . . .
three siblings . . . a risky new spell . . . body
and soul**

"Elysander!" Bryn cried, kicking up the surf as she splashed toward her sister. She threw her arms around the taller woman with such vigor that they both nearly crashed into the sea.

Regaining her balance, Elysander let out a scolding laugh. "Bryn! I don't fancy being soaked tonight!"

Rangar jogged up behind Bryn, lowering his hand from his sword hilt. "Lady Elysander? We had no fore-warning of your arrival."

"I came unannounced," Elysander said, motioning to the colorful Wollin-style scarf covering her hair to disguise her as a Woll noblewoman. "I'm staying in Senna with an innkeeper who has previously worked with some of Jon's associates."

"You got Valenden's message?" Bryn said, proud of Valenden for coming through for them.

Elysander nodded. "He rode to the Dresel border to find us. Once we heard of the situation, Jon and our bandits spread out along the border between the Baersladen and the Mirien, helping villages fight off the berserkir wolves. I was with them for some time. The attacks are brutal. Many have died. And the berserkir wolves are getting smarter—they've learned to evade many of our traps. Then Valenden notified us about the grand parlay, and I left the bandits to deal with the wolves and came here on my own to help."

"King and Queen Grey of Dresel are here."

Elysander nodded. "The Greys must not learn that I am here. As a duchess in their kingdom, they would question my presence. It could cast suspicion on Jon and me. We've worked hard not to reveal ourselves as supporters of a free magical society. Magic is still strictly forbidden in Dresel."

Sand crunched not far away, and Rangar's hand again shot to his sword hilt, but this time the three figures striding down the beach were recognizable. Mars, guided by Illiana, joined them at the chapel ruins along with Prince Anter.

Illiana squeezed Mars's arm and informed him, "Your sister is here, Mars!"

"Bryn," Mars said, reaching out his hand.

Illiana squeezed his arm again. "Yes, Bryn and Rangar are here, but so is—"

"*Elysander?*" Mars finished the sentence with a voice that rose in hope.

Elysander clasped Mars's outstretched hand. Her eyes scoured his face from the blindfold to his gaunt frame. "Brother. By the Saints, you have no idea how happy I was to hear you weren't dead!"

They embraced, and Mars reached out another hand. "Bryn? Bryn, come here. It's finally the three of us together again!"

Bryn broke away from Rangar to join her siblings in the embrace. The rising tide splashed at their feet, but none seemed to care. It had been many long months since the three Lindane siblings had last been together. Their parents had been slaughtered. Their kingdom usurped. Elysander had narrowly escaped the coffin herself, and Mars had faked his own death.

But they were together now, at last.

Tears dampened Bryn's eyes as she thought of everything her siblings and she had endured. And now here they were, no longer children. Mars was king of the richest land in the Eyrie, intending to permit magic to aid the common folk. Elysander lived a daring double life as a Dresel duchess *and* the Forest King, leader of a bandit troupe. And Bryn herself was queen of the Baersladen, a place she could finally call home.

*We've come so far.*

After the reunion, Prince Anter cleared his throat. "Friends, we must discuss the plan for tomorrow."

Bryn's elevated mood dipped at the prospect of the grand parlay. She said, "Rangar and I have made several discoveries regarding the wolf attacks, information we didn't dare reveal except in person. I learned that the wolves mimic a legend—the berserkir beasts—that exists in some form within all the cultures of the Eyrie. The wolves also have black tongues, which harkens back to an ancient spell used by a dark Rumese mage named Zinder, who used a spell called the 'speed-of-dogs' to create vicious hunting dogs."

"It is our belief," Rangar continued, "That the Cheron royal family in Ruma, likely in league with the leaders of Zaradona and Dresel, employed Baron Marmose to modify the speed-of-dogs spell on wolves to create the berserkirs. They then released these wolves in the northern Eyrie region, knowing every kingdom would link the monstrous wolves to the old berserkir legend, and thus intuit dark magic was involved. They did it to sew fear of magic. It's no coincidence the wolf attacks began right after Mars's announcement to permit magic in the Mirien."

Prince Anter let out a curse. Pacing in the sand, he said, "You brought this proof with you?"

Bryn nodded. "I have the books as well as a verbal confession from Marmose, though it's his word against mine."

Anter rested his hands on his hips. "So, we confront them tomorrow at the grand parlay with irrefutable evidence."

"It isn't that simple," Rangar said. "Even if the evidence is clear, Zaradona and Dresel will still side with Ruma."

"There is still the Wollin," Anter argued. "Since Vil-Kevi and Vil-Rossengard each count as half a vote, that makes three kingdoms in support of magic, three against it. The Wollin is the deciding vote. Queen Amelia's mind isn't so far gone that she will ignore clear proof."

Bryn shook her head sadly. "I'm afraid that's exactly what will happen, but it isn't because of her advanced age."

She explained what she and Rangar had discovered about Baron Marmose using an influence hex on Queen Amelia.

Once she had finished, she turned to Illiana. "There must be some way to break the influence hex."

Illiana's mouth remained firmed in deep thought. "There is, but only the original caster can break it, and I doubt you can convince Marmose to do so."

Bryn paced in the surf. "And there is no other way?"

"The influence hex will fade in time, but not before tomorrow. A spell of that nature usually lasts at least three days. Given the queen's weakened mind, it will likely last longer on her. Perhaps a week or more."

"We could attempt to delay the parlay," Mars suggested.

Prince Anter shook his head. "A day, maybe. But the royal families would never agree to an additional week away from their kingdoms. Besides, Baron Marmose might simply extend the spell."

Bryn continued to pace in the surf, letting the steady waves lull her mind into a calm place where she could think through their problem. If they couldn't break the hex, then what could they do? She realized she was absent-mindedly stroking the death slumber hex on the side of her chest. She went still in the water.

"What if . . . what if we fight the hex with another hex?" she asked slowly.

All eyes turned to her. Rangar lifted his chin. "What do you have in mind?"

Wetting her lips, she said, "We could also use a hex on Queen Amelia. Something stronger than the baron's influence hex. He isn't a powerful mage. He's just a basic caster with a few hexmarks."

"A stronger influence hex?" Elysander asked.

Bryn nodded. "That's what I was thinking. Illiana, does such a hexmark exist?"

Illiana began to shake her head, but then her eyes drifted off and to the left. Her lips moved silently as she seemed to think through possibilities. Then, she finally took a quaking break. "Not exactly," she said slowly. "There aren't degrees of influence hexes. It wouldn't be possible to cast a stronger one on the queen; however, I do think Bryn is onto something. There *is* a powerful hex that's been kept secret in my family for many generations of witches. It isn't known widely, so I doubt even a skilled mage would recognize it if they saw it. It would be risky, but it might work."

"What hex is that?" Bryn asked apprehensively.

Illiana looked equally nervous as she said, "A possession hex."

The small group fell silent. The waves crashed as the night wind rustled around them. Finally, Rangar said, "As I understood it, possession hexes were impossible."

"As I said, it's a family secret. My great-grand-mother apprenticed for a mage in one of the lands south of the Great Desert. Their magic is different there. Darker. More powerful."

Bryn's hands suddenly felt sticky from salt water, but the sensation didn't go away no matter how often she wiped them on her dress. She said in a hollowed voice, "How do you envision it working?"

"I know the hexmark's shape and wording," Illiana explained, "Though I've never attempted to carve it before. Still, I believe I can do it. Whoever receives the hexmark will be able to transport their spirit into the body of the first person they see after receiving the mark. They'll wear that person's body like a set of clothes. Speak with their voice, move with their hands."

"So whoever possesses Queen Amelia will make

her support the side of magic when it comes to the vote, just like controlling a puppet," Rangar said.

"Exactly," Illiana said.

"But who will receive the hexmark?" Anter asked.

No one voiced an immediate answer to this, but Bryn felt a stirring in her blood. She was still in her magic apprenticeship with Mage Marna, yet she'd gained much skill in the past few months. She announced, I will."

Rangar's gaze shot to hers. "The hell you will. It's too risky."

"We have no choice," she argued forcefully. "For better or worse, it's the men in the Eyrie who rule. Kings sign their names to a vote, not queens. As king of the Baersladen, you *must* be at the grand parlay. The same goes for you, Mars. And you, Anter."

"My father is the king of Vil-Kevi, not me," Anter said.

"Yes, but you hold the trust of the Viklund family of Vil-Rossengard. If you are not present at the parlay, they will not form a consensus." She motioned to the others. "Illiana cannot perform the possession, as a mage cannot carve a mark upon herself. And Elysander has no magic skill. It has to be me."

"You do not have this particular skill either," Rangar pointed out. "You've never done this hex before."

"I performed the death slumber hex. I can do this one, too."

"Won't everyone wonder at your absence, Bryn?" Elysander said in concern.

"I'll claim to be unwell. Raw oysters are known to cause upset stomachs, and they've served them at every damn meal."

Rangar looked ready to argue again, but as he cast his gaze around the gathered group, he seemed to realize Bryn was right. He rolled his shoulders back, then tightened his jaw. "If I agree to let you do this," he said, "I need to ensure you're entirely safe the whole time. Both your body *and* your spirit."

"I can guard her body," Elysander offered. "I'll disguise myself as a healer and stay in her room with her body, pretending to help her recover from her illness."

"And the rest of us will be at the grand parlay with Queen Amelia," Mars said. "With Bryn's spirit inside the queen, we will be diligent about her safety."

Rangar still didn't look convinced. He paced in the sand, then took Bryn's arm and hauled her a few steps away. Beneath the stars twinkling overhead, he asked, "I've only just taken you for my wife. I swore I wouldn't risk anything to lose you again."

She touched his cheek. "Whether in this body or another, Rangar Barendur, my spirit will always belong to you."

"And if you get trapped inside a ninety-year-old woman's body?"

"Hmm. Then you'll have to be gentler with your kisses."

He growled low at her teasing remark and pressed their foreheads together. "I would love you in any body, my love, but I'm quite particular to *this* one."

He tilted his head so their lips touched. They kissed beneath the glittering stars and swaying palms, and Bryn wondered if this would be the last time she kissed Rangar Barendur with her own lips.

# CHAPTER 34

**A DARK RITUAL . . . blindfolds and blood . . . no longer soulbound . . . five casters . . . auras**

"There's one more thing," Illiana said to the group gathered on the dark beach. "The possession spell is too powerful for any one caster to perform. It requires the amplifier hex and at least five casters. Among us, we only have me, Rangar, and Anter. We need two more."

"Two more who must be of the utmost trustworthiness," Rangar emphasized.

"My father will assist," Anter said. "That leaves the Viklunds of Vil-Rossengard as the only other possible casters: King Hans or Queen Karin."

"I am not well acquainted with either," Mars said. "Which does not incline me to trust them."

"I don't know that we have a choice," Anter said. "Of the two, Queen Karin is more skilled with magic. She was an apprentice mage before marrying Hans."

"Ask her, then," Bryn declared. "It's a risk we'll have to take. The parlay begins at noon tomorrow, so we'll need to perform the spell tonight. Let us return to our rooms and feign going to sleep; after the final servants have gone to bed, sneak out and come to my chamber. Elysander, you'll need to disguise yourself as a healer."

Elysander nodded. "I can steal a healer's uniform from the palace laundry."

The group returned to the palace solo or in couples to dispel any rumors that they'd been conspiring. Back in their bedroom, Bryn shed her dress with its soaked, sandy hem and slid on a white robe.

Once Rangar had changed, he sat on the bed and pulled her into his lap. Circling her waist with one hand, he combed the other through her loose hair. With concern in his eyes, he said, "I don't like this idea."

"Illiana is a skilled witch. Her ability rivals even Mage Marna's."

His thumb grazed her bottom lip, then her chin, as though sealing every detail of her face into his memory. "Yet it is an unknown hex. Granting you the ability to possess Queen Amelia's body is only the first half of the challenge—Illiana will still have to bring you back to your own body."

Bryn shifted on Rangar's lap until she could slide

her hands around his shoulders. Looking him squarely in the eye, she said, "I promise you, Rangar, that by this time tomorrow, we'll be sitting like this again. You in your body, and I in mine."

His eyelids dropped slightly. "I'd rather have you under me, if I'm being honest."

A smile curled on her lips. She kissed him softly, but as fire stoked in her body, it grew more insistent. Rangar gripped the back of her skull and seemed ready to guide her down to the bed when a soft knock came at the door.

"Damn the gods," he muttered, then kissed her harder and faster before breaking away. "Come in."

Illiana entered with a basket of supplies. She began clearing the dining table of their leftover dishes.

"Mars is staying behind in our room," she said. "He's going to make a loud trip to the latrines in about an hour, so it doesn't seem like all our rooms are suspiciously quiet. Now, Bryn, it's best to lay on the floor, so any spilled blood is easy to clean up. I'll use this table for my tools."

While Rangar helped Illiana clear the table, the door opened again. This time, Elysander slipped in. She'd covered her hair with a white scarf and wore the black uniform and gray apron of a healer. She clutched a basket of oranges.

She motioned to the fruit. "I took these from the kitchen. They're supposed to be good for an upset stomach. If anyone comes to check on Bryn, I'll say we need more and send them to the kitchen to get them out of the way."

They made a makeshift bed for Bryn on the floor atop a sheet, and then Illiana handed Bryn a vial. "Drink this. It will help put your mind into a trance. You'll experience strange sensations until your spirit is back in your own body."

As she took the vial, Bryn was reminded of the first time she'd undergone a hexmark carving. Rangar had forbidden her from getting the translation hex, as the spell was untested. Yet she'd gone through with it anyway on the rooftop of Barendur Hold, held down by apprentices, wild visions coming to her from Mage Marna's potion.

She lifted the vial to her lips, but Illiana said, "Wait. One more thing. You'll need a blindfold. Amelia must be the first person you see after receiving the hex. You could possess the wrong person if you see anyone but her." She pulled one of Mars's black silk blindfolds from her pocket and fastened it around Bryn's head.

Someone rapped gently on the door. Rangar's footsteps crossed to let them in. "Anter. King Otto. Queen Karin. Thank you for coming."

Blindfolded, Bryn could not see their company, but she listened carefully for the sounds of their rustling clothes and gave them a nod.

*I can only imagine how Mars feels like this all the time.*

"It's a bold plan," a man's voice said that could

only be King Otto. "We were always led to believe possession was beyond the bounds of magic."

"In the Mirien," Illiana explained, "Magic has been forbidden so long that we weren't able to study the traditional magical masters. We've had to develop our own spells. It's given rise to some hexes no one thought possible."

"And you consent to this, Lady Bryn?" a woman said. It had to be Queen Karin.

Bryn gave a slow nod. "I do."

"We should hurry now that we're all here," Illiana said. "Elysander, you keep watch by the door. Bryn, come. Lay down on the sheet."

Illiana and Rangar helped Bryn down to the sheet, where she lay on her stomach. Illiana unbuttoned the buttons along the back of her dress and smoothed the fabric away from her skin.

"The possession hex requires full use of the caster's back," Illiana said. "It's fortunate that Bryn's back is not yet covered with hexmarks—it would make getting the positioning all the more challenging."

Bryn felt Illiana's confident fingers moving over her back, tracing the shapes she was about to carve. Whatever potion was in the vial was starting to work. Bryn could feel her muscles unwind, and her mind started to float off. She mentally snagged her thoughts, holding them close.

*Don't drift off yet.*

"The hex involves five cuts at these intervals." Illiana pressed her finger on Bryn's shoulder blades, at the base of her neck, and the bottom of each ribcage. "I'll ask each of you to take a place by a mark, then link hands and repeat these words: *Mann desta ka.*"

The skin on Bryn's back prickled in anticipation. Even with the blindfold on, she found herself squeezing her eyes shut. No matter how many hexmarks she received, each one would always feel unpredictable and risky.

She heard the slick ring of a blade as Illiana unsheathed a knife. "Ready, Bryn?"

Bryn swallowed down a hard lump. "Do it."

Whispering a spell under her breath, Illiana pressed the blade to Bryn's left shoulder blade. Pain seared into her skin as Illiana made the first cut, then moved on to the right shoulder blade. As soon as it was done, Prince Anter took up a position by her left side, chanting the possession incantation. When Illiana finished with the second cut and moved on to the one at the base of her right ribcage, Queen Karin took up her position. The queen's voice rang with her heavy accent.

Three cuts.

Then four.

Bryn gritted her teeth against the pain. These cuts felt longer and deeper than any she'd received before, and with each subsequent jab, her mind wanted to drift further away from her body. Already, she was having trouble keeping her attention on the present. Her spirit wanted to run from the pain, run far away . . . and yet it also craved seeking something new.

*Someone* new.

Finally, Illiana moved to the final cut at the base of Bryn's neck. She moved the hair aside again and made the cut. Bryn sucked in a gasp as lines of tingles ran between the five hexmarks making up the possession hex. Her whole back throbbed in a way that went beyond mere pain: it was as though a part of her was trying to claw its way out from the cuts.

The knife clattered as Illiana tossed it aside. "Everyone, hurry. The spell."

All five voices rose in unison.

*"Mann desta ka."*

*"Mann desta ka."*

*"Mann desta ka."*

*"Mann desta ka."*

*"Mann desta ka."*

Bryn's body began to shake uncontrollably. She was aware of it happening, but it felt like it wasn't *her* body. Her spirit felt like it was floating somewhere up near the ceiling, looking down at the five amplifier casters through the black shadow of the blindfold. Yet a small part of her still felt tethered to her body as though by a cord.

"Bryn." Rangar pressed a gentle hand to her shoulder once the recitation was finished. "Can you hear me?"

*I can hear you,* she tried to say but found it didn't quite come out. Watching in that hazy dark light from above, she looked down on Rangar inclined over her body. Her body's lips only murmured a garbled few sounds.

"What's wrong with her?" Rangar snapped.

"Her spirit is separating," Illiana explained. "It's exactly what is supposed to happen. But we must get her to Queen Amelia soon, or else we risk her spirit finding a different body to settle into."

Through the dark clouds, Bryn was shocked to see how much blood was pouring out of her body. Illiana quickly bandaged what she could and applied an herbal poultice, then buttoned up Bryn's dress.

She started to pick up the bloody sheets, but Elysander said, "Go. Take Bryn to Queen Amelia. I'll burn the bloody sheets in the fireplace."

Floating near the ceiling, Bryn watched through the fog as Rangar helped her body to its feet. Her body moved strangely, as though it was drunk or gravely ill. The tether that connected her to it tugged slightly as her body took each shuffling step.

"I'll take her to the queen," Rangar said, urgency in his voice. "The rest of you should return to your rooms. Speak nothing of this."

Prince Anter and his father left, but Queen Karin remained a moment longer, eyes wide as she took in Bryn's nearly-comatose body. "Remarkable."

And then Bryn felt the tether tug more as Rangar guided her body out of the room, and Queen Karin and Illiana and Elysander were left behind. Rangar guided her body into the dark hallway, lit only by a few thick pillar candles.

"All will be well, my love," he reassured in her ear, but it was Bryn's spirit floating above that heard it. In this strange between-body form, she could perceive more than just his words. Rangar was giving off a fiercely protective energy that radiated from his body like the cool blue light of a flame. His thoughts were a scramble flitting around his head: he was concerned for her, he was worried about too many people being involved in the possession hex, he was on alert for any servants who might pass by.

But most of all, she felt his love. It was like a glowing, rainbow-colored blanket of light wrapped around her, protective and all-encompassing, touching every part of her. Her spirit gasped to see something so beautiful.

"I promise you will survive this," Rangar said to her body as he steered her down the wing that contained Queen Amelia's bedroom. "I believe in fate enough for the both of us."

Because they were already in the royal residence wing, fewer guards were posted here. Rangar was able to stick to the shadows and move silently enough not to alert the guards' attention.

Queen Amelia's room had been left open in keeping with Woll tradition; doors and windows of the ailing had to remain open to allow in healing blessings from the Saints. Rangar half-led, half-carried Bryn's body into the dark bedroom.

Drifting along in that foggy darkness overhead,

Bryn saw the queen lying on her four-poster bed. Queen Amelia looked even frailer in her slumber, like a single gust from the open window might turn her pale skin into dust. The queen's aura was weak, too: a faint sea-green light creeping over her body like wooly worms, filled with holes and weak spots from her illness. Was this what a sick person's aura looked like? Did Mage Marna, with her ability to see auras, always see the world like this?

And yet there was a second aura glowing around the old queen: a deep crimson red light pulsing out into the dark bedroom.

*That crimson beam is Baron Marmose's influence hex,* she realized.

And then, while she was still marveling over the queen's multi-hued, layered auras, she saw Rangar untie the silk blindfold from her body's eyes.

Her body looked at Queen Amelia.

Throughout her spirit, Bryn felt a jolt like a strong wave had struck her.

As then, as though sucked into a whirlpool, Bryn's spirit was yanked down by the tether through the dark fog and through the queen's aura light—into the queen's body.

She gasped, struggling for breath. Her body felt both too heavy and too light. Old, chronic pain sank into her bones. Her back ached. Her teeth didn't fit together right in her jaw. She felt a rustle, then a sigh, and then something like a lock slid into place.

Bryn opened her eyes and looked up at the queen's bedroom ceiling.

Her spirit was in a body again—but not her own.

# CHAPTER 35

**FOREIGN BODIES . . . a soft-minded king . . . a weak-bodied queen . . . an iron resolve**

*The rustle, the sigh, the lock.*

Those were the first sensations Bryn experienced as Queen Amelia's own spirit sank into a deeper place of stasis, while Bryn's spirit moved into dominant control of the old woman's body. Now, Bryn blinked into the dark room as her thoughts scrambled. The queen's vision was poor, and the room looked blurry. Amelia's body was so painfully frail that Bryn feared even sitting up might snap some bones. And yet there was a wiry kind of strength left in the Wollin queen. Even at her advanced age, her body was determined to keep going.

"Bryn? Bryn, is that you?" Rangar swept to the edge of the bed, resting a hand on Queen Amelia's shoulder.

Bryn's breath came unevenly as she tried to get used to the feeling of being in a body that wasn't her own. Gazing down at her withered hands, panic started to set in.

*This is wrong. This isn't me!*

She began to shake uncontrollably as her spirit wanted to pull itself out of Queen Amelia and finds its true home again. Her eyes started to roll back in her head.

"Bryn! Focus." Rangar took the queen's head and guided it to focus on his face. He stroked the queen's paper-thin cheeks. "Focus on me."

Bryn's attention locked onto Rangar. *Rangar.* Seeing him steadied the quaking storm clouds rolling through her head. She reminded herself of where she was and what she was doing. Slowly, the shaking subsided.

"Rangar," she rasped. The voice came out in Queen Amelia's pitch.

Rangar's face eased with relief. His big hands felt along the queen's head and shoulders, gently touching her delicate body as though afraid of hurting her.

"It worked," he said.

Bryn nodded, still feeling discombobulated as Queen Amelia's head moved instead of her own. "I was floating up near the ceiling . . . I saw you and Illiana, but everything was a fog . . ."

"Shh. All is well. The hex worked."

Rangar's voice sounded confident, but Bryn could still see a vague outline of his aura, and it was still tinged with fear that she might be stuck inside the old queen's body forever.

"What now?" she said, wincing at her foreign voice.

"Morning comes soon. A servant will come to get you ready for the parlay. As much as I want to stay with you, I can't be seen in Queen Amelia's bedroom. And I need to get your real body back to our bedroom."

She nodded. "Go."

He hesitated. "Elysander will be there the whole time to look after your real body. I'll see you at the grand parlay."

They heard a creak in the hall that could be a servant or guard. Bryn pressed a hand against Rangar's chest, urging him to go, but he hung back one second longer. Tipping the old queen's chin up, he placed a soft kiss on the queen's wrinkled lips.

"Rangar, I'm . . . old," she gasped.

"In whatever body, in whatever age, you're still the woman who has my heart."

And then the creak came again, and Rangar gave her one last long look, his aura radiating out his love, and then crept out of the room. A lady's maid came in not five minutes later, yawning as she started to stack wood in the fireplace.

"Awake all ready, my queen?" the maid said in surprise, noticing her. "I hope I didn't wake you."

"No," Bryn said, aware that she needed to act like Queen Amelia. "No, it's quite all right. I couldn't sleep."

The lady's maid gave her a sympathetic smile. "I'll have breakfast sent up. You need your strength today."

Bryn gave a nod as she leaned back against the pillows, watching the maid stack the logs. Inside, her heart was thumping hard. Had she studied Queen Amelia enough to be able to mimic her mannerisms? Would King Marthin realize there was something wrong with his wife? What if someone else had the aura hex and could see that Amelia's light looked different?

But she forced a regal smile as more servants brought her a tray of tea and scones with clotted cream, and spoke as little as possible.

By the time the servants had fed and dressed her, Bryn was starting to feel more at home in Queen Amelia's body. Maybe not as comfortable as she felt in Barendur Hold, of course, but more like visiting one of the inns along the forest road: it wasn't what she was used to, and there were new rooms and stairs to learn. Still, it was tolerable for a day—even a bit morbidly interesting.

*Only a day*, Bryn reminded herself. *By tonight, I'll be back in my own body.*

She looked in the mirror after the lady's maid finished coiling her hair into a knot at her nape and blinked at her unfamiliar new body. She wore a silk gown in such a light shade of lavender that it was nearly silver, and they'd draped her in strings of salt-water pearls. Bryn felt a sigh from somewhere outside herself; it took her a moment to realize it was Queen Amelia's weakened spirit, tucked aside but watching in the mirror, too.

"I'm sorry," Bryn murmured aloud, hoping the elderly queen could hear her. "It won't be for long."

"My lady?" the lady's maid said. "I didn't catch that."

"Nothing," Bryn said quickly, adjusting the pearls around Amelia's neck. "Is there word on our guests?"

"They're already gathered in the library." A voice from the door made her turn.

King Marthin stood in the doorframe, wearing trousers of the same pale lavender silk and a white shirt beneath a darker silver vest. Bryn's stomach clenched at the sight of him—this was Amelia's husband. If anyone could tell something wasn't right about his wife, it would be him.

"Excellent," Bryn said. "Let us not keep them waiting longer."

Her lady's maid accompanied her to the door, but Marthin waved her away. "I'll escort Amelia, Strella."

Bryn would have much preferred to have the lady's maid's presence as a buffer, but it seemed clear from

Marthin's clipped tone that he wouldn't settle on anything else. She gave the lady's maid a nod.

"Yes, Strella, we're fine."

It took effort to move Amelia's body down the long hallway, not because of the possession hex but simply because Bryn wasn't used to the aches and creaky joints of an elderly woman. She felt immense sympathy for the old queen as well as a large dose of reverence—Queen Amelia hadn't once complained about the chronic pain in her bones.

*I hope I should be so tough in my old age*, Bryn thought.

It also made her flush with anger to think of Baron Marmose using his influence spell on the queen. It rankled Bryn to know the baron's machinations had addled such a formidable woman's mind.

"Amelia," Marthin whispered low. "Did you think more about what we discussed last night?"

*Lords and ladies*, Bryn thought in a panic. What had they discussed? She possessed the queen's body but not her memories—there was no way to know what Marthin referred to.

She cleared her throat. "I have given it thought, husband, but first I should like to know your own mind."

Marthin blinked a few times in pleasant surprise as though he wasn't often asked his opinion, and Bryn hoped he'd take it as flattery instead of a cause for suspicion. Fortunately, Marthin's weak-mindedness didn't appear to be an act. He readily said, "I still believe we should hear out the northern kingdoms before immediately siding with Ruma. I know you said that you felt strongly for that baron's argument to banish magic, but I have yet to hear precisely *why* . . ."

*Ah*, Bryn realized. Poor, sweet, weak-minded Marthin couldn't understand why his normally head-strong wife had decided to back the anti-magic coalition. Of course, Marthin didn't know about Baron Marmose's influence spell. But it was clear now that Marthin and Amelia had already discussed this at length, and Marthin was trying to change her mind back to support the side of magic.

Bryn felt a flutter of tenderness for the old king.

She rested Amelia's hand on his arm. "Perhaps you have a point, Marthin. I will hear all arguments and make my decision then. I mean, then you can make *your* decision."

He looked less distressed as he nodded. "Good. That's good, Amelia." He paused before they entered the library and raised her wrinkled hand to his lips. "Tell me how to vote at recess, and I shall do it."

"You're a good man, Marthin."

He gave a genuine smile—it seemed the old king wasn't used to compliments, either.

As soon as they entered the library, all chatter fell away, and all eyes turned to them. King Cedric Cheron and Queen Yves Cheron of Ruma had arrived so that all eight delegations were present. The Cheron family, along with Baron Marmose, stood by the bookshelves along with the royals from Zaradona and Dresel, while the monarchs from the Mirien, the Baersladen, Vil-Kevi, and Vil-Rossengard waited on the opposite side by the windows.

Tension snapped in the air. Bryn could almost taste it, like the afterburn of fresh-struck lightning.

Baron Marmose immediately swept over, his little dog yapping at his heels. "Queen Amelia. King Marthin. We are honored to have our hosts join us."

Bryn couldn't help but give Baron Marmose a sour look. This pandering, scheming man had put her in her current situation, possessing an elderly woman. There was a chance she might not ever get out of the queen's body. But as much as she wanted to insult him and play it off as an old woman's confusion, she reminded herself she had to act above suspicion.

"Yes, thank you, Marmose. Welcome, everyone. I trust you've all slept well in preparation for a long day of talks . . ." Her eyes drifted around the room and stalled on Rangar, standing by himself by the fireplace.

Bryn's chest clenched to see him through another woman's eyes. Even with the queen's blurry vision, Rangar still looked like a god among men, dark and brooding and devastatingly handsome. By the Saints, how had she gotten so lucky? Her heart tightened like a fist with the sudden urge to run to him and never let go, but she stood her ground.

"King Rangar Barendur of the Baersladen," she asked carefully, "where is your queen?"

Rangar folded his arms. His sizzling eyes fixed on her meaningfully. "Queen Bryn isn't feeling well, your highness. I've left her to rest in our chamber with a healer. She will join us if her health improves."

Baron Marmose stiffened at this news, then scurried over to King Cedric and Queen Yves of Ruma. A few whispers were bandied about.

"Unfortunate," Bryn said, "but perhaps not unexpected. I was told this morning that several of the servants took ill as well. It might have been a batch of the evening's oysters." Bryn clasped her hands together as she'd seen Amelia do. "Well then, my lords and ladies, let the grand parlay begin. Marthin, will you be so good as to outline the rules?"

"Of course," the old king said, clearing his throat, looking comforted by the idea of recitation instead of having to speak impromptu. "Rules of the grand parlay are thus. Number one: All delegates shall have five minutes to deliver their opening points. This hourglass is calibrated for that exact time period. Number two: Subsequent debate must remain civil. Any member who threatens violence shall be removed by our palace guards. Number three: a decision must be reached by the day's end. When the sun sets, this proclamation—" he rested his hand on a scroll laid out on the table, "—will be ratified as the law of the land."

"And if there is no agreement reached in time?" Illiana asked. As a new queen, she wasn't familiar with the archaic laws.

Marthin tapped the parchment once more, firmly.

"Then the guards lock the doors. No one eats, sleeps, or leaves until it's done."

Bryn's legs were starting to ache. She faltered, catching herself on a chair back. Rangar hadn't taken his eyes off her, and at the first sign of weakness, he was by her side in a moment.

"Here, Queen Amelia. Let me help you to a chair."

"Thank you . . . young man," Bryn said as Rangar guided her into one of the settees. His hand lingered an extra moment on her back. Their eyes met. Bryn felt a sharp tug in her chest—not Amelia's—and knew that her spirit wanted nothing more than to be back in her own body, in Rangar's arms. Even now, his aura pulsed with that protective blue energy that meant he'd sacrifice anything for her.

Bryn broke eye contact before anyone might suspect something. She cleared her throat. "Now that we all understand the rules, let us discuss what is at stake. For nearly five hundred years, we have had peace throughout the Eyrie. There have been attacks from foreign lands at the Eyrie's borders. There have been minor skirmishes between our kingdoms, but no full declaration of war. Now, with wolf attacks striking the most vulnerable citizens of many of our lands, and rumors of dark magic, we must decide once and for all what the fate of magic shall be within the Eyrie."

She steadied her gaze on each of the royals in the room. King Grey and his much younger wife from Dresel. Mars and Illiana of the Mirien. King Cedric and Queen Yves of Ruma. Prince Anter and his father from

Vil-Kevi, along with the Viklunds from Vil-Rossengard, and King Salvator of Zaradona with High Priest Red.

And, finally, Rangar.

She motioned to the library table, which would serve as their negotiation table. "Let the grand parlay begin. Take your seats, please, my guests."

# CHAPTER 36

**A ROLL OF THE DICE . . . eight emblems . . . opening arguments . . . sands of the hourglass**

Fifteen delegates from the eight kingdoms of the Eyrie sat around the library table—with one missing seat for Bryn. Baron Marmose, as an unofficial attendee with no voting power, hung back by the library windows, pacing anxiously with his three yapping dogs at his heels.

Seated at the head of the table, Bryn tried to maintain the expression she'd so often seen on Queen Amelia's face: strong, stoic, but with the wandering gaze of a fading mind. Once everyone had taken their places, and the servants had brought wine to facilitate the negotiations, King Marthin rolled an eight-sided die with each of the kingdom's emblems carved on the faces:

The woodland dragon for Vil-Rossengard.

The sea cliff castle of the Baersladen.

The blooming flowers of the Mirien.

The bluebird of Ruma.

The giant lion of Zaradona.

The sparrow of Dresel.

The crashing waves of the Wollin.

The antlers of Vil-Kevi.

It rolled to a halt with Vil-Kevi's antlers emblem facing up. Bryn folded her hands as she announced, "King Otto Jarkkinen of Vil-Kevi. The gods have chosen you to speak first."

She nodded to Marthin, who turned the hourglass timer.

King Otto stood gruffly and pushed his chair back. Though his wild, curly hair and beard had been combed, dark circles hung beneath his eyes. He hadn't gotten much sleep after their amplifier spell. He glanced briefly at Bryn—at Queen Amelia—as though not entirely certain who inhabited the body.

"There are those present who will argue magic is not a right of the Eyrie people, and I would agree with them. It isn't a *right*. A right must be agreed upon and granted by old fools in crowns such as us. Magic needs no agreement. It's a force of nature as sure as the air we breathe, the water flowing in our rivers. You can no sooner deny people magic than you can deny them that very air and water."

There were murmurs of agreement from King Hans Viklund and Queen Karin Viklund.

"Here, here," said Anter, rapping a fist on the table.

Marthin raised a finger. "No debate yet, young prince, and that also goes for voicing support. Each speaks for their allotted time, and the others remain silent."

King Otto finished his speech with an anecdote about how their farmers, plunged in the shade of the forest, couldn't grow crops without magic to amplify sunlight. When the timer ended, Marthin rolled the die again.

"Zaradona," he said when the giant lion emblem came up. "King Salvator Surin, you may speak."

The gray-clad, severe king stood to his full height and said, "I would like to cede my time to High Priest Felisian Red, who may speak on my behalf."

Marthin nodded. "Granted."

As King Salvator took his seat, the priest stood. Ever since his arrival, Felisian Red had given off a dangerously quiet energy that Bryn needed no aura vision to detect. Now, the priest's eyes cut sharply around the table as the hourglass sands fell, seemingly unconcerned about his dwindling time. Bryn's stomach roiled as his eyes glided over her, suddenly afraid he could see through her disguise in Queen Amelia's body and straight into her spirit.

"It is indeed a shame Queen Bryn cannot join us," he said pointedly, and Bryn's eyes shot open wide before she could carefully pull her mask back on.

Did he know who she was? Did he have the ability to see auras?

"And why is that?" Rangar growled from the other end of the table. "You haven't spoken to my wife since our arrival in the Wollin."

"Queen Bryn offers an interesting perspective," the high priest continued, still infuriatingly slow, as though he was utterly unconcerned about the time. "She was raised to abhor magic as a sin in the same way we see it in Zaradona. Now, as queen of the Baersladen, she has embraced magic and even advocates for its use. And yet I wonder, if she were here, what she would say about the wolf attacks. Village after village in her precious new homeland has been attacked. Men, women, and even children were slaughtered. We all know dark magic is behind it—so why would she push for something killing her people? I might say that attitude more in line with her parents' ways."

Both Mars and Rangar shot to their feet, ready to defend Bryn.

"You speak of my sister," Mars said hotly. "May I remind you that she had nothing to do with our parents' reign. Bryn knew nothing of their actions."

Rangar pressed his fists against the table, a deep scowl on his face as he took in the high priest like a wolf stalking its prey. "My wife would risk her life any day for just one of her subjects. You dare to suggest she carelessly allows these murders?"

"Lords," King Marthin scolded, pounding on the table. "Recall the rules! This is not currently a debate!"

It began to dawn on Bryn why High Priest Felisian Red had chosen such a provocative and unusual subject for his opening statement: one king at the table was her brother, and another was her husband. Both men would do anything to defend her honor, as they had all just witnessed.

*The high priest isn't trying to make a logical argument,* she realized. *He's trying to rattle Mars and Rangar. He wants them distracted when it's time to make their own arguments—so they'll use their time refuting him instead of laying out a good case.*

As though Illiana had come to the same conclusion, she gripped Mars by the sleeve and tugged him back down into his seat. "Sit," she hissed. "And ignore the words of fools."

The hourglass ran out, and High Priest Felisian Red gave Rangar a cold, satisfied stare. Bryn wondered if this was why King Salvator had ceded his time to the priest; so that he, as a king, wouldn't have to slander another royal.

Slowly, Rangar sank back into his chair. One hand remained curled into a fist on the table. His attention was fixed on his wine glass, almost as though he was working hard *not* to look at Bryn. But his aura reached out bands of light toward her, wanting to protect her.

Tension snapped even sharper in the room now. Queen Hanna of Dresel shifted uneasily in her seat. King Hans of Vil-Rossengard downed his wine in one long swallow and then signaled to the servants for more.

King Marthin rolled the die again. "King Rangar Barendur of the Baersladen."

Bryn held in a tight breath. Rangar was no fool—he had to know that the priest had been trying to shake him. Still, which would win out—his temper or his reason?

"King Rangar," she said in Amelia's voice. "Please, stand. We would very much like to hear your *measured* opinion."

He met her eyes across the table. The anger in his shoulders seemed to ease as though her words had reminded him why they were here—and it wasn't to punch High Priest Felisian Red in the jaw.

Slowly, he stood. His eyes flickered to the hourglass, but when he spoke, it wasn't rushed. "If my wife were here, I would cede my time to her, as she is a far better speaker than me—not to mention prettier to look at."

Prince Anter good naturally tapped his fist on the table in agreement.

"But in her stead, I shall share her reasons for changing her mind about magic, as you pointed out, High Priest Red. Bryn Lindane was raised in a kingdom where the monarchs had absolute power. Their military controlled every village and road. Their tax collectors heavily regulated what crops could be grown, which harvest could be kept, and which had to be sold. We do not have to debate here whether this was good for the Mir people—the Mir people already answered that question when they rose up and slaughtered King Deothanial and Queen Helena."

He paused for a moment of silence as he let the others consider the inherent threat in his words: If they acted as King Deothanial and Queen Helena had, their heads might end up on the gallows, too.

He continued, "When Bryn came to the Baersladen, she could not speak our language. My aunt gave her that ability through a hexmark. She became a beloved figure in our kingdom, working alongside shepherds. She saw how magic in the hands of our people gave power that the common folk of her homeland lacked. The Baer people, through magic, do not need our military to oversee them, do not need us to tell them what to grow. We are there to guide and to set strategy for the good of the kingdom, not to control every aspect of their lives. My wife saw this. She embraced it. She even became an apprentice with hexes of her own."

Throughout the speech, his eyes never left Bryn's across the table. His words might be for the benefit of everyone else, but his love was all for her.

The hourglass was running out, so Rangar leaned on the table and gave a final word of warning. "If you value your own necks, my advice is this: give your people magic or wait for them to slit your throats. If you value your people's well-being, give them the ability to help themselves. Either way, magic is the answer."

He sat as the final sand ran out.

Baron Marmose, pacing by the bookshelves, threw searching looks toward Bryn in Queen Amelia's body to see how she was reacting to these various speeches. Since he needed to believe she was still under his influence spell, Bryn tried to keep her face carefully neutral, perhaps even with a shadow of doubt for Rangar's words.

Next to speak was King Angus of Dresel, who made the case that the wolf attacks showed that for all the good magic could do, its potential for great evil was too dangerous to let loose without restrictions. Following him was King Hans of Vil-Rossengard, who argued that his ancestors hadn't fought and joined with the other Eyrie kingdoms just to have their basic strength—magic—stripped from them, and that if anything could save them from the berserkir wolves, it was even stronger magic. When Mars spoke, he pointed out that the wolf attacks were not so different from an enemy siege: magic was simply a tool like cannons or warships, and magic shouldn't be banned unless the delegates were prepared to ban all other tools of warfare.

They broke for a recess at midday, with only the delegates from Ruma and the Wollin left to give their arguments. Servants brought in platters of braised mackerel and lemon tarts and more wine, and the various delegates divided into groups to eat around the library, whispering among themselves about the morning's events.

Sitting on the settee with King Marthin, Bryn

couldn't help but look longingly toward Rangar by the far windows, eating alone. She would give anything to be able to swap a few whispered words with him, but she didn't dare approach him. She nibbled her mackerel and only nodded distractedly as King Marthin blathered about the weather.

Her napkin slipped off her lap, and before she could pick it up, Baron Marmose was suddenly by her side.

"Allow me, my queen." He returned the napkin to her with a flourish, a smug smile on his face. "It's been an interesting morning, has it not?"

"Indeed," she said curtly, hoping to signal she didn't wish to speak.

He rested a hand on her chair back as though he had no intention of leaving. Dropping his voice, he said lightly, "I assume we are still in agreement about what we previously discussed?"

Alarm prickled at Bryn's skin. She bought time by chewing a lemon tart, then dabbed at her mouth with her napkin. She gave him a thin smile. "Of course, baron."

He returned her smile smugly, then gave a bow. "My queen."

He sauntered off to sit with the king and queen of Ruma, feeding his dogs a scrap of fish skin, and Bryn suppressed the urge to balk at his hubris.

*He thinks he's already won.*

But the day was only getting started, and Bryn was

looking forward to seeing that smug smile wiped off his face.

# CHAPTER 37

**TWO CHALICES . . . seashell tokens . . . a confident baron . . . suspicious nieces and nephews**

"These wolf attacks are simply unacceptable." It was King Cedric of Ruma's turn to speak, and he had begun with a vociferous condemnation of the attacks. "Any royal who allows their people to suffer, even to die, from dark magic should be hung as treasonous!"

There were a few grumbles among the delegates in the library, but no one outwardly voiced a word, not wanting to get another scolding from King Marthin.

King Cedric pounded his fist on the table. "There's a reason the berserkir beasts are attacking in the north where magic runs rampant, yet we in the south haven't had a single attack. Our lands are pious, not tainted with the sin of magic! We must rid all the Eyrie of this magical scourge that spreads like a disease. We in the south will defend our pious citizens from such violence that the northern realms allow!"

Bryn held in her groan. King Cedric's inflammatory words didn't seem to be going over well if Rangar, the Jarkkinens, and the Viklunds were any indication. All of them threw daggers with their glares in Cedric's direction.

Undeterred, Cedric jabbed his finger at each one of the delegates. "If you allow magic, you have blood on your hands, and you deserve the gallows!"

He sat down heavily before his time had even run out. Rangar bowed over the table, his hair falling over his face to hide his expression, but Bryn could tell from the tight set of his shoulders that he was furious. Even young Queen Hanna of Dresel, whose husband had spoken against magic, looked a little ill at the Rumese king's fervor.

King Marthin waited for the hourglass to run out, then stood and cleared his throat. "Right. The final royal family to speak is my own. You have each made it clear where you stand, and we can all do the math." His brow suddenly wrinkled as though, for a moment, he worried he wasn't actually capable of the simple addition. Then he cleared his throat. "Yes, yes. There is an equal number in support of magic and against it, leaving the Wollin as the deciding vote." He touched his hand on Bryn's back. "I'd like to cede my time to my wife, Queen Amelia Hytooth of the Wollin."

Bryn stiffened, feeling the stirrings of the real Amelia Hytooth's spirit somewhere in the same body. It was hard to gauge what the old queen thought of the proceedings, or if she was even fully cognizant in her current disembodied state. Bryn whispered a silent plea in her head for the queen to be patient; she would get her body back soon.

"Yes, thank you, husband." Bryn folded her frail hands together on the table as she had seen Queen Amelia do. "I appreciate the points that each of you made both for and against magic. As you know, here in the Wollin, magic is not officially sanctioned but nor do we seek out and punish those who choose to practice it. We have always been a kingdom tolerant of others. We take our lessons from the sea, which shows us how fish, whales, sharks, and all sea life coexist peacefully with one another. Until now, it has been our philosophy to let our citizens live as they wish: to practice whatever magic or religion they see fit." She shifted her eyes to Baron Marmose. "Of course, these wolf attacks change things considerably. I will reserve my final decision until after the debates, but I can assure you that by sunset, the decree *will* be signed."

A confident smile curled the baron's lips.

The afternoon erupted into seething arguments between the most vociferous of the delegates. Now that the more formal elements of the grand parlay were gone—the die with eight emblems, the hourglass, Marthin with his rules—accusations were hurled across the room. Bryn watched warily without adding anything, afraid of speaking too much and revealing that she wasn't who she appeared to be.

It was clear that Rangar was attempting to contain his temper so as not to be thrown out by the guards, but he came dangerously close to punching High Priest Felisian Red a time or two. Even Mars once threatened to throw his wine glass in King Cedric's direction until Illiana swiped it out of his hand.

The afternoon recess came a half hour before sunset. Though servants brought in trays of glazed biscuits and fresh wine, hardly anyone touched the refreshments. Everyone's tempers were sharp. Bryn was glad that the rules stipulated that no weapons were allowed at the parlay, because the undercurrent of violence in the room was palpable.

She glanced out the window at the sun falling toward the horizon. *Soon, it will all be over.*

The waves crashing in the distance normally would have soothed her, but today her emotions were too tumultuous. She itched to be out of the old queen's body, hand it back to its rightful owner, and then wake up in her own skin. The longer she inhabited Amelia's body, the more she felt it was binding to her spirit in a way that would be impossible to break.

Declan and Phillipa Hytooth joined them for the recess, bringing everyone a quill and bottle of ink to sign the parchments for the official vote, as well as a handful of tokens carved from seashells, and two silver chalices. Once the supplies had been distributed, the red-haired Hytooths sat next to Bryn.

"Aunt," Phillipa said, taking Bryn's hand tenderly. "I'm worried about you. You don't look like yourself."

Bryn's stomach clenched. It hadn't been too difficult to act as Queen Amelia around the other delegates, who hardly knew her, or even around King Marthin, with his simplistic mind. But Declan and Phillipa Hytooth were sharp and well acquainted with their aunt's mannerisms.

She warred with herself for a moment—Declan and Phillipa were friends of Rangar's and appeared to be allies, yet how would they take the fact that she'd forcefully possessed their aunt's body? It could turn the younger Hytooths against them.

"It's been a long day, dear," Bryn said, patting Phillipa's hand.

"You must push off the remainder of the parlay until tomorrow," Phillipa urged. "So that you can rest and keep up your strength."

"Nonsense," Bryn said. "That's strictly against the rules. Besides, the parlay is almost at its conclusion— I'll have ample rest once a decision has been made."

Phillipa still looked concerned as she squeezed Bryn's hand.

Declan frowned as he looked over the crowd. "Where is Queen Bryn?"

Bryn tried not to let panic show on her face. She glanced across the room to where Rangar was closely watching them from near the fireplace, ready to step in if needed.

He raised an eyebrow, but she shook her head a

tiny amount. "Not feeling well, I'm afraid," Bryn said. "Oysters, they think."

Declan's frown deepened. "I ate a dozen of them and felt fine—"

Bryn cut him off. "I'm sure she'll recover soon."

A servant rang a chime to signal the end of the recess. Bryn glanced out the window to find the sun just kissing the distant ocean horizon, and her heartbeat sped.

The time for the final vote had come.

Declan and Phillipa stood, taking Bryn's empty china plate. Phillipa patted her aunt's shoulder. "Don't let them bully you, aunt."

"I never do."

Phillipa smiled. "I know you don't."

As the servants cleared out to leave only the delegates, the tone was very different as they took their seats once more around the table. The morning had been all formal speeches, the afternoon a wild debate, and now, as the sun fell beyond the windows, a delicate hush filled the room. Tensions had gone from simmering to coalescing into a sharp point like a knife's blade.

Seated behind King Cedric and Queen Yves, Baron Marmose stroked one of his dog's heads while his dark eyes fixed on Bryn.

"Well," King Marthin announced. "We've come to the vote. Our scholars have prepared two versions of the decree. The one here, on the left, lays out the steps that shall be taken should we decide that magic will be forbidden throughout all eight kingdoms of the Eyrie. On the right, it details how magic shall be allowed without infringement. Everything discussed in the afternoon's debates has been added to these two versions. All that remains is for each of us to cast our vote. May I remind you that while a simple majority shall determine the law, monarchs from all eight kingdoms must sign their names to the winning decree whether they voted for it or not."

Baron Marmose's dog jumped out of his lap. The baron crossed his leg casually over his knee, sipping deeply from his wine as though already celebrating his victory.

"We shall vote in the order of this morning's die roll," King Marthin stated. "You've each been given a token. Please place your token in the chalice in front of the decree you wish to vote for and state your decision aloud."

Beginning with King Otto of Vil-Kevi, the delegates stood individually and placed their token into the corresponding chalice.

"For the free use of magic," King Otto declared.

"Against all magic," King Salvator said next.

"For the free use of magic." Rangar dropped his token into the chalice and glared at the delegates from Zaradona and Ruma.

There was a brief moment of hesitancy when King Angus of Dresel went to cast his lot. As he stood, young Queen Hanna snagged him with a sudden grasp and whispered fiercely in his ear, but in the end, King

Angus shook his grizzled head forcefully and dropped his token in the lefthand chalice.

"*Against* all magic," he said, looking sternly at his wife.

Bryn's heart went out to the young Dresel queen, who had given one last-ditch attempt to influence her husband. Queen Hanna hadn't yet learned that in realms such as Dresel, powerful men chose women for their looks and their ability to bear children, not for their advice.

It made her all the more grateful for Rangar. For as stubborn as he could be, he had never seen her as anything less than an equal. Even before her months of study to acquaint herself with history and politics, he had valued her instincts. True, at the beginning of their relationship, he'd forbade her from engaging in any action that might bring her harm, but he'd evolved from that strict attitude, and that was yet another reason why she loved him. Rangar wasn't set in his ways like old King Salvator or King Angus. He could admit when he was wrong.

And he would fight like hell for what he knew was right.

"*For* the free use of magic," King Hans said proudly as he cast his token.

"Strongly agreed. For the use of magic," Mars said as Illiana tossed in their token.

Finally, after King Cedric of Ruma added his token to the left chalice with a gruff, "Against all magic," it was time for the final vote.

The Wollin's.

With his own final token resting in front of him, King Marthin stood and addressed the delegates. "My lords and ladies. Honored guests. It falls to me to cast the final vote, and I do not take this duty lightly. Queen Amelia, our Woll advisors, and our valued nieces and nephews have all weighed in on this decision. We do what we believe is in the best interest of the common folk and royals alike throughout the Eyrie."

He picked up the seashell token, smoothing his wrinkled thumb over its polished surface. Though his chin was held high, his rapid blinks betrayed his uncertainty.

Bryn's heart went out to the old king, and she felt a tenderness coming from the real Queen Amelia, too. All around the table, the delegates remained hushed. Their bodies inclined forward, poised in anticipation, except for Baron Marmose, who sat reclined in the chair off to the side, foot tapping confidently.

From her brief conversation with Marthin earlier that morning, Bryn knew that the real Queen Amelia and King Marthin had already decided before the day's events began that they would vote against magic. Bryn had no idea how Queen Amelia truly felt, though Phillipa and Declan had suggested her mind was open to the free use of magic. But Baron Marmose and his insidious hex had gotten to her first, bending her to his will. And whatever Queen Amelia said, King Marthin would do whether he agreed with her decision or not.

King Marthin held his hand out over the chalices and said, "The Wollin votes for—"

Baron Marmose practically licked his lips while waiting for the words he'd orchestrated.

"Wait." Bryn pushed to her feet, standing at the old queen's full height. The baron's face immediately fell. The other delegates leaned forward even more, shifting uncomfortably in their seats.

Bryn rested the old queen's hand on her husband's arm. Looking him in the eye, she announced, "The Wollin votes for the free use of magic."

She nudged Marthin's hand toward the chalice on the right. His eyebrows shot up, but after a second's pause, he opened his hand.

The token fell into the right chalice.

# CHAPTER 38

**THE GRAND PARLAY...outrages...spells against spells...a clever baron...a library full of magic**

W hat is the meaning of this?" King Cheron shouted, shoving to his feet. His face had turned bright red and wrinkled like an old tomato. He jabbed an accusing finger at Bryn. "A queen has no say in the vote! It is only King Marthin's words that matter!"

"My husband was the one who cast the token," Bryn said evenly, refusing to be intimidated. "And he'll repeat my words about the vote, if you so require it. Marthin?"

Blinking rapidly, Marthin blathered, "Yes, yes, it is as Queen Amelia said. The Wollin votes for the free use of magic."

His voice had taken on more excitement since this surprising turn of events.

Now, King Salvator of Zaradona shot to his feet. "That isn't what you were going to say. We all saw it clear as day; you were about to cast your token in the left chalice!"

"You dare to question your host's vote?" Bryn hissed, resting her hands on the table.

Rangar rose as well, towering over King Salvator. "The votes are cast. Everything was done according to the rules of the grand parlay. You might not like the decision, but you are bound to abide by it."

"This is an outrage!" King Angus of Dresel cried, twisting around in his chair toward Baron Marmose. He threw an accusing scowl. "*Do* something, Marmose!"

Baron Marmose seemed frozen in his seat. As soon as King Marthin had cast his vote for the free use of magic, he'd gone strangely still except for his eyes, which had shot to Queen Amelia and locked there as though trying to pick apart why his influence spell hadn't worked.

*Because you influenced her, you ass*, Bryn thought viciously. *Not me.*

Rangar immediately whirled on King Angus. "What exactly do you want the baron to do, my king? What did he *already* do?"

King Angus's eyes narrowed, but he didn't dare admit to their plan with Ruma and Zaradona to cast a spell on Queen Amelia. Baron Marmose's eyes darted from Rangar to Queen Amelia as his lips pursed in an attempt to figure out what had gone wrong.

"The vote is cast!" Prince Anter announced, his sharp voice cutting through the chatter. "There is no room for further debate. The sun sets as we speak. As King Marthin said, you are bound by the rules of the grand parlay to sign the final decree."

He snatched up the right-hand parchment and unfurled it before his father, King Otto. The room went still again as everyone watched the burly forest king grab a quill and ink. He stabbed the quill into the bottle and then proudly wrote his name across the parchment's bottom.

"Jarkkinen," he barked, passing the document to the king of Vil-Rossengard, who signed his name on one of the eight marks, then passed quill and scroll to Rangar.

Rangar splayed the scroll on the table with one hand while signing his name with the other, glaring at the southern monarchs all the while, daring them to say something. Once he'd signed, he passed the scroll to Illiana. "For King Mars."

As Mars signed his name and handed the scroll to King Grey, the remaining southern rulers began to pace and grunt their displeasure. Queen Yves of Ruma and High Priest Felisian Red rushed off to a corner to speak adamantly with Baron Marmose. Their voices rose and fell in sharp argument.

"I'm not signing that!" King Grey blustered. "I didn't agree to it. Magic will infect our borders!"

"You must sign, husband," Queen Hanna said firmly with simmering resentment in her voice, mixed with a twinge of pleasure to see her elderly husband suffering.

"Your wife is correct," King Marthin said. "The rules were clear."

"If you have any trouble understanding the rules," Rangar added, sidling up behind the old Dresel king with menacing energy, "I'm sure the Woll guards at the door would be willing to explain it to you in the dungeon."

"Wait!" Baron Marmose yelled from across the room. "The rules . . . Yes, King Marthin said if no agreement is made, the negotiations would go on into the night. Don't sign, Grey. We'll keep talking."

"Ah, no, I don't believe you were listening," Marthin said with a rare note of displeasure in his otherwise affable voice. "A decision *was* made. The grand parlay cannot be continued now. All that is left to do is sign, and King Rangar is correct: failing to abide by the rules of the grand parlay can result in imprisonment."

"You can't imprison a king!" the baron shouted.

"Kings are not above the law."

Old King Grey grumbled curses under his breath as he grabbed the quill from Mars' hand and angrily scrawled his name onto the parchment. Derisively, he shoved the scroll in Marthin's direction. "Your turn then, sire. Unless you need your wife to hold your hand as you write your name, as she appears to do everything else for you. I wonder if she even holds your cock while you piss?"

Bryn shot to her feet, insulted on behalf of the queen whose body she inhabited. But she forgot about the queen's infirmity, and her knees buckled.

"My queen!" Rangar rushed to help her before she collapsed back into her chair.

"I'm fine, Rangar," Bryn breathed, then immediately realized her mistake. "*King* Rangar."

Baron Marmose focused sharply on her, having picked up on her calling Rangar directly by his name.

Marthin dropped the quill and went to his wife's side as well. "Amelia? My wife?"

Prince Anter snatched up the quill. "King Marthin, you must sign."

Marthin waved him away. "I will, I will, give me a chance to attend to my wife!"

Prince Anter turned toward King Salvator of Zaradona instead. "Then it's your turn, Salvator."

King Salvator looked furious enough to burst apart at the seams. His lips pursed as though ready to refuse, but then the doors opened for additional armed soldiers whom the servants must have summoned, and the thought of the dungeon cowed him.

He signed his name in disgust.

"That only leaves Marthin and you, Cedric," Rangar barked, grabbing the scroll and slamming it down in front of the Rumese king.

King Cedric Cheron looked like the hounds of hell were about to tear him apart and he had no idea what to do. His attention darted between his wife and Baron Marmose whispering furiously in the corner, the armed guards, and the little dogs yapping at his feet.

He picked up the quill with an uncertain hand.

At the same time, Declan Hytooth came striding into the library with a worried look on his face. Oblivious to the tension in the room, he searched among the delegates until his eyes settled on Rangar.

"King Rangar? I went to check on Queen Bryn. You must go to her—she's in some kind of comatose state. The healer looking out for her tried to tell me it's nothing, but my own eyes tell me differently."

Bryn's lips parted silently as she realized what was happening. Declan Hytooth thought he was saving her life . . . but he was ruining everything!

Rangar's gaze shot to Bryn's; his jaw clenched. After an unspoken look passed between them, he said to Declan, "Yes. Of course. I already signed the vote—I should be free to attend to my wife."

"Wait!" Baron Marmose shoved past Queen Yves and High Priest Felisian Red to approach Declan. Eyes narrowed in suspicion, the baron asked, "You say Queen Bryn is comatose?"

"That's right," Declan said, clearly concerned. "I've never seen anything like it."

The baron dropped his voice, but Bryn was close enough to hear. "Would you say she's in a trance?"

"A trance? I wouldn't know. Only that her healer seems unsuited to address the severity of whatever ails her . . ."

Baron Marmose held out a sharp hand for Declan to be silent. His urgent, searching gaze scanned from Rangar, to Prince Anter, to Mars and Illiana, and then settled on Bryn in Queen Amelia's body.

A dangerous light gleamed in his eye.

"Don't sign that parchment, King Cedric," the baron ordered.

Bryn's heart shot to her throat, and she had to try to mask her fear as indignation. "You do not set the rules here, Baron Marmose—"

"Nor do you, *Queen Amelia.*"

Bryn heard all she needed in his tone to know that he'd figured out their ruse or at least come close enough to the truth. Her body froze as her mind spun in different possibilities.

*I could order the guards to drag him out.*

*I could threaten King Cedric with the dungeon.*

*I could use a hex . . .*

But could she? She was in Queen Amelia's body, not her own, and the queen had no hexmarks that Bryn had seen. Another tremor of fear entered her mind as she thought of her real body back in their chamber, guarded by Elysander. Her sister was a fierce fighter, but she was only one woman with no magic. If Baron Marmose sent guards to her room, Elysander wouldn't be able to stop them.

"What is the meaning of this?" King Otto thundered.

Baron Marmose swept a hand over the table, knocking the inkwell to the carpet. Queen Hanna gasped as ink stained her slippered feet. Then, the baron pulled a dagger from a hidden pocket of his vest.

Queen Yves gasped at the flash of steel.

Thrusting the dagger in Bryn's direction, Baron Marmose said, "Queen Amelia is, in fact—"

He was cut off when Rangar grabbed a sword from the nearest guard and sliced it through the air, pausing the blade an inch from Baron Marmose's throat. The baron's jaw slackened, his eyes wide.

"King Rangar!" King Marthin said. "The rule is no weapons!"

"Marmose was the first to draw a blade," Rangar said steadily, keeping the sword's blade flush with the baron's exposed neck. "He smuggled in a weapon, going against the rules, and what's more, he just threatened our host and the reigning queen of the Wollin. Your own wife, my king. It is within my right to defend everyone in this room against this blackguard."

Though it was a stretch to say the baron's small blade posed an immediate threat to Bryn's life, King Marthin was clearly persuaded by Rangar's words. He turned to Bryn with deep concern in his eyes and indignity that she suffered such a fright.

"My wife. Are you all right?"

"Yes," Bryn said, fluttering her hand to her chest. "But King Rangar is right. The baron has proven himself dishonest and must be removed immediately!"

"There's dark magic at work here—" Baron

Marmose started, until Rangar pressed the blade to his throat, and he silenced. Grimacing against the kiss of steel, the baron then whispered under his breath while his eyes scoured the room.

It took Bryn a moment too long to notice his hand subtly tracing a hex shape at his side. His gaze landed on Queen Karin. "Her! She knows something. I can sense deception in her—"

Rangar thrust his free hand over Marmose's mouth while the blade remained against his neck. The baron gave some muffled, illegible cries, motioning between High Priest Felisian Red and Queen Karin.

The high priest's eyes snapped to Queen Karin. His lips moved silently while his hand traced the same symbol by his side, such small movements as to be nearly unnoticeable.

"Rangar," Bryn gasped. "They're using magic!"

"Magic?" King Marthin said in a voice rising in surprise, and Bryn silenced a groan. The batty old king had to be the only one in the room who wasn't entirely aware that the majority of royals had hexmarks, whether they preached their use as a sin or not.

But Rangar was too busy silencing the struggling Baron Marmose to stop High Priest Felisian Red, who strode across the library in great steps toward Queen Karin, whose eyes went wide as she backed into a corner. The priest grabbed her by the throat.

"*Ultha na ragus,*" he said low.

The queen's eyes rolled back in her head as whatever spell he'd cast took her over.

King Hans, her husband, thundered across the room in defense of his wife. He threw out a hand, whispering his own hex.

*"Kora yoquin tertin."*

The flames from the nearby fireplace swelled twice their size, threatening to burn the priest where he'd backed the queen into a corner.

"Release her at once, Red!" King Hans roared.

The priest moved as far from the flames as possible while not releasing Queen Karin's throat. "Say it," he growled to Queen Karin. "The truth. You're hiding something. What spell have you used?"

Bryn gripped the edge of the table with white knuckles.

*Don't say it*, she urged the queen. Half the people in the room already knew about the possession spell, and the other half suspected it, but as long as the words weren't uttered aloud, there was no way to prove it.

Though Queen Karin struggled to fight High Priest Red's hex, whatever truth-telling spell he'd cast over her exceeded her own magical ability. Peeling back her lips in a grimace, she hissed through her clenched jaw, "We used the amplifier spell."

The priest's pinched face twisted in a scowl. Bryn felt a surge of relief and pride in the Vil-Rossengard queen for her quick thinking to mention the secondary spell instead of the main one.

Before High Priest Felisian Red could ply Queen Karin with another truth-telling spell, King Hans reached him. He shoved a heavy hand on the priest's shoulder, spinning him away from his wife.

"*Kora yoquin tertin.*" The fireplace's flames swelled, singing the priest's crimson robes. The priest cried out and stumbled away from the fireplace, his fingers quick to unfasten his outer cloak and toss it onto the ground, stamping out the flames.

"What is the meaning of all this?" King Marthin wailed, turning to Bryn with horror on his slackened face.

"War," Bryn said in a voice that sounded fierce even in Queen Amelia's throat. "It means war, Marthin."

# CHAPTER 39

**A ROYAL BATTLE . . . magic, swords, and wits . . . dog bites . . . broken glass . . . slashed throats . . . a new queen**

"Guards! Stop this madness!" Marthin cried. The Woll soldiers stationed at the door rushed into the library, drawing their swords as they approached the crowd. Prince Anter blocked the path of the closest one, wrestling the sword out of his hand before the guard could even finish drawing it. Anter thrusted his open hand toward the guard, shaking his head firmly.

"This isn't your fight. Stay back."

The unarmed Woll soldier looked torn, but seeing the other soldiers surround the royals, he gained courage and tried to take his sword back. Anter punched the man in the face, knocking him out.

"Anter!" Rangar called as he struggled to subdue Baron Marmose. "Get King Cedric! There's only his signature and Marthin's left to sign. Make Cedric sign it, and this all ends!"

As soon as Rangar finished speaking, one of the baron's dogs let loose a folly of vicious barks and bit Rangar on the ankle. It stole Rangar's attention long enough for Baron Marmose to twist out of his grasp and back away from his sword's blade.

"You repulsive snake," Rangar growled. "This was all you. The wolves, everything."

The baron snorted derisively, though his heaving chest betrayed his nerves. His eyes flashed to Bryn. He made a lunge in her direction. Rangar jumped forward to cut him off.

"*Queen Amelia,*" Rangar called with enough presence of mind to use the queen's name. "Get to Illiana—she'll protect you!"

But Bryn was blocked behind the table on one side by the baron, and the other side by Queen Yves, who yanked a hidden blade out of the massive silver charm on her necklace. Bryn's heart thundered.

*If only I had my magic!*

Trapped in a ninety-year-old body, unable to fight or flee without the hexmarks she'd worked so hard to earn, her mind clawed for a solution.

"Queen Amelia, duck your head!" Illiana shouted from the opposite side of the table. She raised her hands, speaking a levitation spell. One by one, books flew off the library shelves and slammed into Queen Yves' body. Pummeled by the heavy volumes, the Rumese queen sheltered herself just long enough for Bryn to rush past her. Queen Yves blindly slashed her small knife, wounding Bryn's arm.

Illiana grabbed Bryn, guiding her to the safety of the spiral staircase in the library's corner. "Climb. Hurry. I'll keep them away."

Blood trickled from Bryn's arm. It was a wound that, in her normal body, would have been barely a scratch, but the old queen's body was far more delicate. She clamped one hand over the bleeding wound as she took the spiral stairs two at a time, around and around until she reached the balcony overlooking the library's lower level.

From there, she looked down at a shocking scene.

In a matter of mere minutes, a true battle had broken out in Hytooth Palace. Woll guards clashed with whoever appeared as a threat, confused themselves about which side they were supposed to defend, so they settled for surrounding King Marthin with raised swords. Rangar and Anter, both formidable warriors and both now armed, were the next obvious targets. The guards' swords clattered as they fought with the northern royals.

"Stop!" Bryn shouted, but from across the room, her voice was lost in the clash of steel.

"What is this? What's happening?" Phillipa rushed through the open library doors with her cousin Declan just behind. At the sight of drawn swords, she pressed a hand to her mouth.

Bryn saw her opportunity.

"Phillipa! Declan!" she called from the balcony. "The families from Ruma, Zaradona, and Dresel have declared war—command the guards to arrest them! They can't hear me over the noise!"

Phillipa's eyes went large, but she nodded. Declan drew his own sword as he strode toward the soldiers. "Stop this!" he cried. "King Rangar and Prince Anter are not our enemies!"

One of the soldiers, caught up in the struggle, elbowed Declan in the face before he realized who he was. Phillipa gasped. She hefted one of the heavy iron candlesticks from a reading table and tossed it with all her strength into the center of the fight.

The soldiers jumped back from the sparks, buying Declan enough time to insert himself into the fray again. "Dammit, the aggressors are the southern kingdoms! Arrest them!"

The soldiers pivoted to face the Ruma, Zaradona, and Dresel royal families. "As Lord Declan says," the lead soldier commanded, and they strode forward.

King Salvator immediately fled behind a settee, calling, "Felisian! Do something!"

High Priest Felisian Red was already striding forward in his singed robes. He raised his hands and whispered a spell. "*Enon ella vind.*"

Outside, a great wind rushed off the ocean and pummeled the floor-to-ceiling windows. The panes rattled in their frames, harder and harder, until the glass shattered. A burst of glass shards rained over the Woll guards, who fell to their knees amid yells and painful wails.

A shard of glass lodged deep in King Marthin's neck. The old king gripped his throat as a gargle escaped his lips.

Bryn cried out, "No!"

With a roar, King Otto summoned a rival wind spell, swirling his hand in a circular hexmark shape. The broken glass that littered the floor was swept up into a magical whirlwind. Once he had control of the wind, King Otto thrust the glass back toward King Salvator and High Priest Red. The glass shot swiftly through the air, but the two men managed to duck behind a sofa in time.

Pacing on the balcony, Bryn began pulling books off the upper shelves and tossing them down onto the royal's heads. Marthin needed immediate help, or he'd bleed to death from the gash.

"Get Queen Amelia!" King Cedric cried, wincing from a heavy tome that had crashed into his bald skull. "Bring her down here!"

King Angus and Queen Yves both pitched their heads up at Bryn with barred teeth. The two rushed toward the spiral stairs, but Illiana blocked their path.

"*Spectra ka hypony*," Illiana said forcefully at Queen Yves.

The Rumese queen's body immediately sagged as her eyes drooped. *The sleeping spell*, Bryn realized. But

Illiana could only cast one spell at a time, and King Angus simply stepped over his slumped wife as he grabbed Illiana by the wrists.

"Try casting with broken wrists, witch," he growled as his fists tightened over Illiana's delicate bones. Illiana cried out painfully.

"Illiana!" Mars called at the sound of his wife's cry. There was little Mars could do without his sight, but he felt his way around the table. King Angus wrenched Illiana's wrists painfully. A *snap* cracked through the air as one of the bones broke. Mars finished making his way around the table and felt along the wall until his hand collided with a fire poker. He jabbed the poker in King Angus's direction. It missed, but it distracted Angus long enough for Hanna, Angus's wife, to grab the poker from Mars's hands and slam it down on her husband's arms.

Crying out, King Angus released Illiana, who collapsed against the stairs, cradling her broken wrist. Angus shrieked at his wife. "You bitch!"

Pressing a hand to her head, Bryn looked over the battle with a deep sense of dread. Blood coated King Marthin's clothes as he slumped against the sofa. Rangar was battling Baron Marmose, who had gotten a sword off one of the soldiers and was proving to be a formidable swordsman. Prince Anter had cornered King Cedric by the map stand in one corner, holding off all means of escape, and Queen Karin was rushing to fetch the parchment and quill. At the threat of Anter's blade, they forced King Cedric to sign.

That left only Marthin to sign—but Marthin was dying.

The Hytooth cousins tried to reach their wounded uncle but were blocked by a wall of fire summoned by High Priest Felisian Red. Everyone in the room was locked in battle, and the only one spared from it was Bryn.

She had no magic in this body.

She had no ability to fight.

So, what did the old queen have at the ready?

Bryn's mind finally stopped on one possibility.

"Phillipa!" she called down from the balcony with as much strength as the old queen's throat could muster.

Phillipa pitched her head up.

"Phillipa Hytooth!" Bryn repeated. "I have decided on my succession! Effective immediately, you will take over as queen of the Wollin, as I am abdicating my throne right now. Those here shall serve as witnesses!"

Phillipa blinked up in shock. "Aunt..."

"Sign the damn scroll!" Bryn shouted. "Marthin is incapacitated, which means the queen may sign in his stead. As serving queen, *you* can sign!"

Phillipa still appeared confused, but Declan grabbed her shoulders, shaking her. "Do it, Phillipa." His eyes went to King Salvator, who was already stalking forward to stop them. "I'll cover you."

Rangar smashed his sword hilt into Baron Marmose's face, then strode across the room, taking the scroll from where Queen Karin held it out to him.

Rangar set the scroll down on the table, then thrust the quill at Phillipa.

Phillipa's shock quickly gave way to determination. She grabbed the quill and poised it over the scroll, then stopped. "There's no ink—it all spilled out."

Growling, Rangar sliced his blade over his arm and offered her his blood. To her credit, Phillipa didn't balk as she dipped the quill in Rangar's blood and signed her name to the scroll.

"There," Bryn said, breathless, as she looked down over the wrecked library. "It's done!"

The royals on the far side of the library paused their fighting with mixed looks of incredulity and outrage on their faces.

"Magic shall prevail throughout the Eyrie!" Bryn announced from the balcony. "For too long, magic has been seen as a sin while secretly being used among the ruling class. But for the Eyrie to thrive, we must empower all our people—not just the elite few in this room. Yes, magic can be a tool of destruction, but it also has the power to heal. We must not fear it but embrace it." She took a deep breath before finishing. "The wolves among us shall prevail no longer!"

She gazed down upon the battle that they had won. The Viklund family had cornered King Angus of Dresel with the help of his wife, Hanna. Prince Anter and King Otto had captured King Cedric and Queen Yves of Ruma. And Mars had managed to get a blade to the neck of King Salvator, while Illiana—with her one good wrist—was poised to cast the sleeping spell at High Priest Felisian Red should he try to attack.

*We prevailed,* Bryn thought with a fierce flush of pride. *And so did the way of magic.* Her eyes fell on Rangar. Blood streaked his arm, soot smeared his face, and his hair tangled over his scars. Her heart swelled with pride that he had never once doubted them.

But then Rangar's brows narrowed. He glanced back at where Baron Marmose's body had fallen . . .

Only to find no body.

At the same time, Bryn felt a shadow creep up behind her.

In a flash, she realized what had happened. During her speech, Baron Marmose had climbed up the library balcony and used the bookshelves as cover to make his way to where Bryn stood.

"My queen!" Rangar yelled.

Baron Marmose descended upon Bryn with outstretched arms to push her off the balcony.

# CHAPTER 40

**ROYAL SOULS . . . death to the traitor . . . a grieving family . . . helpful memories . . . a borrowed body**

Everything happened so fast that Bryn's mind briefly traveled to another place. For a moment, her spirit and Queen Amelia's were one. She glimpsed all of Amelia's memories, knew everything the old queen knew. Amelia's spirit flashed a single memory into Bryn's mind:

*Queen Amelia, barely older than Bryn was now, standing here on the library balcony, yet it was only half-finished. Workmen were installing the railing. They left a portion hinged in the event they ever needed to haul up furniture or large shipments of books, but cleverly disguised the latch so no one would accidentally unlock it.*

Now, Bryn gazed down at the small divot in the

otherwise smooth railing. Just as Baron Marmose's hands closed in on her, her thumb felt for the hidden catch and flipped it.

*Hold on, for the gods' sakes!* Queen Amelia's voice rang in her mind.

Bryn curled the old queen's wiry hands around the railing as the hinged portion suddenly swung open. She gasped as her feet left the balcony, and then suddenly, she was swinging out into nothing, dangling by her arms.

Baron Marmose didn't have time to slow his momentum. The shock of the suddenly open section of railing made his face contort, but it was too late. He plunged through, falling past Bryn with a cry on his lips. Hurtling downward head-first, there was a terrible *thud* as he collided with the table below. Queen Hanna screamed. The baron gave a weak groan, filled with pain.

Out of the corner of Bryn's eye, as she clutched the railing with all her might, Bryn saw Rangar swiftly draw his sword.

"He tried to kill Queen Amelia," Rangar announced. "We all witnessed it! The sentence for that is death."

Rangar brought down the point of his sword into the center of Marmose's back, hard enough to lodge the blade into the table beneath him. With a strangled cry, the baron slumped lifelessly.

Bryn clenched her teeth as she adjusted her grip. Queen Amelia was ninety years old; her body couldn't hold on long. Her hands were slipping . . .

"Drop down!" Rangar called. "I'll catch you!"

She didn't have a choice. The queen's hands gave out, and Bryn plunged downward—

Into Rangar's arms. Cradling her, he drew her in tightly to his chest, whispering a prayer of gratitude under his breath. She gazed up at him with so many things to say, yet had to maintain the farce that she was Queen Amelia for the benefit of the Woll soldiers and King Marthin.

"My queen," Rangar purred, his throat bobbing as he swallowed. "It's over now."

Declan pushed forward as Rangar set Bryn down on her feet. "Aunt! By the gods, you aren't twenty years old anymore! You cannot do such brazen acts!"

"I'm quite all right, Declan. But Marthin . . ."

Declan's face sagged. "I'm so sorry, aunt. He's . . . he's gone."

Bryn didn't have to act to show genuine grief. King Marthin had proven himself to have a good heart even if his mind was dulled. Pressing a hand to her chest, she said, "I need rest . . . I can't take this shock . . . Oh, poor Marthin."

Declan motioned to two guards. "Help the queen to her chamber."

"Wait. First, the scroll . . ." Bryn turned toward the table. Phillipa handed her the paper. Bryn confirmed that all eight signatures were at the bottom, then felt her body ease. Her eyes briefly closed.

*It's really done.*

"Did you mean what you said, aunt? That I shall be your heir, effective immediately?" Phillipa seemed concerned not for her own future on the throne, but for Queen Amelia's soundness of mind.

Bryn pressed her lips together as she tried to figure out how to answer. She'd borrowed the old queen's body without permission; she'd made the old woman dangle from a balcony . . . could she really now make a promise as serious as succession on Amelia's behalf?

*Please, child,* Amelia's spirit whispered in Bryn's mind. *I haven't had this much fun in fifty years! And Phillipa earned it. Now, give me back my body. I wish to grieve my poor husband.*

Bryn smiled inwardly while she squeezed Phillipa's hand. "Indeed, my niece. We shall work out the details with the Wollin's advisors after Marthin is laid to rest. I should very much like to find a way to allow a woman to rule whether she is married or not."

Phillipa smiled, though it was heavy with grief over her uncle's death.

Bryn let herself be fussed over by the guards, who helped her make her way down the hall to the queen's chambers. As she sank back into the bed, her whole body—as well as the queen's spirit—seemed to give a sigh of relief mixed with grief.

As soon as servants had attended to her minor scrapes, Bryn faced the bedroom mirror. Capturing her own gaze, she whispered, "Your body shall be yours again soon, Amelia. I'm sorry. And thank you."

Not long after, the door creaked open, and Illiana slipped in. She sat on the bed at Bryn's side, squeezing her hand. "Bryn. You're all right?"

"Yes, though I'm sorry for Mathin's loss. Obviously, I'm not nearly as sorry for Marmose's."

"When you swung off the railing like that . . . I thought you'd lost your mind!"

"Amelia showed me her memories of the railing's hidden hinges."

Illiana shook her head in wonder. "Everyone has finally left the library after much argument. The Cherons stormed out—they're already on their way back to Ruma, and they took Baron Marmose's body with them to bury it. The Grays, along with King Salvator and his priest, are leaving first thing in the morning. King Otto wanted them arrested for treason, but they agreed to leave peacefully and not contest the decree they signed. Much blame fell on Baron Marmose—he could hardly defend himself since he's dead."

"And Rangar?" Bryn asked.

Illiana smiled. "He's with your real body right now, ready to shower it with a sinful amount of kisses once you awaken. He wanted to come here, but he's too closely watched. Thankfully, no one called for his arrest after he killed Marmose—Marmose's crimes were clear—but the Woll guards are keeping a close eye on him just the same."

Bryn took a deep breath, rubbing her tired eyes.

Illiana patted her shoulder gently. "Tonight, as

soon as the palace retires and we can ensure privacy, I'll restore you to your real body. I'll perform the ritual from the other bedroom, where your body is, so you might not feel anything until you're back in your own skin."

Bryn nodded, though she was impatient to be back in her body. She wished to be with Rangar, gazing at him with her own eyes, clutching him with her own arms. Illiana left, and Bryn fell into a troubled sleep. Caught somewhere between the waking world and the dream one, images came to her in a tangled knot: Amelia's memories, Bryn's own memories, and dreams of oceans of blood with wolves prowling the beach.

Not long after a soft chime in the palace's bell tower signaled day's end, she felt a sudden sharp *tug* like a seamstress ripping apart a dress at the seam. She gasped. *Illiana must have started the spell.* Her spirit snapped away from Queen Amelia's body, not all at once, but like individual threads breaking, one by one, and then Bryn was back floating somewhere near the ceiling, disembodied, gazing down at the sleeping Queen Amelia.

Amelia's body twitched for a few moments, the old woman's face crinkling as though she had bad dreams, and then suddenly, all the tension eased off her face. Her features settled into a peaceful sleep, her spirit alone now in her rightful body.

Bryn gazed in wonder at the elderly queen, who had proven to be far tougher than anyone had believed.

*I hope I should be as strong*, she thought.

Then she felt another tug, softer this time, guiding her toward the open door. It was the same sensation as the finding spell, almost like a delicious scent leading her to a room full of fresh-baked cakes. Letting her spirit float along in the pull's direction, she found herself slowly transported down the hallway, past guards chatting amongst themselves about the old queen's daring move, and through the cracked doorway of her chamber.

Her spirit gave a great exhalation to see her true body lying in bed.

Her face was deathly pale, her chest barely rose with breath; it was clear why Declan Hytooth had been so concerned for her health that he'd interrupted the grand parlay. Rangar sat on the bed next to her, clutching one of her hands and, with his other, stroking her hair off her temples.

Elysander and Illiana loomed over the table where Illiana's supplies were laid out, preparing a draught. "Quick, give her this to drink," Illiana said, passing a bottle to Elysander. "Rub it on her lips, so she doesn't choke."

Elysander hurried to the other side of the bed and fed Bryn the elixir, sip by sip. At first, high up near the ceiling, Bryn watched them in fascination like they were characters in a play. Elysander had grown so strong and confident since leaving Castle Mir; Bryn felt in awe of all her older sister had accomplished. And Rangar . . . well, what else was there to possibly say about Rangar Barendur? How could she put into words the passionate feelings inside her chest?

Gazing down at him, Bryn studied him from a new perspective. Months ago, when they'd first reunited at the Low Sun Gathering, he'd been stooped and sulking, ashamed of his scars. Now, he held himself like a true king: back straight, shoulders proud, hair combed off his scars as though daring the world to judge him.

Her heart clenched with more love than she'd ever thought possible.

Illiana said to Elysander, "Where are the others? We can't wait much longer. We need them to amplify the spell."

The note of worry in Illiana's voice made Bryn snap back to the present. Now, she looked more intently at what was happening in the room:

Illiana's pinched brow.

Rangar's clenched jaw.

Elysander's pacing by the door, glancing out every few moments.

*They're afraid,* she realized.

Just as fear started to curdle in Bryn's chest, Prince Anter appeared at the door, out of breath. "I'm sorry. After King Marthin and Baron Marmose's murders, there are guards everywhere. It was hard to get away."

"Your father?" Illiana said.

"On his way."

They waited with baited breaths until Queen Karin slipped in, wearing a black robe with a scarf covering her hair. "I had to use a shadow spell to get past the guards," she said breathlessly.

A few painful moments passed before heavy footsteps sounded, and then King Otto finally appeared in the doorway. He shut the door behind him, looking grave. "We must do this quickly. The guards are suspicious—they found me in the halls and thought I was secretly meeting someone. They've started checking each room."

"Quick, then," Illiana said, waving everyone toward the bed. "Join hands."

The five casters held hands near the bottom of the bed while Illiana rolled over Bryn's body. She peeled off the bandages on Bryn's back, then began to rub an elixir into the five fresh hexmarks.

"*Mann desta ka ra,*" the five casters chanted in unison.

Floating above them, Bryn couldn't tear her eyes off her body. Every piece of her spirit wanted to sink back into her familiar skin. Yet she didn't seem to be getting closer. She felt a strange, cold sensation, almost like a preternatural wind at the door—only instead of blowing her toward her body, it was wafting her *away* from it.

"What's happening?" Rangar paused the recitation to ask Illiana. "Why isn't she waking?"

"Just keep chanting," Illiana said with a note of panic.

Rangar did as bidden, but his shoulders were now set tensely. His eyes flashed down over Bryn's body with fear in them. Another round of the chanted spell passed, and Bryn only felt colder, like her spirit was drifting even further from her body.

"This isn't working," Rangar hissed.

"I know it isn't!" Illiana cried. "I told you this spell has never been done before!"

"You separated her soul from her body," Rangar said tensely. "You should be able to put it back in!"

"I don't know how!" Illiana sputtered. "I thought it would be like tucking a bookmark into a book, but it's more like water spilled from a glass. Once it's out, it can't be put back in!"

"What are you saying?" Rangar growled, dropping his hands from the amplifier group. The others fell silent, their eyes wide. "You can't put her soul back in her body?"

"I'm trying!" Tears welled in Illiana's eyes. "I've done all I know how to!" She swallowed hard, her throat bobbing as she admitted, "Rangar, I don't know what else to do."

# CHAPTER 41

**TRUE LOVE'S KISS . . . real magic . . . sun and moon and stars . . . bound forever**

"Move aside," Rangar ordered as he waved his hand at Illiana and the casters. "All of you, get out. Now. Leave me with Bryn."

Despite his sharp command, no one in the room moved. With Bryn's lifeless body face-down on the bed, she looked as good as dead.

*That's what I'll be if I can't get back into my body.*

Existing in her spirit form no longer felt fascinating and ethereal; now, it was terrifying. She felt hollow, like a leaf tossed in the wind. There was no way for her to communicate to the others that she was right there, over their heads, watching everything happening.

"Rangar," Elysander said softly. "I know this is painful—"

"Leave us!" he ordered again. "Illiana's not the only one who knows something of magic. I was raised on hexes. I have the scars cut into my chest to prove it."

His voice was so forceful that the others finally complied. Though they seemed hesitant, Queen Karin and the Jarkkinens left, taking care to avoid the guards in the halls.

Illiana started to pack up her supplies, but Rangar said softer, "Leave your things, Illiana. Go to Mars. Should I need you, I'll come to find you."

Illiana nodded as she wiped away some tears. She spared a moment to briefly touch Bryn's bare back with the carved hexmarks, then left.

"You, too, Elysander," Rangar said.

Elysander folded her arms. "She's my sister. I won't leave her side."

"You have done much for Bryn," Rangar conceded. "And for that, I owe you deeply. But she is my Saved. Since we were children, her soul has been bound to mine. Bryn shall belong to me for all eternity, as I shall belong to her."

Taking a deep breath, Elysander finally relented. "I wish you luck, then, Rangar. But should you be unsuccessful, know that my sister loved you deeply. What the two of you shared is rare in this world. Many would be lucky to know a love like yours even for so brief a time."

Rangar's jaw clenched hard at the insinuation that Bryn might never return to her body. He didn't look at Elysander as she slipped from the room, leaving him alone. He drew in a deep breath, then huffed out an exhalation. Leaning over the bed, he hovered his hand an inch above Bryn's exposed back, almost as though he was afraid he might hurt her by touching her.

"My love," he whispered. "My Saved. My soul-bound. I know you are here. I can feel your presence. The room smells like maiden roses when you are near."

Bryn gasped slightly, reaching out her ghostly hand, wishing nothing more than to touch him. Rangar gently rolled Bryn's body over, so she was face up. He stroked the hair away from her face.

"Ten years ago, I followed a girl into the woods on a whim," he murmured while gently running his hands through her hair. "Something about her boldness caught my attention. I saw her plunge into the forest at an hour when only predators should be about, and sure enough, I soon saw the wolves' tracks in the mud."

Taking a deep breath, he hung his head. "I should have moved faster. I should have gotten to you before they did."

Bryn wanted desperately to cling to Rangar and kiss away all his unfounded guilt. *You saved my life,* she wanted to say. *What are a few scars?*

"When I carried you back to Castle Mir after the attack," Rangar continued in a whisper, "I wasn't thinking of the *fralen* bond. I was thinking only of getting you to safety. And yet, even at that moment, a piece of me felt bound to you. Your brother had to pry you out of my arms. You felt so slight and delicate, and yet I could sense your toughness. As they laid you out on the table to tend to your wounds, I saw the gashes across your chest, and then later that night, as I was cleaning my cuts, I realized they were the exact same scars. The same wolf claws. And that's when I knew that you and I would always be in each other's lives."

Rangar's hand cupped Bryn's near-lifeless face. It was rare for him to display the measure of vulnerability that his voice carried. He drew in an unsteady breath.

"I never stopped wondering about you. At night, I would dream of that glen and the wolves and the fair-haired princess with the scars that matched my own. When I grew older, I started to think of you differently. I was so curious to know the young woman you'd grown into, if there was a lover in your life, or if perhaps you . . . you ever thought of me."

His voice broke on the final words as he swiped a hand over his damp eyes.

"I finally saw you again when my brothers and I snuck to the Mir Harvest Gathering. You were even more radiant than in my dreams. You'd grown into a young woman as luminous as the sun, as beguiling as the moon, as graceful as a midnight stream. I knew then and there that I wanted you. That I loved you. That I would do anything in my power to protect you. And I tried, Bryn. The gods know how I tried. And yet, I failed."

He curled over as a sob escaped his lips. His hands caressed Bryn's nearly lifeless body as though trying to shape unwieldy clay into a vase.

"Bryn. You are the stars in the sky, the water in the ocean. You are the light in my dark days, the fire in my cold nights. You are my everything. In the old Baer tongue, *fra na mag* means "my dearest of all," and that is truly what you are to me. There is no life without you. Your love has made me stronger and braver than I ever thought possible. You are my soul's other half. And I will go on loving you for every moment of every day that I live on this earth."

He lowered his trembling lips to hers in a tender kiss. Bryn's ghost-like lips tingled as though she could feel his touch, and she breathed in a shaky inhalation.

*You are my everything, too, Rangar Barendur. And I refuse to be apart from you any longer.*

"Come back to me, Bryn," Rangar whispered.

Bryn gathered every ounce of her determination. She had no hexes in this ethereal form. She knew no spells for returning to one's body. And yet, a piece of her felt connected to a deep well of magic that was older than spells, that predated hexes. The magic of the sea and stars. The magic of two fated mates fighting to unite against all odds.

Stilling her thoughts, she surrendered herself to

the deep thrum of magic singing in the air. She poured every bit of her strength into the faint tingle of Rangar's kiss on her lips. She visualized being back in her body, having his lips touch hers. Feeling his love for her pour from his heart into hers, giving her back her life.

And slowly, her spirit began to tingle a little more. She felt her extremities growing warmer. Rangar brushed his thumb over her body's cheek, and she felt it even in her spirit form.

*Yes*, she thought. *I can feel you, Rangar!*

He continued to gently kiss her, and Bryn clung to that spark like a rope and pulled herself back into her body inch by inch. Warmth blossomed throughout her. She felt the thump of a heartbeat in her chest. Her lungs filled and emptied.

Then, she sank back into her body like slipping into a cool bath.

She sucked in a sudden breath.

Her eyes snapped open.

Rangar drew back in shock, his thumb still touching her cheek. His wide eyes searched hers as though he didn't dare believe he wasn't dreaming. "Bryn?" he whispered as though speaking to a ghost. "Bryn, are you . . ."

"It's me, Rangar." Breathless, she sat up, grabbing him around the shoulders and kneading her fingers into his muscles, needing to feel that he was real, too. "I'm back!"

His head shook slightly in disbelief. "How is that possible?"

"I heard you," she whispered, touching her forehead to his. "I felt your kiss. It reached through the trance and gave me a way to pull myself out."

He gripped her shoulders, holding her a few inches away so he could look over her face and body as though needing to verify it. He touched her forehead, her cheeks, her chin.

"You're back?"

A smile broke across her face. "I'm back."

"Dear gods." He wrapped her in a fierce embrace, burying his face in her hair. "You've brought her back to me. I thank you with every word I've ever spoken."

He finally released her. "But it wasn't the gods, was it? *You* did this, Bryn. You are a warrior at heart, connected to magic in ways I've never seen, a true queen of the Baersladen."

He kissed her as though they had been apart for years. He kissed her like the first crocus bloom after a long winter. He kissed her like she was the crackling warmth of a fire during a blustering storm. The kiss was a song, each touch, each movement, a beautiful melody played out in perfect harmony.

When they finally parted, both breathless and smiling, Bryn could feel their hearts beating as one.

"I made a vow to you, Rangar," she said softly. "That we would be together forever. I meant that promise. And though I had to break all the rules of magic, I kept it."

"You didn't break the rules of magic," Rangar replied, gazing at her with reverence. "You discovered a new way. A new path. You made your own rules, and magic rallied around you."

They kissed again in a tangle of limbs. Now that Bryn was back in her body, she wanted nothing more than to experience every sensation she could. She wanted to touch Rangar everywhere, to feel him touch her. She wanted to breathe in his woodsmoke scent. Wanted to hear the blood rush in his veins. Wanted to taste his kisses, salty from his dried tears.

Once they had quenched their desire and lay on the bed, hands intertwined, Bryn's head resting on Rangar's chest.

"We did it," Rangar said finally.

"You mean ratifying the decree?"

"The decree, yes. Outsmarting the southern kingdoms, yes. Opening the Eyrie to the free use of magic, yes. But more than that, Bryn. We proved to ourselves, to everyone here, and to the gods that we have earned our place as king and queen of the Baersladen."

She rolled over, resting her chin on his chest. "My king."

He stroked her hair. "My queen."

She leaned into his palm, then closed her eyes. "There's only one thing left to do. Something that the forces that be—the gods, the Saints, magic itself— seem to keep returning us to."

"What is that?" he asked.

"You saved me from wolves once, Rangar. Now we

must stop the wolves one final time before they destroy the Eyrie."

# CHAPTER 42

**HEX OF THE WOLF . . . the Ardmoor gathering . . . princes and common folk . . . a caged beast . . . snowfall**

Two weeks later, an entourage from the Baersladen arrived at the market town of Ardmoor under cover of darkness. Oliver and a fleet of Baer guards led the small traveling party, their swords prominently on display should any of the town's riffraff get the wrong idea. Rangar, riding Legend, rode behind the guards with no hood covering his bronze crown this time. Bryn rode behind him on Fable, her eyes keen as she took in the town that had once caused her so much trouble.

"Last time we were here," Valenden said from atop his horse behind Bryn, "I was calling you my wife."

Bryn hissed wryly, "You'd better hope Rangar doesn't overhear you."

"I *did* hear that," Rangar called from ahead, barely glancing over his shoulder. "And you'd best keep in mind that *my* ring is on her finger now, Val, if you value keeping all of *your* fingers."

Valenden snorted at his brother's threat. "Come, Rangar, that's not very kingly of you."

"I was a warrior long before I was king."

Bryn sighed fondly as the two brothers bickered. For all his faults, Valenden had proved himself to be an essential and highly effective ruler in Rangar's stead. During the time they were in the Wollin for the grand parlay, Valenden had orchestrated a system of defensive traps around the villages to protect the Baer people from berserkir wolves, had dealt with a shortage of fishing hauls, and had settled a land dispute between two prominent Baer families.

But more than his accomplishments, Valenden had proven his loyalty. With Rangar and Bryn far away in the Wollin, it would have been easy for Valenden to have stolen the Baer throne if he'd so wished. As the elder brother, he had some arguable claim to it, and some people would have supported that claim. And yet, when Bryn and Rangar had returned to Barendur Hold, Valenden had ceded power to them without incident. When Rangar had asked if he'd liked the taste of rulership, Valenden had only laughed.

"Not half as much as I like the taste of freedom," he'd said.

Ever since then, the two Baer brothers had been closer than ever. Bryn was grateful that their obstacles had only solidified their bond, and now the two of them moved in lockstep: Rangar making decisions, Valenden helping to carry them out.

As queen, Bryn had been heavily involved in their decision-making about the kingdom, but lately, she'd found herself distracted.

She pressed a hand to her belly. A small smile graced her lips.

Oliver turned to Rangar and asked, "Shall we settle in at the inn first?"

"No," Rangar said, "Directly to the arena. I fear we don't have time to rest before the gathering is set to begin."

"Yes, my king."

Oliver signaled to the other soldiers, who steered the traveling party down a thoroughfare lined with vendors. Even at the late hour, the streets of Ardmoor were crowded. In a busy market town at a crossroads, they'd known their presence would garner much attention, yet it was the most logical meeting place. Given the heavy snowfall that had recently fallen in the north, travel there was too difficult. And meeting too close to the southern kingdoms—who were still disgruntled after the results of the grand parlay— could be dangerous.

So, Ardmoor it was.

A large stone structure loomed ahead, lit by torches. A chiseled sign declared "Ardmoor Grand

Arena" with painted murals of warriors locked in combat. Though the fighting competitions were finished for the day, the arena gates remained open.

Two figures flanked the gate with swords drawn. When they saw the Baer party arriving, they lowered their swords. A man and woman disguised as market vendors stepped forward.

"Elysander!" Bryn said, dismounting from Fable and hurrying over to embrace her sister. "And Jon. Thank you for coming."

"Of course," Elysander said. "The others are already waiting inside. You're the last group to arrive. Our bandits are spread out in the nearby streets to keep away any troublemakers who might get curious about what's happening in the arena after hours."

"We are grateful for your assistance," Rangar said as he and Valenden dismounted. "Our guards will wait here at the gates with you."

Bryn's heart kicked up as they entered the arena. She'd only ever heard of fighting competitions for money, where spectators placed bets on who would win and lose. The arena had the aura of danger even though it was currently quiet. Bryn could practically hear the echo of the crowd cheering on someone's violent end earlier in the day.

As though wanting to shelter her from such a disreputable place, Rangar wrapped an arm around her waist. "It's just through here."

As they passed beneath archways, more torchlight appeared ahead. Finally, they stepped out into the arena floor covered with sand. A small cluster of people congregated in the center of the arena, speaking low and urgently amongst themselves.

Bryn immediately recognized some of the people who had come for this gathering: besides Elysander and Jon Dryden, Illiana was there, and Prince Anter Jarkkinen from Vil-Kevi, along with Mage Albia. But there were many faces she didn't know. A handful of mages and apprentices in robes from Vil-Rossengard, two raven-haired women whose clothes looked Zaradonish, and common folk in farmers' and laborers' garb, among others.

Looking over the crowd, Bryn's skin danced with the promise of magic.

Rangar strode to the head of the crowd, signaling for Bryn and Valenden to join him. Once they took their place, the rest of the crowd quieted.

"Friends," Rangar announced. "I thank you for your willingness to travel here for this important occasion. Each of you has come from far and wide, leaving behind your homes to join us. Your sacrifice is not taken lightly; we are honored to call you allies."

He took Bryn's hand, squeezing it tightly.

"The berserkir wolf attacks have gone on too long," he declared. "All of us in this room have lost neighbors, friends, and family to their scourge. In the Wollin, we discovered the source of the wolves, and now it is time to end the wolves themselves. Prince Anter, have you brought the beast?"

Prince Anter signaled to two men, who carted out

an iron cage. The berserkir wolf they'd examined in Higharbor Keep paced in the cage, snarling. The Vil-Kevi soldiers set the wolf in the middle of the arena.

The closest people drew back, whispering amongst themselves again, and Bryn realized it was the first time some of them had seen one of the black-eyed berserkir beasts up close.

"We have invited each of you here today because of your magical abilities," Rangar said. "From princes to common folk, you each hold amplifier hexes that can unite to defeat this great evil and bring peace to the land once more."

Some of the common folk shifted nervously. The two refugee Zaradonish women clutched hands. There had to be about twenty-five casters gathered in all, and most of them had kept their magic secret until now. The Zaradonish witches would have been sentenced to death if their abilities had ever come to light in their restrictive kingdom, but even the common folk from the Mirien and the Wollin had risked much to practice magic secretly.

When Rangar had sent messengers throughout the kingdoms looking for casters of all abilities, Bryn had been worried none would dare to respond, afraid that the decree for the free use of magic wasn't trustwor-thy. But King Mars, in the Mirien, and Queen Phillipa, in the Wollin, had taken steps to demonstrate to their people that magic was no longer a sin—and some brave souls had believed them and come.

Rangar held up Bryn's hand. "My wife, Queen

Bryn, has assumed the title of the Mage Queen in our land. Though she is still in the apprentice phase, she is working to take over as head mage from my aunt, who remains behind to protect our land in our absence." He met Bryn's gaze with one filled with pride. "Our Mage Queen shall lead the amplifier hex today."

Bryn's stomach tightened with excitement and a twinge of fear. For the last two weeks, she had worked diligently with Mage Marna and Ren to devise a spell that might put an end to the berserkir wolves, and now was her chance to prove herself not just to her people but to all of the Eyrie, royals and common folk alike.

Bryn cleared her throat. The attendees fell silent, awaiting her words. Rumors had spread about her possession spell and her miraculous return to her body, and she'd been met with awe and reverence from fellow casters ever since.

"Friends," she said. "The berserkir wolves were created with a dark magic spell adapted from an ancient Rumese incantation to strengthen hunting dogs. The intention was to scare off the populace from using magic, and many still fear magic's use despite the decree now allowing it. Today, we will not only stop the wolf attacks but show the people of the Eyrie that magic has the capability for great good." She extended her hands on either side. "Everyone, please hold hands around the caged wolf."

Rangar and Valenden grasped her hands, and the

group stretched out in a wide circle as everyone clasped hands.

"With all of our voices chanting the amplifier spell, I will put an end to these wolves." She squeezed Rangar's hand. "If you're ready, begin."

Rangar led the chant. "*Arnan ka spartha. Arnan ka spartha . . .* " Twenty-five voices rose to match his as they recited the words in unison. A crackle of energy spread throughout the arena. The torchlights flickered. The caged wolf snarled as though sensing the change in the air.

Their voices fell into a perfect rhythm, and Bryn's eyes sank closed.

*Now*, she told herself. *It's up to me.*

In the Baersladen, she, Mage Marna, and Ren had run through countless possibilities to defeat the wolves. They had studied the original Rumese spell that had created them, but attempting to reverse it hadn't worked. Ren had finally come up with an idea inspired by Calista, whose specialty had been controlling the natural elements. "We need something that can touch all corners of the Eyrie at once," Ren had said. "That no wolves can run or hide from."

Now, Bryn touched her left shoulder blade, where Mage Marna had bandaged a fresh hexmark before they'd left. Taking a deep breath to center herself, she spoke the new spell's words.

"*Nevnon ka.*"

The casters continued chanting the amplifier hex,

and she felt the amplifying energy crackling, swelling, strengthening her own spell.

Closing her eyes, she recited hers again. "*Nevnon ka.*"

Their voices continued, unwavering, into the night. A spell to encompass all eight kingdoms of the Eyrie required not only this large group of casters—the largest group gathered in recent history—but also time. They chanted long after midnight until their voices were hoarse.

Slowly, a strange chill spread over the arena. A breeze blustered in from its high open arches with the promise of frost. Though snow wasn't unheard of in Ardmoor, no snow clouds had hung overhead earlier that day.

Now, however, a few snowflakes swirled on the breeze. They had an odd bluish tint to them.

*It's working!* Bryn thought and recited her spell with even more focus.

More blue-tinged snow blew in from the arena's open arches. Though it landed harmlessly on the casters' hair and clothing, the wolf began to spasm when touched by the magical snow. It twitched several times, then gave a contorted yawn.

As they chanted, more of the enchanted snow blew in. As it collected in the wolf's fur, the beast curled up in the bottom of the cage. It yawned again and then seemed to fall asleep. Its body gave another few twitches, and then with a strange sigh, the beast stopped moving entirely.

Elysander, watching from the side, ducked beneath Valenden and Bryn's clasped hands and ran to the cage. With a knife in hand out of caution, she reached in to test the wolf's breath. She peeled open one of its eyes.

"It's dead!" Elysander confirmed. "Dead, and back to normal, too. No more black eyes or black tongue."

An excited murmur spread throughout the crowd, but Bryn shushed them urgently. "Keep chanting! We must ensure all the wolves are put to sleep!"

Clasping hands again, the group returned to their spell with even more enthusiasm. Bryn could hear shouts from outside the arena as Ardmoor's townspeople remarked on the strange blue snow.

Finally, a cloud rolled over the moon, and Bryn stopped as exhaustion overtook her. The other casters, also tired, dropped hands with one another. Bryn pressed her hand to her throat, raw from having chanted for so long.

Rangar supported her, looking at her with concern. "You wore yourself out."

"I'm fine." Her voice was hoarse.

Valenden looked out the high arches at the night sky, where the final snowflakes were swirling down. "Do you think it worked over all the Eyrie?"

The spell Ren had come up with created an enchanted snowfall that would put the berserkir wolves to sleep—then quietly to death—while not harming people or livestock. Only creatures affected by the original spell would be affected by the snow.

And though snow never occurred in the southern kingdoms, it would today. It would cover every glen and mountain and field of the Eyrie until every last berserkir wolf lay curled and still on the ground, covered in bluish flakes.

Bryn looked up at the sky, feeling a flutter of hope in her chest. "We'll have to find out," she said, "but the wind is whispering to me that we won."

# CHAPTER 43

**THE MAGE QUEEN . . . blue snowfall . . . finally home . . . an end to terror . . . a new beginning**

Bryn saw the results of the Ardmoor gathering with her own eyes as their traveling party made their way back north to the Baersladen. The faintly bluish snowfall blanketed every inch of road and forest within eyesight, even to the distant mountains that gleamed with the bluish cast. By the second day of their return journey, when they reached the Vil-Kevi border, the snow had mostly melted. And yet when they stopped at The Chestnut Inn to rest, the mood couldn't be more different than it had been on their previous visit.

Instead of somber diners distrustful of anything

with a whiff of magic, the patrons in the inn's tavern buzzed excitedly.

As Bryn, Rangar, and Valenden took their seats—in plain traveling clothes to hide their titles—while the guards patrolled outside, the old innkeeper came up with rounds of ale. "On the house!" she declared.

"I've never known inns to give away ale for free, good madam," Valenden said. "What is the occasion?"

"Mester Harrow, one of our foragers, found a den of those monstrous berserkir wolves in the forest—dead! All of them! Asleep and cold as ice! And that's not all; we've heard similar stories from nearby villages."

Bryn couldn't hide her smile. "I'm so relieved to hear that."

"Could it be the berserkir attacks are finished?" the innkeeper speculated.

Bryn touched her chest in a sign of hope. "Let us pray to the gods and Saints alike that is so."

The innkeeper leaned in conspiratorially. "Word reached us too about the decree for the free use of magic. By the Saints, you best believe I'm going to learn a hex or two! I've needed more help since my grandchildren moved away, and I thought to myself, why can't *I* see what magic can do?"

"As well you should," Rangar said. "Last time we came through here, your patrons did not appear to be supporters of magic."

"Oh, pish." She made a *pfft* sound. "Then they don't

have to practice it, do they? But this is good for the rest of us. The town's leaders are discussing setting up lessons for the villagers to learn the rudimentary hexes. Apparently, there was a witch living in secret just three towns away! Can you believe it? Now that she doesn't have to hide her abilities anymore, she's going to teach others."

"We are glad," Bryn said and meant every word.

Sure enough, once they returned to the road and crossed into the Baersladen lands, they were met with more reports of berserkir wolves found dead in forests and fields. By the time they reached Elderwall, they hadn't seen a "No Magic" sign in miles. They stopped at the dairy farm to greet Jonnah and let the horses rest, where the farmer's two little girls brought them pitchers of warm, creamy milk.

"And you haven't had more berserkir attacks, I take it?" Rangar asked.

"No, my king," Jonnah said with a twinkle in his eye. "It's a strange thing, you know. As you passed south on your urgent trek a few days ago, the wolves were constantly attacking, and only Prince Valenden's traps kept us safe. And now, just a few days later, you return through Elderwall, and the wolves have all perished after that strange snowfall."

Bryn, Rangar, and Valenden exchanged a knowing look.

Rangar finally cleared his throat and said, "We're as relieved as anyone to hear about the end of the violent wolf attacks."

Jonnah only smiled and offered the accompanying soldiers milk and bread.

As they rode along the final valley road back toward Barendur Hold, Bryn asked, "Do you think more people than just Jonnah suspect that we're behind the berserkir wolves' end?"

"My guess is rumors are already spreading," Rangar answered.

Valenden scoffed. "I don't see why you don't just come out and take credit. It's one of the greatest victories of the last decade."

Rangar stated, "It was a collective effort of all people of the Eyrie, royals and common folk alike. Rather than individuals taking credit, better to let rumors spread about the mythical enchanted snowfall. People will know that magic stopped the wolves; that is enough."

Bryn felt a flush of pride in what they'd accomplished.

*As Rangar says, let legends grow on their own. Those are the best kind.*

They crested a hill, and Barendur Hold appeared in the distance, backdropped by the sea. She drew Fable to a stop as she gazed at her home.

She pressed a hand to her belly, smiling.

"Bryn?" Rangar asked, stopping Legend. "Are you all right?"

She smiled. "Oh yes. I just wanted a good long look at my home."

Once they returned to Barendur Hold and settled back in after the journey, Bryn went to Mage Marna to confirm what she had recently come to suspect. The white-haired mage, not known for easy smiles, offered a grin when she felt Bryn's stomach.

"When will you tell Rangar?"

"As soon as he returns from patrolling the forest to make sure all the berserkir beasts are dead," Bryn said, beaming, though her smile faltered. "Will this change anything about my mage apprenticeship?"

"Of course not. All types of women have become mages at all stages of life. Motherhood is no exception."

While Bryn impatiently waited for Rangar to return, she visited Saraj in the falconry mews. Zephyr spotted her first, giving a sharp *caw*, and Saraj whirled around from where she'd been fixing a broken perch.

"Bryn! You're back!" Saraj threw her arms around her. With a wide smile, she lowered her voice and said, "Your bold plan seems to have worked."

"No berserkir wolf attacks in days," Bryn agreed. "If there are no attacks the following week, we can officially declare the threat over."

"How was it?" Saraj asked breathlessly. "The mage gathering?"

"Like nothing I've ever experienced," Bryn said dreamily, reflecting on the raw power of all that collective magic. "Twenty-five casters all working together in unison. The energy was palpable."

"I'm sorry I couldn't join you."

"We were grateful you stayed behind to defend against the wolves." A sly look crossed Bryn's face. "You know, Oliver is back from the trek, too."

Saraj's cheeks pinkened. She cleared her throat a few times. "Oh?"

"He's practically lovesick for you," Bryn teased. "You should show the poor man some mercy."

Saraj bit her lip, looking conflicted.

Bryn took her friend's hand gently. "Trei would want you to move on, Saraj. He would wish for your happiness. For you to find love, and with someone he cared about, too."

Saraj turned back to the broken perch distractedly. "Oliver asked if we might take a walk together when he returned . . . perhaps I will accept."

Bryn let out an excited squeal and gave her friend another hug. Her hand fell to her belly as she considered sharing her news with Saraj, but she resisted. As much as the good news nearly burst from her lips, she owed it to Rangar that he be the first to hear.

She visited the castle workers in the laundry and armory, then went to the barn to greet the shepherdesses and stable workers, then strolled down to the docks to speak with the fishermen. Everyone shared good reports about the end of the wolf attacks, and a few even praised Valenden's leadership in their absence. She was finishing a visit with

Mam Delice in the kitchen when she heard the castle's guards discussing Rangar's impending return.

Gasping, she jumped up from the kitchen table. "Excuse me, Mam Delice, but I must speak with Rangar."

The cook's elderly eyes skimmed over Bryn's plumper, softened body with a knowing look. "Take these biscuits, my queen." She wrapped a handful of honey biscuits in a cloth napkin and pressed the bundle on Bryn. "Something tells me the two of you might have a reason to celebrate tonight."

Blushing, Bryn raced up to their chamber, where she set out the honey biscuits and then examined herself in the mirror, adjusting her dress where it was growing snug over her midsection. Then she went to the window to anxiously look over the village square below.

Rangar and his men rode into the square and dismounted. They seemed in good spirits, which meant they must have found no signs of living berserkir wolves. Rangar clapped Oliver on the back, who then led Legend and the other horses to the stable while throwing glances toward the falconry mews.

Bryn paced the room, hands clutched lovingly on her belly while she tried to quell the rising excitement in her chest. She'd intended to tell Rangar the news in a calm, queenly manner—and yet the moment he swung open the door, delicate white snowflakes still tangled in his dark hair, she threw herself into his arms.

"Whoa, there," he said, laughing, as though he was still speaking to Legend. His hand wrapped around her back. "What have I done to earn this embrace?"

Bryn pulled back to meet his eyes, biting her lip. She took a moment to drink in every detail about him. His scars, which matched her own. His simmering brown eyes. His jaw edged like a sword's blade.

*We've come so far*, she thought. *And yet it's still only the beginning.*

Breaking into a smile, she nudged him toward the chair. "Sit. I have something to tell you."

Raising his eyebrows, he dropped into the chair and eyed the plate of honey biscuits. "What's this about?"

"First, tell me what you found in the forest."

"Nothing." His eyes lit up. "Which was exactly what we hoped to find. No traps or bait stations showed any sign of berserkir wolves, only regular wolves and other forest animals. I believe it's safe to say the berserkirs are all gone from this land."

"Good."

He leaned back, eyeing her suspiciously. "You don't want to talk about the wolves, though, do you?"

She answered with a broader, secretive smile. She took a deep breath and said, "Do you remember on our travels, we discussed having Mage Marna prepare a tea to keep me from falling pregnant until we were ready for children?"

Rangar's eyes widened slightly as a curious look crossed his face. "I do."

Bryn splayed her hands on her belly. "Well, we didn't ask for the tea soon enough."

There was a moment of silence, and then Rangar bolted upright from the chair. Towering over Bryn, his gaze raked up and down her body as his eyes widened further.

"You mean . . ."

"You're going to be a father, Rangar."

He stood in stunned silence, his lips slightly parted. Bryn's heart began to thump extra hard. She'd felt certain he would be pleased with this news, yet now, a hint of doubt crept into her mind.

"Rangar?" she prompted.

He blinked, then closed his mouth. "By the gods, Bryn. Do you mean it? Are you sure?"

She nodded.

A wide smile broke across his otherwise brooding face. Before she knew it, he swept her up in his arms. Laughing, she clung to him around the neck as he swung her in a circle. When he finally set her down, he captured her face between his hands and looked her squarely in the eye.

"We're to be parents? You're truly pregnant?"

Her grin grew wider. "Mage Marna confirmed it when we returned from Ardmoor."

Rangar pressed a hand to his forehead in disbelief. "How did this happen?"

She gave a soft snort. "How do you *think* it happened?"

He remained speechless, staring at her in awe.

"You're pleased?" she asked.

His hand fell as his gaze shot to her, serious now. "Am I *pleased?* Bryn Barendur, the gods alone know how great my joy is at this news. When you wished to delay having children, I understood your reasons, though I did not share them. Knowing that my child grows in your belly is the greatest blessing I could ever receive."

He stroked his thumb over the hill of her cheek, his eyes filled with adoration. "But how do you feel, my love?" he asked concernedly. "I know this was not your wish."

She shook her head gently. "You speak so often of fate, and I rarely share your views. Yet something about this child feels fateful. This child is a symbol of the love we share. And I know I have many who will help raise it. I couldn't be happier."

Rangar tipped her head up, his gaze falling to her lips. "You are my everything, Bryn. I swear to dedicate my life to protecting you and our baby."

They kissed in the candlelight with the sweet smell of honey biscuits hanging in the air. The kiss began softly, but their hands became more insistent as they stroked one another. Rangar picked Bryn up by the waist and carried her to the bed, laying her down gently. He skimmed his hand along her neckline, fumbling with the uppermost button.

"I suppose we need not worry about you falling pregnant anymore," he purred. "So, we can be free with our affections."

Bryn raked her fingernails through his hair, pulling his head down into another kiss. As his fingers undid her buttons, she untucked his shirt from his trousers. She tugged it over his head and gazed admiringly at his body.

"That is true, Rangar Barendur. You can't get me pregnant twice, though if any man could, it would be you."

"I'm more than happy to try."

He smoothed her blouse off her shoulders and covered her skin with kisses. Her head tipped back as pleasure sparked throughout her body. Her hands ran over his bare chest, fingers tracing his hexmark scars.

"We brought magic to the Eyrie," she whispered, "And now we're bringing new life."

He kissed her again, fierce and loving and possessive and tender. In the distance, a wolf howled far in the forest. For a second, the kiss broke apart, and their eyes met.

"A regular wolf," Rangar reassured her. "Nothing to fear."

Bryn gripped his shoulder, pulling him back down to her. "I stopped fearing wolves long ago, Rangar. Ever since a wild prince swore to keep their claws and teeth away, and then did just that."

She kissed him with all the love of the sea and stars. She kissed the boy he'd been when he'd saved her, and the man he'd grown into. She kissed him as king of the Baersladen, and father to her future child.

"You're mine," she whispered in his ear. "As I am yours."

"Now," Rangar murmured. "And forever."

~

**Ready for your next read? For a modern fantasy romance between a human nanny and a billionaire fae, try my Wilde City series!**

~

**To claim your Scarlight bonus scenes, join my author mailing list!**

# Appendix

# Appendix
## The Noble Families of the Eyrie Kingdoms

**THE MIRIEN**

King Mars Lindane and Queen Illiana Lindane

Princess Bryn Lindane

Princess Elysander Lindane


**THE BAERSLADEN**

King Aleth Barendur and

Queen Anathalda Barendur (deceased)

Princes Trei, Valenden, and Rangar Barendur

Mage Marna Barendur


**RUMA**

King Cedric Cheron and Queen Yves Cheron

Baron Marmose


**VIL-KEVI**

Prince Anter Jarkkinen

King Otto Jarkkinen

Lady Enis

**DRESEL**

King Angus Gray and Queen Hanna Gray

Duke Jon Dreyden

**THE WOLLIN**

Queen Amelia Hytooth and King Marthin Hytooth

Declan and Phillippa Hytooth

**ZARADONA**

King Salvator Surin

High Priest Felisian Red

**VIL-ROSSENGARD**

King Hans Viklund and Queen Karin Viklund

# A Note from Evie

Dear Reader,

Thank you for reading the final book in the Castles of the Eyrie series. I loved every minute of writing the forbidden romance between Bryn and Rangar!

Was this a 3, 4, or 5 star read for you? If you enjoyed this book, help fellow readers discover their next binge-worthy read by leaving a rating!

xo,
    Evie

# About the Author

Evie Marceau writes fantasies to satisfy her nagging curiosity that there is more out there just beyond the veil. She is the author of romantic fantasies with a touch of darkness and hint of magic.

www.eviemarceau.com

Join Evie's FB Reader Group! https://www.facebook.com/groups/344599161310206

www.eviemarceau.com/newsletter
(PS: get exclusive bonus scenes when you join!)